The Secret Clan

HIGHLAND
BRIDE

This Large Print Book carries the
Seal of Approval of N.A.V.H.

AMANDA SCOTT

The Secret Clan
HIGHLAND BRIDE

WHEELER
PUBLISHING

LP
c.1

Published in 2003 by arrangement with Warner Books, Inc.

Wheeler Large Print Romance Series.

The text of this Large Print edition is unabridged.
Other aspects of the book may vary from the original edition.

Set in 16 pt. Plantin by Ramona A. Watson.

Printed in the United States on permanent paper.

Library of Congress Cataloging-in-Publication Data

Scott, Amanda
    Highland bride
        p. cm.
        ISBN 1-58724-445-4 (lg. print : hc : alk. paper)
                                                        2003052516

To Terry & Jim,
who make it all worthwhile,
always

Author's Note

According to the *Collins Encyclopedia of Scotland*, in 1541 (and indeed until the reorganization of local governments in 1975) Inverness-shire was Scotland's largest county, comprising 4,211 square miles. It stretched from Nigg, on the Moray Firth just east of Inverness, down Glen Mor (the Great Glen) to Fort William, and then northwest through the Isle of Skye and the lower Outer Hebrides south of Lewis, out to St. Kilda, 100 miles from the Scottish mainland. In other words, it comprised most of the western Highlands, including Kintail.

Prologue

With the coming of darkness, an eerie, creeping mist began to drift across the glassy surface of Loch Ness, quickly thickening and rising to blend with mist from the surrounding rain-soaked hillsides until dense fog carpeted Glen Mor — the Great Glen — and cloaked the darkly menacing mountains that flanked it to east and west.

Occasionally an errant breeze would stir for no apparent reason, swirling the mist enough to reveal a pale, silvery glow from the full moon above. Otherwise, the Great Glen lay shrouded in impenetrable darkness of the sort that kept wise men indoors, because men of lesser wisdom had been known to disappear on such nights, never to be seen again, as if the monster of the loch had taken those lost souls to one of its secret caves in the murky depths.

Thus, it was that four local men had sought shelter at an isolated alehouse near the western shore of the loch some ten miles south of Inverness. The alemaster, Ian Fraser, was a barrel-chested man of middle years, well able to keep a peaceful house. Moreover, he knew all four

7

men and although one was a young trouble-maker of the first order who was ever too quick to draw his sword, the other three usually knew better than to stir his temper.

All might have remained peaceable had the conversation not taken an unfortunate turn.

At a pause in what had been aimless discourse, one of the men muttered with a sigh, "Faith, lads, but this be a night fit only for ducks and fish."

"Aye, sure, and mayhap for foxes," suggested another with a quiet chuckle.

"Do not speak to me about accursed foxes," growled the troublemaker. He was a young man, still in his twenties, and handsome despite the sour look on his face. It was said that young women found him charming, but the other men in the alehouse had seen little if any of that charm.

"Peace, lad," the oldest of the four, a grizzle-bearded, burly man said calmly. "We'll talk o' summat else."

"Mayhap I do not travel with my usual tail of men tonight, Rory Malcolm, but you'll address me properly nonetheless. Moreover, I ken fine what you are thinking. You've all heard what that vulpine villain did at Bothyn, have you not?"

Silence greeted his words.

"Well? Have you not?"

"Aye, we heard," Malcolm said in his peaceable way. " 'Twas nobbut a prank, and no harm meant."

"No harm?" The speaker's voice rose. "No harm, you say! Did the villain not sneak into Bothyn Castle, stronghold of the sheriff's own family, and manage by unnatural arts or other villainy to enter at dead o' night and arrange for buckets full of excrement to be emptied over me as I rode out next morning?"

"I'd say he did ye a kindness," declared the fourth man. "Is your father no the new Sheriff o' Inverness-shire, and are ye yourself no his sheriff-substitute?"

"You know that I am," the troublemaker said belligerently. "But my father is scarcely new to his position. He has been sheriff for nigh onto six months now."

"Aye, well, but his lordship were sheriff for thirty years and more afore him," the alemaster said.

"And his lordship's own cousin a murderer, I'd remind you."

"Perhaps, but *Sionnach Dubh* were mostly peaceable whilst his lordship looked to the law hereabouts, and now he do be stirring again," Malcolm said.

"I told you," the other snapped, "I don't want to hear about the Black Fox!"

"Aye, sure, but he only worked a bit o' mischief at Bothyn," Fraser said. "I'm thinkin' ye should be grateful he were content wi' just showing ye that your defenses required refinement, and didna slit your throats."

"Aye," said the man who had first mentioned

foxes, having kept silent since. "Ye should guard your home better, lad. 'Tis only sensible, that, particularly since ye now ha' the duty to live in and look after Sheriff's House in Inverness, as well."

"Do you dare suggest we do not guard our residences? We do, and well, but the Fox is the devil's own spawn, or he would not slither through keyholes in the dead of night. He would face his enemies, man to man and sword to sword."

Fraser chuckled.

Instantly, the troublemaker's temper flared. Leaping to his feet, he snarled, "By Jesu, do you dare to laugh at me?"

"Peace, lad," Fraser said. "I didna laugh at ye but at the silly notion that the Fox be afraid to meet any man wi' a sword. 'Tis said, and truly, that he be the finest swordsman in all Scotland."

"A myth, I tell you, a nonsense! I warrant you'll next believe that he rides the Loch Ness monster, waving his sword as he plunges with it down to its lair."

"We'd believe nowt o' the sort, only that the man's a grand swordsman."

"I am the best-trained swordsman in the glens," he declared. "Or do you forget that I trained in Italy? Moreover, my sword is the finest in the Highlands."

Whipping his weapon from its scabbard, he waved it menacingly.

"Mind what ye're about now, lad," Fraser warned sternly.

"Call me 'sir,' damn you! I say the Black Fox is a damnable coward! Does anyone dare deny that?"

The others remained prudently silent.

"By Jesu, then, I tell you he is a thief and a murderer, and as soon as I get the chance, I'll show him and all Scotland who is the better swordsman."

"Shout *hallelujah* then, ye ill-natured puppy," snapped a deep voice from the back of the room. "God has granted your foolish wish."

So fixed had everyone's attention been on the flashing sword and the swordsman's complaints that no one had noticed the door slowly opening.

Even now, the light of the little fire barely reached the figure that filled the doorway, making him seem to be just a shadow against the mist. Like the night behind him, he was cloaked in black, and either the hood of his cloak or some sort of mask concealed his features, for only his eyes, glittering with reflected firelight, were visible to his startled audience. Then, deftly swirling his cloak, he revealed the pistol he held in his left hand and the sleek-looking sword in his right.

"We'll ha' a fair fight, lads," he said, gently gesturing with the pistol.

"Dinna burden yourself, sir," Malcolm said. "We're a peaceable lot, and we favor fair play."

11

Nodding, the intruder slipped the pistol back beneath his cloak. "Come at me then," he said softly to the troublemaker, "if your feet will carry ye."

The sheriff's son seemed to have lost both his voice and his bluster, but at this taunt, he recovered swiftly and lunged at the newcomer.

A deft parry slid his blade aside, and in the flurry that followed, the men silently watching soon saw that the Fox toyed with his opponent. No matter what the sheriff's son did, the Fox easily deflected his strokes.

"I see ye ha' studied your swordplay in Italy," he said at one point.

"Aye, to your cost!"

The masked man's eyes danced merrily. "The Italians make fine swords, and your Italian masters taught ye well how to thrust, but Italians ken gey little about defense, my lad. Ye'd ha' done better to take your fine Italian sword into France to study the art," he added as he deftly parried another thrust.

The other was clearly tiring, but the Fox fought on, the merriment in his eyes fading as he forced the sheriff's son to defend himself. A moment later, he said grimly, "The sword be a gentleman's weapon, but ye and your trouble-some father ha' been using yours to torment people in the glens, and ye dare to do so under the false claim that ye act for his grace, the King."

"We do represent the King," the other insisted, gasping. "My father is Sheriff of Inverness, appointed by the King, and I am his sworn deputy."

"Ye seek only to curry favor wi' them who would realign the Highland kirk more securely wi' Rome. Appointed or no, ye dinna represent his grace. In any event, the pair o' ye disgrace the titles ye hold, and this be what I think o' ye," he added as he suddenly knocked the other man's sword up, closed with him long enough to tweak his nose with his free hand, and then leaped back again.

Their audience erupted in laughter.

The sheriff's son shot them a murderous look, whereupon the Fox, with a flick of his wrist, sent the fine Italian sword clattering into the fireplace, scattering coals and embers onto the hearth.

As the Fox held his stunned opponent at sword point, the alemaster rushed to rescue the latter's sword and to kick the burning embers back into the fireplace.

"On your knees, my lad," the Fox ordered, "unless ye want to meet your Maker and discuss His lack o' wisdom tonight in granting your wish."

Glowering resentfully, the sheriff's son did as he was commanded.

"Now, put your head to the floor and beg the pardon o' all here for so discourteously disrupting the peace o' this house."

"I won't!"

13

The sword point moved to his throat, rendering him stiffly motionless, and then pricked him just enough to draw blood. "Now," said the Fox sternly.

The other swiftly put his head to the floor, but he did not speak until the flat of the sword smacked him hard across the buttocks, making him yelp.

"Aye, then," he shrieked, "I beg pardon!"

"Consider yourself fortunate that I dinna take a whip to ye as ye've done to the unfortunate folk ye seek to reform," his nemesis said.

"Righteous men should honor the Pope and attend virtuously to the holy sacraments, and priests should neither marry nor have children as they do throughout Scotland," he wailed.

The sword whacked him again. "That isna for ye to decide. Take it up wi' the Kirk in Scotland or with his eminence, Cardinal Beaton, who men do say ye claim as a great friend o' yours. Tell his eminence that if he requires reform in his Kirk, he should take it up openly and begin wi' his ain house."

"By heaven, one day I'll make you swallow your impudence," muttered the other man, still staring at the floor. "See if I don't!"

But he spoke to air, for the intruder was gone. Realizing this, the sheriff's son scrambled to his feet and ran to the open door with the others close behind him.

A breeze stirred, and they saw the man and his horse as black shadows against the silvery, mist-shrouded moonlight. Then the mist swallowed them.

"We'll meet again, you villain," the sheriff's son said, shaking his fist.

The others shook their heads at him, turning back to the fire.

Suddenly, Ian Fraser said, "Look here, what's this?" Bending near the spot where the sheriff's son had knelt, he picked something up from the floor and held it out for the others to see.

It was a silver coin with a stem of Highland heather engraved on one side and a fox's mask on the other.

The Bay of Biscay, that same night

Lightning flashed, thunder cracked, and heavy seas crashed against the sides of the ship, tossing it about as if it were no more than a wee fishing coble. Strong, experienced seamen were sick as cats everywhere, and he would have been no exception had there been anything left in his stomach to spew.

He was exhausted and starving, and had he had a choice, he would have crawled into bed and slept for a month, but he was given no choice. Officers strode about — at least as well as they could stride, considering that they had to grab standing rigging or anything else they could grab to remain upright — bellowing orders and trying to act as if they knew how to keep the storm from sweeping them all to destruction and death somewhere on the formidable French coast.

To be sure, the *Marion Ogilvy* was a stout ship, constructed of modern carvel planking with three masts, lateen rigged fore and aft. But the strength of the wild winds had forced them to furl the sails over an hour ago, and despite the anchors' struggle to slow the ship's speed, it rode the lightning-lit sea now at the mercy of the storm and the hand of God.

He had climbed the mizzenmast earlier to help furl the sails and was standing in the mizzen-topcastle, clinging to the mast with one hand while he fought with the other to lash the furled topsail to its yardarm, when the ship listed to port and the man performing the same task on the mainmast plunged into the angry sea.

No one attempted a rescue, although with the wild pitching and yawing of the ship, he felt as if he were dipping low enough in his topcastle to reach out and pluck the fellow from the water if he popped up again in the right place before the ship righted itself. Instead, the hapless victim vanished beneath the churning waves before terrified officers and men on the deck below realized what had happened.

It was a wonder he had not fallen in himself, as weak as he felt. There was a moment, just a single moment, when he had thought he might let go of the mast and follow the other man into the sea. But the moment had passed, and the anger that had sustained him for so long that it had become part of him stirred to life again. He had descended to the deck without incident and had been working furiously since then to keep things tied down and himself from being swept overboard.

A particularly fierce wave knocked him onto his backside, but a panicked grab and a death grip on the capstan saved him. He clung to it, gasping for breath.

"Lad, come along o' me now," Tam's familiar voice muttered gruffly close to his ear as the Borderer's powerful hand clamped tight to his arm and hauled him upright. "Ye mun get clear o' this place afore one o' them masts comes down."

"Gibson said I was to stay on deck," he said, referring to the first officer.

"Nay, we'll tell 'im one o' the cannons below needs lashing. Come now."

He went without further argument, content for once to let someone else decide his fate.

Chapter 1

The Highlands, a week after Easter Sunday, 1541

The party of riders made its way uphill under a heavily overcast sky, their narrow pathway flanked by steep, bluebell-laden woods. The air was cold, damp, and heavy, the gloom perfectly reflecting the mood of at least one of the riders.

Barbara MacRae, Bab to her family and close friends, was bored and fed up with behaving politely when she felt murderous. She would rather have stayed at court with her brother and friends to continue celebrating the end of Lent and the recent birth of the Duke of Albany, the King's second son, but Sir Patrick MacRae had taken one of his rare pets and ordered her home to the Highlands instead.

Somehow, Patrick had got it into his head that she did not belong at court, that she had cozened their mother into taking her there and then into leaving her there when Lady MacRae returned home to Ardintoul. Some of what he believed was perfectly true, of course, but what had he expected? Had he not left home eight months before without so much as telling her where he was going?

Surely he had not expected her to live forever

at Ardintoul like a nun in a cloister, but he had not even done her the courtesy of letting her know that he was returning or, worse, that he was returning with a wife. Of course, if he had sent a message home, Bab would not have been there to receive it, but she knew he had not sent one, so that was a mere bagatelle.

"Barbara, my dear," Lady Chisholm said gently, "you should put up your hood, for it is chilly with the snow still clinging to the mountains as it is, and I believe it is coming on to drizzle again."

Bab managed a smile as she reached obediently for the hood of her crimson cloak, saying, "I vow, madam, 'tis a miserable day for traveling. Sir Alex was wise to remain at Stirling. Indeed, I am sure we all should have stayed there, for I warrant the castle's hall fires are blazing away, keeping everyone warm and dry."

"It is true enough that our Alex will be warm, wherever he is," Lady Chisholm said with a chuckle. "He is a man who always looks out for his own comfort. But to be fair, my dear, your brother did ask him to linger, and we agreed that his lordship would more swiftly recover his customary health and good spirits at Dundreggan, well away from all the political turmoil."

Lady Chisholm cast a worried glance at her husband, who had rejected his son's suggestion of a litter or chair carried by running gillies, and had opted instead to ride with his wife, their servants, and Mistress MacRae. Bab had not heard until earlier that day that he had been ill, and she could see little sign of it other than a certain lassitude and her ladyship's occasional, narrow-eyed, measuring looks.

Their plodding pace tried Bab's patience. They had been traveling for a sennight, and if they continued at this pace, they would be lucky to arrive at Dundreggan before the fire festival of Beltane on the first day of May.

She was an excellent horsewoman, and she wanted to gallop, if only long enough to blow the fidgets from her mind. But she knew that her companions would forbid her to ride ahead even if she suggested taking along one or two of the half dozen men-at-arms that Sir Alex had provided to protect them.

He had said he did not expect them to encounter trouble, but then Sir Alex, a hedonist to the bone, never expected to meet trouble anywhere. He was far more interested in seeing to his own gentle pleasures.

Before meeting him recently at court, she had not seen him since just before Patrick had gone away. Chisholm and his lady had invited them both to take part in the welcoming party when the newly styled Sir Alex returned after two years of traveling on the Continent. At the time, the family was still reeling from the deaths of his two older brothers, which had occurred that previous Easter Sunday, when Sir Robert Chisholm and his brother Michael apparently died at the hands of a cousin who had gone mad, murdered them, and then had disappeared. Sir Alex's welcome at Dundreggan had therefore been a quiet one, but Lord and Lady Chisholm had wanted to celebrate the return of their sole surviving son, now Chisholm's heir, and Sir Alex had seemed glad to be home.

Bab had thought the continental journey an energetic, even uncharacteristic undertaking for the young man she knew as a friend of her brother's. To be sure, Alex had gone at his father's behest to represent the family at the proxy wedding of James, High King of Scots, to Marie de Guise at the Cathedral of Notre Dame in Paris. But Bab knew that his brothers and hers had teased Alex unmercifully before he left, assuring him that Chisholm was at outs with the King and thus had decided to send the least of his sons to attend him. They told him as well that they were certain he would never reach Paris in time for the ceremony, that he would get lost along the way or be overcome by thieves or murderers.

Bab knew that Patrick, Robert, and Michael had frequently teased Alex so because he scorned to engage in most of the pastimes that they enjoyed. Patrick was an expert with a sword, dirk, longbow, and crossbow, and his reputation as a falconer was of one with an almost magical way with birds of prey. The elder Chisholm brothers had likewise been expert

21

swordsmen and fighters, but Patrick had said that Alex barely knew one end of a sword from the other.

Thus, the two seemed oddly matched as friends, but they had known each other from childhood and Patrick admired Alex's wit and his social skills. Bab, however, preferred men of action like her brother and their friend Fin Mackenzie, Laird of Kintail, while Sir Alex apparently had spent his time on the Continent seeking out the finest tailors and dancing masters. Although she knew Alex had also studied at the famed Sorbonne in Paris, the plain truth was that he had become too Frenchified for the plainspoken Mistress MacRae, and as their recent encounter at Stirling had demonstrated, a year at home had done nothing to improve him.

Lady Chisholm was again narrowly observing his lordship.

To Bab, Chisholm looked as he always did, although he had aged a good deal in the past nine months. He was tall like his son, but Sir Alex was slender and glib, while Chisholm was burly and blunt-spoken. For many years, she knew, his lordship had served as the Sheriff of Inverness-shire, and his customary brusque manner was that of a man who expected instant obedience. That brusqueness was missing today, but he sat straight in his saddle, his continued grim silence the only indication of his weariness.

At least the rain that had fallen intermittently

since morning had not yet begun again. "How much farther do we travel today?" she asked Lady Chisholm.

"Not far, thank heaven," her ladyship replied quietly. "We are to stay the night with friends in the next glen. Indeed, if I thought Chisholm would agree to it, I'd claim hospitality there for several days to let him rest."

"Would he not agree?"

"There is not the slightest chance," Lady Chisholm said, still speaking in an undertone that would not carry to his ears. "Once he is on his way home, it is all I can do to persuade him to halt each night long enough to —"

She broke off with a cry of dismay when her horse reared, nearly unseating her, as a half dozen armed riders burst out of the woods ahead of them.

Bab reacted swiftly, controlling her own mount with one hand as she reached with the other and grabbed the rearing horse's bridle.

"Giorsal, Clarice, this way," she shouted to the two waiting women who accompanied them. "Madam, follow me!"

Wheeling her horse and noting with satisfaction that the attackers were fully engaged in fighting the armed men of the Chisholm party, and that Lady Chisholm had regained control of her horse, she led the women back the way they had come. As she spurred, she murmured a brief prayer that her ladyship, who favored a padded, boxlike woman's saddle, would not be thrown from it by such rough riding.

"Hurry," Bab cried over her shoulder. "The men can fight harder to protect his lordship if we are out of their way!"

"We're right behind you," Lady Chisholm shouted.

Bab's bay gelding was willing, but the track was steep, rutted, and rocky. Knowing better than to ride too fast, for the horses' sake as well as her own and Lady Chisholm's, she searched the thick shrubbery ahead for an opening that would let them seek shelter in the dense woodland.

At the first such place, however, four more riders emerged from the forest and blocked the path. Their leader wore a black cloak and mask.

Bab had no choice but to rein in, but when he yanked off his mask, revealing his face, she exclaimed in relief, "Thank God, Francis Dalcross! I vow, I have never in my life been so glad to see anyone. Ruffians attacked our party down in that glen. You must ride at once to help them!"

"I doubt they'll need my help," he replied blandly, staying where he was.

"Don't be —"

Something in his expression silenced her, and she gazed warily from him to the men flanking him.

Francis Dalcross was tall and broad shouldered with light brown hair, blue eyes, and a charming smile. At Stirling, she had found him fascinating. Indeed, he had been her most ardent suitor there and the most favored — except, of course, by Patrick, who favored no man unless one counted the faintly amused preference he showed Sir Alex Chisholm. And one never counted Sir Alex.

Now Dalcross sat easily on his chestnut horse, regarding her thoughtfully with a slight smile, but any charm that smile had ever suggested to her was gone.

Uneasily, she glanced at Lady Chisholm, who like their two waiting women, remained silent. Her ladyship was staring fixedly at Francis Dalcross, her expression wooden except for a muscle twitching high in her cheek.

"What means this, sir?" Bab demanded. "Why do you not help us?"

"Well, you see, my sweet, those ruffians you mentioned are my ruffians."

"Yours! But why?"

"For you, of course." His blue eyes twinkled as he added, "You did tell me more than once, did you not, how you long for adventure. Have you not heard of *Sionnach Dubh*, the Black Fox of the Highlands?" He bowed, grinning now.

She gaped at him. "Don't be absurd," she snapped when she could speak. "*Sionnach Dubh* is a bairn's tale, not a real person! In any event, you cannot be such an iron-witted daffy as to think I meant you to do anything so outrageous as this! If those horrid men of yours have hurt his lordship or anyone else, I vow I . . . I —" She broke off, unable to think of a punishment severe enough for such a crime.

"I am real enough, mistress," he said evenly. Then, to the men with him, he said, "Take Lady Chisholm and her women back to their party, lads. I'll keep my lass with me. Chisholm and his people may continue their journey to Dundreggan, but do not let them try to follow us, and mention the Fox as often as you like."

"Wait!" Bab cried as his men moved to obey. "What are you going to do?"

"Why, nothing dreadful, my sweet. You will simply come with me, which I promise you will find more entertaining than life at Dundreggan Castle. 'Tis a dour and dreary pile, believe me, well suited to the dreary Chisholms and their ilk."

"But I don't want to go with you!"

"Sakes, mistress," he said, "I expected you to be thrilled by my daring rescue. You cannot want to molder away at Dundreggan, putting up with that sappie-headed bletherskate, Alex Chisholm, whilst you wait for your brother to collect you and bury you alive at Ardintoul."

Although she had been bemoaning this exact fate less than a quarter-hour before, Bab disliked the alternative more. Watching his men lead the other women off down the trail, she said curtly, "Do you want to ruin me?"

"I want to marry you, my sweet, to add to my consequence in the shire, and if you will but consider a moment, you will realize my cleverness. Even if her ladyship does not believe that I am the Black Fox, the rumor will quickly spread that the Fox fell tail over top in love with you and carried you off."

"Patrick does not believe in the Fox. He will kill you for this."

"Then he will hang for his crime," Dalcross retorted. "My father is the Sheriff of Inverness-shire, after all, and I am his deputy."

"Nonsense, even I know that Chisholm serves as Sheriff of Inverness."

"He has not for almost a year. I assumed you knew that he had retired."

"I didn't know any such thing," she said. "Nor do I know it now."

"Well, it is true."

"I do not pay much heed to politics," Bab admitted, "and news from Inverness rarely reaches us at Ardintoul." Sarcastically, she added, "Does Sheriff Dalcross know that his only son goes about claiming to be the Black Fox?"

He smiled enigmatically but said only, "My father wisely allows himself to be guided by me, so in due time, I expect to succeed him as sheriff. I warrant you will enjoy the increased status of being the sheriff's lady."

"By heaven, if you succeed in this wretched plan, I will kill you myself!"

"We hang women, too, my sweet, but you may try your worst. I believe I can defend myself, whatever you do."

"Does it not occur to you that, even if your plan should succeed, an unwilling wife might prove to be an uncomfortable one?"

"She will soon learn to conform to my wishes, however," he replied, reaching to take her reins from her hands. "If she does not, I will make her sorry."

Bab ground her teeth but said no more. As he turned their horses, it occurred to her that had anyone suggested half an hour before that she would be wishing for her brother's presence now, she would have laughed, but she could think of no grander sight than that of Patrick or Wild Fin Mackenzie leading an army of Kintail men to rescue her. It would not happen, though. They were in Stirling, days away.

Francis Dalcross rode ahead, leading Bab's bay gelding by its reins, leaving her nothing to do but think. A knot of fear had settled in her midsection, but she strove to ignore it, refusing to let him see that she felt anything other than fury.

She was no coward. For as long as history had recorded such matters, the MacRaes had guarded the Mackenzies and fought for them, serving them without being servants to them. Just as Patrick served Fin Mackenzie as his constable and friend, her father had served Fin's father and had died at his side in battle. The MacRaes did not sire weaklings, and she was true to her breeding.

As they rode, her thoughts raced, but although her mind was willing and able, the result was small. She knew the lands and tracks of Kintail through and through, but she had rarely visited the Great Glen or its environs — only twice in her life, in fact — and she had never been on this path before today. She and her mother had not traveled by road to Stirling. Instead, they had gone from Kintail down the west coast to Dumbarton in a sea galley rowed by strong oarsmen and aided by lugsails and a stiff wind from the north. From Dumbarton, they had hired horses and men-at-arms to take them to Stirling Castle.

So far, at least, she knew how to get back to where Dalcross had caught her. Although he turned uphill through dense woodland that soon hid the path from view behind them, she still did not worry, because she knew the path followed the glen. She could easily find it again, and since Lady Chisholm had said they would stay with friends in the next glen, she was sure she could find them again too, if she could just get away from Francis before he got her totally lost.

His horse was large, well muscled, and undoubtedly fresher than hers, which was tired from days of traveling. They had not changed horses, because Chisholm had insisted that the slow pace would not tax even the oldest nag, that a few hours' rest each night was all they needed, but she knew that horses did not

rest any better than humans in strange surroundings. Thus, she judged her chances of
outrunning Dalcross to be small and tried to
imagine instead how she could outwit him.

Her usually quick mind seemed sluggish. She
knew she was tired, but she knew, too, that if
the men who had attacked the Chisholm party
rejoined them, even the slimmest chance to escape would disappear. She would have to think
quickly.

Dalcross clearly knew where he was going.
Near the top of the ridge, where patches of
snow still lingered amongst the bluebells, he
followed a deer track for a time before he dismounted to lead both horses through a narrow,
rocky pass. The mountains here were like a
maze and as steep as the mountains of Kintail.

"Hold tight, my sweet," he said. "I don't
want you to fall, and this next bit is steep. Even
if these rocks are not icy, they will still be slip-
pery from the rain."

They had left the trees behind. Melting snow
banks were larger and more precipitous, because the pass was barren and boulder-strewn,
but at last, from the other side, she gazed down
on a glen much like the one they had left, albeit
with fewer trees and more heather. The slopes
were purple with it, dull now under the gray
sky but doubtless splendid in sunlight. She
could hear a burn rushing below.

"It is beautiful here, is it not?" Dalcross said.

"It's cold. Where are we?"

" 'Tis my own place. No one else kens its existence."

Scornfully, she said, "Surely others have been here."

He shrugged. "I have never seen another human here. It is my place."

She hoped that meant his men would not join them, because he would have to sleep sometime, and she could escape then. Looking around, memorizing the landscape, she searched for distinctive boulders and trees. Although she often had to think to remember which was her right hand and which was her left, let alone to tell north from south, Patrick had long since trained her to find her way in the mountains, where getting lost could amount to a death sentence.

When they were out of the loose, tumbling scree, Dalcross mounted again and led the way down through a scattering of trees into foliage that grew thicker as they neared the burn. For a time the greenery was so thick that Bab could glimpse only flashes of light on the rushing water, but then the trees and bushes thinned and she saw a thatched cottage near the water's edge ahead.

"I thought you said no one else was here."

"There is no one," he said. "I built the cottage myself for my own pleasure."

The look he gave her then made icy fingers tickle her spine. He was not as large as Patrick or Fin, but he was larger than she was, and she had no weapon. She had only her damp cloak and the other clothing she wore, because Chisholm's sumpter ponies carried all her baggage. She did not even carry her riding whip, not having needed it in such plodding company.

Dismounting, Dalcross dropped her reins to the ground while he tied his to a bush near the cottage entrance. Then, without bothering to pick hers up again, he turned toward her, his eyes gleaming with anticipation.

She sat still until he reached for her. Then, giving sudden spur to her horse, she grabbed a handful of its mane and leaned forward, spurring hard to urge it on.

His hand flashed up, catching the bridle and yanking the gelding to a halt before it had taken two steps. With his other hand, he grabbed her wrist and gave it a vicious twist.

Stifling a cry of pain, she snatched her hand away, but he caught her waist in both hands and lifted her from the saddle. Instead of setting her down, he slung her over his shoulder as if she had been a sack of meal and strode to the cottage.

His bony shoulder bit into her side and stomach, bruising her, but she struggled nonetheless, screaming and pounding his back with her fists.

Ignoring her blows, he carried her inside and dumped her onto a pallet of furs and fleeces, knocking the wind out of her.

The cottage had no windows, so Dalcross

loomed over her like a dark, evil shadow outlined in the dim light from the doorway behind
him.

"Before you strike someone, you should consider the likely penalty," he said grimly as he
unbuckled his sword belt and cast it aside. "If
you ever raise a hand to me again, mistress, I
will beat you until you scream your remorse to
the four winds, and then I will beat you some
more. Do you understand me?"

"Aye," she said. "What I do not understand
is why I liked you at Stirling. It is a penance
just to know that Patrick judged you more accurately than I did."

"Get up."

She glowered at him, not moving.

"Do as I bid you," he snapped. "You have already given me cause to punish you, and I do
not let such things pass. Do not add to your offense."

The threat made her shiver this time, but as
she sat up, she said, "You will do as you please,
I expect, since there is no one here to stop
you."

"I'm glad you understand that," he said,
bending to grab her forearm and jerking her to
her feet.

Fighting increasing fear, she looked him in
the eye and said, "You will have to force me,
Francis Dalcross. I will never submit to you
willingly."

"I'll enjoy forcing you, lass. I'll also enjoy

schooling you to obey me," he added, catching her by the shoulders and pulling her close.

Seeing his intent, she ducked her head, but he caught her chin, forcing her face up, and then brought his mouth down hard against hers.

Bab struggled to free herself, but he just held her tighter, and when she raised a knee sharply, he sidestepped it, leaned back, and slapped her across the face.

As she put a hand to her stinging cheek, he jerked loose the strings of her cloak, pushed it from her shoulders, and reached for her bodice. Clutching the material in both hands, he tore the gown and the shift beneath it, baring her to the waist. Then, grabbing her by the shoulders again, his grip cruelly tight, he shook her and said harshly, "If you ever try that trick again, I'll strip you naked and take my whip to you." Then his mouth crushed against hers again.

"Release her," a deep, unfamiliar voice snapped from behind him, "or her soft lips will be the last thing ye touch in this life afore I send ye to the devil!"

Dalcross whirled around. "You!"

"Aye, ye spawn o' Satan, 'tis me, indeed."

With her attention on Dalcross, Bab had not noticed that the light from the doorway had dimmed, blocked by the figure of a man whose head nearly touched the lintel and whose shoulders barely fit between the upright posts. Cloaked in black, his face hidden beneath a hoodlike mask, he held a menacing basket-hilt sword in his right hand, and his eyes flashed through the holes in his mask.

"Did this snaffling gallows bird dare to hurt ye, lass?" he demanded.

"No," Bab said, regaining her wits as relief and unfamiliar heat surged through her in equal measure. She was safe now, come what may, for her rescuer could only be the true *Sionnach Dubh*, the greatest swordsman in all Scotland — perhaps in all the world. She had heard tales about him since her childhood, but she had believed he was only a legend. Clearly, amazingly, he was real.

Chapter 2

With one hand still clutching Bab's arm, Dalcross snarled at the newcomer, "My men are all around this house, but if you leave at once, you may escape them."

The Fox laughed, an infectious sound from deep in his throat that sent more of those odd feelings coursing through Bab's body. "Ye always come to this place alone, Francis Dalcross," he said. "Your men followed Chisholm and his party, and my men are following yours. All of them, that is, but for the ones who came here wi' me and now guard this wee glen against undesirable intruders."

"Do you mean to murder me then?" Dalcross demanded, his voice unsteady. He glanced at Bab, and although she still watched the Fox, she could see enough of his expression to know that Francis wondered if she knew he was afraid.

No longer fearful of him, she focused her attention on her rescuer, trying to judge his size and detect any other trait that might reveal something of the man beneath the cloak and mask. His accent was common to the area, albeit not as heavy as some, and he still blocked the doorway, so the dusky light in the cottage

36

revealed as little about him as his voice did. She could not even tell the color of his eyes.

These thoughts flashed through her mind in the moment of silence before the Fox said easily, "I expect I *could* kill ye, Dalcross. Ye deserve it for the things ye've done in the name o' his grace the King. I willna do it, but ye'll benefit from another wee lesson in manners, so come away outside wi' me, and I'll give ye yet one more chance to best me wi' yon Italian pig sticker ye call a sword."

"By heaven, you'll soon be sped yourself then, you insolent cockerel!" Snatching up his sword belt, Dalcross whipped the weapon from its sheath, making Bab gasp and look quickly at the Fox to see if he had anticipated such a move.

He simply stepped back out of the doorway to wait outside, clearly unconcerned about any trick Francis Dalcross might attempt to pull.

When the latter strode out to confront him, Bab followed, remembering her torn gown only when the breeze kissed her bare skin. Then, dismayed to think that both the Fox and Francis had seen her bare breasts, she clutched the remnants tightly together. Her cloak lay on the floor behind her, but she left it there, not wanting to miss a second of what transpired outside and wishing she had a pistol so that she could shoot Francis if he even looked like he might hurt the Black Fox.

Both men held their swords at the ready now

and circled, narrow-eyed, each clearly measuring the other's fighting state. The Fox had
swept his dark cloak back over his right
shoulder to keep it from tangling his blade, but
it still seemed to Bab as if it might encumber
him. She wished he would take it off.

She could see now that he was well built, that
his powerful torso tapered to a slim waist and
strong thighs. His black boots were nearly knee
high but fit so snugly that she could see the
lines of his muscular calves. He moved lightly,
with feline grace, his steps muffled on the soft,
damp ground.

Suddenly Francis lunged.

Bab clapped a hand to her mouth to stifle the
cry that rose to her lips, but the Fox parried the
thrust with ease, and although Francis fought
hard and with evident skill, she soon saw that
the Fox was more proficient. She had often
watched Patrick at practice and recognized in
the Fox the same easy grace and dexterity.

Just as that thought passed through her
mind, Dalcross leaped forward and forced the
Fox's blade aside with a deft flick of his wrist,
and then thrust toward his heart. She barely
had time to gasp at the move, however, before
it was deflected.

The Fox employed no offensive tactics until
his opponent began sweating heavily. Then,
abruptly, in a few flashing flurries, it was over.
The sword that had looked like an extension of
Francis's hand one moment went sailing

through the air the next, whipped adroitly away by his opponent, whose own sword point now pressed against Francis Dalcross's throat.

Scarcely daring to breathe, Bab could not look away.

"Don't," she said quietly. "Don't kill him."

"I am no killer, lass," the Fox said just as quietly. "However, this shameless varlet dared to rip your gown." His sword tip dipped lower, touching the top button of Francis Dalcross's doublet. "Dinna ye move now, varlet."

The blade slid inside and up, slicing through threads, while Dalcross stood stiffly, his brow beaded with sweat. Then the sword slipped down to his belt and breeks. In moments, the sharp edge had reduced his fine clothing to rags.

"Ye'll step out o' your boots now if ye please," the Fox said politely.

Dalcross glowered at him but dared not argue with that gleaming blade.

When he had removed his boots, his nemesis said, "Now strip off what's left o' them rags and set them tidily by yon boots."

"I'll not stand naked before the lass!"

"Ye had no regrets about baring the lass, so ye'll bare yourself, or I'll bare ye, choose how. She can turn away if she doesna want to gaze on your puny body."

Bab could not have turned away unless her own life had depended on it, but although she could see them both easily enough, her gaze was fixed on the Fox, not on Francis Dalcross. Her rescuer did not look at her, however, until Dalcross had obeyed him and stepped naked away from the pile of clothing.

"Now, then, start walking, varlet, and give thought to your bad manners and to them ye've stripped o' their goods and turned out o' their homes just for living as they ha' done for hundreds o' years. See how ye like bein' without, yourself."

"You cannot —"

"I can. I do." Flipping a silver coin through the air toward the man, he added, "Take that. Mayhap 'twill buy ye a shirt from someone wiling to sell ye one. Meantime, the lass and I will look after your horse. Now, move along, or I'll assist ye wi' the flat o' me blade as I did last time." He hefted the weapon threateningly.

After Dalcross bent hastily to pick up the coin and dashed barefoot to the cover of the thicker foliage near the burn, the Fox moved to recover the fallen sword. Only then did he say to Bab, "Ye'd best collect your cloak, lass, for unless ye've a needle and thread by ye, ye'll need it to cover yourself. Ye canna safely ride a horse if ye ha' to clutch your dress like that."

Still gripping her torn bodice, Bab went into the cottage and picked up her cloak, putting it on and fastening enough of the clasps to protect her modesty. Stepping back outside, she came face-to-face with the Fox.

She had already seen that he was tall, but

standing so close to her, he seemed larger than life.

He reached toward her, placing his hands gently on her shoulders, but even so light a touch sent a wave of heat to her very core.

His gaze met hers and held it, his eyes gleaming with intent. She saw at last that they were light gray, almost colorless, but the knowledge was of little help, since more Highland folk than not had blue eyes or gray. If his were unusual, it was only that they were particularly light and particularly clear, only darkening at the outermost rim of the iris.

He gazed into her eyes as if he were also trying to determine their color, which was absurd, since she knew they were just ordinary dark blue.

Still she could do nothing but stare back at him.

Gently he reached for the ribbons of her hood although she had not even put it up. He tied them in a bow beneath her chin, his knuckles gently brushing her skin as he did. When she did not move or protest he put one hand on her left shoulder, slowly drawing her closer. Then, with the other hand, he eased the lower part of his mask up as he bent his head and kissed her on the lips.

She could smell the dusty material of his mask and saw his light gray eyes close to hers. His lips tasted salty, but they were smooth and soft, and they moved gently against hers, as if they savored the taste of her.

No man had ever before dared to take her willingness for granted until Francis Dalcross had done so that day, but it did not occur to her to protest. It was not the first time she had been kissed, of course, but any man who had kissed her before had first sought her permission, and those kisses — although daring, since she was yet a maiden — had been chaste and gentlemanly. This one was neither, although she could not have explained just why it was not.

Perhaps the energy emanating from him made his kisses seem unusual.

As the thought crossed her mind, the hand that touched her shoulder slid to the small of her back, somehow increasing the heat in her body as his other hand eased around to the hollow between her shoulder blades, pulling her harder against him. At the same time, the pressure of his lips against hers intensified.

Lower down, she felt his body stir against hers.

Bab closed her eyes, relishing every sensation.

His kiss grew hungrier, more demanding, and her lips moved in response.

His hands slid over her body, exploring and caressing her as no man's hands had ever done before, and yet she did not try to stop him even when his tongue slipped into her mouth.

Involuntarily she gasped, but his tongue felt warm, and her body welcomed the penetration with another rush of pleasure. Without a thought for what she was doing, she pressed harder against him, moaning softly in her throat.

He raised his head, and both hands moved back to her shoulders, holding her firmly as if he knew that her knees were weak and might not hold her.

She stared at him blankly, wondering why he had stopped.

"Now that," he said softly, "is how a man should kiss a woman."

Her throat felt tight, and she was not sure she could speak, let alone speak sensibly, but since he seemed to expect a response, she murmured, "Is it?"

"Aye, so if ye're sensible, lass, ye'll ha' no more to do wi' Francis Dalcross. He's not nearly enough man for ye."

"No," she said, agreeing with him and realizing that it did not disturb her in the least to know that he would now abduct her just as Dalcross had.

He gestured toward the two horses tethered near the cottage. "The bay would be yours, mistress, would it not?"

"Aye," Bab said. "The chestnut is his."

"Ha' ye aught else inside to collect afore we go?"

"Nay." She had a dozen questions she wanted to ask him, but the words would not form sensibly on her tongue. She could only stare at him.

Without looking away, he gave a low whistle. At first she thought he expected it to mean something to her, but then she heard movement in the nearby thicket, and a splendid horse appeared, all black except for a narrow white stripe extending from just above its eyes to its nostrils. Trotting to the Fox, it nuzzled his shoulder as he stroked its nose.

"What's his name?" she asked.

"Merry Dancer."

"Like one of the Northern Lights?"

"Aye, for he's magnificent, beautiful, and strong, just as they are."

"How did you find me?"

His eyes twinkled, and she knew he must be smiling. "Ha' ye no heard, lass? *Sionnach Dubh* kens all, sees all, and rescues them that suffer from injustice."

"I have heard that," she admitted. "Are the tales all true, then?"

"Need ye ask?" He reached for her shoulder again, but his touch was casual this time as he turned her toward her horse. "We'd best be going," he said. "I doubt that yon Dalcross will soon find his lads or let them see him as bare as he is, but if I'm wrong and he leads them back here, we're sped."

"Surely, if you know all and see all . . ."

He chuckled. "I'll ha' none o' your backchat, lassie."

"But did you not say that you left some of your men watching?"

44

"I did, so now ye ken me for as grand a liar as Dalcross," he said as he lifted her onto her saddle. "Will ye still love me even so?"

Feeling flames in her cheeks, she said sternly, "You should not jest about love, sir. Where are you taking me?"

"To rejoin the rest o' your party. Where else would I take ye?"

Since she would rather have died than admit she had hoped he was abducting her, Bab did not answer, but her cheeks felt hotter than ever.

He untied the gelding and handed her its reins. Then he untied the chestnut that Francis Dalcross had ridden, and with its reins in his hand, mounted the black and guided it to stand next to hers. "Ready?"

"Aye," she murmured.

He said no more, and she remained silent, too, as they rode back up the hill. The questions she wanted to ask seemed impossible under the circumstances. A well-bred young woman simply did not ask a masked man why he did not wish to abduct her, and doubtless it would also be unmannerly to ask him to remove the mask. He had rescued her from a horrid fate, after all. The least she could do was respect his privacy as he apparently expected.

Honesty stepped in then. The truth was that she did not want him to refuse her request, and she was certain he would. Thus, they rode in silence until they reached the track she and the others had been following when Francis's men attacked them. It occurred to her then that the Fox might leave her there, expecting her to rejoin the Chisholm party without further help.

Glancing at him, she nearly blurted the question, but he forestalled her.

"I'll see ye safe afore I leave ye, mistress."

"Thank you," she said. "I should have thanked you before, for rescuing me."

"Aye, but ye did," he said, and she heard laughter in his voice. "However, if ye think the one wee kiss were insufficient, mayhap we should bargain a bit."

She felt her heart pound at the thought of what he might mean, but she had regained her wits and would not have him guess that she had nearly lost them. "I do not bargain with men," she said.

"That be a good attitude to take wi' most men," he said amiably.

"Is it, indeed?" she said, nearly adding *sir* out of habit. Something about him reminded her of her brother and Fin Mackenzie. He had the same ease of command and the posture and bearing of a man who knew his worth. He spoke like a common man, to be sure, but she had noted, too, that he often phrased things as his betters might, so he clearly aimed to improve himself.

"Aye, lass," he said, repeating provocatively, " 'twould work wi' most men."

She knew that he did not count himself among "most men," nor should he. His voice was so deep that it seemed to vibrate when he spoke, and the vibrations touched responsive chords in her body.

They came to a branching glen, and he gestured toward a narrow path jutting upward at an angle from the track they followed. "We'll go that way," he said.

"Why?"

" 'Tis the way your people went," he said.

"But how can you know that? There are hoof prints everywhere in this mud, and just as many fresh tracks lead onward as lead up that hill."

"Aye, for Dalcross's men will ha' left your people here," he said.

"But how do you know which ones went which way?"

He gestured toward a nearby tree. "That mark yonder," he said.

She saw it at once, a slash in the bark of a tree. It did not cut through the outer layer, but it was visible once he had pointed it out. So he did have henchmen of one sort or another, at least one of whom had followed Lord and Lady Chisholm.

"Lead on," he said. "I'll follow until we see the gates, and then I'll watch until ye be safe within."

She did not ask how he knew there would be gates, thinking that perhaps in this area everyone had them, but they came into view all too soon. Built of stout timber and ironbound, the double gates formed part of a high, stone wall, and she could see the steeply pitched roof of a house beyond.

They reined in, and she turned to him. "Thank you again. He would have ruined me had he succeeded in his plan. If ever you need aught of —"

"Dinna say it, lass," he cautioned. "Ye shouldna make promises to men ye dinna ken, even them that play hero now and again. Ride on now, and if ye do have a care for me, ride quickly, so I needna tarry here long. Ah, but wait now. I ha' a wee gift for ye to remember me by."

He reached inside his cloak and withdrew a silver coin. Pressing it into her hand, he closed her fingers over it and said, "Go quickly now, and don't look back!"

Clutching the coin, not daring to look at it lest some guard at the gate demand to know what she carried, she obeyed him, spurring the gelding to urge it to speed. Nor did she glance back to see if he lingered. She was not so obedient by nature, but if the guards had not seen him, she did not want to alert them to his presence. Let them think she rode alone, desperately hard though it was to keep her gaze fixed firmly ahead.

He watched her from the shelter of the trees until the ironbound gates of Gorthleck House opened and swallowed her. What a lass she was! Stunningly beautiful but without guile or vanity, and she had a head on her shoulders and courage in her heart. He had thought it too much to expect that she would resist looking back, but she had surprised him, making him even more thankful that he had sent Hugo to keep watch over the Chisholm party. The decision had seemed only sensible at the time, and he had been confident of his abilities against Dalcross, but his stomach churned now at the thought that had he been wrong and had Dalcross bested him, the villain would have succeeded in his evil intent.

He could still taste her lips on his, and he mentally shook his head at his foolhardiness in kissing her. No sooner had he touched her than his usual quick wits and survival instinct had deserted him, for she might easily have unmasked him when he kissed her, and had she done so, it would have jeopardized everything.

Knowing she was safe now, or as safe as any lass could be these days in the Highlands, he forced his thoughts back to the present and the necessity to take every care. Riding back to the main track, leading Dalcross's horse, he forded the burn that tumbled through the center of the glen and rode into the trees on the other side.

Elsewhere and in their own time

As Brown Claud entered the misty place members of the Secret Clan called the High

Glen, music filled the air. It was so infectious that his feet begin to tingle, reminding him of another day and the beguiling Lucy Fittletrot, who had enticed him to a fair where he danced as he had never danced before. He had liked Lucy.

But Lucy had disappointed him, and despite his tingling toes, he did not feel like dancing. It was a long time since he had been to the High Glen, and he entered reluctantly and only because he dared not ignore the summons to present himself before the High Circle. In his experience, such a summons portended nothing good.

The music grew louder as he walked down the hill into the mist, and despite his fears, the sound eased his spirits. He began to look forward just a little to the Beltane fair and the gathering of the tribes, if not to the meeting of the Circle.

At first, he was aware only of the lush, mist-laden shrubbery around him and the enthralling music, but as he moved deeper into the Glen, although the music grew louder and more alluring, he heard laughter, too.

Moments later, the mist dissipated, and he saw the fair in a clearing ahead. Colorful tents and banners emerged from the densely growing trees and shrubbery. A greensward in the center teemed with dancers, and folk who were not dancing tapped a foot or nodded to the music.

He recognized members of different tribes by their apparel and appearance as hailing from the lowlands, the hills, or from points in between, as well as others whose antecedents he could not so readily discern.

He chuckled, his spirits increasingly buoyed by the music. Until he found his mother, he would not even know why he had been summoned. He watched eagerly for her, but although he searched the merry crowd, he could not find her, and soon his determination to do so faded, as did his worries about why he was there, until he was aware of nothing but music and gaiety.

Maggie Malloch was aware of her son Claud's arrival, had known the moment he entered the High Glen, and she knew what he was feeling, but she had other things on her mind. The annual spring festival of Beltane had already begun for the Secret Clan, and as a fire festival, Beltane was a time when the members' powers were at their strongest, when tempers flashed and mischief stalked the shadowlands. And at present, she was enduring a more private meeting of her own.

"What were ye thinking, woman?"

She stiffened and looked the questioner straight in the eye, although she had to look up a considerable distance to do so. He was much taller than she, reed thin, white-bearded, and a wizard of the first order whose eyes were

51

known to flash real sparks when he was angry. He was also Chief of the Secret Clan, but the only thing that gave him greater power than hers was her sworn fealty to him. "I were thinking I'd a job tae do, like always," she said.

"Aye, sure," he agreed. "Still, ye ken our rules, and ye ha' overstepped them by a wide margin wi' this last business."

Rolling her eyes toward the ether as though she sought patience there, she made a rude noise, which was met by grim silence.

Meeting his stern gaze again, she saw that his pupils glowed like smoldering coals. Her temper stirred, but for once she drew a deep breath to bank it down before she said, "I ken fine what I did. Ye'll recollect, though, that the odds were high, the opposition unmannerly if not downright evil, and the outcome excellent."

His grim expression did not soften. "The outcome doesna concern me," he said. "What does concern me is your evident belief that our rules dinna pertain tae ye. Did ye no warn your own son that he should do naught tae draw attention tae himself or tae Lucy Fittletrot, that wee Border baggage he's mad about?"

"I did," Maggie replied.

"And were ye no casting spells right and left even afore then, the results o' which anyone wi' half an eye could see?"

"Even an I did do such a thing," she said, "ye can be sure I saw tae all the pertinent details afterward. There be nae one able tae

52

speak o' those events, nor will there be, for none will recall aught but his or her own role that night."

"Sakes, woman, ye took a common serving lass, clad her in a grand dress, decked her wi' jewels fit for a queen, and sent her tae a royal ball. Are ye so daft that ye thought nae one would notice her there?"

Maggie shrugged. "Only good came o' that in the end. She married happily."

He was silent, but his eyes remained fiery, and the air was thick with his displeasure. At last, quietly, he said, "Ye caused a riot."

"I solved a problem nae one else could ha' solved and in the face o' grand wickedness, too," she retorted. "When ye recall what I did, mind ye recall what that villain Jonah Bonewits tried tae do, as well."

"Aye, Maggie, I ken fine that Jonah Bonewits ha' tried ye sorely over the years, but what I'm trying tae tell ye now, if ye'd but listen tae me, is that although we ha' banned him from the Circle, he still has allies here."

"Toadies, more like!"

"Aye, sure, call them what ye will. Still, they'll no stand for ye tae walk clear o' this business when he did not, not when they can say, and fairly, too, that ye ha' made nae progress on the other wee task we set for ye."

"I ken that, too," she admitted. "But mending rifts betwixt the Merry Folk and the Helping Hands be a gey difficult task, which is why ye set me tae do it. The mischief lies wi' their determined unwillingness tae come tae any agreement."

"I understand that. Still, ye'd best understand that what comes o' this will come tae ye. Ye'll ha' tae answer for your actions and for the lack o' them, too."

"Aye," she said, folding her arms across her breast and glowering at him. "Let them try their worst."

Aboard the Marion Ogilvy, *outside the Strait of Gibraltar*

The storm that prevented the *Marion Ogilvy* from entering the Mediterranean reminded him of the first storm he had endured at sea, except that he no longer cared much one way or another if the ship stayed afloat or plunged to the bottom. He had not been ashore since his boarding, bound and gagged, when he had learned that his fate was to serve aboard her until he died.

The *Marion Ogilvy* would be heading for Rome and then Brindisi and Venice when she could sail through the Strait, but it did not matter where she went. One port or another, it was all the same to him.

Bab's arrival at Gorthleck House, home of Malcolm and Fiona Mackintosh, the friends of Lord and Lady Chisholm with whom they were to pass the night, was the cause of profound relief and delight, particularly after she assured her hostess and Lady Chisholm that she was unharmed.

"I vow, I should not have known what to say to Sir Patrick had you not returned safely to us, my dear," Lady Chisholm exclaimed, hugging her. "I was terrified, and I promise you, his lordship wanted to send men at once to look for you, and he would have had those villains not threatened to murder us all if anyone so much as stirred a foot to do so."

"I am just glad to see that you are all safe," Bab said sincerely.

"You have had a dreadful ordeal," Fiona Mackintosh exclaimed. She was a slender woman of an age with Lady Chisholm. Her personality was effervescent and her delight in Bab's safe arrival at Gorthleck House was warm and sincere.

"Indeed we have," Lady Chisholm agreed. "Only two of our men were injured, and neither seriously, I'm glad to say."

His lordship entered with his host and the Mackintoshes' son Eric, to express their relief at Bab's safety, so the subject was changed, and later, when his lordship asked how she had escaped, she said calmly, "A stranger intervened, and I was able to get away, my lord. Fortunately, her ladyship had told me where you meant to pass the night, so I rode until I found the path that led to this house. I can tell you," she added with a laugh, "I was prodigiously re-lieved to learn from the guards at the gate that you were actually here."

The deceitful answer tugged at her con-science, but something told her the Fox would be safer if she did not tell all and sundry that he was in the vicinity. Doubtless, Francis Dalcross was ripe for murder, and as his father's deputy, he must command any number of men-at-arms, so the less he knew or could learn about the Fox's movements, the better.

Another mental vision stirred to tickle her sense of the ridiculous, for it presented her with a picture of Francis, striding up naked to a group of his armed men and ordering them to ride out at once in search of the Fox and not return until they could bring him the man's masked head on a pikestaff.

Exhausted from her long day, she excused herself after supper and went to bed, barely ex-changing more than a few words with her waiting woman, despite that worthy's clear de-sire to learn every detail of the afternoon ad-venture.

"All you need know of it, Giorsal, is that Dalcross did nothing horrid and I am safe and sound," Bab said crisply when the woman per-sisted in her questions.

"Aye, Mistress Bab, mayhap that be true, but when ye returned, ye had the odd look about ye, and no the sort a lass usually has when she ha' been abducted."

"Have you known so many abducted women, then?" she asked, grinning.

As Giorsal sputtered her insistence that it was no such thing but only worry about her mistress, Bab said, "I had an adventure, that's all. If he had harmed me, I'd have cause to look glum, but since he did not . . ." She shrugged.

Giorsal snorted. "Adventure, is it? I warrant Sir Patrick wouldna think it so. I dinna want to hear what he will say about it, I promise ye."

"Well, Patrick will know naught about it until he comes to fetch me, and since he will see then for himself that I am unharmed, he will doubtless only laugh at the whole affair."

She did not really believe that Patrick would laugh, but he would not feel obliged to seek out Francis Dalcross so long after the fact either, whereas he might feel so were he presently at hand. For that, above all else, she was grateful.

As slowly as the Chisholm party traveled, she had half-expected him to overtake them on the way, because he had promised not to dally but to fetch her as soon as he was able. Now it occurred to her that he might already have returned to Kintail. Had he sailed on a Highland galley, as she and her mother had, traveling to Stirling, he might have reached Ardintoul by now or even already be awaiting them at Dundreggan. She rather hoped he was. Although she liked Lady Chisholm, and his lordship had been kind to her, she would feel more comfortable at home.

As expected, Lady Chisholm failed to persuade his lordship to remain more than one night with their friends, and they departed the following day, reaching the Great Glen before noon. From there, their journey along the western shore of Loch Ness and west into Glen Urquhart and Glen Affric, consumed nearly four more days, although Bab was sure she could have ridden it in one.

Indeed, she was certain she could have walked the distance more quickly, but Lady Chisholm called for frequent rest periods and always insisted that they stop for the day by four o'clock. She said it was for his lordship's benefit, but Bab, sensing his lordship's impatience, thought the slow pace taxed him more than would a faster pace. She had learned enough, however, to realize it was more likely her ladyship's own indolent nature that demanded the former.

Still that pace made it more likely that Patrick would be at Dundreggan to meet her when she arrived. So when the formidable red-and-white-stone castle hove into sight at last on the triangular granite promontory where the River Affric met another swiftly rushing burn, her heart began to pound with a mixture of eager anticipation to see him and apprehension for what he was likely to say when he learned of her adventure. It was thus a disappointment to find that he was not waiting in the graveled bailey when they rode through the arched gateway.

Bab had visited the castle before, so she settled in quickly, but finding that Lady Chisholm looked askance on any venturing outside the high stone curtain wall, she chafed at having too little to do. So, she explored the castle again, revisiting the splendid little chapel that adjoined the massive keep and inspecting the dairy, bakehouse, and kitchens.

She strolled the length of the long gallery above the great hall, and peeped through the laird's peek to see what was happening below, knowing no one there could see her. She also spent a good deal of time in Lady Chisholm's comfortable bower, accessed through a door at the back of the great-hall dais, where she chatted with her hostess, whose cheery kindness made the tedious hours pass more quickly.

Still, Bab longed for activity, so when riders arrived two days later, on the eve of Beltane, she hurried downstairs, telling herself that it must be Patrick at last.

Dashing into the bailey, she stopped short at the sight of six running gillies carrying a large, covered chair on long poles. As she stared in amazement, the men came to a stop, breathing heavily as they lowered the chair to the ground.

Its curtains parted. Then one silk shod foot emerged and gently touched the ground, followed by a second one as the chair's occupant stepped out.

Sir Alex Chisholm had returned home to Dundreggan.

Chapter 3

Bab gazed wryly at the crisp, well-dressed vision before her, remembering how dusty and tired she had been at the end of each day and how grateful she had been to see Dundreggan's walls when at last they had loomed ahead of her.

Sir Alex was tall, graceful, and splendidly attired, almost as if he had meant to present himself at court instead of at his own ancestral home in one of the more isolated glens in the Highlands. Silver lace edged his dark blue velvet doublet, and his trunk hose was splashed and puffed with a lighter blue silk, from which the fashionable, ruffled edging of his collar had been made to match. He wore clocked stockings, and his velvet shoes boasted modish pointed toes and silver trimming.

His dark hair was cut fashionably short in the German style. In the sunlight, its russet highlights gleamed. His handsome face was clean-shaven, and his features well formed, but in Bab's opinion, his drooping eyelids and a weakness in the look of his mouth and chin sadly reduced his beauty. She shook her head at him.

"Really, sir," she said.

"I am delighted to see that you and my parents arrived safely, Mistress MacRae," he drawled. "Are you not equally overjoyed to see me?"

His voice was higher-pitched than she liked to hear in a man, but she thought she would not mind if it did not sound as if he might fall asleep midway through a sentence. She felt a familiar impulse to shake him, to see if she could wake him up.

As it was, she said more sharply than she had intended, "Yes, of course, we arrived safely. What on earth is that thing you were riding in?"

He looked at the chair and then back at her, clearly puzzled. "But you can see what it is, mistress. I thought it a clever notion, myself. Suggested it to my father, don't you recall, but he scorned such comfort for himself."

"I cannot imagine why you should need such pampering."

He shrugged. "Since you are one of the many who account me an indifferent horseman, I thought you would approve. Indeed, you should try it yourself when you return to Ardintoul. I promise you, such a conveyance, with its cushions and fur rugs, is far more comfortable than any saddle could be."

"Where is Patrick?" she demanded, tiring of the subject.

"Faith, I haven't a notion. Must we stand out here in the sun like this? You seem to forget that I've endured a tedious long journey."

"I warrant you are nigh onto fainting with fatigue," she snapped.

"Aye, well, I doubt I shall faint," he said, his eyes nearly closed, his posture flagging, "but I received a prodigious shock two days ago when I reached Gorthleck House and learned of your abduction. I have been nigh sick with worry ever since."

"Indeed, sir."

"Aye, mistress." He covered a yawn before adding, "I regret that such a wretched inconvenience should occur whilst you were under my father's protection. I warrant you were terrified."

"It proved to be a little more than an interesting adventure," she said airily. "Moreover, I do not believe for one minute that it can have worried you overmuch, sir, since you took two days to get here after hearing about it."

"But that in itself proves I *did* hurry," he protested. "Experience makes me certain, you see, that the same journey took you at least four days."

"Aye, but your father is ailing. That is why we traveled so slowly."

"Do you think so?" He regarded her quizzically, adding gently, "Now, I have found that my mother always travels at a sensible pace, whether any of her companions is ailing or not, but doubtless you know best. Are you certain that your ordeal caused no lasting harm?"

"Certainly not, sir, I promise you."

"Well, I shan't press you further, as it is clear from your sharp tone that the ordeal distressed you more than you like to say. You will be safe enough at Dundreggan, though. We harbor no vulgar villains here to trouble you."

Annoyed, she said, "Since my abductor was Francis Dalcross, the son of the Sheriff of Inverness, he is no mere vulgar villain."

"But of course he is. I knew it was Dalcross, of course, thanks to the ever loquacious and generally informative Fiona Mackintosh and her son Eric, who is a friend of mine; but what I do not understand is what can have possessed Dalcross to do something so cock-brained as to abduct a young lady from my father's party."

"He said he expected to impress me," Bab said. "I met him at Stirling, as you must know, and I'm afraid I once confided to him that I long for adventure."

"Do you, indeed?"

"Aye, but not the sort he intended, I promise you. That is not the real reason he wanted me, anyway. He said he wants to marry me to increase his consequence in Inverness. I don't call that adventurous at all!"

"Adventure of any sort is tiresome," he said, putting a hand gently beneath her right elbow and urging her toward the entrance to the castle keep. "I infinitely prefer life to run a perfectly gentle, predictable course."

She had two choices. She could either walk with him or pull her elbow away. The latter seemed rude, so she allowed him to take her inside.

As a minion leaped to open the door for them, Sir Alex said in a puzzled tone, "It must have been high adventure, indeed, if you were able to escape from Dalcross. I should have thought him a match for any woman, even one of your undoubted resourcefulness, but Eric mentioned that you had encountered a stranger who intervened, thus allowing your escape. You neglected to provide even the stranger's description, however, which seems somewhat remiss of you."

She glanced at him, wondering what resourcefulness he thought she possessed, but it seemed wiser just then not to ask. Instead, she said, "I did have help, sir, but I should prefer not to discuss it, if you please."

"As you wish, mistress. I am persuaded that my father and mother will be eager to tell me all about it. You need not exert yourself to do so, since I cannot doubt that you must have told them more than you seem to have told Eric or Fiona."

Bab grounded her teeth in frustration. The others had all been polite enough not to question her about the details, but if he brought up the subject now, his parents would likely deluge her with questions. His lordship might even become a trifle testy, because although he had seemed distant of late, his temperament was uncertain and he was not a man known to take rebuff lightly.

"If you must know," she said tartly, "my rescuer was *Sionnach Dubh*."

He regarded her with an air of mild surprise. "But, dear me, he is as great a scoundrel as Dalcross. Faith, mistress, had I known you were forced to endure such uncivil company —"

"Oh, don't be a noddy! He was quite civil and behaved like a gentleman." As she snapped the words at him, she remembered the kiss she had enjoyed so much and knew she was blushing furiously at the memory.

Cocking his head, he smiled his disbelief. "You *liked* him?"

"I did," she said, on firm ground again. "He is kind, and he showed every indication of a keen intelligence and a discerning wit. Moreover, he speedily vanquished Francis Dalcross, and —"

"Did he murder the poor chap, then? Is that how he helped you escape?"

"No, he did not." Reminded of Francis's fate, she felt a sudden impulse to laugh. "They say he is the greatest swordsman in Scotland, and I believe it, for I think he is even more skilled than Patrick. Moreover, he displays the speed and grace of a cat and lightning finesse with his blade. He actually undressed Francis Dalcross with it before he sent him on his way, and he kept his horse. Then he escorted me as far as the Gorthleck House gates and saw me safely inside them."

"Well, he's always seemed a tiresome sort of

fellow to me," Sir Alex said with a sigh as they entered the great hall, where servants were setting up trestles for the evening's supper. Glancing around, he added in a low tone, "I would suggest, mistress, that you do not speak too freely of your acquaintance with that fellow."

Since she had not intended to speak of it at all until he practically forced her to, this unfair command immediately set up her hackles. "And why should I not speak of him?" she demanded.

"Well, I may be overly cautious," he said, "but I should think it might be dangerous. He tends to take the law into his own hands, you know, and not everyone appreciates his methods. Word travels quickly hereabouts, and I think it would be unwise to let his enemies suspect that you can identify him."

"They will be disappointed if they think any such thing," Bab informed him, adding on a more wistful note, "I doubt that I shall ever lay eyes on him again."

"Faith, mistress, do you want to?"

She shrugged, seeing no reason to confide her wishes to Sir Alex Chisholm. He certainly would not encourage her to hope that she would meet the Fox again, nor be pleased to know that she wanted to.

The coin the Fox had given her lay safely hidden amidst her belongings, where even Giorsal would not find it. Bab liked knowing she had it, but she felt a bit chagrined, too, knowing that according to the legends, he generally presented it to his enemies as a reminder of whom they had to thank after he had bested them. But perhaps he also gave it to those he had helped, to remind them, too.

"At least, he helps people," she said tartly. "I have heard tale after tale, both during our journey here and since we arrived, of how Sheriff Dalcross and his men mistreat your people hereabouts and in Glen Mor. Surely, you and others like you should do something to stop them."

"Me? Faith, mistress, what would you expect me to do?"

"Your father was the previous sheriff, was he not?"

"Aye, but the past has naught to do with the present. He resigned after my brothers died, and Sheriff Dalcross presented his papers of appointment less than a fortnight later. Even if my father were healthy enough to take up arms against him now, and did so, Dalcross would say — and rightly, too — that he was greatly overstepping his authority."

His drawling tone seemed even more irritating than usual.

"I did not mean that he should do anything but that you should," she said. "They are your people, too, are they not?"

"Aye, but what you think I could accomplish to the purpose, I know not." He looked about as he spoke, and then, frowning, he added, "Where are my parents? I expected to find them both here in the hall at this hour."

"Your father has only just begun to leave his chamber for meals," Bab told him. "He was exhausted when we arrived, and your mother has been a careful nurse. She cannot always make him mind her, of course, but he has rested a good deal. I warrant they will both be here soon if they have learned of your arrival."

"You have been good company for them, I believe," he said.

"Indeed, I hope so, sir."

"Certainly, my mother must enjoy your company. You doubtless spend most of your time with her and must be a great help to her with the household, too."

Increasingly irritated by this mild discourse, Bab shot him a narrow look. "I warrant your mother would be very much surprised to learn that you think she requires help running this household, Sir Alex, and I am certain that my brother did not expect me to put myself forward in such a way when he consigned me to your parents' care. I will certainly obey your mother's wishes, but she has made it clear that I am to be her guest. I expect to behave much as I would at Ardintoul."

"Do you? And how do you spend your days when you are at home?"

"I do as I please, of course."

"But surely you have duties to perform. Every-one does."

"Yes, but my burdens are light, because our servants are efficient and capable. I ride and I hunt. I visit friends, and they visit us. If I were at home now, I would doubtless be overseeing the preparation of oatmeal bannocks for the Beltane festivities tomorrow, but your cook and his minions are attending to that."

"But you must do as you please here, too," he said amiably. "I hope I have not distressed you by suggesting that you must be an excellent companion for my mother. That was not my in-tention."

"Of course, you have not distressed me," she said, wondering how she could feel guilty and at the same time feel like throwing something at him. It was not the first time he had made her feel so, either. Somehow, whenever they were to-gether, he managed to turn the tables like this, to make her feel as if she had put a foot wrong when she had done nothing of the kind.

"I adore your mother," she added firmly. "She is one of the kindest people I know, and I am grateful for her hospitality. I merely wanted to make clear to you that I prefer to be out doing things and not just sitting quietly, stitching seams. I was wondering, in fact, if it might be possible to send someone to Ardintoul to fetch one or two of my horses to ride whilst I am here. Since we traveled to Dumbarton by sea, I have ridden only borrowed horses since I left home."

"We can mount you perfectly well here, mistress. There is no need to send someone so far merely to fetch a horse or two."

"But —"

"Perhaps you would care to explain to my father that you do not find any of his mounts suitable for you," he murmured with a twinkling look. "Since he takes great pride in his stable, I would not want to do that myself. I find his temper tantrums utterly exhausting."

Lord and Lady Chisholm entered the hall together just then, and her ladyship hurried forward to greet Sir Alex, sparing Bab the need to reply, which was just as well. Since the thought of Chisholm in a temper was not one she wanted to contemplate, she decided she would be wise to see what choice of horseflesh the Chisholm stables could provide. The horses she had ridden since leaving Stirling had not impressed her, but horses employed for long journeys were chosen for their strength, stamina, and good manners, not for their speed or spirit.

If she did find a suitable mount, she could ride out and see for herself what was happening in Glen Affric and perhaps even venture into Glen Mor. And if she should chance to meet the Fox again . . .

That delicious thought brought a smile to her lips.

Sir Alex, although enveloped in his mother's fond embrace, did not fail to note Mistress

MacRae's secret smile or to wonder what she was thinking. That she was angry with him was clear, but he never seemed able to please her, so that did not distress him. Her anger heightened the roses in her cheeks and added sparkle to her beautiful dark blue eyes, which must always be accounted to her credit.

When Sir Patrick MacRae had decided to send her home to the Highlands and had asked him to arrange for her to accompany his parents to Dundreggan and to remain there until Patrick could fetch her home to Ardintoul, Alex had agreed with alacrity. Until the previous summer, when he had returned to Scotland after two years spent roaming the Continent, he had not seen Mistress MacRae since she was a thin, gawky twelve- or thirteen-year old. Despite the tragedy that had brought him home and the grief that still engulfed his parents, the change in her had staggered him, and he had wondered how he might get to know her better.

Recently, at Stirling, he had learned that she had a volatile temper and that she had little in common with the more predictable ladies of the court. Her intelligence and quick tongue set her apart, as did her way of saying exactly what she thought when she thought it. He had found her entertaining and a bit of a puzzle, and for some reason, it amused him to stir that temper.

She was clearly a lass who enjoyed life. Just being in her presence gave one a fresh look at the world through her eyes. He had thought himself jaded beyond redemption by all he had seen before, during, and after his travels on the Continent and his visits to various royal courts. He had even journeyed to the Vatican and had learned to his astonishment that it was nothing more than one more court, with the same protocols, political games, and poisonous mischief that typified all the others. He had not been to London, for the English court was no safe place for a Scotsman these days, but he had heard enough about Henry the Eighth and his court, and he had visited others at Paris, Rome, Brussels, Amsterdam, and Stirling. With steadily increasing cynicism, he had found them all tediously boring.

Life was not boring now, however, and he doubted that it would become so again as long as Mistress Barbara MacRae remained a part of it.

The members of the High Circle gathered in the Great Chamber, and when Maggie Malloch took her customary place, no other member greeted her. When the chief entered, they straightened into a line, flanking him — four on one side, five on the other — leaving her to face them all.

It was not the first time they had done such a thing, for great power stirred jealousy and resentment in its wake, but the rearrangement irritated her.

Although their usual number was twelve, only the ten others were present, for they had done nothing to replace Jonah Bonewits, the powerful, shape-shifting wizard who had nearly defeated her more than once. His most recent attempt had resulted in his banishment, but she was certain he would not remain quietly in exile.

The only light in the Great Chamber was the golden-orange glow in the center that illuminated the members, but movement in the blackness beyond it told her that other members of the Clan were entering, witnesses perhaps, as Claud would be, and watchers. Knowing that her son might be called to bear witness against her stirred the coals of her temper nearly to ignition point, but she knew she would be wise to reserve her energy until she could identify exactly what she faced.

The hushed, shuffling movements behind her ceased at last, and for a long moment, the air was thick with the silence. Then the chief declared abruptly, "There be business afore the Circle. Who will speak first?"

"I will," said one of the dark-cloaked ten. Maggie recognized the reed thin voice of Red Annis, who represented the Jolly Gentry, a Highland pixie tribe allied with the mischievous Merry Folk.

"Maggie Malloch broke our rules," Red Annis said shrilly. "She must be banished. I vote therefore to hand her over to the Evil Host!"

A chill washed over Claud at these words, for he feared the Host above all things, and the thought that the Circle might give his mother to them terrified him. He could see nothing of Red Annis's face or tiny figure inside the voluminous cloak, although he could see the chief's face and the other members flanking him.

A man with a fringe of green beard immediately to the chief's right declared gruffly, "She ha' caused strife, and more, I say. We o' the Circle set ye a task, Maggie Malloch, tae make peace betwixt certain warring tribes. Ye ha' done nowt that I can see tae achieve it."

Claud saw Maggie tense and knew she had clamped a lid on her temper.

She said icily, "If I ha' failed tae make peace betwixt your Merry Folk and our Helping Hands, 'twere the fault o' the Merry Folk. The plain fact be that the Helping Hands see their duties clear and attend tae them, whilst the Merry Folk make mischief for the fun o' it and shirk every duty they can manage tae shirk. 'Tis a scandal, and did I ha' my way, I'd demand punishment for the whole tribe."

Several members tried to talk, but the chief silenced them with a gesture and said, "Fir Darrig, chieftain o' the Merry Folk, be ye present as I commanded?"

"Aye," declared a voice near Claud as a little old man stepped into the golden glow. He had long gray hair streaked with red, a wrinkled face, and he wore a scarlet sugar-loaf hat and a

74

long scarlet coat that reached to the floor.

"How d'ye answer the charge Maggie Malloch makes against your tribe?" the chief asked.

"I'll tell ye how," Fir Darrig said. "I challenge the fashious woman to name any member who has shirked any duty."

"The challenge would be tae name one who has not," Maggie muttered.

"Give us a name, then, Maggie," the chief commanded.

"The sly, wanton lass called Catriona," she snapped, shooting a memory into Claud's mind that instantly stirred his libido. "Her duty," Maggie said, "be tae serve mortals o' the Mackenzie clan, tae keep them safe and watch over their lands and goods. Instead, the parlous slut seduced a lad o' me own Good Neighbor tribe and cozened him into conjuring things he had nae business conjuring, tae serve her."

The chief said, "How d'ye respond, Fir Darrig?"

The chieftain of the Merry Folk had no response.

"Verra well, then," the chief said. "Ye'll hail forth the lass, Catriona, tae answer for herself, and we'll adjourn this meeting until ye do. And ye'll none o' ye here speak a word o' this matter in the meantime, or ye'll answer tae me."

As Bab watched Sir Alex that afternoon with his parents, she wondered what it was about him that so quickly stirred her temper when

75

she did nothing to stir his.

Then, bowing to honesty again, she realized that she had tried to do just that by poking at him as she had. Still, the thought of him confronting the sheriff or his son was ludicrous. Like most gentlemen of fashion, he wore a short sword at his side, but she doubted that he had any notion how to use it and feared he would cut himself rather than his opponent if he tried to defend himself with it.

Conversation over supper was good-natured at first but not stimulating. When asked about events at Stirling after their departure, Sir Alex said only that he believed Patrick had finished his business in good form and had headed south with his bride so that he could look into some matter or other at Dunsithe, the Border stronghold owned by Mackenzie of Kintail, where Patrick served as constable.

"Pray, sir," Bab said at last, goaded, "why did he go to Dunsithe when he said he would be coming here as soon as possible?"

"You'd do better to ask him about it when he arrives to take you home," he said, gesturing casually to a gilly to refill his goblet with claret. Then, without waiting for her to respond, he said to his father, "You are looking better than you did in Stirling, sir. I collect you are not sorry to have returned home."

"Nay, not in the least," Chisholm said. "All that political bustle and stew, and like as not over matters having naught to do with us here

in the Highlands. It becomes increasingly difficult to identify the players in each new game."

"Are there so many players then?" Sir Alex
asked blandly.

"You should know that there are," his father
said, his tone hardening. "The people of the
glen are your people, Alex, and one day you
will have to lead them. That is to say, you will
have the *duty* to do so, and to protect them,
too. If you do not understand the fundamental
changes taking place both here and in Stirling,
you will be of little use to the House of Chisholm."

"I am doubtless, in my own way, as great a
villain as Dalcross, sir, but I am persuaded that
the ladies cannot wish to be subjected to a
dreary discussion of royal or even local politics
at the supper table."

"I do not mind," Bab said sweetly. "I like to
know what is happening around me. Indeed, I
found the intrigue at court fascinating. Such a
lot of scheming and plotting, even at balls and
festivals!"

Chisholm smiled cynically, displaying more
of his customary nature than he had since
leaving Stirling. "*Especially* at balls and festivals," he said. Turning back to his son, he
added, "I do not count you a villain, lad, but
our entire Highland way of life is weakening,
our Gaelic ways dying, and something must be
done. Whilst the Lords of the Isles held sway,
they encouraged high standards in the Gaelic

arts, but Sheriff Dalcross had a man flogged not long since for no greater crime than carving his mother's grave slab in the Celtic fashion."

"The King is now Lord of the Isles," Sir Alex said. "You are not suggesting that the Islemen should attempt to take back their lordship, I hope."

"I do not," Chisholm said with asperity. "I say that Dalcross and his even more villainous son overstep their authority in trying to influence fundamental matters and stir chaos in their wake."

Sir Alex's eyebrows lifted slightly. "Does not every generation complain about the old ways dying out, sir?" he said. "New customs have always replaced old ones just as new fashions do, so surely this is only more of that sort of thing. I promise you, I heard complaints of much the same nature from my various hosts wherever I traveled."

"Doubtless that is true, my dear," Lady Chisholm said, "but surely the French and Italians have not taken to destroying their ancient artworks to make way for newer ones. Sheriff Dalcross and his men exert their authority in just that way. You must have heard tales of such travesties yourself."

"Those rumors may well have been put about by malcontents," he said. "Change always brings complaint, but without change there can be no progress."

"Is it true that your sheriff flogs priests, too,

my lord?" Bab asked. "I have heard it said that he does, but I could scarcely credit the truth of such talk."

"It is certainly true," Chisholm said. "Dalcross and his supporters want to reform the Scottish Kirk to conform with demands from Rome, although in my opinion and that of many others, such reforms do not suit our people. Young Dalcross says that Cardinal Beaton supports them. To that I say, let Beaton tidy up his own corrupt house before he imposes unnecessary alterations in mine."

"You make a good point, my lord," Sir Alex sipped his claret and then said to Bab, "Would it amuse you, mistress, to see more of Glen Affric tomorrow?"

Surprised, she could not help saying, "Faith, sir, would you exert yourself so soon after your long and tedious journey?"

"I had thought rather of arranging for an escort to show you some of the countryside," he drawled, meeting her gaze with a mocking look.

"You will do no such thing, sir," Chisholm said sharply. "Simple good manners dictate that you should take Mistress MacRae about yourself. I only wish that my present state of health permitted me to do so."

"Thank you, my lord," Bab said, smiling demurely. "I am persuaded that you could tell me much more about the history and people here than Sir Alex will, but I confess, I am more interested in visiting your mews. I hope you will be well enough soon to show them to me. Patrick said you have some famous hunting birds."

"I do, indeed."

"Patrick has taught me much of hawking and falconry," she said. "After so many days of plodding along, I am eager for more stimulating exercise. Indeed, sir, I wonder if you would be so kind as to permit me to hunt."

Chisholm nodded thoughtfully. "Your brother is renowned for his skill with birds of prey, mistress. If he has taught you, I am certain you must know what you are about. My chief falconer, Alasdair Mackinnon, is a skilled man, too. He and Alex shall take you out tomorrow if you like."

Shooting a glance at Sir Alex, Bab was pleased to see a muscle jump in his cheek. Although she suspected that he did not much like having his day planned for him, she thought it would be good for him to have to exert himself a bit. "Thank you, my lord," she said happily. "I will enjoy that very much."

Sir Alex said, "With respect, sir, I had forgotten that tomorrow is the feast of Beltane. I'd not be surprised should Francis Dalcross and his men decide to make mischief with the revelers. Do you think it is safe for her to ride outside our wall?"

"Faith, Alex, you were just saying they mean no harm, and they will hardly disturb you whilst you are hunting. Show some backbone for once in your life!"

Sir Alex fell silent, his expression wooden, and Bab felt sorry that she had ever raised the subject of hunting. Conversation languished after that, and after supper, she found herself in Lady Chisholm's bower with only her ladyship, Giorsal, and Clarice for company.

Chapter 4

To Claud, the time between the adjournment and the reconvening of the High Circle was so brief as to be nonexistent. One moment everyone was leaving and he heard the music outside; the next moment he was back in the blackness surrounding the golden-orange glow, watching the Circle straighten into a line again. The only difference was that Maggie no longer faced them alone, because the lovely, golden-haired Catriona stood beside her, albeit at a discreet distance.

Claud's memories of Catriona had dimmed, but they flooded back when he saw her. She was as beautiful as ever, standing regally before the hooded figures, the panels of her gilt-trimmed green gown flowing like rivers of soft gauze over the enticing curves of her body. Like all her gowns, it was cut low to reveal her plump, beautiful breasts. He remembered how soft they were, and how easily her gowns slipped off. He remembered, too, the wonderful things she had done to him, and with him, and he felt his body stir in anticipation of enjoying her charms again.

He realized that Maggie had come to the end of her catalogue of Catriona's crimes only when the chief demanded that the lass respond.

Catriona's stubborn little chin lifted defiantly. "Maggie Malloch hates me because her son adores me. That's all there be to the matter."

"Indeed," the chief said. To Fir Darrig, he said, "As ye see, the lass doesna deny the charge, so Maggie has answered your challenge. What say ye now?"

The wrinkles in his face deepening into a grimace, Fir Darrig said, "I'll agree that Catriona were in the wrong, but her actions ha' naught to do wi' the strife betwixt our tribe and the Helping Hands. 'Tis but an unfair diversion, that."

"How d'ye identify the cause, then?" the chief asked.

"We say that hill folk shouldna ha' to look after mortals like the Gordons, the Chisholms, and their ilk, wha' ha' their roots in the Borders. Such clans, and any that mix or marry wi' them should be seen to by them wha' guard their roots."

"Then I say ye dinna want peace at all," Maggie declared. "There be many Highland clans rooted snug in the Borders. D'ye truly want our folk tae move tae the Highlands tae look after any o' our mortals that mix or marry wi' yours? How will ye like it when there be more o' us throughout your land than there be o' ye? And, too, will ye send your folk tae the Borders when your mortals mix or marry there? Mind, we

83

dinna ask your folk tae come, nor do we want ye there."

Silence reigned until a new voice growled, "Do we no be getting off the subject?" The speaker scowled fiercely. His large head emerged from his cloak like a shaggy plant from an odd black pot, revealing twisted ropes of dark unkempt hair that framed a high, leathery brow, piercing dark eyes, a bulbous nose, and thick red lips. "We ha' gathered to reprimand this woman for breaking our rules, ha' we not? Did we no banish Jonah Bonewits for the same crime? I say Red Annis be right. Maggie Malloch must suffer banishment or the Clan's rules mean nowt."

The chief said, "Can ye resolve the dispute then, Grogan Capelthwaite?"

"He canna do it," Maggie snapped. "Nor could any o' ye."

"Hold your whisst, ye venomous woman!" Grogan Capelthwaite snarled. "Ha' ye no done enough damage, causing Jonah Bonewits to forfeit his place here?"

"He forfeited it by his own actions," Maggie said.

"Silence," snapped the chief. "I ha' heard enough."

"But we ha' witnesses yet to question," Red Annis protested.

"I ken well enough what they will say, and I dinna need tae hear them. This be my decision, and any who fails tae keep faith with it will suffer the gravest punishment." He glowered from one to another, daring them to defy him.

No one spoke.

Satisfied, he said quietly, "I decree that Maggie Malloch shall settle a peace betwixt the Merry Folk and the Helping Hands afore our next meeting, and do so without breaking any rules or face banishment equal tae that o' Jonah Bonewits."

"Now that's good, that is," Red Annis said shrilly.

"Aye, well, I'm glad ye approve," the chief said.

"I, too," Maggie said. "I accept your challenge, and I set one in return. As I must render service tae the hill tribes, Catriona should ha' tae render service tae a clan wi' its roots in the Borders. Since ye named the Chisholms earlier and there be trouble brewing up for them o' Glen Affric, I say Catriona must render them a true service, and without getting up tae any o' her usual mischief."

"Here now, I dinna answer to you," Catriona exclaimed. "What's more, 'tis your own Good Neighbor tribe that must look after Gordons and their ilk, and that includes yon Chisholms o' Glen Affric!"

Maggie added steadily, "If she refuses, she should also face punishment, for if I am tae resolve the strife betwixt the tribes, my judgment in associated matters must be accepted. That were agreed afore and should stand now."

"Aye, it does stand," the chief said. "And so shall it be."

Outraged, Catriona opened her mouth to protest again, but Fir Darrig placed a quelling hand on her shoulder.

"One moment," he said. "I'd remind ye all that in settling the dispute Maggie Malloch be rendering service to both sides equally. Therefore, if Catriona must render service for which Maggie's tribe is responsible, then someone from that tribe must serve a hill clan and face the same consequence for failure."

"Fair enough," the chief said, turning to Maggie. "A good notion, in fact. I further decree that your son Claud shall render an equal service tae a Mackenzie or a MacRae and that he shall suffer the same punishment as Catriona if he fails."

"Agreed," Maggie said. "But I must retain the right tae intervene if one or the other makes a muck o' things, lest the peacemaking process suffer as a result."

As she said the last word, the golden light went out, and with a bright flash of lightning that filled the chamber, a deep, thundering voice roared, "Ye'll fail, Mag! I'll see to it, lass!" Then all went black and still.

Tension filled the darkness until the golden glow slowly returned, revealing the figures of the High Circle, slightly shaken but still in their places.

"There be only one wha' could ha' done

that," Maggie Malloch muttered. "That were Jonah Bonewits, and he ha' dared tae challenge me afore ye all."

The chief frowned, saying, "Aye, he has, but me decree stands, Maggie. Still, I agree ye must ha' the right tae intervene if aught goes amiss. If ye do, however, ye must give equal attention tae both sides, and only if ye believe there be mischief afoot. As tae punishment if Claud or Catriona fails, we'll determine that in the event. But if the pair o' them dare tae create even half as much mischief as they did last time," he added grimly, "I'll give them both over tae the Evil Host."

Claud stared, horror-stricken. He had done nothing but sit quietly and watch, and now his fate depended upon completing a task about which he knew nothing and with which he could apparently request no help. Moreover, for his own sake, he would have to stay away from Catriona.

Since all she had to do was crook her little finger at him to make him forget everything else, he was certainly doomed to failure and thus doomed to fly with the wicked Host until all his sins were expiated, which effectively meant that he would fly with them to the end of time.

"I hope you do not find life at Dundreggan too tedious, Barbara," Lady Chisholm said with a smile when they were comfortably settled in her bower that evening. "It sounds to me as if you are accustomed to a more active life than I am."

"I am sure I shall not find it tedious, madam," Bab said politely. She already had, but one simply did not admit such things to one's hostess.

"I did not realize that the women of Kintail hunted with their menfolk. Surely, your mother does not."

"No, madam," Bab said, smiling at the thought of the eccentric Lady MacRae riding out with a hawk or falcon on her fist. "I believe she did enjoy such activities in her youth, but as you must have seen for yourself at Stirling, she has not behaved in her customary manner since my father's death two years ago."

"One could not help but notice that she had altered considerably," Lady Chisholm agreed, "but one supposed that since she had not attended court for some years she had simply mislaid the gift of social converse. One does that, you know."

"In truth, madam, my mother converses more with herself or with imaginary wee folk than with anyone else these days," Bab said. "I own, it worries me."

"You will forgive me then if I speak plainly, my dear. It surprises me that she did exert herself to such an extent as to journey to Stirling."

"Oh, she enjoyed herself, I believe," Bab said lightly, feeling a twinge of guilt as she recalled how hard she had fought to persuade her mother to make the journey. "I think it did her a great deal of good to get away from Ardintoul even for a short time, to reacquaint herself with old friends."

"It certainly was a short time," Lady Chisholm agreed. " 'Twas but a sennight before she returned to Ardintoul. It surprised me, too, that she left without you."

"I expect her actions surprised many people," Bab admitted, "but —"

"Doubtless Lady MacRae, knowing she was leaving her daughter in Kintail's capable hands, believed it was safe to do so," Sir Alex drawled from the doorway, where he leaned gracefully with one hand against the jamb, the other resting on his sword hilt. "She could thus enjoy a respite from Mistress Bab's lively presence."

"Do join us, my dear," Lady Chisholm said with a smile. "I feared you might spend the whole evening conversing with your father and quite wear him out."

"No, for he is still vexed with me, and when he discovered that my chess game has not improved since the last time we played, he decided to retire early."

"Oh, that was clever of you," Lady Chisholm exclaimed. "If you had beaten him, he would have insisted on staying up until he won. This way, he will enjoy an excellent night's repose."

"Do you suggest, sir, that my mother gets on better without my company?" Bab asked evenly.

"Faith, how you do take a fellow up," he said, moving forward gracefully when his mother patted the sofa beside her invitingly. "I meant only to suggest that her ladyship's generosity in allowing you to extend your visit to court was soundly based." As he adjusted his sword so it would not interfere with the elegant folds of his fashionably puffed trunk hose when he sat, he added, "But mayhap I misjudge you, mistress, and you are more a restful person at Ardintoul than in other settings."

She made a face at him.

Lady Chisholm looked sternly at her son. "You should not speak so to our guest, Alex. Surely, if Sir Patrick and Lady MacRae saw nothing amiss in Barbara's remaining at Stirling, it can be no business of yours to criticize her."

"I criticize no one," he said. "Tolerance is easier on one's temperament."

Bab snorted.

In the same amiable tone, he said, "I came only to ask what time you would like to depart in the morning, mistress. If you hope to be off by first light, you should doubtless retire soon. I shall certainly do so."

She would have liked to contradict him, to tell him that she required little sleep, but the truth was otherwise. She knew that to enjoy the hunt the next day, she would be wise to retire earlier than usual. Nevertheless, she would not allow him to send her to bed like a child.

"I do think we should leave early, sir," she said. "But although I know that you have had a tiring day today, I have scarcely exerted myself at all. I shall sit with your mother a little longer, I think, for if I were to go up so soon after supper I doubt that I should fall asleep. Shall we meet at six o'clock?"

He yawned. " 'Tis a devilish early hour," he complained. "Mayhap half past six would be better. That will give us both a chance to break our fast before we go."

"I require only an apple and some salted beef to take with me," she said, "but I will meet you in the stables at half past six if that plan will suit you better."

"Then I will bid you both goodnight," he said, kissing her ladyship's cheek and adding lightly, "I think you have worried about my father more than you need, madam. He wasted no time in taking me to task, as you saw, and that must always be a sign of returning energy. Sleep well."

Lady Chisholm smiled. " 'Tis good to have you home again, my dear."

He bowed with his customary grace and left them, but Bab made a point of staying another half hour. Her ladyship enjoyed talking about friends she had seen at Stirling and others from the Highlands, but Bab had heard many of her anecdotes during the journey from Stirling to Dundreggan, and to work up enthusiasm about people whom one barely knew or did not know at all was difficult. Her mother was the same, though, talking with eagerness about times gone by when she deigned to talk sensibly at all, and Bab did not mind lending an ear now, particularly since she liked Lady Chisholm and deeply appreciated her kindness.

At last, however, she bade her hostess an affectionate goodnight and retired to her bedchamber, realizing only as she approached the room that she had not sent word to Giorsal of her intent to retire early. Doubtless the woman was still below, gossiping with the household servants, and would not come until her usual time unless Bab went to fetch her. It would be easier, she decided, to undress herself.

Pushing the bedchamber door open, she realized only as she stepped into the room that Giorsal had apparently closed the curtains already but had neglected to light candles or the ready-laid fire. It was not long after dusk, but still the woman ought not to have left her mistress to enter a dark room by performing the one task without properly seeing to the others.

As these thoughts crossed her mind, the door swung shut behind her, a warm hand clapped over her mouth, and a familiar deep masculine voice murmured in her ear, "Dinna shriek, lass. 'Tis only me."

Though she had stiffened with shock, at the sound of his voice she relaxed.

The Fox released her, and she heard him step toward the dark fireplace. Next, she heard coals settling, saw a spark, and moments later, flames leaped. When he stood and turned to face her, he held a lighted taper in one hand.

"Where is your maid?" he asked, his deep voice stirring coals inside her, too.

"Downstairs with the other servants, I think," she said, her voice sounding strained and rather hoarse. "You should not be here. Someone might see you!"

"No one will see me," he said, stepping toward her. "They do say the witches be abroad tonight, and the wee folk, too. I wanted to see for myself that ye be safe."

Her skin tingled, but her limbs seemed frozen in place. She licked suddenly dry lips and forced herself to draw a long breath, hoping it would steady her. It did not. His presence in her bedchamber overwhelmed her ordinary calm. It was scandalous behavior. Her reputation would be ruined if anyone should walk in and find him with her.

He was so large, especially with the long cloak swirling about him and outlined as he was by the golden glow of the fire behind him.

Involuntarily, she stepped backward, not even realizing she had done so until she bumped against the door.

"You should not be in here," she repeated.

"Art afraid of me, sweetheart?"

"N-no, of course I am not afraid. You saved my life. I cannot believe you would harm me now. But —"

She broke off when he reached out to stroke her cheek with his knuckles, his leather glove soft against her skin.

Had she noticed the glove when his hand clapped against her mouth? She could not remember, and somehow the trivial point seemed important, but she could not focus her mind. The rest of her body was too aware of how near he was. Even through the glove, his hand felt warm against her cheek.

Her breath was ragged. He was bending toward her, his lips only inches away. Already her body sang in response to his, and she felt as if the energy in his were drawing her irresistibly closer to him. She raised her chin and parted her lips, and the door bumped into her, startling her nearly out of her wits.

"Mistress?"

"Giorsal!"

In a heartbeat, he thrust the candle into her hand, crossed the room in three long strides, and disappeared behind the curtains. The door bumped against her again, and she stepped aside to let the woman into the room, saying, "What a start you gave me, Giorsal! I nearly dropped my candle."

"Why were ye standing against the door?"

She had not thought of a reason, but the candle's glow illuminated an object that gave her one. "I wanted to light that cresset," she said, indicating the iron basketlike holder suspended from its jutting hook on the wall by the door. "I did not think you would come upstairs so early since I did not send for you."

"Her ladyship sent for Clarice and the gilly who came for her said ye had already gone up. Ye should ha' sent someone for me straight-away, mistress."

"One does not like to order other people's servants about so casually."

Giorsal looked at her in astonishment, and no wonder, Bab thought, since she had rarely hesitated to make her wishes known in any other household. One learned from childhood how to do so without giving offense to one's host. She gazed limpidly back nonetheless, content to keep Giorsal's attention fixed on her lest the woman realize that someone else was in the room with them.

"I'll light that cresset, and then I'll fetch out your night clothes," Giorsal said, taking the candle from her.

As soon as Giorsal's attention shifted to the cresset, Bab looked toward the window and felt some relief when she saw nothing to indicate his presence behind the curtains. She knew he must still be there, because the room was nearly three stories above the graveled bailey. Somehow, she would have to get Giorsal out of the room long enough for him to escape.

What, she wondered, had he been thinking? His daring but foolhardy act appalled her, be-cause the first person to enter might as easily have been Giorsal as herself — more easily, in fact. The man was clearly a lunatic but a fascinating one. Whatever would he dare next?

"I can fetch my nightdress myself if you will go and tell a gilly to bring me some hot water," she said casually.

Giorsal had managed to light the wick in the oil-filled cresset. The flame flared up brightly, casting more shadows on the walls and giving her face a yellowish cast reminiscent of the witches the Fox had said were abroad, as she turned and said bluntly, "I kent well that ye'd want hot water, mistress. I've already given the order. Indeed, and do I no be mistaken, that'll be the lad with it now."

Bab heard him, too, and the clumping footsteps made her wonder why she had not heard Giorsal's approach. When the gilly entered, however, and she saw the contrast between his heavy boots and Giorsal's light slippers, she realized how fortunate it was that she and the Fox had not spoken for several moments before the woman's arrival. Surely, she would have heard them as easily through the door as Bab had heard the gilly's approach.

"Pour that out for us, an ye please," Giorsal said to the lad, following in his wake and watching critically as he poured hot water from the pail he carried, first into the basin on the washstand and then into the ewer beside it.

Giorsal dipped a testing finger into the basin, nodded dismissal to the lad, and then, to Bab's horror, walked to the curtains as the lad strode to the door. Before Bab could think of a way to stop her, Giorsal swept aside one curtain and looked askance at the open window beyond it.

"This room be gey cold, and nae wonder," she said, leaning out, yanking the shutter closed, and firmly latching it. "Surely, ye didna open that, mistress."

"The room was just like this when I came in," Bab said truthfully. She could scarcely breathe and hoped fervently that Giorsal would not touch the other curtain.

With relief, she watched the gilly shut the door after himself. At least now, if Giorsal found the Fox, they would only have to deal with her, and although Bab was not certain that she could persuade the woman to keep a still tongue in her head, she knew it would be easier if they had no other witness.

Giorsal said, "I warrant one o' his lordship's gillies opened yon window, thinking he were being helpful. Mayhap the fire smoked a wee bit when he lit it, and he hoped to air out the smoke afore ye came up. Had ye come at the usual time, he'd ha' had time to shut it again and let the room warm up for ye."

Bab did not reply. She could not have spoken had she wanted to, for while Giorsal was talking, she was inspecting the curtain she had held back as if to see whether it had been properly shaken, and Bab knew as well as if the woman had said so that next she would inspect its mate.

"Isn't it too dark over there to see anything?" she asked hastily.

"Ye dinna want to sleep in a room littered wi' cobwebs," Giorsal pointed out. "Ye'd likely ha' one o' their inhabitants crawling over your nose in the dark."

Wrinkling her nose at the unpleasant thought, she tried again. "I need a towel, Giorsal."

"On the washstand rod," Giorsal said, turning to the second curtain and whisking it back from the wall and window.

Bab gasped.

No one was there.

The Fox had vanished, and unless he had melted magically into the wall, he had flown just as magically out through the window before Giorsal had shut it. In either event, he was clearly no ordinary man, and Bab decided that if she were to learn that a Beltane witch had collected him on her broomstick and swept him away with her to the moon it would not astonish her in the least.

Half an hour later, as she lay sleepless in her bed, she realized that she had neglected to tell Giorsal to awaken her early. Indeed, upon discovering that the Fox had vanished after diving behind the curtains, she had said little to the woman, scarcely trusting herself to make ordinary conversation. Instead, she had quickly washed her face, donned her nightdress, and jumped into bed, whereupon Giorsal had drawn the bed curtains and bidden her goodnight without further comment.

Staring now into the blackness overhead, Bab tried to recapture the feelings she had experienced before Giorsal's arrival, but she was quickly coming to believe that the whole incident must have been a dream. Remembering Giorsal's bumping the door into her was another matter. Just thinking about that sent a shiver dancing up her spine. Had she not been in front of the door — bang up against it, in fact — Giorsal would have walked right in and set up a screech before they could stop her.

Bab had not noticed before that the woman walked as softly as a cat. But if Giorsal moved softly, the Fox had moved more softly yet. How, she wondered, had he managed to disappear like that?

She would have liked to discuss that with someone, anyone, but she dared not trust a soul with the information she had. The danger to him and to herself was too great. In any case, she doubted that the Fox would return after so near a disaster, and thus it was pointless to keep thinking about it. Despite this resolution, she still could not fall asleep though, because she jumped at every least little sound.

After she had popped her head through the opening between the bed curtains for the fourth time to see if anyone was there, she realized that she had no confidence in his behaving sensibly. At last, she got up and opened the curtains all the way, deciding that it was better to be able to see what she could by the glow of the fire, even at the risk of catching a chill when it died, than not to see anything and risk having him reach through the curtains and into the bed to waken her.

That thought made her smile. She decided that he would not really do that, but even as she reassured herself, a niggling voice in the back of her mind whispered that he certainly might. The man had nerve enough for anything.

Chapter 5

Even without Giorsal's help, Bab awoke early, but she could not compliment herself on the achievement since she had awakened frequently during the night, wondering on each occasion if it were time yet to arise. Sunrise at this season began shortly before six, however, so when she saw that it was light at last, she jumped out of bed and splashed cold water on her face. What Giorsal would think when she came in at her usual time to wake her, she did not want to contemplate.

"I am too old to worry about being scolded by a servant," she muttered to the ambient air as she brushed her dark curls. She had been muttering such things for years, but when one's personal servant had been present at one's birth, it was hard to achieve grown-up independence.

Scrambling into her favorite riding dress, an elegant rig of gray-green velvet with dark blue trim to match her eyes, she was glad she had ordered it to fit without corsets so she could ride as she liked instead of having to sit stiffly in the manner required of proper ladies, because that made it easier to dress herself. Patrick had taught her to ride astride as nearly all women did in the Borders, deeming a cross saddle safer than a heavily padded, boxlike sidesaddle, but it occurred to her that Sir Alex might assume she preferred the latter. She had never ridden with him, and his mother used the lady's sidesaddle. His people would remember though, surely.

Twisting her hair into a knot at the back of her head, she pinned her hat in place, picked up her riding gloves and whip, glanced in the looking-glass to be sure she had not forgotten anything important, and hurried downstairs, wondering if he would be ready or if she would have to wait. Although she had said she would meet him at the stables, she doubted that he would be out there yet.

He was not in the chilly hall when she entered, but he strolled in only a moment or two later with a half-eaten apple in one hand.

"I'd forgotten Beltane means they had to put out the kitchen and hall fires before retiring last night," he said, adding with a grimace, "They've let the others die, too. That's why it's so devilish cold in here. Even if we return by noon for our dinner, we'll get nothing hot until someone lays all new fires and renews their flames from a Beltane need-fire tonight."

"The festival will be fun though," she said.

He stared at her. "Faith, did you expect to attend? You'd never catch my parents at such an accursed revelry. I doubt my father will hear of your going."

She noted that he did not suggest taking her himself, and indeed, if his parents did not attend, for her to go with him would be most improper, for it would suggest a far closer relationship than the one they had.

He looked splendid, quite unlike Patrick ever looked when he was about to hunt, because Patrick always wore plain leather breeks and a tan jerkin. Sir Alex wore an elegant doublet of cornflower blue, slashed with white silk and tied with gold ribbons. He even wore a matching hat with a pointed brim and a white plume.

"It is a good thing we are not hunting deer," Bab said with a teasing smile. "Seeing that bright blue and gold would startle them all into the next shire."

"Do you think so?" He looked down at himself. "I thought it was the perfect rig, myself. Blue to match the spring bluebells in the woods and gold for the sun if we see any today. I did think at first, though, that I might wear emerald green to match the new spring leaves. Do you think I should change?"

"I think you are being absurd," she said bluntly, certain that it would take him an hour or more to change. "You need not ride with me at all if you do not wish to do so. I am perfectly accustomed to hunting with only gillies to accompany me, so I could easily do that here. Indeed, all I really need is a lad to help me retrieve the hawk if I run into difficulty and a

103

falconer's lad to teach me its calls and what it's used to until I grow accustomed to the bird and the bird to me."

"So you do intend to hunt," he said with a sigh. "I was hoping we might just roam the countryside for a short while until you grew weary of the scenery."

"My dear sir," she said with asperity, "I have done enough plodding about on horseback this past fortnight to last me an age. I want to gallop, and I want to hunt. When Patrick told me about your father's excellent mews, I hoped his lordship would permit me to fly one of his hawks, but since he is still not enjoying his usual good health, I feared I would see little hunting, especially since you . . ."

She shrugged, unable to think of a tactful way to say what she thought of him, and added only, "Well, it does seem a shame for all those birds just to be sitting there day in and day out."

"But surely our falconer must take them out now and again for exercise," he said. "That certainly seems a logical duty for him to perform."

"Of course he does," she said, striving to maintain a civil tone but wanting yet again to shake him. "They must be exercised and hunted frequently until late spring, or they will mope themselves to death."

"All that sounds a most energetic business," he complained.

"I think you had better stay here," she said.

"If you will summon a lad to show me to the mews, I am sure I can manage very well on my own."

He sighed. "An excellent notion, but our chief falconer, Alasdair Mackinnon, would complain to my father of my inattention to you, so I had better go along."

"Well, you need not. I shall speak to his lordship myself if you like and tell him that I'd prefer to go without you."

"That would put him off his feed for a sennight," Sir Alex said. "I shall just have to exert myself, but I am sorry that you do not want me to accompany you."

Bab suppressed an impulse to soothe his injured feelings, to assure him that it was not so much not wanting him as feeling annoyed that she had put him in a position where he believed he had to exert himself. That impulse increased the annoyance she already felt, however, because a truly civil man who did not want to accompany her would not let his feelings show, and he certainly would not show them merely to make her feel guilty, which she was certain Sir Alex had done.

When he politely offered his arm, she would have liked to pretend not to notice, but one could hardly criticize a man for behaving uncivilly and then behave childishly oneself, so she accepted the arm with grace, as a gilly hurried to open the door for them. They crossed the bailey to the stable, where they found a lad bridling a buttermilk-colored mare, and Bab noted with approval that the saddle was exactly the sort she liked. A handsome, well-muscled dun gelding — that is to say a cream-colored one with a black mane and tail — stood ready in a nearby stall.

Her first impression was that although the mare was lovely, it was small, but her experienced eye took note of its fine lines, the alert look in its eyes, and the impatient way it pawed the ground, as if it were telling the gilly to get on with it. When she approached, the mare snorted and pushed her shoulder with its nose.

Bab chuckled and glanced at Sir Alex, to find him eyeing her in much the same alert, curious way that the mare had.

"Do you like her?" he asked.

"She's beautiful," Bab said.

"I feared you might insist on riding some great, thundering beast so you could show me its heels," he said.

Stroking the mare's nose, Bab said, "She looks as if she could manage the ground hereabouts better than any great, thundering beast could. That gelding looks to be a fine animal, too."

He eyed it cautiously. "He's handsome enough, I expect. I haven't ridden him before, so we can only hope his manners match his looks."

She refused to respond to that, finding it difficult to believe that he was as poor a horseman as he consistently suggested he was. Her brother would tolerate many faults in a close friend, but Patrick would have small opinion of any Highland gentleman who could not sit a horse properly.

Unseen, Claud watched the two mortals curiously from his perch on the well-house roof nearby. His natural instinct drew him more strongly to study Sir Alexander Chisholm, who was a connection of the Border Gordons his tribe had served for so long, but his present duty was to the lass, the MacRae, and despite some small experience with Mackenzies, he knew little about her or her family.

"I can help ye," a seductive, familiar voice murmured beside him.

Starting, Claud stared in dismay at Catriona, who smiled entrancingly at him.

"What be ye a-doing here?" he demanded.

"Why, I am to help the Chisholms," she said innocently. "D'ye no recall the bargain, Claud? I can tell ye much about the MacRaes if ye like."

"I ken wha' I need tae ken already, and that be that I must keep clear o' ye, Catriona," he said firmly, looking about in fear that some other member of the Clan might have seen them together.

"Nae one said ye must keep clear o' me," she protested, snuggling closer.

"Aye, but I must or I'm sped. I ken that right enough!"

"We're alone, laddie," she said, leaning closer yet to kiss him warmly on the cheek. Her plump breasts billowed above the lacy edge of her gown, beckoning. Her hand moved to his thigh.

He jumped as if he had been burned. "Dinna do that!"

"D'ye no like me anymore, Claud?"

"Aye, I do, and that's the rub, for I canna think when ye touch me like that, and I must think, Catriona."

"But that is just why we should talk together, Claud. Ye must tell me all ye ken o' Chisholms, whilst in return, I'll tell ye what I ken o' the MacRaes."

He shook his head fiercely. "Ye're just going tae muddle me again, Catriona. I ha' decided tae ha' nowt tae do wi' lasses till I've done my part o' this business."

"But, Claud —"

"Nay, it be nae use tae cozen me." He looked shrewdly at her, noting that her long gauzy green gown covered her feet. "See here, Catriona, be ye a Glaistig?"

She stiffened. "Who told ye such a thing?"

"Some'un once told me ye ha' the goat's feet o' a Glaistig. Do ye?"

"What a horrid thing to say! Just for that, Brown Claud, I willna help ye one bit wi' your task, and if the Evil Host seizes ye and carries ye off, too bad!"

Catriona vanished on the words, leaving Claud to wonder if he had just made a horrible mistake or had just narrowly avoided letting her twist and distort his thinking again as she had so easily in the past.

After Bab and Sir Alex had briefly admired the horses, she said, "Do we not go to the mews? Where are the birds?"

"Alasdair Mackinnon will bring them to us here."

"But I shall need a hawking glove."

"Faith, but I expected you to have one tucked up your pretty sleeve."

She wrinkled her nose at him, but the falconer approached just then through a door at the back of the stables, carrying a hooded white gyrfalcon. A minion with him carried a smaller peregrine. Bells tinkled lightly as the men moved.

Bab exclaimed in delight at the sight of the birds, but particularly the gyr. Gyrfalcons were Arctic birds and quite rare, and although she had often heard tales of their beauty and size, she had never seen one up close before. In truth, she was more accustomed to hawks than to falcons, but she understood the latter well enough, and the idea of hunting with such fine specimens as these delighted her.

"Dear me, Alasdair," Sir Alex said. "I thought I told you to fetch a merlin for the lady and the robin hobby for me."

Bab nearly protested aloud. Merlins were small ladies' falcons and all very well in their way, but it was no day for skylarking. She did not care what bird Sir Alex took, but she wanted to fly the gyr.

The falconer, a wiry, stern-looking man of middle years, gave Sir Alex a direct look from under bushy salt-and-pepper eyebrows and said, "Nay, Master Alex, 'twere the peregrine and the gyr ye requested. Whistle up them dogs for us now, Will," he called to one of the gillies in the yard.

Alasdair clearly expected to accompany them. His horse would be ready in a trice, he said as he watched the lad, Will, whistle two brown and white spaniels to heel. In the meantime, perhaps Mistress MacRae would like to try on the several gloves he had in his falconer's bag to see which of them suited her best.

Pleased, Bab quickly found a hawking gauntlet of thick buckskin that fit perfectly. Alasdair waited until she had mounted and then let her take the peregrine on her left fist. She carefully entwined its leather jesses around her fingers, glad the gauntlet was thick enough to protect her from its sharp talons and beak.

The bird was much lighter than it looked, but she could tell by the alert way it perched that it was hungry and ready to hunt.

"Will ye tak' Duchess here on your fist, sir?" the falconer said, gesturing toward the much larger gyrfalcon.

"Dear me, no," Sir Alex said. " 'Tis far too fatiguing to ride whilst constantly holding one's arm up. She likes you better than she likes me, anyway, Alasdair."

"Aye, sir," Alasdair Falconer said with a fond twinkle.

It was not the first time Bab had noted that Sir Alex's servants were very fond of him, but that did little to mitigate her impatience with his affectations.

"I'd like to take the gyr then if you will permit me," she said quietly. "I have flown peregrines before but never a gyrfalcon."

The falconer shot her a measuring look, then glanced at his master, who shrugged. Turning back to Bab, the falconer said diffidently, "Wi' respect, mistress, I'd like to see how ye manage the peregrine afore I let ye fly the gyr. 'Twould be as much as me place be worth did aught happen to her."

She nodded, having expected nothing else. Alasdair was Chisholm's chief falconer, and a man did not reach such a high position without being certain of his authority. She turned her attention to Sir Alex as he mounted the dun gelding.

He mounted easily, and she saw, as she had expected, that he demonstrated a graceful agility in the saddle. Still, he soon revealed that he was not as skilled as her brother. He was not a poor horseman, just one who lacked enthusiasm for horses or riding. He glanced around to see if everyone was ready, then gave the signal to start.

Outside the walls of the castle, a thin, curling mist hung over Glen Affric. It was chilly and damp, and the falcons ruffled their feathers and hunched their wings, whether because of the mist or because they looked forward to the hunt, Bab did not know. She was neither cold nor uncomfortable, but she wondered if Sir Alex had purposely ordered falcons instead of hawks on such a day just to aggravate her.

Hawks hunted from the fist and stayed low to the ground, their prey mostly woodland birds and small animals like rabbits and squirrels. A good hawk could take its prey in high grass or in woodland, but a falcon stooped from great heights, relying on its amazing eyesight to spy out prey far below. Not that mist meant the falcons would starve, of course, because they would soar above it and could easily hunt above it too, taking smaller birds on the wing. The problem, as she understood it, lay in recalling a falcon afterward. One generally did so by swinging a lure and whistling, but if the bird could not see through the mist, it could not see the lure.

She kept these thoughts to herself, certain that Sir Alex would not risk losing the gyr and believing he hoped she would complain so he could suggest returning to the castle. In any case, her silence was rewarded when they emerged from the mist halfway up the ridge. The sun shone brightly above it, and puffy white cumulus clouds drifted gently overhead.

Soon they came to a wide, flat moor in a saddle at the top of the ridge, which provided an excellent view of nearby glens.

When Bab noted several men carrying armloads of wood to piles of logs in the center of the moor, she shot a look of inquiry at Sir Alex.

"For the Beltane need-fires tonight," he said. "Folks from miles around will trudge up here to rekindle their home-fires at the festival."

"Won't those woodsmen disturb the falcons?"

"No more than we will," he said. "The moor is wide enough for all of us, and these birds are well accustomed to humans prowling about whilst they hunt."

Looking back toward the castle, she could just make out its gray-and-red-stone towers jutting through still-clinging mist. They looked mysterious, even fairy-talelike, with their damp turrets glistening in the sunlight.

The falcon on her fist tensed in anticipation of the hunt, and even through the glove, she could feel its body humming.

"They be sharp set, the pair o' them," Alasdair said.

"Aye," Sir Alex agreed. "Everyone seems shockingly full of energy today. I expect you lads had best whistle those dogs back until the first bird throws up."

The peregrine began bobbing her head and making a low chortling sound.

"She be ready," Alasdair said, keeping an eye

on the dogs as they raced back in response to their whistle.

"Do I wait for the lure, or will she fly from my fist?" Bab asked.

"She kens her business, mistress. When ye unhood her, hold tight to the jesses till I tell ye. Then, loose them and raise your fist."

Bab nodded. She knew what to do. Gently, she loosened the hood's braces with her right hand and slipped it off by its plume. The peregrine observed her with its alert, dark brown eyes, but Bab avoided meeting that look directly lest the bird, unaccustomed to her, think she challenged it.

"Now?" she said quietly.

"Aye, mistress, when ye're ready."

Bab raised her left hand and released the jesses.

Needing no further invitation, the peregrine lifted its powerful wings and shot skyward, the tiny bells on its legs tinkling as it circled higher and higher with astonishing speed, the sounds soon fading in the distance.

Alasdair waved to the gillies, who released the dogs. Making up in enthusiasm what they lacked in finesse, the spaniels darted forward, barking madly, and soon flushed a covey of grouse.

Will whistled the dogs to heel again, his whistling making an odd musical harmony with the mad clacking of the grouse as they flapped upward out of the shrubbery that had concealed them. But Bab had shaded her eyes against the sun and was watching the falcon, so high above them now that she was afraid to look away lest she lose sight of it and never see it again.

"Would ye no like tae fly wi' yon falcon, Claud?"

"Lucy!"

So fixed had his attention been on the beautifully soaring bird that once again Claud nearly jumped out of his skin. He grabbed the mare's mane to steady himself, having nestled comfortably in its tresses to watch the hunt.

Lucy Fittletrot perched on Sir Alex's near shoulder, looking as light as thistledown in a pale lavender gown of a soft material that caressed her body and legs as she moved. She gazed limpidly at Claud. "Aye, 'tis m'self," she said in her musical voice with her tinkling chuckle. "Didst miss me, Claud?"

Her hair was like fine corn silk, long and flowing softly in the breeze. Her eyes were like dark forest pools, drawing him into their depths, and her attraction was as strong as it had ever been.

He blinked, struggling to free himself from the spell she always cast over him. "Ye shouldna be here," he muttered. "I've nowt tae say tae ye."

"Oh, Claud, ye were no so cruel tae me the last time. What ha' I done?"

"Ye ken fine what ye done. Ye lied, Lucy! Ye

told me ye were daughter tae Tom Tit Tot, the fiddler, when instead that fiend Jonah Bonewits be your sire."

"Nay, Claud, Jonah Bonewits be your father, not mine. He told your mam so himself, so dinna be a daffy."

"I wouldna trust that villain's word, now, or yours, for anything," he said. "Ye could be me own sister, Lucy. Ye canna get from it."

She grimaced, but unlike Catriona, she did not disappear. Instead, her expression grew stubborn, and although Claud was sure he was right about their odd relationship, he knew, too, that it would not keep Lucy from trying to persuade him otherwise if it was in her interest to do so.

The peregrine stooped, diving straight for the earth. As she came into sight, in the seconds before she struck, Bab saw that her wings had closed. Then she heard a thunk and saw a puff of golden feathers fly from the grouse. The falcon opened its wings and swooped away, leaving the grouse to fall to the ground.

"She's playful, that one," Alasdair said as one of the gillies ran to retrieve the grouse and bag it.

As he did, Bab saw the falcon turn, close her wings again, and with a second thunk and puff of feathers came the demise of a second grouse.

"She's quick, too," Bab said, laughing with pure joy at this fine display of nature in action.

"Take care, she's going to feed this time!"

"The lads will keep her off," Alasdair said. "When they've got that second grouse safely bagged, I'll whistle her in."

"Faith, does she return to the fist, then? That is most unusual, I believe."

"But most convenient for the falconer, don't you agree?" Alex said lazily.

Bab grinned. "What I think, sir, is that your father enjoys an excellent chief falconer. Patrick has told me how difficult it is to train a falcon to return to the fist."

"I suppose you'd like it to return to yours," he said teasingly.

Delight leaped within her, and she looked questioningly at the falconer. "Would she do that?"

"Aye, sure, mistress," Alasdair said. "She'll return to the glove that's offered to her. Just hold it out as ye would for a hawk, and mind ye dinna start or jerk it away when she comes for it."

"I know," Bab said, barely able to contain her delight. Patrick had restricted her to retrieving his falcons from the grass, which was the normal way to recover one after its kill.

"I've a quail's wing ye may give her when ye've got her safe again," Alasdair said. "She'll be expecting it." Then he whistled a tune different from the ones used to direct the dogs. The falcon, on the ground now between the two gillies and eyeing their actions narrowly in the clear hope of seizing its share of the grouse, raised its head at the sound of the whistle and spread its wings.

Sir Alex said quietly, "Turn your face away, mistress."

She heard him, but she waited, watching, with her fist held up and out until the last minute, until the falcon threw its wings back and up, spread its tail to brake its speed, and thrust its talons forward. Then, holding her fist as steadily as she could, she looked away and held her breath. The powerful talons clamped onto her hand and wrist, and one powerful wing brushed the side of her face.

Turning back to look at the magnificent bird, she remembered the hood clutched in her right hand. "Should I hood her now?"

"Nay," the falconer said. "She'll rest quiet, but hold her jesses till we're ready to fly her again. We canna fly her wi' the gyr."

Nodding, she reached for the quail wing that he held out.

The bird's beak was already open, its talons twitching. It took the wing as its due and, holding it against her glove with one talon, began tearing into it.

Bab realized that she was grinning widely, and she turned to Sir Alex, her delight spilling over as she exclaimed, "She is magnificent!"

Her cheeks were flushed with color, her dark blue eyes bright with pleasure, and as he smiled in response, Alex thought, *she certainly is.* And he was not thinking about the falcon.

When Alasdair looked to him for permission to let her fly the gyr after the lass had said she wanted to, he had wondered if he were being a fool even to consider it. He would be annoyed with himself if she came to any harm — and, again, he realized, he was not thinking about the falcon.

Perhaps she would be tired now, though. She had risen well before the hour she had been accustomed to rise at court, so maybe she would agree to wait until next time. Even as the hope crossed his mind, he knew it was a forlorn one. He had only to consider her present delight to know what she hoped to do.

He sighed, but it was no more than he had expected. He had been sure it would amuse him to have Mistress Barbara MacRae as a guest at Dundreggan, and so far she had not disappointed him. She was enchanting.

Regarding her from beneath hooded eyelids, he said nonetheless in his customary, teasing drawl, "Are you ready to return to Dundreggan now, mistress? I confess that this morning's exercise has made me yearn for a nap."

She gave an unladylike snort. "You speak an infinite amount of nonsense, sir, for it cannot have done anything of the kind. That gelding's pace would suit a newborn babe, and you have not lifted a finger except to hold your reins, because the horse seemed to know his own way to this moor. Unless you want me to think you the greatest beast in nature, we are not going anywhere until I have flown that gyr. I'll be happy to do so at once, however. Unless, of course, you want to fly it first to wear it out a bit before I take it in hand," she added provocatively.

Hiding his amusement, he shot a speculative look at the quiet gyr and made his decision. "You must do as you like, mistress. I warrant that if I should try to take her from Alasdair, she would douse me with a stream of her mutes just as she did the last time I took her on my fist. Not only would the odor offend us all the way back to Dundreggan, but this rig is much too fine to spoil."

She rolled her eyes and shook her head, but her annoyance with him was clearly small compared to her yearning to fly the gyr. She turned to Alasdair. "Should I know anything in particular about flying her?"

"Nay, mistress, 'tis plain that Sir Patrick has trained ye well."

"I dislike casting a pall over this cheerful gathering," Alex said, "but the gyr will not return to your first, mistress, nor, for that matter, should you be the one to make to her after she kills. You will allow Alasdair or his men to retrieve her."

"Mayhap we should ride to the end o' the moor," Alasdair said. "Happen I recollect a pond where we might see some heron. The gyr be particular to heron."

"She'll take what she finds," Alex said. "I prefer to stay where we have a clear view in all directions, since we cannot know what mischief-makers might be about today, and we have brought no men-at-arms with us."

"Nor have we seen anyone but a few log carriers," the lass said tartly.

"Aye," he said, "but there are some who may use Beltane as an excuse, you see, and I'd as lief not meet with trouble here. Hand the gyr to Mistress MacRae, Alasdair, so we may have done with this soon enough to return in time for dinner."

Clearly not caring where they did it as long as she could fly the gyr, the lass said to Alasdair, "Does she know her business as well as the peregrine?"

"Aye, mistress. She'll fly from your fist just as a hawk would. Indeed, she differs from the peregrine only in that although she may soar up and wait on, as the peregrine did, like as not, she'll swoop low — more as a hawk does — and seek squirrels, voles, and herons or their like near the ground."

"Oh." She sounded disappointed, Alex thought, and he thought, too, that he understood. One expected mightier deeds from so splendid a creature. But then, reality so often failed to measure up to one's expectation.

He wondered if the reality of Mistress Barbara MacRae would disappoint him in the end. Watching her and seeing her enthusiastic smile as she handed the peregrine to Will and took the gyr from Alasdair, he rather thought she would continue to prove delightful.

Lucy and Claud paid no heed to the gyrfalcon. Lucy had flitted down to nestle beside him in the mare's pale, thick mane, and now she rested her elbows on her knees and her chin on her hands and peered at him wistfully.

He stared off into space, trying to close his ears to her insistent voice.

"Ye must believe me, Claud," she said. "The magical fiddler Tom Tit Tot certainly do be my father, just as I told ye he were."

Claud shrugged, wondering how she could say such a thing when he had seen the truth for himself the day he had watched Tom Tit Tot turn into Jonah Bonewits before his very eyes, and merely because he had spoken Jonah Bonewits's name to Tom Tit Tot.

Lucy said persistently, "D'ye forget that Jonah Bonewits be a powerful wizard and one, moreover, wi' grand shape-shifting powers?"

Claud blinked. That was just what he had been thinking. Some said Jonah Bonewits was as powerful in every way as Maggie Malloch, maybe even more so.

When Lucy said no more, another thought occurred to him. "D'ye mean tae tell me he just took the shape o' Tom Tit Tot and *pretended* tae be your dad?"

"Aye, for 'tis true. Under his spell, me poor

dad were stuck in the cage as a fiddling cricket in some faraway land where men wear long plaits down their backs. And Jonah Bonewits cast his spell over me, too, Claud, but I be free now."

Claud's spirits lightened considerably. If Lucy was free, that put a new light on things. When she rested a hand on his thigh, he grinned at her.

Chapter 6

Since the gyr was more spectacular in appearance than the peregrine, Bab had expected it to be more spectacular in flight, but she was glad when it swooped low as Alasdair had suggested it might, instead of seeking the heron. In her opinion, heron were nearly as spectacular themselves and were rather tough birds for eating.

After the gyr made its kill, she let the gillies make to it, watching critically as the one called Will knelt to bag the game while the other lad gently put a gloved fist to the gyr's belly. The bird stepped obediently onto it, accepted the bait he offered, and made no objection when he laced the jesses around his fingers.

They flew each of the birds several times more, then whistled up the dogs, and Bab made no objection when Sir Alex asked patiently if she had enjoyed enough hunting for the day. She could scarcely complain, but she felt a twinge of disappointment and wished he shared her zest for the sport.

She could not resist saying with a mocking smile, "Doubtless you fear you will get sunburned and spoil your pretty looks."

"You are so perceptive, mistress. That is exactly my fear, but I can see that I have annoyed you again, and I do most sincerely apologize for it."

"If you are hoping to burden me with a guilty conscience, Sir Alex, I must warn you that such meekness is likely to cast me into an ill temper instead."

"I feared it might," he said. His eyes twinkled, and in the sunlight, she noticed that their color matched the brilliant cornflower blue of his doublet. As lazily hooded as they usually were, she had not realized before how bright and clear a blue they were.

"Master Alex, have done," Alasdair Falconer said curtly. "What would his lordship ha' to say about such goings-on?"

When Sir Alex looked taken aback, Bab had all she could do not to laugh, realizing that he too was cursed with servants who had known him from birth, just as she was.

"The fact is, I'm a man sorely beset by women," Claud said with a deep sigh when Lucy leaned over and kissed him.

"Women? I'm but one wee lass, Claud, and I'm no besetting ye."

"Aye, but Catriona were here no long ago, too, ye see."

"Catriona? Och, aye, the Glaistig your mam calls the wee Highland slut," Lucy said helpfully. "Well, we dinna need her. I'll get rid o' her for ye."

"Nay, then," Claud said doubtfully. "I dinna ken but it might be as well tae make a bargain wi' the lass, just tae be safe."

"What sort o' bargain?"

"She'll tell me about the MacRaes and I'll tell her about the Gordons and Chisholms. 'Twould be tae give us both a better chance at success, dinna ye think?"

"I do not," Lucy retorted, stroking his thigh in just such a way as to stir tingling sensations throughout his body. "We ken all we need tae ken about anyone, Claud. I'll rid us o' that baggage, never ye fear. I've helped ye afore, ye ken, and what's more, I be Border bred like yourself so nae one can cavil at me helping ye."

"Aye, perhaps, but what o' Jonah Bonewits?"

"What about him?" she demanded, tilting her chin. "He ha' been expelled, which means his spells be nae more, and that be that, Claud."

"Nay, he were but banished from the Circle, not expelled from the Clan!"

It occurred to him as her hand moved up his thigh that even if Jonah Bonewits's spells had been weakened, the spell that Lucy Fittletrot cast over Maggie Malloch's son, Brown Claud, was stronger than ever. Without another thought, he gave himself up to the magic in her fingers and her rosy little mouth.

The hunters' return to Dundreggan was uneventful, perhaps because their conversation was limited to comments on the day's increasingly fine weather and Sir Alex's wondering aloud more than once what the menu would be for their noonday dinner since there would be no fires at the castle. The afternoon and evening likewise passed without incident, because Bab did not see him again until suppertime, and immediately after partaking of that cold meal, Chisholm agreed vaguely to let Alex try again to beat him at chess.

That left Bab to pass the evening with Lady Chisholm in her bower. While their time was spent comfortably in pleasant conversation, she found it dull entertainment, even more so by comparison with the Beltane festivities doubtless taking place that night on the high moor and other sites throughout the glens.

She had attended such festivals every year of her life and could easily imagine the kindling of the need-fires without seeing them. The men of each village would twirl an oak windle in a hole bored in an oak plank until sparks flew. Then they would feed the sparks with fungus that grew on old birch trees and, bit by bit, add wood from the nine sacred trees until the fire roared. After rituals celebrating the power of the sacred fires to purify, there would be music and dancing.

From that point on, representatives of each household would step forward to light the torches they would take home to rekindle their own fires. The atmosphere would be merry and far more entertaining than conversation with

Lady Chisholm. The fact that entertainment at Ardintoul would be even less stimulating when she returned made Bab wonder if Fate intended the rest of her life to be long or mercifully short before it allowed her to die of boredom.

Lady Chisholm recalled her attention by asking what she thought of a particular pattern of embroidery she was attempting, and Bab put her melancholy thoughts aside to discuss it with her.

Above the high moor, the sky was dark, for the moon was new and too shy to show its face, but stars blazed overhead and the revelry was loud and merry. Two need-fires flamed high, shooting crackling sparks into the black night, while pipes and fiddles played for the dancers.

Lowing cattle in the distance suggested that the ritual blessing of the beasts had already taken place, and here and there couples prepared to take their coupling leaps as soon as one or the other of the fires burned low enough to do so without risking self-immolation. Already, a few folks who had no wish to remain on the high moor until midnight had lined up to light the torches and brands they would use to rekindle their home fires for the new Celtic year. In a short time, parades of them would be wending their way back down into the nearby glens.

With attention on the dancers, the piping, and the fiddling, the merrymakers failed to see five horsemen ride onto the moor from a track to the east. Not until the men showed themselves in the fire's ambient glow did anyone take note of them.

The pipers stopped first and then the fiddlers, and soon all that anyone could hear was the sharp crackling of the fires.

Francis Dalcross, astride a muscular bay, shouted out, "This is an unlawful, pagan gathering. You must all disperse at once to your homes."

Somewhere in the midst of the revelers a man shouted back, "What be unlawful about Beltane? 'Tis a celebration we hold every year."

"Aye," shouted others. "And for hundreds o' years afore now!"

Dalcross bellowed back, " 'Tis a pagan celebration, disapproved by the Roman Church. We mean to put an end to it once and for all."

"Ye dinna ha' the right to do that!"

Others echoed that shout across the moor, but Dalcross stood his ground, and when the shouts died away to silence, he pointed at one of the men who had dared to defy him and snapped, "Arrest that man and those two others nearest him."

A general gasp met the order, but Dalcross had his sword unsheathed and his companions held pistols at the ready, so the three victims were quickly arrested, their hands bound behind them, and rope collars rigged around their necks. Another, much longer rope looped from collar to collar, and one of the men-at-arms yanked the free end, forcing the three to stumble along behind his horse when he turned it and rode back toward the eastern track. A second man-at-arms followed.

Turning back to the crowd, Dalcross snapped, "You will put out these fires at once and return to your homes. You may rekindle your home fires as you will."

"What about them lads ye've taken away?"

"The sheriff will hang them for indulging in pagan rites as a lesson to the rest of you that we will no longer tolerate such goings-on. And on Sunday next when you show yourselves in the Kirk, you should pray for your souls, every last one of you, and pray that our Almighty God above forgives this dreadful sin."

With angry muttering, several men in the gathering stepped forward, but since the muttering ones were unarmed, threatening gestures from Dalcross and the two still with him stopped them in their tracks.

The crowd was silent, allowing the deep voice that spoke from the shadows to be easily heard: "Stop where ye are, Francis Dalcross. I see ye ha' replaced the fine Italian sword I deprived ye of wi' another just as fine, but my men in the trees ha' longbows and guns, and their aim be true. One move from ye or your lads and I promise by the word o' *Sionnach Dubh* it will be your last."

Everyone turned toward the voice, and a

130

large black stallion moved just far enough into the ambient glow for them all to see it and to see the faint outline of the cloaked figure astride it. The silvery blade he held aloft was shiny enough to catch the flickering firelight, making it twinkle as brightly as the stars overhead.

"Sionnach Dubh!"

What began as a whisper soon grew to an audible murmur that swept across the high moor.

Dalcross glowered at the dark figure. "There are five of us, you scoundrel. Surely, you don't rate your skills so high that you'd dare take us all on at once."

"Mayhap not five ordinary, well-armed men," the Fox said. "But three with as little skill as ye and your men possess should not distress us."

"Three?"

"Aye, for I've already dealt with the two louts ye sent off wi' your three victims, and those victims be free. Ye'll no see them again yet a while, for I've explained to them that they must keep clear o' ye."

Dalcross looked over his shoulder, but the two soldiers who had led the three men away, and the men themselves, had disappeared.

As he looked back, the man to his left raised his pistol and kicked his mount forward, sending villagers scrambling for safety. Before he could shoot, an arrow from the darkness pierced his shoulder, and as he dropped his gun with a shriek, a few erstwhile celebrants yanked him from his saddle and quickly subdued him.

Others, taking advantage of the diversion, snatched Dalcross's sword and that of the man beside him, and their pistols, and dragged both men to the ground.

"Take care, lads," the Fox said, his voice carrying above the glee. "Francis Dalcross carries a dirk in his left boot and may ha' other such toys scattered about his person, so search him and his men well. Keep all their weapons but then escort them to the edge o' the moor and set them free."

As several men moved to search the captives and did the job so thoroughly that their heavy jacks of plate and belts were ripped off and cast into the shrubbery, another voice was heard to snap, "We'd do better to hang the lot o' them!"

"Nay, for we dinna be murderers," the Fox said. "We seek only to retain our lives and traditions and persuade the likes o' Dalcross here to let us be."

"But if we set them free, they'll only come back!"

"Ye'll keep their horses and send the men off down the track. If they go carefully, the stars will guide them safely back to Glen Mor and Inverness."

"But what if they linger?"

"I doubt they'll be so daft to stay after making so many enemies," he said. "Still, if they give ye trouble, take their boots. I'd warn ye, too, Francis Dalcross, that folks betwixt here and Glen Mor dinna take kindly to strangers. Ye'd do well to keep off the main tracks, since ye nae longer ha' your weapons."

Laughing now, the villagers hastened Dalcross and his men on their way. When they returned to the still blazing need-fires, they saw the great black stallion rear high as *Sionnach Dubh* vanished into the night.

When Lady Chisholm announced that it was time to retire, Bab made no demur. She had been yawning for half an hour, and looked forward to a full night's repose. Tomorrow, perhaps, Patrick would come to take her home.

The notion had its merits, but when she realized that it would not disturb her much if he failed her, she did not try to analyze her feelings.

Reaching the door to her chamber, she remembered the previous night, but despite her faint hopes, she felt no surprise to find Giorsal in sole possession of the bedchamber. Water steamed on the washstand, and Bab's nightclothes lay ready for her. With a sigh, she let Giorsal help her prepare for bed.

Before she sat down to let the woman brush out her hair, however, she knelt to put another log on the fire.

Noting this, Giorsal said, "It be gey cold tonight, mistress. That fire were burning when I come in, but the heat doesna seem to stir beyond the fireplace."

"I'll get into bed soon, but you may go as soon as you brush my hair," Bab said, sitting. "I mean to stay by the fire and toast my toes for a few minutes."

"I've already warmed your bed wi' yon warming pan," Giorsal said. "Ye'd best hop in as soon as I'm done here, whilst it still be warm."

"Very well," Bab said, knowing better than to argue. Five minutes later, she climbed into the warm bed, let Giorsal tuck her in, and bade the woman goodnight.

Giorsal drew the bed curtains, and a moment later, Bab heard the door shut quietly. In a trice, she was up and sweeping the bed curtains back again so that she could watch the flickering firelight. But the fire burned down quickly.

Still not ready to sleep, she got up and knelt to put on another log.

Brushing off her hands, she straightened and turned, only to walk into a large, muscular, black-cloaked body. Strong arms enfolded her.

It was all that she could do not to scream, for she had not heard the least sound to warn her of his arrival and would have crumpled right down to the floor but for his arms closing tightly around her. But when they did, the shock of his touch left her stiff and still, scarcely able to breathe.

"Sorry, lass," he murmured close to her ear. "I didna meant to startle ye."

She swallowed, still speechless. As tall as he was, and the way one hand held the back of her head, her left ear pressed flat against his chest and she could hear his steady heartbeat. Compared to her own heart, thundering away in her chest, his was beating strong and slow.

The hand cupping her head eased its grasp.

Finding her breath at last, she looked up at him. He was wearing the hoodlike mask, and by the fire's glow, she could see only the indistinct shape of his head. Reaching up, she touched the mask's hem between her thumb and forefinger, but he caught her hand and held it tight.

"You have got to stop sneaking up on me like that," she muttered fiercely. "You frightened the liver and lights right out of me."

"Never that, sweetheart. Ye're a canny lass, and ye didna even shriek." His hand tightened around hers when she tried to move the mask edge higher.

"I want to see you," she said. "You should not even be here, but since you are, I want to see your face."

"Nay, lass, that would not be safe for either of us."

"Do you not trust me?" That he could sneak into her bedchamber, twice, and then not trust her to protect his identity was hurtful. "I would never betray you," she said quietly, striving to make the declaration sound as sincere as she felt.

"I believe ye," he said just as quietly, his deep

135

voice touching those chords inside her as it had before, making her blood hum as it coursed through her veins. "I ken fine that ye wouldna willingly betray me, but under certain circumstances, no one can trust himself to remain silent, let alone trust someone else to do so."

The humming changed to an icy chill as his meaning struck home. "Do you fear they might torture me?"

"Neither Dalcross nor his son be known for mercy," he said. "They say they speak for the King, but they believe they speak for the Pope and for God himself."

"Faith, then why did you come here?"

" 'Tis a fair question," he replied, "especially since it becomes clearer each time we meet that ye represent grave danger to me."

"And you to me if what you said about the torture is true," she murmured.

"Aye, but only if Francis Dalcross should persuade himself that ye ken all he wants to ken about me. At this present, ye need only assure him that ye ha' never seen my face. Can ye do that an he questions ye, lass?"

"You speak only of Francis Dalcross. What about his father?"

"Francis pays more heed to ye than his father does. What's more, I think he yearns more for power than does Sheriff Dalcross and seeks a route to it through Cardinal Beaton and his lust for keeping the Highland Kirk under Rome's domain."

"I met him — Francis, that is — at Stirling," she admitted. "I . . . I liked him."

"Aye, well, he can be likeable an he chooses."

"Patrick did not like him. I hate it when Patrick is right and I am not."

He chuckled but made no further comment. He still held her hand clasped warmly in his, and his other arm felt snug around her waist.

"That sounded petulant," she said with a sigh. "I am not usually so irritable."

"Doubtless your ill humor arises from too much time spent in the company of yon noddy, Alex Chisholm," he said.

"I don't know that I would say that," she said.

"I say it. Ye asked why I came here tonight, remember?"

"Aye," she said, wishing again that she could see his face. It was hard to read his thoughts or even his tone when she could not see his expression.

"I came because I couldna stay away," he said. "Ye draw me like a lodestone, lass. I saw ye riding wi' him, and I was sorely tempted to snatch ye away, fearing ye might die o' boredom afore I could enjoy your company again."

Intrigued, she said, "Where did you see us?"

"On the ridge when ye rode onto the high moor to hunt. Although I were on the watch for Beltane mischief even then, I couldna stay away from ye then any more than I could stay away tonight."

"But if it is so dangerous —"

"I'd ha' dared anything to see ye tonight, sweetheart."

Both the repeated endearment and his passionate tone delighted her, but fear of discovery tempered that delight, and common sense stirred her to say, "I fear you flatter me, sir. I once told Francis Dalcross how I longed for adventure. Perhaps he mentioned that to others, and you somehow came to hear of it."

"We dinna move in the same circles, Dalcross and me," he said. "Still, I ken fine that ye seek adventure, lass, for I do myself, and one adventurer be bound to recognize another. 'Tis why I also believe ye ha' nae more use than I have for yon sniveling coward, Alex Chisholm."

Bab stiffened. She had let the earlier insult pass, but although she did wish Sir Alex would bestir himself to find a way to help his people, and had certainly said as much to him, she had never called him a coward or thought him one.

The word hung heavily between them.

She realized that her companion must be aware of the tension in her body. "Did you hear something just then?" she asked, hoping to divert him and thus not have to explain feelings that she did not yet understand. "I thought I heard a noise."

"Nay, lass, I heard naught. Ye were saying . . . about yon Chisholm . . ." He paused expectantly, leaving her no choice but to reply.

Drawing breath, she equivocated, saying,

"He has been kind to me, but in truth, I do find it dull here. If only women could enjoy such adventures as men enjoy, I might have done as Patrick has. He does not boast about his adventures, of course, but other men boast of theirs, and I should like very much to perform daring deeds to protect those who cannot protect themselves."

"You can safely leave the protection of the people of Glen Affric and Glen Mor to me, sweetheart," he said softly.

"Can I?" Her breathing was ragged again.

"Aye." Still holding her hand, he moved his other one to her shoulder and turned her, then put his fist gently under her chin so that she looked up at him. "I want to kiss you again," he said. "Can I trust you not to touch my mask?"

"Aye," she said, the word no more than a whisper. Thinking he might not have heard, she added, "I won't touch it, truly."

He let go of her hand, and she slipped it beneath his cloak, encircling his waist with her arms, feeling the hard muscles there.

In the glow from the fire, she saw him put a hand to his mask, and as his head bent toward hers, he eased the cloth upward. She saw nothing useful though, because his mouth touched hers at once, and although his eyes gleamed and stared straight into her own, she saw none of his other features.

She closed her eyes, savoring the moment, but unlike the first time he had kissed her, this time she tried to pay more heed to what she could learn about him.

His chin was smooth where it touched her, so she could tell he was clean-shaven, but that told her little, because many Highland men, fashionable and otherwise, cut their hair short and forbore to wear beards.

The thought checked itself in the stream of her consciousness. Why had her judgment suddenly linked him, even briefly, with men of fashion? As he kissed her, a part of her mind played with that thought, but its importance quickly faded.

Her lips were warm and soft. He had not expected her to respond so swiftly or with such ardor and wondered briefly if she might be more experienced than he had guessed. He doubted that any man had held her so closely before though, unless one counted that contemptible scoundrel Francis Dalcross, and clearly, that experience had not dampened her passion. Just then, he did not care a whit for the whys of her behavior. He wanted to kiss her, to explore her supple body with his hands. A voice inside his head whispered that he was a villain and no mistake and there would be dire consequences, but the lass was willing and he wanted her.

A lesser man would simply scoop her into his arms, carry her to the bed, and slake his passion with her. Her Giorsal would not return until morning, so a lesser man could enjoy a fine night if the lass remained willing.

Her thin nightdress concealed little of her slender, gently curved body. He wanted to touch her bare skin, to see if the skin of her belly and hips was as smooth as that of her cheeks and throat. The warning voice in his head muttered again.

Holding her easily in the curve of one arm, he let his free hand move to cup one soft breast and touched its nipple with his thumb.

She gasped but did not try to pull away. Still, that single little intake of air was enough. She thought of him as being only half real, he knew, and thus unlike any true gentleman, but in spite of that perception, or because of it, the lass trusted him. That trust represented something of a burden, too, and one that he had not experienced before. His previous experience had been solely with ladies as sophisticated in the arts of love as he was himself.

He moved his hand from her breast to the curve of her waist, but he allowed his kisses to become more demanding. He did not want to stop tasting her.

Bab melted against him. She did not want to think about what she was doing, or heed the potential consequences. She just wanted to enjoy the feelings coursing through her. He was warm and tender, and his kisses stirred her more than she had imagined kisses could stir any woman. The few stolen ones she had enjoyed in the past were as nothing to his.

No one had ever held her so closely before or taken such liberties as he took with her. Certainly, no man had ever touched her body in the same possessive way. What if Patrick should find out . . . ? Although she pushed the thought away, she reminded herself that she should be resistant, even shocked. Instead of following her own dictates, however, she wished he had not stopped caressing her breast.

Both of his hands moved from her shoulders to her waist and then to her buttocks, cupping them through her thin bedgown and pulling her body closer to his. Even then, she did not protest. She was certain she could trust him, for he had saved her from Francis Dalcross's evil intentions. He would not betray her now.

He held her so tightly against him that she could feel his body stir against hers, and she was hugging him now, too. His sword belt pressed against her ribs hard enough to leave marks, but the thought that it might be marking her was less distressing than the sure knowledge that any marks would fade before the room would be light enough again to see them.

One of his hands moved to caress her cheek, and she heard him groan deep in his throat. Then both hands gripped her shoulders again, and he gave her one last kiss before holding her away to look into her eyes. That look penetrated deep, and she could not summon words to speak. Her lips parted, but she could only stare silently back at him.

"I must go," he said. His voice sounded hoarse.

"No." The word leaped out, and she had an impulse to snatch it back lest it make him think less of her. But one could not snatch spoken words from the air, and in any event, the plain truth was that she did not want him to go.

" 'Tis the hardest thing I have ever done, sweetheart," he said as if he echoed her thoughts. "Yet I must if you are to retain your virtue and I my self-respect."

"But —"

"I'll tuck you in first," he interjected, scooping her into his arms.

She put hers around his neck, and a memory stirred from deep within of her father picking her up so and carrying her to her bed in the same manner.

The thought made her blink back sudden tears, tears that had not welled up to surprise her so in nearly a year, although before that, from the day she had learned of Sir Gilchrist MacRae's death while fighting beside the present Laird of Kintail's father, she had only to think about him to shed tears for his loss.

Her feelings now were different. It was as if the sense of security she had always felt when her father carried her had returned, shaking her emotions but only for a moment. She rested

143

her head against the Fox's shoulder, and when he laid her upon her bed and gently drew the covers up to her chin, she smiled and murmured, "Will you come back soon?"

Without answering the question, he bent and kissed her cheek, murmuring, "I'll shut the bed curtains, sweetheart."

"No, don't," she said. "I like to watch the firelight."

He nodded, then strode to the window and disappeared between the curtains. A breeze furled them as he thrust the shutter open, and then came silence.

Leaping from the bed, Bab hurried to look out the window, but when she did, she saw only darkness. The night was moonless and cloudy, so it took several moments for her eyes to adjust to the thick darkness after the fire's glow in the bedchamber. Hearing a slight sound from above, she wondered if it were possible that he had climbed to the roof, but then she heard the cooing of a night bird and decided that that was what she had heard before.

Closing the shutter and climbing back into bed, she lay for a long time watching the firelight play with shadows in the room and letting her imagination dance with them. At last, though, she slept and did not waken until Giorsal entered the next morning to open the curtains and shutters to a new, sun-laden morning.

Full of energy, Bab dressed quickly and went

downstairs to the hall where she took an apple from the table and hurried out to the stables. Running the chief stableman to earth, she asked him to have someone saddle a horse for her.

"His lordship didna say nowt about saddling nae horses this morning, mistress," the man replied brusquely.

Chapter 7

"You know perfectly well that I am his lordship's guest," Bab said to the stable man with a friendly smile. "You must have seen me ride out yesterday with Sir Alex and Alasdair Mackinnon."

"Aye, but that were yesterday, mistress, afore witches was flying, and wi' Sir Alex, too. This be another day and didna nae one say nowt about nae horses."

Suppressing the indignation that arose in the face of this bland but stubborn attitude, she said, "I do not mean to ride far, but I am accustomed to taking morning exercise. Every morning," she added bluntly.

"His lordship doesna hold wi' womenfolk riding out alone, mistress, and since they do say Beltane witches and *Sionnach Dubh* was all riding last night —"

"The Fox would not hurt me," she said instantly.

"Nay, then, he would not," the man agreed. "Did he no rescue three lads what were taken up by the sheriff's villainous son only yestereve for nae more than celebrating Beltane wi' the others, and did the Fox no set them free again?"

"Did he, indeed?"

"Aye, and that Francis Dalcross did search for him throughout the night, but he didna catch him, nor anyone else, come to that, since he and his men wasted their efforts a-searching for the Fox. The sheriff dinna hold wi' Beltane, saying it be a heathen festival and no approved by the Kirk, which be foolishness since Beltane been part o' our lives here since time began. Some say *Sionnach Dubh* be nobbut an outlaw, but I'm thinking it be just as well he took a hand in that business."

Though she was delighted to think that the Fox trusted her not to betray him to Francis Dalcross or anyone else, Bab kept her voice carefully even as she said, "I am sure that the Fox is a good man, so his being in the area can be no danger to me. As to Beltane witches, why, Beltane is over, and all witches fly by night."

"Nay, then, mistress, 'tis no the Fox nor the witches that concern us, nor anyone but the sheriff's lads."

"Then send a pair of gillies with me," Bab suggested. "I am sure that arrangement would meet with his lordship's approval."

"I canna do it without he orders it, mistress."

"Then I shall go and ask him," Bab said, fighting for patience.

"Likely, he'll still be abed, mistress, for her ladyship did say as nae one were to waken him betimes. He should get his rest, she said."

"Yes, of course. I'll just speak to Sir Alex then."

"Aye, that would be the thing to do, that would," the man agreed. "Likely he'll be up and about in an hour or two, and ye can fix it wi' him then."

"An hour or two!"

"Aye, for he doesna show his face till ten or later, most days."

"But yesterday he was up quite early."

"Aye, and ye could ha' knocked me down wi' a willow wand when I saw that. Told me missus ye must ha' lit a fire in his bed to stir him out so early."

"I see," Bab said, giving up for the moment but intending to put the matter to Lord Chisholm at the earliest opportunity.

Unfortunately, that opportunity did not arise until much later in the morning, and when it did, she could not call it a successful venture. His lordship said vaguely that he was sure Alex would be happy to escort her again but then warned her sternly that it was dangerous for a woman to ride out alone.

"I could not reconcile it with my conscience if aught should happen to you through my carelessness, mistress," he said. "Your mother and Sir Patrick expect me to keep you safe whilst you remain at Dundreggan."

Resigned to the inevitable, she spent yet another hour waiting for Alex to descend from his bedchamber. He did so at last, however, dressed in an elegant pale blue and silver doublet and matching hose. She knew he was partial to blue, since he had often worn it at Stirling, and the shade he had chosen today seemed to have been selected to match his eyes without the sun to aid their brilliance. The outfit was not one that any gentleman would wear to ride out into the rugged glen.

Responding to his greeting with a frustrated grimace, she said, "Do you always lie abed until the day is nearly over and then dress like a courtier?"

His eyebrows rose. "It is not even noon yet, mistress. I rarely arise so early as this. Surely, you did not mistake that outrageous hour yesterday for my habit!"

"I would like to ride," she said, striving to keep her tone civil.

"Certainly," he said. "Ah . . . have you broached this subject to my mother?"

"I have not," she said. "You know perfectly well that she does not enjoy such exercise unless she must, and then she plods along."

"Then I'll have to take you," he said. "My father has just informed me that he is sending a running gilly to Fort William, so I must write some letters before he departs, but when I have finished, I'll be happy to ride out with you. That is . . ."

"What?"

"Well, I shan't finish before we sit down to the midday meal, and you would not want to depart without your dinner, particularly since it will be the first hot meal we have enjoyed since

Saturday. Will two o'clock satisfy you?"

She had, perforce, to agree, but by one o'clock the clouds from the previous night had returned and the sky had grown dark and threatening, so she was not surprised when Sir Alex sent word that he was sure she would not want to risk a wetting merely for a bit of exercise. She would have liked to inform him that a little rain would not hurt them, but she knew he would just come up with another excuse. Sir Alex was not a man to brave the elements unnecessarily.

The following sennight passed in much the same manner as those first two days, except that the Fox did not deign to visit her again and the rain seemed to conspire against any but the shortest of outings. To his credit, Sir Alex did exert himself to take her riding whenever the weather permitted and was as kind as anyone could be the rest of the time, even teaching her to play chess one afternoon and allowing her to beat him twice. He said he had not let her win, that she had simply taken him by surprise, but she knew she was not yet skilled enough to have done so. Her delight when she realized that she had successfully placed his king in a fatal predicament, however, was nonetheless real.

Even so, she was soon chafing to return to Ardintoul. At least, there, she told herself, she could do as she liked when she liked.

On Tuesday, it rained again, and Sir Alex spent most of the day closeted with Lord Chisholm. By afternoon, thoroughly bored with inactivity, Bab complained to Giorsal, saying, "I vow, I did not feel so constrained as this even at court."

"Aye, sure, but ye needna sit glowering at yon drizzle, mistress. Black looks willna chase the clouds away."

"It is not the clouds or the rain," Bab snapped. "It is having nothing of interest to do. At home, this drizzle would not keep me indoors. You know it would not, and at Stirling there were always things to do, rain or no rain."

"Ye be a guest in this house, mistress. Ye must obey his lordship's wishes."

"I know that, but it is not his lordship who keeps me so close. Indeed, he scarcely speaks and seems to take interest in nothing. It is Sir Alex who calls the tune here, I believe, for all that everyone pretends that his father does."

Giorsal chuckled. "That Sir Alex! They say he pays heed to naught but his clothing and correspondence. Shuts himself up half the day, most days, writing letters and such. He says he be looking over accounts, too, but others do say —"

"You should not gossip with Chisholm's servants," Bab said, cutting her off with a sigh and some regret, since she would have liked to hear the rest but knew it was bad manners to gossip with her woman about her host's household. "I should not do it, either," she added conscientiously. "Indeed, I am surprised that you would tempt me like this. I just wish Patrick would come. I want to go home."

"Aye, well, mistress, doubtless he will be here soon."

Claud was just wondering to himself if he should chase the clouds away so that Mistress Bab could have some sunlight when Lucy danced into view, her dark eyes twinkling with suppressed laughter. He recognized the look, and it gave him no encouragement to return her smile.

"What ha' ye been up tae now?" he demanded.

"Are ye no going tae bring out the sun then?" she asked, dimpling again.

He stared at her. "How d'ye ken I were thinking o' that?"

Lucy shrugged. "Ye were gazing up at them dark clouds wi' a gey thoughtful look, Claud. I'd ha' tae be a noddy m'self no tae ken what ye were thinking on such a dour day as this. Shall I help ye clear them away?"

"Nay, we'd best not," he said. "The lass will only get herself into mischief, like as no. At least wi' the rain, she willna wander far afield."

"D'ye think ye need only keep her out o' mischief?" Lucy asked. "Why, I recall how ye ha' contrived more than one wedding afore, me lad. Will ye no find a man for your Mistress Bab, too?"

152

"Mayhap I ha' already found one," he said. "Did ye no think o' that?"

Lucy dimpled again.

"Look here," he said, "what ha' ye been doing, Lucy?"

"I fixed things so that slut Catriona canna distract ye."

"Here now, what did ye do to her?"

"That would be telling," Lucy said, grinning impishly. "I did nowt tae harm her. O' course, if she refuses tae do as she's bid . . ."

Claud gave her a sharp look. "I dinna believe ye. Ye ha' nae power over Catriona. If she's gone about her ain business, ye may be sure 'tis because me mam sent her off wi' a flea in her ear. She'll be sulking somewhere, that's all."

"Aye, well, it be all the same, then," Lucy said agreeably. "So now, Claud, since ye needna worry about Catriona, and Miss Bab be safe within the walls o' Dundreggan, mayhap ye can think o' summat else tae to." Grabbing one of his ears, she pulled his head around and kissed him hard on the mouth.

Laughing, Claud caught her to him and proceeded to teach her better manners, an exercise that proved enjoyable to them both.

Wednesday afternoon, while Bab was sitting with Lady Chisholm in her bower, practicing patience as her ladyship's conversation ambled idly from topic to topic, a gilly entered and said with a bow, "We ha' visitors, my lady.

153

They did ask for his lordship, but I told them he be taking his wee nap, so they asked for you."

"How pleasant," her ladyship exclaimed. "Do show them in at once!"

Elated, certain that Patrick had arrived at last, Bab patted her hair into place and smoothed her skirt.

Hearing the gilly's return, she jumped to her feet, only to hear him say solemnly as he entered, "The Laird o' Kintail, my lady, and Lady Kintail."

"But where is Patrick?" Bab demanded when Molly and Fin entered on his heels and she realized they were alone.

"Mind your manners, brat, or I'll not give you the letter I brought from him," Fin said as he made his bow to Lady Chisholm. "Your servant, my lady. We have come to collect this baggage and take her off your hands."

"Pay him no heed, madam," Molly said, making her curtsy with her red-gold curls tumbling free of the snood that had barely contained them at the best of times, since she refused to wear a proper headdress on all but the most formal occasions. Smiling brightly, she added, "I warrant you will miss Bab when she has gone."

"I will, indeed," Lady Chisholm said. "I so rarely have opportunity to enjoy feminine company. I'd like to have had a daughter or two, but we had only sons, and now, of course, we've only our dear Alex left to us. Must you take her away?"

"Aye, we must," Fin said, shooting a stern look at Bab who was struggling to contain her impatience.

She made a wry face at him as she hugged Molly. "But where is Patrick?" she asked again. "I am delighted to see you both, of course, but he did say he would come for me."

"My dear Barbara," Lady Chisholm said with a fond smile, "do let them sit down before you demand all the gossip from Stirling and beyond."

"Yes, madam, I beg your pardon." Obediently Bab sat down again.

"Patrick is at Dunsithe," Fin said, referring to the border stronghold that had come into his possession upon his marriage to Molly. "I asked him to stay there."

Knowing that the Laird of Kintail's request was as good as a command, Bab said with a sigh, "Isn't he coming at all, Fin?"

"Not straightaway," he said. "Jamie is gathering forces in the Borders, hoping to keep his uncle Henry of England on his own side of the line, and Patrick must stay at Dunsithe until I raise men in Kintail and we ride south to join him."

"But what about me? Am I to go to Dunsithe then, too?"

"Nay, lass," Fin said. "I'm taking you home to Ardintoul."

155

Bab sighed. The worst part about being a woman, she decided, was that no one ever asked for her opinion or considered that she might want to choose her own course.

Aboard the Marion Ogilvy *in the Tyrrhenian Sea*

When shouts came for all hands to assemble on deck, he calculated that they were off the west coast of Italy, nearing Rome. The *Marion Ogilvy* had no regular route that he could work out. She seemed to sail at the whim of her owner or captain and was certainly no mere merchant's ship.

He had long ago deduced the identity of the ship's owner from various bits of information, not least of which was the name *Marion Ogilvy*. More than a decade had passed since Davy Beaton had decided to take holy orders with an eye to replacing his uncle, then Archbishop of St. Andrews. But when he had decided upon that course, he set aside his wife, Marion, and their several children with the full dispensation of the Holy See in Rome, to become a priest.

The whole business had created a scandal the length and breadth of Scotland. Even so, most folks discredited the notion that such a jumped-up priest could ever become an archbishop. But Davy had fooled them, taking his uncle's place upon that gentleman's death just as he had said he would and then going on to

156

become Cardinal Beaton and the Lateran Legate in Scotland, all without having set Marion Ogilvy and his children aside in any way other than name.

He was turning to answer the call for all hands when Tam intercepted him.

"Lad, we must do summat. Gibson's going tae flog Willie Armstrong!"

"Young Willie? What for?"

"For nowt," Tam said with disgust. "That bastard Gibson goes for 'im every chance he gets. They do both be Border bred, so 'tis just feuding, like as not."

That made sense if anything aboard the *Marion Ogilvy* made sense. He followed Tam to the main deck, where hands were still shuffling into place and where Gibson, the first officer, stood by the grating smirking as he waited for them to bring Willie Armstrong for his punishment. The sun was shining, the shrouds creaked, and white tops flew from the waves in showers of spray.

Watching two burly sailors drag the skinny little Borderer forward and fling him against the iron grating made something snap in him. Angrily, he strode forward and confronted Gibson.

"That lad has done naught to warrant this, Gibson, and you know it. If you must flog someone today, how about me?"

The first officer glowered at him, but he had to look up nearly a foot to do so. "I be Lieutenant Gibson tae ye, ye scrofulous malcontent, or sir. And it would be a right pleasure tae flog ye, so dinna tempt me."

He glowered right back, his arms folded across his chest.

Gibson glanced at Willie Armstrong. "Ye'd really take his place?"

"I said I would."

"D'ye ken what penalty he faces?"

He shrugged.

"A hundred lashes for insubordination. Ye still want tae take it for him?"

His skin crawled at the thought of what a hundred lashes would do to it. He had too little meat on his bones to protect them, if anything could protect a man against a bullwhip, but Gibson's lads would kill Willie with such a flogging. He gestured to them to pull the lad aside, and then he strode to the grating.

As the two were shackling him to the grating, the bosun shouted from the forecastle, "Land ho off the larboard bow! All hands to for losing way!"

Gibson chuckled. "Aye, well then, ye can wait yet a while, me lad. We've business and all tae tend afore we tend tae ye. Release him, lads, and we'll get a bit more work out o' the man afore we give him his hiding."

In minutes, they had dropped the anchors, furled the sails, and the swarm of men in the rigging had descended to the deck. The *Marion Ogilvy*'s banners and flags still flew gaily, and her officers leaned over the bulwarks and waved.

On the shore, vendors had already gathered. He saw men selling chickens and pigs, women in bright dresses, and children and dogs darting everywhere. Some of the women wore the bright yellow wrappers and veils that, as he had learned on his first trip, marked them as prostitutes. Not that the knowledge could do him any good even if he were a man who indulged himself with strumpets, for here as in all other ports, he would remain aboard ship.

Before sundown, they had chained his leg irons to the standing rigging to ensure that he would not try to jump ship, and soon afterward, a Venetian galley dropped anchor nearby. In the dusky light, he could see galley slaves taking the air on its deck, their high red bonnets and bare backs marking them clearly for what they were so one would not mistake them for honest crewmembers.

"D'ye see them lads?" Gibson said with a sneer as he checked the shackles. "I can arrange for ye tae join them if ye continue wi' your insolence. How'd ye like tae be chained tae an oar sixteen hours out o' twenty-four and flogged whenever they want more speed out o' your oar?"

"If we are to speak of preferences . . ."

"Och, aye, ye'd prefer tae take Willie Armstrong's flogging. I remember. Well, barring any bad omen, such as a crow in the rig-

159

ging or news that a crew member ha' dreamed o' black goats, we'll be away wi' the morning tide, and ye can ha' your flogging then."

"We're here only overnight?"

"I ken fine that ye'd prefer a long visit," Gibson said with a chuckle. "But ye dinna give the orders, and Rome provides nae safe harbor, so we're off tae Naples tomorrow. 'Tis a hundred miles, so we'll ha' plenty o' time for a good flogging."

"Don't you want to go home, Bab?" Molly asked at supper that evening, after they had spent the afternoon in a flurry of packing.

Fin frowned as if he disapproved of the suggestion that Bab might not want to do as she was bid, but Molly gave him a look, and he held his peace.

In that moment, Bab realized she did not know what she wanted. Although she chafed at the confinement and the lack of things to do at Dundreggan, she was no longer so sure she wanted to leave. She certainly had reason to go, though.

Much as she liked Lady Chisholm, she was bored. Thanks to her ladyship's preference for indolence, Dundreggan provided few outlets for her energy. Chisholm slept much of the day and spent his waking hours staring at the fire or looking through documents or accounts that Sir Alex placed before him, but he never so much as questioned them, let alone found any fault.

Sir Alex was kind to her and slightly more entertaining, but even when he rode out with her, his idea of exercise was to ride aimlessly along one track or another without any particular goal in mind, except perhaps to hurry back within doors before it rained and spoiled his doublet.

She told herself that she would be happier at Ardintoul, but on the other hand, the Fox was active in Glen Affric and Glen Mor, both many miles from Kintail and Ardintoul. He had never, to Bab's knowledge, shown himself in Kintail, and she had barely had a chance to become acquainted with him.

Recalling what he had said about being drawn to her, she wondered if he would follow her home. But despite his words, he had not managed to steal even a few more moments with her at Dundreggan, so the likelihood was that if she went home, she would never see him again.

"Bab?"

She looked blankly at Molly, who gazed expectantly back at her. Realizing that she was still waiting for her to tell them what she wanted to do, Bab said, "Will Patrick stay at Dunsithe until King Henry returns to London?"

"He will stay as long as I want him to say," Fin said. "Dunsithe is near the English line, so Henry might decide to add it to his holdings if he invades as he threatens to do at any moment now. He has been waiting impatiently at York for our Jamie, but Jamie has better sense than to join him so far inside his own boundaries."

"Then Molly will stay at Eilean Donan," Bab said, referring to Kintail's primary seat at the mouth of Loch Duich, some miles to the west.

"Nay, she will not," he said. "My lass stays with me."

"Then I should go to Dunsithe, too." As soon as she said it, she realized the notion held no appeal, so she was just as glad when Fin shook his head.

He said flatly, "As you have seen by his letter, Patrick's orders are that you are to remain at Ardintoul with your mother, and I've promised to take you there."

Bab opened her mouth to protest out of habit rather than from any wish to change his mind, but before she could speak, Molly said swiftly, "You know your mother would never agree to leave home again so soon, Bab, and in any event, she would refuse to make the long journey into the Borders."

That point was unarguable. Bab had had all she could do to persuade her mother to journey comfortably by sea to Dumbarton and thence on horseback the short distance to Stirling. Even then, Lady MacRae had stayed barely a sennight before returning to the Highlands, and Bab knew that she had hated every minute she had spent at the royal castle.

In truth, Bab had no wish to leave the Highlands even if Fin would permit it. And since Patrick had decided she was to stay at Ardintoul with their mother, as he had made clear in his letter, she would never persuade Fin to any other course. Patrick had also written to Sir Alex, and although something in that letter had made Alex chuckle, he had not shared what Patrick had written with the rest of them.

At least, Kintail had not asked her yet about her journey from Stirling to Dundreggan, so she had not had to tell him about her abduction and rescue. She did not want to contemplate what he might say about that incident.

He was in a great hurry to begin gathering his men, and so early Thursday morning, Bab took fond leave of her hostess, the only one of the Chisholms up at that hour to bid her farewell, and set out for home.

Claud was sitting quietly in his mother's little parlor when she entered and said abruptly, "I see your lass be leaving Dundreggan."

Claud said swiftly, "Ye're no tae help me wi' this, Mam!"

"I ha' nae intention o' helping ye," Maggie said tartly. "For once, things be marching peaceably betwixt yon Merry Folk and our Helping Hands whilst they wait tae judge whether ye and that fractious slut Catriona succeed in your tasks, so I came tae see that all here were in order. However . . ."

He sighed, knowing she could never keep out of his business. It was a sickness with mothers, he thought. "What?"

"A wee bird told me that ye did meet wi' that wagtail Catriona again."

"Aye, I did, and then ye spirited her away," Claud said grimly. "Dinna think I couldna see your fine hand in that."

"Spirited her away?"

"Aye, dinna try tae hide your teeth, woman. She were there one minute, suggesting we should exchange information for our common good, and the next she vanished. I havena seen her since."

"By your troth?"

Claud nodded, realizing that he had said nothing about meeting Lucy, nor had Maggie mentioned her. He did not think he would tell her now, though, especially since she was frowning heavily.

After a long moment, Maggie said, "I ha' had nowt tae do wi' Catriona's vanishing, lad. I only just heard that the shameless callet had been at ye again."

Claud looked narrowly at her. Maggie's power allowed her to do many things. Her temper was legendary, her methods of punishment terrifying.

But she did not lie to him.

Aboard the Marion Ogilvy

Overnight a good deal of activity ensued, and before the new dawn glowed in the east, someone released him to climb the rigging with the swarm so they could begin unfurling the sails. He watched for Gibson, certain the man would wait only until the ship was underway before ordering him back to the grating.

Before then, he noted a new face gazing up at him from the quarterdeck. The man wore clothing that set him apart from all but the captain, and he bore an air of distinction that would not have been out of place at any court.

Twenty minutes later, with the ship underway, the expected order came.

"Stretch him tight," Gibson said to the sailors who chained him in place.

Focused as he was on his immediate fate, it was a moment before he heard the angry buzzing or identified it as muttered protest from the hands gathered on deck to watch his flogging. The sound grew louder.

Hands clutched his saffron shirt to rend it from his back.

"Hold there," an unfamiliar voice snapped. "Release that man."

"Wi' respect, sir, this be ship's business," Gibson growled.

"I'm told this man committed no offense."

"That be for me as first officer tae decide," Gibson retorted.

"Release him."

And to his shock, the hands clutching his shirt released it to unchain him. As he struggled to his feet, the man he had seen earlier on

165

the quarterdeck beckoned to him. Glancing at Gibson and receiving no order to the contrary, he moved to obey the summons. The relief he felt at avoiding the flogging made his knees feel weak.

"Do you know who I am?" his benefactor asked when he stood before him. Of medium height and slender build, he had the casual air of authority that bespoke breeding, and displayed none of the bluster that was Gibson's stock in trade.

"Nay, sir, I dinna ken your name."

"Nor I yours."

"They call me Kit, sir, or Devil's Kit. I ha' nae other name."

A slight frown creased the other's brow, but he said only, "I am Sir Kenneth Lindsay. My uncle is Scotland's ambassador to the Holy See."

"What d'ye want wi' the likes o' me, sir?"

"I noted the shackles last night when I came aboard and asked a few questions. I'm told your first officer treats some men more brutally than others."

"D'ye ken I be a prisoner, sir, bound tae serve me life aboard this ship?"

"Aye, I do, but one man does not stand in for another's punishment."

"Willie Armstrong didna warrant flogging, and they'd ha' killed him!"

"I agree. Gibson must contemplate his practice of leveling more punishment against men

166

of certain Border surnames, and I trust he'll do so with an eye to changing that behavior. I'll not have unfair treatment whilst I'm aboard this ship."

"Then I hope ye'll stay aboard her a good long time, sir."

Lindsay chuckled. "Only until we reach Dumbarton, I'm afraid."

"Aye, well, that'll be a wee while yet. We're for Naples, Brindisi, and Venice yet afore we turn for home."

"There has been a change of plan, because I've messages that must reach Cardinal Beaton as soon as possible. We're bound for Scotland with all due speed, and I'm a compassionate man, so if you've any message you'd like to get to your people once we're home, I'll be glad to see it reaches them straightaway."

"Thank ye, sir, but I'll send nae message."

Chapter 8

Kintail's party traveled by the shortest route possible to Eilean Donan, a journey of twenty-five miles through rugged landscape made treacherous all along the way by melting snowbanks and fast-flowing rivers. It took them only two days, because Kintail knew the terrain and traveled fast. He, Molly, and their personal attendants had brought a minimum of baggage with them to Dundreggan, having sent their sumpter ponies on to Eilean Donan from Glen Mor by way of Glen Moriston and Glen Shiel. Bab and Giorsal carried only minimum baggage too.

Kintail had arranged with Chisholm to lend the two women suitable mounts and to send the rest of their things the longer way by sumpter ponies.

Their present route lay through high, steep-sided, rocky glens, first following the River Affric to the head of the glen, then through the high pass, down into the even steeper Glen Lichd, and along the River Croe into Kintail. Rain and snowmelt swollen rivers raced alongside them, and numerous waterfalls in full spate roared at them along the way. In many places, the riders had to dismount and lead

their horses, but in general, the nimble Highland ponies managed the route with ease.

After a long, tiring day, they took shelter
Thursday night with Mackenzie kinsmen near
the head of Glen Lichd and then set out again
shortly after dawn.

Mountains towered on all sides as they followed the river down to the broad flatness of
Strath Croe, while the high peaks known as the
Five Sisters stood guard over them to the
south. Bab had known the Sisters from her
childhood, because whenever she took a boat
onto Loch Duich she could see their sharp
peaks notching the horizon at the head of the
loch. The perspective from Loch Duich was far
different from Glen Croe's, however, and when
Fin told her that she was looking at the backside of her beloved Sisters, she found it hard at
first to believe him.

They reached Loch Duich late Friday afternoon. The familiar journey along the loch
passed quickly, but it was nearly dark when
they reached Eilean Donan.

"You'd best stay the night here," Fin said
when they arrived. "I'll take you across to
Ardintoul in the morning."

Asleep on her feet, Bab agreed. She had
spent many a night at Eilean Donan, which was
practically her second home, and she did not
stand on ceremony. Giorsal fetched soup and
bread from the kitchen for her, and when she
had eaten, she slept.

* * *

Claud had found it difficult to guard Mistress Bab's progress and search for Lucy at the same time, so he was glad when the former fell asleep and he knew she would stay put for a while.

After that, finding Lucy was quick work, because she danced into view accompanied by her rippling, musical laughter.

He loved to watch her dance. It was as if her own music accompanied her everywhere, and he remembered when he had first heard it for himself. She had told him then that the music was hers but not so fine as what her father could play on his fiddle, and then she had whirled him away to hear Tom Tit Tot play.

He put the thought away with a shudder and made no objection when she danced up to him and snuggled at his side. Better that she should snuggle than that she should dance him away and make him forget all he had to remember if the Circle was not to make a gift of him to the Evil Host.

Remembering what Maggie had said, he waited until Lucy was comfortable, struggling to ignore the tantalizing sensations her moving fingers created wherever they touched him. Then he said, "Lucy, what exactly did ye do tae Catriona?"

Lucy chuckled. "So ye believe now that I did summat tae her, do ye?"

"Aye, I do, so tell me what ye did."

"Let me show ye a wee thing first that I ha' learned since the last time we played together, Claud."

As she spoke, she shrugged the soft lavender gown off her shoulders and let it fall to her waist. "Put your head down here, laddie. Ye'll like it, I promise."

He did.

The morning mist had dissipated and the day was clear, sunny, and peaceful when Kintail, his lady, Bab, and Giorsal set out across the loch in a flat-bottomed fishing coble rowed by two strong oarsmen. The only sounds to break the silence were cries of the birds overhead and someone hammering in Dornie village on the northern shore of the loch, across the tidal channel from Eilean Donan.

Just enough wind blew to fill the lugsail, and although it blew from the northwest, the oars-men's skill guided the boat swiftly across the water. The four passengers, content to enjoy the peace, did not converse.

Watching the soaring gulls and listening to the wind in the sail and the water lapping the sides of the boat, Bab soaked up sunlight and inhaled the fresh sea air, knowing she was home again and delighting in each familiar sound and sensation.

Neither Fin nor Molly had asked yet about her journey to Dundreggan from Stirling, so she had begun to hope that Lady Chisholm, Sir

Alex, or even Chisholm himself had explained what had happened and had asked them not to distress her by discussing it further. Such restraint seemed unusual for both Fin and Molly, but they had talked little on the journey, and Bab had no wish to initiate any discussion now.

Fin had sent a gilly across in a boat the night before to warn Ardintoul that Mistress Bab was returning, with the result that a servant met them at the beach with horses. The journey from that point was little more than a mile along a woodland trail to the natural, easily defended approach to the castle itself.

Ardintoul's gray stone walls formed part of a precipitous outcropping of rock on the inside of a horseshoe-shaped ridge surrounded on the outside by dense woodland. The trough ran northeast to southwest with its opening at the southern end, its upper slopes steep enough to shield most of Ardintoul from the heavy winds that swept in from the north and frequently turned the waters of Loch Alsh into a maelstrom. Even so, from the heights of the tower battlements, one had a clear view northwest along the length of Loch Alsh, as well as southwest across Kyle Rhea to the Isle of Skye and northeast to Eilean Donan. From outside the trough, an enemy would face a steep pile of loose scree, impossible for horses to ascend and easily defended from above against men on foot. It also provided a natural escape route for the castle's inhabitants, rendering it an unlikely target for siege. Ardintoul was, in fact, one of the most easily defended fortresses in the Highlands.

To the south, high granite peaks and sharp, serrated ridges guarded the landscape, making it nearly impossible for any Macdonalds or Mackintoshes who might covet Mackenzie or MacRae lands to attack without warning. Gentler, thickly wooded ridges to the east blocked the view of Loch Duich from Ardintoul, but the Mackenzie of Kintail who had deeded land for the castle to his MacRae constable had done so not only because of MacRae loyalty but also because putting MacRaes on that strategic site added significantly to Eilean Donan's security.

Kintail's seat occupied the islet at the mouth of Loch Duich where the loch met Loch Alsh to the west and Loch Long to the north. With the rugged Highlands to the east and south making access difficult from either direction, when Eilean Donan fell under attack, it most often came from Loch Alsh or Kyle Rhea. Located near the convergence of the two, Ardintoul made an excellent watchtower.

As they approached its gates, Bab saw Kintail look around speculatively.

"What's amiss, Fin?" she asked. "You don't expect trouble here, do you? No one has ever attacked Ardintoul."

"Nay, lass, I'm just wondering how many men I can take south for the King from here.

This place is safe enough unless Eilean Donan itself falls, and presently any enemies of mine who might attack are busily making friends with Henry of England and adding their resources to his."

Bab nodded. She had heard as much from others. Most clans in the Highlands powerful enough to attack each other had allied themselves with either Henry or with James of Scotland to help him prevent the invasion that Henry so eagerly sought. The action would remain far south of Ardintoul though, so it did not worry her in the least, and in any event, the Scots would prevail. They always did, and with the Lordship of the Isles no longer in dispute, the likelihood seemed small at present that anyone would dispute the peace of Kintail.

The iron gates guarding the entrance to Ardintoul swung open, and they rode through the arched gateway into the flagstone-paved yard. It was not nearly as busy or noisy there as in the graveled bailey at Dundreggan, so their horses' hooves echoed hollowly on the flags. As she dismounted, Bab called a greeting to each of several servants who emerged to bid her welcome home.

Crossing quickly to the wide stone steps leading to the entrance, she caught up her skirts and ran up them as a gilly opened the stout, ironbound door. The heavy yett, a massive iron-grill on heavy hinges that would reinforce the door at times of attack, rested against the wall behind the open door, as usual. The only time in Bab's memory that Ardintoul had closed and bolted its yett had been the year her father died, after he and his master had left for Kinlochewe to fight the Macdonalds.

Inside the great hall, all was tidy and a fire burned cheerfully, for despite the bright sunlight outside, the interior of the stone tower was nearly always chilly.

"I want to speak to Duncan," Fin said, referring to Patrick's steward. "You go and find your mother, Bab. I am sure you must be eager to see her."

"I'll go with you," Molly said, smiling. "Giorsal can see to your things."

"Aye," Bab said, adding, "You won't take Duncan with you, will you, Fin?"

"Nay, lass, he's too far past the age mark to enjoy the journey, although I'm sure he'd disagree with me. In any event, he is more useful here. Patrick and I can trust him to look after you and your mother and to keep things running smoothly."

She nodded, satisfied, and went with Molly to look for Lady MacRae.

Encountering Duncan's wife Florrie, their housekeeper, on the way, Bab gave her a hug and asked where she would find Lady MacRae.

"Bless ye, Mistress Bab, she'll be up top o' the tower like always."

"At the top of the tower?"

"Aye, for she sits up there day in and day out,

gazing out across Loch Alsh as if she expects to see them ships sailing up it again."

A chill shot up Bab's spine as she caught Molly's sympathetic gaze.

Twelve ships had sailed up Loch Alsh in August of the previous year, carrying the High King of the Scots and Cardinal Beaton to Eilean Donan, where the King had demanded that Kintail accompany him back to Stirling. Despite the MacRaes' and Mackenzies' unswerving loyalty to the Crown, James had decided that the Laird of Kintail should be one of his many Highland hostages, and had attacked Eilean Donan with cannon fire to force Fin's surrender.

Bab knew that the incident had sorely distressed Lady MacRae, as had Patrick's leaving shortly afterward with Molly for Stirling, so that Molly could join her husband in confinement there. And although Lady MacRae had seen for herself that Kintail and Molly were safe at Stirling, and knew now that Patrick was safe too, her distress had eased but little with that knowledge. Bab knew too that at first, when the King's ships had sailed into Loch Alsh, Lady MacRae had hoped briefly that one of them might be bringing Sir Gilchrist MacRae home again.

From the day two years before, when Sir Gilchrist had ridden north with Fin's father through lightly falling February snow, Lady MacRae had lived in constant hope of his homecoming and had refused to accept that his body had returned and lay buried in Ardintoul's little cemetery in the woods outside the gate. Although she had stood shivering at the graveside with Bab and Patrick while the priest spoke solemn farewell prayers, she had not spoken, nor had she given the slightest sign then or afterward that she was aware of what had transpired there.

Catching Molly's gaze now, Bab said, "Perhaps I should go up to her first."

"I'm coming with you," Molly said firmly, and Bab did not argue. She was glad to have her company.

They went up the spiral stone stairway, past Patrick's bedchamber and that of Lady MacRae, up more stairs past Bab's chamber, and then up the final, steeper flight to the battlements. Pushing open the door at the top, Bab stepped onto the walkway, which at that point faced due south. Looking first to the west and then to the east, she saw no sign of her mother.

The wind had increased, still blowing from the northwest and whipping around the corners of the ramparts. Feeling chilled despite the cheerful sunlight and the sheltering crenelated parapet, Bab wrapped her arms around herself, trying to keep warm, and saw Molly do the same.

From each corner of the parapet jutted forth a rounded turret, or bartizan, that provided protection for the ever-present guards on the ramparts. Because the area had been peaceful for some time, a single man-at-arms patrolled now, and Bab did not see him until she had reached the southeast bartizan. From there, she saw him walking toward her along the eastern walkway.

He smiled. "Welcome home, Mistress Bab," he said. "Ye'll be wanting her ladyship, I'll wager."

"Aye," Bab said. "Where is she?"

"Yonder, mistress, working her stitchery."

Glancing back at Molly, Bab slipped past him into the next bartizan. From there, she could see her mother in the next one, sitting on the little stone bench, gazing through the angled gun loop at Loch Alsh with her needlework in her lap.

About to call out a greeting, Bab changed her mind. Realizing that her mother had no idea she was there and fearing to startle her, she waited until she neared the bartizan before saying quietly, "Good morning, madam."

Lady MacRae turned her head and smiled. A slender, dark-haired woman, she wore a dark green day dress and had a gray cloak draped over her shoulders. When she smiled, she bore so striking a resemblance to her daughter that folks never had to guess from which parent Bab had inherited her beauty. Her ladyship's dark hair showed streaks of silver, and her complexion was much paler than Bab's, but the resemblance remained clear.

"They have not come yet," Lady MacRae said matter-of-factly as if in response to a question Bab had asked, "I warrant it will not be long now though. Certainly they will come before I have finished stitching this cushion cover."

Watching her ladyship slip the needle aimlessly into the fabric and pull it through again, Bab felt a lump in her throat when the blue thread came all the way through and she realized it had no knot. No matter how many stitches Lady MacRae took, she would never finish the cushion cover if she failed to knot her thread.

"Madam, Kintail and his lady have returned from Stirling, and have come to pay their respects to you," Bab said gently. "I pray you, descend to the hall with me now to receive them. You are blue with cold."

Although Lady MacRae did not acknowledge her concern, neither did she object when Bab put an arm under her elbow and urged her gently to her feet. Between them, she and Molly guided her safely downstairs to the hall and settled her comfortably in Sir Patrick's armchair before the fire, where she continued her aimless stitching but stared into the flames.

"Where is her woman?" Molly asked quietly.

"I do not know, but I will find out," Bab said. "She seems much worse, Molly. I had hoped that by persuading her to accompany me to Stirling, I could stir her from her lethargy, but I only caused more damage. It was horrid of me to let her come home alone."

"Don't be foolish, Bab. Had she behaved like this then, do you think either Fin or I would have allowed you to stay with us when she returned, or that you would have been content to let her go?"

"But you cannot deny she is worse," Bab said.

"No, nor can I deny that she behaved much more like her old self at Stirling. She was much as she has been any other time she had to appear at court, for as you know well, she has always disliked court life. You will recall that even your father had difficulty persuading her to attend court with him the few times he went."

That being undeniable, Bab said no more about the matter, ordering refreshment for them all instead and hoping that her return to Ardintoul would serve to stir her mother from her fantasies.

She indulged that hope until a blunt conversation with Ada MacReedy, Lady MacRae's waiting woman, dampened it considerably.

"I dinna ken what be the trouble, mistress," Ada said. "Time was, I thought she missed ye and Sir Patrick, but she doesna fret nor worry. She just watches the loch and stitches, and betimes, she talks to herself or to others nae one else can see."

Bab nodded. Lady MacRae had talked to

herself even before Sir Gilchrist's death, so that was nothing new. Bab had been about seven or eight the first time she had noticed that her mother often muttered to herself when no one else was about.

"Who are you talking to?" she had once asked.

"Why, to myself, dearling," Lady MacRae had answered matter-of-factly.

"But why?"

"Well, from time to time, you see, one grows tired of talking to servants and children and likes to speak to someone who can be depended on to understand exactly what one is saying."

Suspecting mockery, Bab had nodded wisely and run away, but she remembered that conversation now and wondered sadly if Lady MacRae still believed that no one else understood her thoughts or feelings. To be sure, Bab had felt that way more than once in her life, but she feared that her mother had somehow left the real world and now inhabited some strange world of her own.

From the ramparts, Bab watched the boat carrying Molly and Fin back across to Eilean Donan and felt bereft. They would not leave at once for Dunsithe, so she would see Molly again and be able to visit with her and seek her advice at least once or twice in the meantime. But it occurred to her that when they had gone, she would be in that position her mother had described to her so long ago of having no one in their right senses but servants and children with whom to talk, and that meant she would have no one with whom to talk about personal matters.

It took less than two days for her to realize that if she had been bored at Dundreggan it was as nothing to what she faced in the coming months at Ardintoul. She was able to ride out those first days, as she had been accustomed to do all her life, because the weather remained sunny until midday Monday, but Chisholm's sumpter ponies had no sooner arrived from Dundreggan with her baggage and Giorsal's than a battering rainsquall swept in from the sea. By late that afternoon, the rain had diminished to a steady patter that threatened to continue for days.

Conferring with Florrie MacRae and Ada MacReedy, Bab found as expected that she had nothing to complain about in the running of the household. Both women were supremely capable and required no more assistance than they received from the maids and gillies who had long served Ardintoul. Thus, she found herself again with little to do but to bear her mother company and watch with sadness while Lady MacRae muttered to herself and continued her endless stitching.

"Ye've more trouble brewing here than first meets the eye," Maggie Malloch said sternly to her son. "What be ye doing about it?"

Claud had sensed her presence for once before she spoke, so he was able to retain his dignity as he said, "Mam, d'ye no trust me tae
look after yon lass?"

"I do trust ye," Maggie said. "But I canna be
easy in mind until I ken what's become o' that
idle weed, Catriona."

Claud rolled his eyes. "Ye ken right well
where she be. She be looking after Chisholms
like ye said. She doesna want tae face punishment any more than I do."

"Aye, well there be nae sign o' her anywhere
near Dundreggan, I can tell ye, and she's
needed there, Claud. There be grand mischief
a-boilin' up, ye see, and 'tis her business tae see
that it all comes right in the end."

"D'ye want I should search for her?"

"I dinna want nowt o' the sort," she snapped.
"If I canna find her, ye won't. Ye keep away
from all the wenches, Claud, or ye'll fall in lust
again, and then we'll all find ourselves in the
suds."

Clearly, this was not the time to tell her that
Lucy Fittletrot was back, although in truth he
was surprised Maggie apparently did not know
that she was. It was just plain luck that Lucy
had flitted off earlier on business of her own. In
any event, he would ask Lucy again about
Catriona as soon as he had the chance. First, it
was imperative to learn what Maggie's plan
was.

"Are ye going tae be peepin' over me shoulder every minute, Mam?"

"I've nae time for such, but I canna leave the Chisholms on their own just because that dissembling harlot canna be bothered wi' them. And ye'll recall that if I help one side, I must give equal attention tae the other."

"But, Mam — !"

She grimaced. "Hold your whisst, will ye? I willna interfere wi' ye an ye dinna require it. Your business be wi' Mistress Barbara. I'll take nae hand wi' her."

With that, he had to be satisfied, but he hoped Lucy would return quickly.

Aboard the Marion Ogilvy

They were off the southern coast of Portugal when the wind shifted. For nearly a sennight, crossing the Mediterranean, it had been steady from the larboard quarter or southeast, an unusually fortunate occurrence. What was more common, Kit knew, was for a ship to fight headwinds when sailing west, which required men to be constantly in the rigging, hoisting, lowering, and trimming sails to catch wind when and where they could. They had been under full sail, running with the wind nearly the whole distance, making excellent time with remarkably little effort.

Sir Kenneth Lindsay had told Kit only that

morning that because of their commendable speed, they would not put in to shore again for fresh water and supplies until they reached La Coruña, on the northern tip of Spain.

Lindsay had spoken to him several times along the way but briefly, because he had not encouraged the man's attention. That attention had clearly aided him so far, if only because Gibson had kept his distance, but he knew that Gibson was only biding his time until he could be rid of the ambassador's nephew. Then things would doubtless grow worse than before.

Gibson also kept clear of Willie Armstrong. Indeed, the atmosphere aboard the *Marion Ogilvy* was more cheerful and less tension-filled than Kit could remember its being since he had come aboard. It was not so happy, however, that he wanted to remain aboard her for the rest of his life.

He was in no hurry, for his time was not his own and he was watched too closely to attempt an escape yet. In any case, he expected the ship to find itself becalmed somewhere along the way. Indeed, with the wind blowing constantly from the east and southeast, he had thought they would slow considerably on turning north. And so they had yesterday, after passing through the Strait of Gibraltar.

Now, though, as he watched breakers crash against the Portuguese coast, the sounds of wind straining the sails above him and shouts of the men scrambling to adjust the running rigging, told him the wind had shifted at last.

It blew now from the south, pushing them steadily northward as if God Almighty were as eager as Sir Kenneth was to see the latter's messages delivered swiftly into Cardinal Beaton's hands.

Either that, Kit thought morosely, or they were all speeding toward perdition.

By Friday, the end of her first sennight at Ardintoul, Bab had begun to sense a change in her mother. If she asked a question or made a comment, Lady MacRae would sometimes respond in a normal fashion. But just as Bab began to hope that her mother was emerging from the misty world she had chosen to inhabit, her ladyship got up in the middle of a comment she was making and walked out of the room. Following, Bab found her on the ramparts again, staring through the bartizan arrow loop at rain pouring down on Loch Alsh.

When the rain stopped that afternoon, unable to bear being cooped up any longer, Bab ordered her favorite gray gelding saddled, rejected an escort, and left the confines of Ardintoul for the peaceful quiet of its surrounding woodland.

She knew the area well and knew that she would be safe, certainly while Kintail was in residence at Eilean Donan. He was not called Wild Fin Mackenzie for naught, and the one thing guaranteed to arouse his temper and stir his men to action was a threat against anyone under his protection.

Fin, like Patrick, might have something unpleasant to say to her about riding out alone, but he was across the loch and Patrick was in the Borders, and even when both were at home, she often defied what she perceived to be their more arbitrary commands, the ones issued out of habit rather than necessity. The people of Kintail knew her as well as they knew Fin and Patrick, and she could take care of herself.

She rode through still-dripping woodland, retracing the track that they had followed the previous week from the beach, and when she reached the shore of the loch, she turned east toward Loch Duich. From its shore, riding uphill through trees and shrubbery to the high meadows was easier than trying to reach them through the rock-strewn glens. She enjoyed the solitude so much that it was not until a drifting cloud crossed the sun that she realized how low it had sunk in the western sky.

Turning toward home, she wondered guiltily how her mother had fared without her. But Ada MacReedy was an excellent companion as well as an experienced waiting woman, and Florrie was a MacRae as well as being their housekeeper, so Bab knew that Lady MacRae was safe and well cared for.

She tried to tell herself that it was good for her mother to have her daughter home again, but persuading herself of that was hard. The fact was that although Bab worried, her worry did no good, for she did not know what ailed her mother or how to help restore her to the woman she had been before Sir Gilchrist's death.

As she rode out of the trees toward the shore of Loch Duich, she saw another rider emerge from woodland a short distance away. The sun was dropping swiftly behind the Isle of Skye, so its light was slanted and dusky, and the woods were deeply shadowed. Lost as she was in her thoughts, she might not have noticed him but for an instinctive awareness that she was no longer alone.

At first, he was no more than a solid shadow in the flickering depths of the forest, but as he rode nearer, she knew without question who it was, and her heart began to sing.

Chapter 9

A natural sense of caution reminded Bab that at least one impostor, Francis Dalcross, had pretended to be *Sionnach Dubh,* but even as the thought flitted into her mind, she knew that where the true Fox was concerned no pretender could fool her. Something about him stirred recognition, something she would know in the darkest night and without his speaking a word, an intimate, inexplicable signal that hummed between them, offering both comfort and the promise of increasing awareness and more intimate knowledge.

She reined in her horse and waited for him to come near.

"You came all the way to Kintail," she said when she knew he would hear.

"Aye, sweetheart, to make sure ye reached home safely."

Smiling at the feeling his voice stirred within her, she said, "As you see."

"What I see is a young woman out riding without suitable protection."

Despite the stern tone, she continued to smile. "We Macraes are perfectly safe on our own land," she said. "Moreover, Kintail land surrounds us and Kintail is in residence. Were there strangers about, we would receive warning long before they could do us harm."

"I am a stranger."

"Aye, but even if someone saw you, no one would complain about the presence in Kintail of *Sionnach Dubh*."

"Perhaps not, but how could anyone be certain of my identity?"

Suddenly shy, not wanting to tell him she would always know, she said only, "There are but two choices, sir. Either you are a lone rider and thus small danger to Kintail, or you are *Sionnach Dubh* and no danger to anyone who behaves himself and does not cause harm to law-abiding folks."

As she said the words, she realized that his next argument would doubtless be that even a lone rider could cause harm to an unprotected female. Surely, that was what Fin or Patrick would say, for it was exactly what they had said in the past.

But he did not. Instead, he reached out gently and brushed her cheek with the knuckles of his gloved left hand.

The stallion stood so still that it might have been inanimate black marble.

"The fresh air agrees wi' ye, lass," he said. "It has put color in your cheeks and a sparkle in your eyes."

And heat, suddenly, in her cheeks. She nibbled her lower lip, uncertain what to say to him and realizing there were dangers for unprotected women that she had not considered. Speaking the first words to come into her head, she said, "I thought you would scold as Patrick would."

"I dinna ha' that right, sweetheart. Nor, if I did, ha' ye yet given me cause. I wanted to see ye, so it would be gey hypocritical to scold ye for riding out alone when it affords me exactly what I'd hoped for and gives me such pleasure besides."

"Aye, but I did not expect you to admit that."

She thought she heard him chuckle, but she could not be sure. How she wished she could see his face and read his expression. She was sure he must be handsome, but even if he wore the mask to cover scars or an otherwise hideous countenance, it would not matter. Her reactions would remain the same.

He moved his hand away from her cheek, and she wished he had not. It occurred to her as it had the first day they met that if he were to sweep her off her saddle and carry her to his lair, she would not care one whit.

"How is your mother?"

The question startled her. "She . . . she is well, thank you."

"Don't offer me polite chatter, lass. I ken fine that she is not well and has not been well for many months, and I ken, too, that her state must be distressing. How fares she since your return to Ardintoul?"

Even to him, she would not say all that was in

her heart but neither would she lie. "She does not seem aware of much that happens around her," she said. "She spends hours each day sitting on the ramparts watching Loch Alsh as if she still expects my father to return, but I think she is a little better now. Last night, after supper, she complained that the chicken was stringy."

He chuckled. "Is that so unusual?"

"Aye, for she rarely speaks of food or other ordinary things. She mostly talks to herself, and when she does seem to talk to others, she says odd things."

"Does she?"

"She told Florrie MacRae — our housekeeper — that she thought the new turf near the fairy ring would be ready for cutting in a sennight's time."

"Well, it is springtime, after all."

"Aye, but we plant no turf, for Ardintoul does not lend itself to such luxuries. The land is either too rocky or too wooded, so we have never planted a lawn. And if there is a fairy ring hereabouts, I have never seen it."

It was easy to talk to him, easier even than she had expected, and although she did not voice her greatest fear, that her mother would disappear forever into the odd world that she occupied for so many hours each day, she had a notion that he understood without needing to hear the words.

"I heard about the incident at the Beltane

192

fire," she said, turning the subject away from Ardintoul. "Are those men you rescued still safe?"

"Aye," he said. "They'll keep themselves scarce until Francis Dalcross and his men find other mischief to occupy their time."

"It was good of you to help them," she said.

His body stiffened, and she could see his gray eyes narrow. She could even detect the glimmer of anger in them and wondered what she had said to ignite it.

"It is not a matter of goodness but of justice," he said. "Our self-righteous sheriff and his power-mad son have taken extraordinary liberties with folks too well accustomed to freedom to relinquish it easily, and when one sees what Francis Dalcross does in the open, one wonders what else he has done in the shadows."

"You said he acts only to enhance his personal power," she reminded him, "but does he not also act in the name of Rome and his grace, the King?"

"Aye, and power is heady stuff, lass. Even good men fall victim to its lures. Villains like the sheriff and his son use it as a weapon."

"But is that not what politics is all about? Patrick says politics is just fighting to control others and to seize power. Is that not exactly what the Dalcrosses do?"

"Nay, lass, this has become personal, whilst politics tend to be factional. To have a political motive, both Dalcrosses would really have to represent the King, the Pope, or some other recognizable faction, but despite words to the contrary, they take no more interest than most Highlanders do in Jamie's court or the Pope's."

"Francis cares more for his own consequence," Bab said.

"Aye," he agreed. "He also seeks to ally himself with powerful men, specifically Cardinal Beaton and the Pope, even when it sets him in opposition to his own people. We Highlanders cling to our ancient traditions, but we try to practice tolerance and common sense, too, allowing for differences and necessity of circumstance. For example, we allow a marriage to take place without a priest, so that folks can marry even when a priest can't get to them because of weather or distance. According to Dalcross at present, all men should worship, marry, and die with the exact same rituals, whether they worship in Rome or Stirling or London."

"Mercy, sir, you sound most knowledgeable! Does all this mean that you agree with King Henry that Scotland should have her own Kirk?"

He chuckled, his posture relaxing, and his eyes twinkling. "Ye ken fine that I hold nae such belief. Henry be exactly the same as Dalcross, for he wants what he wants when he wants it. He dismissed Rome and formed his own Kirk in England merely so he could discard a wife who couldna give him sons to marry one he thought would. When the hapless

Anne Boleyn produced a daughter instead, he cut off her head and married a third time. He's now on his fifth wife, and the only son he's begotten is a weakling brat. D'ye see our Jamie acting in such a daft way?"

"His grace has had two wives," she pointed out.

"Aye, but only because his first and most beloved died soon after arriving in Scotland. And he now has two legitimate sons, both presently strong and healthy, and may they remain so."

"So what will happen?"

"To Scotland? I dinna ken. To the Dalcrosses? An they go on as they ha' begun, they'll be lucky to hang. Folks in these parts lack leadership presently, wi' so many o' their menfolk gone south to help Jamie keep Henry in England. But those men will return, and when they do, the Dalcrosses' reign will be short. In the meantime, those o' us that remain do what we can."

It occurred to her to wonder how he had avoided riding south to fight the English, but she knew that men had stayed behind for many reasons. No one could risk sending all his armed men away, and she knew that even some chieftains, if not clan chiefs, had stayed to keep their own homes safe. Even so, few households would be at full strength again until the men in the south came home.

"Will ye no offer a man a reward for his long journey, lass?"

His words startled her from her half-formed thoughts. With most people, one had warning of speech to come, but with his mask, one had none. Moreover, she was comfortable with him even in silence. With most people, silences grew awkward, forcing speech.

She knew what he wanted from her and would give it gladly, but she wanted him to say the words. Innocently, she said, "What reward do you seek?"

"Just a kiss, sweetheart, as ye ken verra well."

The stallion moved closer, although she had detected no signal from rider to horse; and although he had once called her a lodestone, it was she this time who felt drawn to him. She longed to feel his arms around her again.

Thus she scarcely breathed as he put one warm hand on her shoulder and bent near, lifting his mask with the other as his lips met hers.

The kiss was soft, warm, and gentle, but then the hand on her shoulder tightened, and he pressed harder. His lips savored hers, and his tongue darted forth to taste her and then to explore the interior of her mouth.

She moaned softly as she kissed him back and felt her body respond. It fairly cried out to him to caress it, to take her from her horse and work his will with her. But as quickly as the kiss had come, it was over.

"I must go, lass," he murmured. "I dare not trust myself too far."

"I trust you," she said, exerting every ounce of restraint she could summon to avoid begging him to stay. She would not beg any man, not even him.

"I know ye think ye do," he said. " 'Tis one reason I dare not trust myself. Ye'll be safe for now, I warrant."

"Will you come again?"

"Aye, lass, I told ye. I canna stay away."

And with that, he turned the stallion and rode into the woods, leaving her to stare after him until a chilly gust of wind and thickening dusk reminded her that she had to return to Ardintoul soon or they would send searchers out to look for her.

Now that he was gone, her common sense stirred, and she realized that she had probably hovered within aim's ace of making a great fool of herself. Boredom and worry about her mother had made it far too tempting to seek adventure with a man like the Fox, but there could be no future in such a relationship. Still, being with him was exciting, and she looked forward to seeing more of him. For the first time, she began to look forward to Fin and Molly's departure for Dunsithe.

Elsewhere, shafts of late-afternoon sunlight still filtered through a dense green forest canopy into a small, trackless glade, playing on the moss-covered ground and sparkling on the calm green water of the little pool in the center.

A trickling mossy stream fed the pool, and if one stayed perfectly still and no breeze rustled the leaves, one could hear the water bubbling as it flowed. The emerald glade was silent when Brown Claud arrived, just as he remembered it. The figure lying on a mossy bed beside the stream was not, however, the figure he had hoped to see. Her lavender gown clashed with the greenery.

"Lucy, wake up," he said sharply, shaking her shoulder.

She opened her eyes, grinned at him mischievously, and he knew she had been awake all the time. "Did ye miss me, Claud?" she said.

"Aye, and I ha' been looking for ye, too, but I didna expect tae find ye here."

"Then why come here?" she asked archly.

" 'Cause I be looking for Catriona, too, and this be her bower. Ye shouldna be here, Lucy. Members o' her tribe might be wroth wi' ye, and me mam be having enough trouble making peace 'twixt the hill folk and our own."

"I like it here," Lucy said. "Come lie with me, Claud."

"Nay, not till ye tell me what ye did wi' Catriona," he said, folding his arms across his chest, determined to stand firm.

Lucy shrugged. "I put a wee spell on her, is all."

"What spell?"

The gamin grin peeped out again. "It'll make her goat's feet show if she goes near

198

Dundreggan. If she be willing tae let them show, she can do as she pleases."

"But she hasna got any goat's feet!"

"She will if she goes anywhere near Dundreggan," Lucy said. "It will keep her from making mischief, Claud."

"But ye're making mischief instead!"

"I'm preventing her mischief, Claud, that's all."

The logic sounded reasonable, so why, Claud wondered, did he feel as if there were trouble afoot? Women confused him, which was why he preferred having to deal with only one at a time. With two flitting about, plus his mother, he was bound to have difficulty. He would certainly have to keep his wits about him.

The next morning, when Bab descended to Ardintoul's great hall to break her fast, she found a grim-faced Kintail awaiting her.

Her first thought, thanks to her guilty conscience, was that he had somehow learned of her meeting the previous afternoon with the Fox, but his opening statement banished that fear.

"A boat of mine arrived with bad news this morning, lass."

She gasped. "Not about Patrick!"

"Nay, and I'm a fool for frightening you so," he exclaimed. "I should have known you'd fear instantly for him. 'Tis bad enough though, for the boat came from Dumbarton. The King's sons are dead."

She stared at him in shock. "Both of them! But how?"

"A fever, they say. James and her grace were returning from Aberdeenshire and Angus, where they had been encouraging the local nobility to support him against England, when an urgent messenger reached them with the dire tidings from the Keeper at Stirling. The baby, Arthur, was dying. His older brother, the Duke of Rothesay, was sick too, vomiting and eating nothing. I need scarcely say that Jamie and Marie hastened to their sides, but they arrived too late. Both lads were gone."

Tears sprang to Bab's eyes. One of the reasons for her journey to Stirling, and the one that had finally persuaded her mother to make the trip, had been the anticipated birth and subsequent christening of the King's second son. James had a litter of illegitimate offspring scattered about, but he had sired only two legitimate sons, and the entire country would mourn their loss.

"This changes things, lass," Fin went on.

"Aye, I'm sure it will," she said, deciding she would not tell her mother. Such news, if Lady MacRae were even able to absorb it, would only cause her pain.

He said flatly, "I cannot let you and her ladyship stay here at Ardintoul now with only a few lads to guard your safety."

"Then you'll take us to Dunsithe after all?"

"Nay, for her ladyship would not agree to go,

200

and in her present state the journey would not be good for her. You must see that, Bab."

She nodded. "Then what? Do we stay at Eilean Donan?"

" 'Tis no better defended than Ardintoul," he said with a half smile. The measuring look he shot her warned her that she would not like what he said next. "I'm going to take you back to Dundreggan," he said. "The journey will not be too hard on your mother, and Chisholm will keep you safe. Dundreggan is a fortress."

Bab swallowed hard, not knowing how to respond. The first words that leaped to her tongue were clearly ineligible.

Kintail expected a response, though, and she realized that letting her anger show would avail her nothing. "My mother will not agree to go to Glen Affric either," she said at last with commendable calm.

He frowned, and she was glad she had not snapped an outright refusal at him. She knew that much of her anger arose from the fact that she had been home barely a sennight and now he meant to whisk her back to Glen Affric. Still, it was never wise to defy him, and today Molly had not accompanied him and so would not be at hand to soothe his temper if Bab ignited it.

She held her tongue, hoping his concern for her mother would persuade him.

"It is most important that you and her ladyship be safe, lass," he said at last, his tone calmer than she had expected. "The deaths of the princes will stir chaos. There is talk already of fear that the Islesmen may take advantage of James's troubles to try winning back the Lordship of the Isles. Added to the tales of unrest in the glens that I've heard so often of late —"

"But the center of that unrest is Inverness, so Glen Affric is even closer to it, and that is where you want to send us," she pointed out.

"Only because if you stay here, I shall have to leave more men to look after you than I want to leave, and I will not be certain of your safety even then," he said. "The deaths of the princes greatly complicate matters, because if Jamie should die, every powerful noble in Scotland will be striving again to control the throne. We must do all we can to help him beat Henry if only to stabilize this realm."

"But that fighting is all far from here," Bab said.

"Aye, and perhaps it will remain so, but perhaps not," he said. "We may find that the other Highland lairds are not so quick now to join Jamie or so willing to fight at his side. Some may decide to bide their time and see if Henry prevails."

"The King angered many Highland clans last year when he took their chiefs and chieftains hostage," Bab said, remembering.

"We of Kintail will follow him now, because he is our king," Fin said, "but 'tis true that others are not so loyal."

Bab sighed but did not argue. She had learned long since that when matters of loyalty arose, there could be no argument with the men of Kintail.

"Shall we go to Lady MacRae now?" he said quietly.

"Aye, but I'm telling you, Fin, she will never agree to go to Dundreggan."

He did not reply, and she wondered what he would do when her mother defied or simply ignored his command. Lady MacRae was perfectly capable of doing either if what Bab had seen of her in past days was any indication. And if Fin tried to bully her . . . That would be another matter, Bab decided. She would not stand for it, even if it meant infuriating him herself.

They found Lady MacRae in her comfortable bower just above the great hall. The chamber faced east, and the rising sun spilled golden paths across the floor. Her ladyship, in a light gray day robe and simple white veil, sat at a table that held a bowl of apples, a jug of ale, a manchet loaf, and various condiments. Clearly, she was breaking her fast, but she smiled vaguely at Fin when he made his bow.

"Dear me," she said to Bab, "have we guests today, dearling? You or Ada should have told me, for I am not properly attired to receive company."

Bab shot a glance at plump Ada, who sat on a nearby stool with her embroidery in her capacious lap. Encountering a grimace and a headshake, she said gently, "It is only Kintail come to call, madam, and he will not stay long, for he has much to do. Nonetheless, he wanted to pay his respects."

"I shall not change then if he does not object," Lady MacRae said, nodding. "I do not want to return to my bedchamber until the wildcat is gone."

"Wildcat!" Bab and Fin exclaimed as one.

"Why, yes, curled up right on my bed as if it owned the place."

"Madam," Ada MacReedy said, setting down her embroidery and moving to refill Lady MacRae's mug with ale. "I told ye, 'twere only a bad dream ye had. There were nae wildcat there when I stepped into the room."

"Mayhap you did not see it, Ada, but it was there, and I warrant it is still there, awaiting my return. I'd as lief not go back until the beast is gone."

With a speaking look at Fin, Ada said evenly, "I'll send one o' the lads up to shoo it off afore I let her ladyship return to her bedchamber."

Bab saw Fin's frown and hoped that now that he'd had a taste of her ladyship's fantasies, he would think twice about removing them to Dundreggan.

Surely, her mother would fare better at home in familiar surroundings.

"Did ye hear what the woman said, Lucy?" Claud demanded, pulling Lucy back behind a window curtain. "Me mam's nearby!"

"How d'ye ken that?"

"That wildcat. She always makes it appear wi' her when she first makes herself visible tae mortals. Says it scares them more than seeing a member o' our Clan does, so when they see she can control the cat, they dinna fear her."

"I'd no ha' come here wi' ye had I thought Maggie Malloch would learn o' it," Lucy said with a frown. "I hope ye didna tell her I'm helping ye."

"Nay, I did not," Claud said. "Moreover, I dinna want her tae see either one o' us, nor Kintail neither."

"Why d'ye no want her tae see Kintail?"

"Ye misunderstand me, lass. I dinna want *him* tae see *us!*"

"Are ye saying he has the Sight?"

"Aye, he does," Claud explained. "He doesna like admitting it, so he'll no speak o' us, and he'll no recall any o' our folk he's met before, in any event. Still, I'm thinking it will be as well an he doesna see us at all, so take care."

"Aye," Lucy said, smiling seductively. "Mayhap we should think o' summat quiet tae do, Claud."

In Lady MacRae's bower, Fin approached her ladyship, saying politely, "Good morning, madam; may I sit?"

"To be sure, sir. Draw up that stool yonder and take a mug of ale with me."

Bab relaxed as she too drew up a stool and took her place between them. At least her mother seemed willing to converse sensibly.

"I need your help," Fin said as he accepted the mug of ale Ada poured him.

"We MacRaes are at your service, sir, as ever," Lady MacRae said.

"Trouble is brewing in the Highlands, my lady, and I have promised to supply men to aid the King in his fight against an English invasion," he said.

"Then you must take men from Ardintoul."

"Aye, madam," he agreed, "and because of that . . ."

Here it came, Bab thought, watching her mother narrowly.

". . . I intend to escort you and your daughter to Dundreggan and place you under the protection of Lord Chisholm until my return."

To Bab's shock, her mother did not protest. Instead, she frowned and then said in the muttering tone she used when she talked to herself or to some unseen entity, " 'Tis understandable, albeit not yet the best time of the year. Indeed, I should prefer to wait until the days grow warmer, but mayhap they will warm themselves soon, and 'twill take some little time to organize, after all."

"To organize what, madam?" Bab asked.

"Why, the wedding, of course."

"Wedding! What wedding?"

With visible bewilderment, Lady MacRae

looked at Fin and then back at Bab. "Why, your wedding, of course."

"But I am not getting married," Bab said, exchanging a baffled look with Fin. "No one has even courted me."

"Nonsense, my dear, you are going to marry Lord Chisholm's son. Your father and Chisholm discussed the matter long since, and now apparently Kintail has settled it. Why else should he take us to Dundreggan?"

As Bab drew breath to explain, Fin put a quelling hand on her arm and said, "I will set everything in train then, madam, and you would please me best if you could be ready to depart early Monday morning."

"Do you hear, Ada?" Lady MacRae asked. "Can we be ready so soon?"

"Aye, my lady. I'll see to it."

"Excellent," Fin said. "Now, Bab, if you will come with me —"

"But —"

"I want to talk to you," he said in a tone that brooked no refusal. "We will leave your mother and Ada to begin their packing."

She still hesitated, but his grip on her arm was insistent.

"Oh, very well," she said with a sigh, "but if you think for one moment . . ." A glance at his stern face silenced her until they were downstairs again in the empty hall. But then she said hotly, "Fin Mackenzie, if you think for one minute that I am going to marry Alex Chisholm —"

"Hush, lass, I don't think anything of the kind, but even if I were inclined to leave you and your mother alone here, I certainly cannot do so when she is in such an odd state of mind. And if you think it will be easier to travel with her if she goes to Dundreggan against her will than if she goes believing she is about to plan your wedding, I'd advise you to think again."

"But what will Lord and Lady Chisholm think? My father and his lordship never made any agreement, and even if they had, I wouldn't!"

"I'd not be surprised to learn that they discussed such a union," Fin said thoughtfully. "But any talk they might have had never went further than talk, because my father would have known if they had fixed an agreement between them. Moreover, we'd have the signed and witnessed documents right here at hand."

"There was no such agreement," she repeated, measuring her words.

"No, because everything of that sort was in good order before my father left for Kinlochewe," Fin said. "Knowing he might fall in battle, he explained all such matters to me, and to Patrick too, since the possibility existed that my father and I might both fall. Then it would have been Patrick's duty to inform the next heir and explain to him any commitments that my father had made before his death."

"Well, I cannot imagine why my father would even have talked about my marriage," Bab said.

"Faith, sir, I was only fourteen then."

"Nearly fifteen and quite old enough," he said with a grin. "You forget that Chisholm's land adjoins my eastern boundary. The match would be excellent for you and good for the Mackenzies and MacRaes, too."

Angrily, she exclaimed, "I don't care about the Mac—"

"That's enough, Bab."

Biting off the words with a near sob, she pressed her lips together.

"Think about your mother for once, and not just about yourself."

"I wasn't!" But she knew that was not true, and heat flooded her cheeks with the shame of the knowledge.

"Rest easy, lass," Fin said in a gentler tone. "If she goes to Glen Affric believing in this marriage, the journey will be easier for her, and you must both go. Patrick and I will be able to attend to our duties more easily if we need not worry about you. And, pray, do not try telling me you've not been worried about her, because I have known you all your life and I can sense the worry in you."

"Aye," she said, feeling only relief in admitting it. "She has been so strange since I returned, Fin. Indeed, this morning she appears nearly normal in comparison to what I usually see."

"Then when you arrive at Dundreggan, you should discuss your concerns with Lady Chisholm. She is an indolent creature, but she is kind and wise, and I warrant she will be glad to help. Your mother's condition is not something you should try to deal with alone, Bab. If Molly were going to be here, it would be another matter, but we simply cannot take Lady MacRae all the way to Dunsithe."

"No," she said.

"Good," he said. "Then here is what we'll do. If you and her ladyship can be ready to leave first thing Monday morning, I'll take you myself. My lads can have everyone who means to go south with me ready to go within the week, so Molly and I can meet them on the road after we've seen you safe at Dundreggan. I'll warn your people before I leave that I'll want ten men who mean to ride with me to escort you to the head of the loch on Monday. You can meet me there at nine o'clock."

Bab nodded, still stunned by her mother's unexpected reaction and the complications in her own life that this absurd wedding notion was bound to cause.

Chapter 10

The return journey to Dundreggan took Kintail's party twice as long as their journey to Eilean Donan, because in deference to Lady MacRae, he followed the more traveled track through Glen Shiel and Glen Moriston to the Great Glen, and then along the west coast of Loch Ness to Glen Urquhart and west again into Glen Affric. Thus, they followed three sides of a rectangle, the fourth side of which comprised the more direct route they had traveled before, a route far too steep and treacherous to risk with her ladyship and with Chisholm's laden sumpter ponies.

Bab rode her favorite gray gelding, the sumpters carried their baggage, and the accommodations for the intervening nights were far more comfortable than before, because they stayed with friends of their own station.

To Bab's astonishments and relief, Lady MacRae weathered the journey well, only occasionally chatting with unseen spirits along the way and observing once, to everyone's consternation, that a little lady whom she claimed to have seen in her bedchamber with the wildcat was riding pillion with Molly Mackenzie.

At the time, Fin was leading the way along

the narrow Glen Shiel track, followed by Molly and Bab, with Lady MacRae riding behind them, followed by Giorsal and Ada MacReedy. A small party of men-at-arms rode a half-mile ahead and another, larger party of such men followed.

Not surprisingly, Molly looked over her shoulder when Lady MacRae made the odd comment, but of course, there was no little woman to be seen.

However, instead of simply saying so, Molly glanced at Fin, who shrugged and shook his head, whereupon the pair of them turned as one to look speculatively at Lady MacRae and then at Bab.

"What?" she demanded in an undertone with a sidelong look at her mother to be certain she was paying them no heed. "For mercy's sake, do not encourage her."

"Does she often say things like that?" Molly asked.

"Aye, of course she does," Bab replied. "She talks to animals as if they were human, sees fairies riding dust motes in the hall and peeking out from under leaves in the woods, she saw this fictional wildcat in her bedchamber yesterday, and now this little woman. She has talked of such things since I was small, but she began doing it more often after my father died. One of her complaints at Stirling was that the wee folk had not visited her and she missed them. You know she has always been eccentric,

Molly. Pray, do not encourage her to become more so."

Fin chuckled. "I suppose she also claims to have the gift of second sight then," he said mildly.

"She has claimed no such thing, so I beg you, do not put the notion in her head. It is bad enough that I'll have to explain her conduct to Lady Chisholm. She noticed at Stirling that it had altered considerably, because she told me so."

"What did you say to that?" Molly asked.

"Only that I was a little worried but thought Stirling had done her good. Now, I am not so sure about that, and I doubt that her ladyship will think so if she hears her talking about little women and imaginary wildcats. More likely, she will think me the worst of daughters to have persuaded Mother to make the journey."

"Don't puff things up to be worse than they are, Bab," Fin said. "Is it only the fairies she sees that distress you, or have there been other things?"

Glancing back again to make sure that Ada and Giorsal were keeping a close eye on Lady MacRae, she said, "There is a good deal more. Although she talks to people who are not there, she rarely talks to me or to the servants, and she sits up on the battlement walk day in and day out, watching for a ship that will never come."

"She conversed with me quite sensibly yesterday," he pointed out.

"Aye, and she has occasionally spoken sensibly to me, too, but those occasions are the exception, sir, not the rule. For the most part, she seems to live in another world, taking notice of this one only in passing. I live in constant fear that she will stop noticing this one altogether."

"Then keep her occupied at Dundreggan," Molly said. "I agree with Fin, though, that the case may not be as bad as you fear. You are so close to her and care so much, I think, that you tend to fear the worst. Do not dismiss her beliefs out of hand. Many people believe in the wee folk, and who is to say they are wrong?"

"But she is planning my wedding," Bab protested. "What am I to do about that, if you please?"

"Speak to Lady Chisholm," Fin said again. "If planning a wedding will bring your mother more into this world and out of the other, you should encourage her. You could do much worse than to marry Alex Chisholm, after all."

"But I don't want to marry him!"

"If your father had made the agreement with his father, you would have little choice in the matter," Fin reminded her. "For that matter, if Patrick were to decide that marrying you to Alex is the appropriate thing to do —"

"He wouldn't dare!"

Fin gave her a look that warned her to guard her tongue, but she was too angry to be silent. "Patrick would not force me to marry a man I do not love."

"No, he would not, nor have I suggested that he should. I merely point out to you that you could do worse. Chisholm has only the one heir now, and Chisholm is very well to pass. Moreover, he has always been an ally of ours, and his lands abound mine. If Patrick were to ask my opinion, I'd certainly support the match."

Bab swallowed hard. The last thing she wanted was for Fin to tell Patrick *that* when they met at Dunsithe.

She liked Sir Alex well enough. He was a kind host and an excellent dancer. He would certainly take his wife to court at least once a year, and his wife would dress well and would have all the pin money she required. But asset though he might be at court, his general behavior was far too tame and Frenchified for her. Moreover, Sir Alex was not the man who invaded her dreams, and Sir Alex was not the man she wanted to find standing beside her bed when she awoke suddenly in the night thinking someone was in her room.

She could say none of this to Fin or Molly, however, lest they think her as demented as her mother. Indeed, if she were so daft as to tell them of her meetings with the Fox, they might assume that she had behaved in such a way as to ruin her reputation and thus make any good marriage impossible. She did not want to endure the sort of interview with Fin that such a suspicion would generate, so she held her tongue and hoped consultation with Lady Chisholm would prove more fruitful.

The rest of the journey passed without incident, and they arrived at Dundreggan late Thursday afternoon. If the servants and men-at-arms who greeted them in the bailey were surprised to see them, they were too well trained to show it. They helped the women dismount and began immediately to unload the sumpter ponies, which were doubtless happy to see their home stables again.

Chisholm's steward greeted them inside and suggested that Giorsal and Lady MacRae's Ada be shown at once to suitable bedchambers where they could begin to stow their ladies' baggage as soon as gillies had carried it upstairs. In the meantime, he showed Fin, Molly, Lady MacRae, and Bab into the great hall, where he bade them make themselves comfortable while he went to inform Lord and Lady Chisholm of their arrival.

Lady MacRae went directly to a settle near the fire, where she sat, carefully arranged her skirts, and stared calmly into the flames.

Bab shot Fin a speaking look, but Molly smiled at her and sat beside Lady MacRae, holding out her hands to warm them and speaking quietly to her.

"What will you tell them?" Bab muttered to Fin in an undertone.

"The truth, of course," he said, and then there was no more time to talk, for Lady Chisholm bustled in, full of delight at having company again.

"Oh, my dear, you cannot imagine how much I have missed you this past fortnight," she said to Bab after she had greeted Fin and Molly. "It has been as dull as can be without you. And you, madam, are as welcome to Dundreggan as the springtime," she added, moving to hug Lady MacRae. "How very delightful that you have chosen to pay us a visit."

Lady MacRae acknowledged her hug with little more than a nod but said matter-of-factly, "Why, Nora, I could do nothing less. If we put our heads together, you know, they can easily be married by Trinity Sunday."

Lady Chisholm blinked, then looked to Bab for enlightenment.

Knowing her face must be as red as fire, for it certainly felt as hot, Bab looked at Fin.

He said matter-of-factly, "I would have sent word to you of our intended arrival, madam, but I knew you would not fail me and believed I could explain matters more frankly in person."

"I am sure you can," her ladyship said, casting another, more speculative glance at Lady MacRae. "My dearest Arabella, you must have a mug of something hot to refresh yourself and I know you will want to wash before we take supper."

"Oh, yes, that would be pleasant," Lady MacRae said.

"Let me show you to your bedchamber, so I

may be sure you will be comfortable. I'll have something sent in for the rest of you, too, if someone has not already arranged it," she added as she gently urged her chief guest from the room.

Lucy began to follow them, but Claud grabbed the back of her gown and held tight. "Where be ye going?" he demanded, "Kintail might see ye."

"Nay, I'll keep clear o' him, but your lass's mam be going tae plan her wedding, Claud, and I'm thinking one o' us should keep an eye on her."

"Aye, well, remember me mam's somewhere about and keep clear o' her, too, or we'll both find ourselves in the suds."

"I will," Lucy assured him. "Ye just keep watch o'er your lass."

Claud nodded but when she was gone, he found it hard to focus on Mistress Bab, because he was worried about what Lucy might be up to, and still worried, too, about Catriona.

He had not seen a sign of her since she had suggested trading information, and much as Lucy fascinated and delighted him, he knew he would do better not to trust her, particularly where Catriona was concerned. Even so, he did not know where else he could look for his Highland lass, especially since he had a duty to watch over Mistress Bab, and since his temperamental mother was nearby.

All in all, he decided, women made a chap's life very difficult.

"How much of the truth will you tell Lady Chisholm?" Bab asked once she was alone with Fin and Molly.

"As much as necessary," he replied with a touch of impatience.

"But she is bound to think —"

"What she will think is no more than what is perfectly true," he said, his tone gentler now. "Nora Chisholm is fond of your mother, Bab, and she can help both of you more if she understands from the outset how matters stand."

Bab knew he was right, but she felt all control of her life slipping away again just as she had begun to think she might regain it, and she did not know how she could do that at Dundreggan. Perhaps, though, Chisholm would have other plans now that Sir Alex was his heir, for that could not have been the case when the two fathers talked — if they had. Before Sir Robert Chisholm and his brother Michael had died, any such discussion must have referred to the alliance of a youngest son. That Chisholm might look higher for his son's wife now that Sir Alex would one day own Dundreggan and all Chisholm's other estates could not astonish anyone.

Her ladyship soon returned, saying, "My people are bringing ale and apple juice for us, and Arabella and her woman are getting nicely settled in her rooms."

"Thank you, madam," Bab said. "I fear we have imposed upon your good nature to a shocking degree."

"Nonsense, my dear, I am delighted to see you all. But perhaps, Kintail, you would like to tell me now what brings you all to us like this, for although Arabella is full of wedding plans, I do not think that can be it. Chisholm has mentioned nothing to me about any wedding, and nor has Alexander."

"No, madam, and I will explain," he said. "But first, I bring bad news that I doubt you can have heard yet. Sunday morning, one of my boats arrived from Dumbarton, carrying word that both of the young princes have died."

"Mercy on us," she exclaimed. "How dreadful for James and his Queen, and just when we all had hoped two healthy heirs would bring peace to the realm!"

"Just so," Fin said. "I had supposed that Lady MacRae and Bab would be safe at Ardintoul whilst Patrick and I stay at Dunsithe, but this news alters things, especially in light of the recent troubles in Inverness-shire."

"Yes, I understand," Lady Chisholm said. "If James falls to Henry, all will be at risk. You are quite right to bring them here, sir. Chisholm has sent only a few men to support the King, because he worries about what the Dalcrosses may do here. We are but a minority against them as it is. So far we follow the law, of course — at least, most of us do," she added with a smile.

"Aye, I've heard that *Sionnach Dubh* has been active again," Kintail said.

Lady Chisholm smiled at Bab. "Then you did tell him. I realized after you had gone that the subject never came up and feared you might fail to tell him."

"Tell me what?" Fin demanded, looking at Bab.

She shut her eyes, wishing she could snap her fingers and magically whisk herself back to Stirling, well out of his reach.

"Well?" Fin's tone indicated his rapidly diminishing patience.

Bab opened her eyes but avoided his gaze, saying to Lady Chisholm instead, "I did not tell him, madam, but only because I thought you or Sir Alex must have done so." Then, risking a wary look at Fin, she added, "When neither he nor Molly mentioned it, I thought they were being tactful. I should have known better."

"What is this?" he demanded. "What did you fail to tell me?"

"We did not converse a great deal, sir, if you will recall, neither here nor on the way home. Our journey was swift, and when we stopped at night, we were all so tired that we scarcely spoke over supper and fell asleep directly afterward."

"Don't prevaricate, lass. If there was aught of import to tell me, you should have done so straightaway."

"Truly, sir, I thought you knew."

"You salved your conscience thus, at all events," he retorted, unappeased.

Molly said, "What is it, Bab? What happened?"

With a sigh, she said, "Francis Dalcross abducted me on the way here, but —"

"Bab!" Molly exclaimed. "How could you possibly imagine that we might learn of such a dreadful event and not mention it? Did he . . . that is —"

"He did not harm me," Bab said, still eyeing Fin.

"You want beating," he said grimly. "You didn't tell us because you did not want to hear what I'd say about it and very likely feared what I might do about it. I think you had better tell us the whole tale, my lass, and right quickly, too."

Meeting a sympathetic look from Lady Chisholm, Bab hastened to describe her abduction and its aftermath, sliding glibly over Francis's behavior at the cottage and the Fox's behavior after Francis's departure, emphasizing her rescuer's heroism instead. But if Fin was pleased to learn of her rescue, he showed no sign of it.

"What makes you think this fellow is any better than Dalcross or that he could really be *Sionnach Dubh?*" he demanded when she finished. "The Fox is no more than a bairn's tale, lass. Some prankster has been making game of the Dalcrosses, and now it seems that he has made one of you, too."

"Pray, do not scold her, sir," Molly said. "Whoever the man is, he rescued her from what must have been a shocking ordeal. Recall that she greatly admired Francis Dalcross at Stirling."

"I do recall it, and although I did not encounter him at court myself, I recall perfectly well that Patrick did *not* admire him."

Lady Chisholm said diplomatically, "I cannot express the relief I felt when she assured us she had suffered no harm at that villain's hands."

"Someone ought to thrash him, too," Fin said grimly.

"Oh, indeed, sir," Lady Chisholm agreed. "I wish someone would, and his father, too, but we of Dundreggan cannot say much on that head, you know."

"Why not?" Fin asked. "Chisholm was our previous sheriff. I should think he might say quite a lot."

"Aye, and so he did at first, but Sheriff Dalcross just shrugged it off and said that different men handle being sheriff in different ways. He said that since Chisholm had done naught to curb the excesses of the Kirk in these parts whilst he was sheriff, he should hold his tongue and not criticize others."

"At least with Chisholm, life was peaceful hereabouts," Kintail said.

"Aye, it was," she agreed.

"He must have retained considerable influence."

"You forget, sir, how devastated he was by the deaths of our sons," Lady Chisholm said with tears welling into her eyes.

"Forgive me, my lady. I did not intend to distress you."

"My point is that he lost interest in everything after Rob and Michael were killed," she said, quickly recovering her usual poise. "That is how Sheriff Dalcross came to take over so quickly, you see."

"It was quick," Fin agreed.

"Less than a fortnight," she said, nodding. "The arrest and confession made all the difference, of course."

"What confession? I heard nothing of this."

"It was the final straw for my husband," she said with a sigh. "Francis Dalcross caught young Christopher Chisholm, you see, and when Christopher admitted killing his cousins, declaring that he hoped thereby to inherit more of the Chisholm wealth than what he stood to inherit from his own father —"

"By our lady," Fin breathed. "He said that?"

"Francis Dalcross and his men all swore to it," she said, "and no one was able to ask Christopher, because they said he escaped from them that very night and no one has seen him since. But the confession was all Francis Dalcross needed to persuade James to appoint his father in Chisholm's place. Their seat,

Bothyn Castle, lies near Inverness, and they have many men to support their authority. Moreover, they are kin to the Sinclairs, and Francis is particularly friendly with Oliver Sinclair, who as you know is the King's present favorite."

"In that event, I'm surprised James did not name Francis himself sheriff."

Lady Chisholm smiled wryly. "I believe Francis would have liked that, but he is certainly too young for such a large and important job."

Fin shook his head. "We may think so, madam, knowing him, but recall that James himself is not yet thirty. I just wish I had known all this at the time."

"Recall, sir, that you were still dealing with Macdonalds then, and soon afterward you became a royal hostage. There was naught you could have done. Indeed, Chisholm was out and Dalcross in so quickly that practically no one noticed until it was over. Chisholm told no one. He was just grateful that the Dalcrosses managed everything about Christopher with as little scandal as they did."

"I do recall that, and I don't know that they can claim credit for it," Kintail said. "Folks were so shocked that they scarcely spoke of the tragedy except to express astonishment. Christopher Chisholm was well liked hereabouts, and many believe to this day that he must have been killed, too. As for Rob and Michael . . ."

"They were much beloved," Lady Chisholm said with a sad smile.

"Aye, madam, I believe they were."

A brief silence fell, and although Bab was grateful for any diversion that took Fin's mind off her abduction and his clear if unreasonable desire to scold her for it, she was relieved when Molly said gently, "Forgive me, but should we not discuss this notion Lady MacRae has taken regarding Bab's wedding?"

"We must explain to her that she has made a mistake," Bab said firmly.

"Is there to be no wedding, then?" Lady Chisholm asked, smiling wistfully.

Bab stared. "Surely, you did not think there would be!"

"I certainly would not object to one, my dear. I think you would make our Alexander a wonderful wife."

"He has not even asked me!"

"I do seem to recall now, however, that your father and Chisholm did once discuss some such possibility."

"But there was no arrangement," Bab said desperately. She could not bring herself to declare, as she had to Fin and Molly, that she did not want to marry Sir Alex. One simply could not say such a thing to his gently spoken mother.

"You must ask Chisholm," Lady Chisholm said. "Oh, and I do believe that Alex had a letter from Sir Patrick, did he not?" She looked hopefully at Kintail. "Did you not bring him such a letter when you came to fetch Barbara, sir?"

"Aye," Kintail said, "but I doubt that Patrick wrote of any marriage contract, my lady. I'd know if he had knowledge of any arrangement or present intent."

A brief silence fell before Lady Chisholm turned to Bab and said with a rueful smile, "You know, my dear, your mother is very tired from her journey, and as none of us wants to distress her . . ."

"We don't, of course," Bab said reluctantly when the pause lengthened until it became clear that her ladyship expected a response. "But neither do I want her to become so accustomed to the notion that she will not let go of it, my lady. This whole business is very awkward, as you must agree."

"I can see that you think so, my dear," Lady Chisholm said kindly. "However, if you will heed my advice, I think we should let her rest comfortably tonight and see how matters stand in the morning."

"Where is Sir Alex?" Bab asked, wondering how he would react to the notion that he was to marry her, and fairly certain she would not want to hear it.

"He has been away several times since you left," Lady Chisholm said. "His father asked him to visit some of our people, you see. After that business at the Beltane fire, everyone is taking particular care to avoid the sheriff's men, but Chisholm thought it as well to send Alex out to be sure everyone is safe. You know how Chisholm tries to impress upon him his duty to look after our folk."

"I should think Alex is well aware of his duty," Fin said.

"Aye, sir, but just as different sheriffs act differently, so do men in general, and the plain fact is that as much as Alexander tries to please his father, their methods will never be the same. Rob or Michael, now . . . but there, I begin to sound like Chisholm, and that I do not wish to do. Indeed, I do not know how he can demand that Alexander 'do something' and then grow angry when another man takes the law into his hands. But I always loved my sons equally, and although death encourages us to make saints of our loved ones, neither Rob nor Michael would qualify for sainthood either before or after his demise. The best any of my sons can hope for is to have been good men and true, and that all three have been."

"When will he return?" Bab asked.

"He just left again yesterday, but I expect he'll return soon."

With that Bab had to be content, but she quickly learned that she had underestimated the strength of Lady MacRae's belief in her arranged marriage.

Early Friday morning, after breaking her fast with Molly and Fin and walking out with them into the bailey to bid them farewell, Bab returned to the great hall after twenty minutes' absence to find both Lady Chisholm and Lady MacRae at the table with their heads together while servants scurried to bring them food.

Startled, since she had supposed they were both still sound asleep, she paused at the threshold.

Lady MacRae was talking but broke off upon seeing her to exclaim, "Oh, my dearling, we thought you were still abed. Do come and sit with us, for we are discussing your wedding dress."

Blinking at this cheerful, articulate stream of words from a woman who had scarcely spoken above a murmur for months, Bab shot a look at Lady Chisholm before she said warily, "Wedding dress?"

"Aye, for you must have a new gown for the occasion, you know, and whilst I am sure that Ada and Giorsal can create one for you quickly, you should look to see if there is anything that you cannot like in this pattern we have devised."

"Pattern?"

Lady MacRae looked more narrowly at her. "Are you quite awake, dearling? You sound as if you were talking in your sleep."

"I am wholly awake, madam. Indeed, I have been up this past hour and more, because Kintail and Molly left only a few minutes ago. Had they known you were on the point of descending to break your fast," she said to Lady Chisholm, "I know they would have waited to express their thanks personally for your hospitality. As it is, I am charged with that duty."

"They both thanked me profusely last night," she said with a chuckle. "I told them then as I tell you now that you have little for which to be grateful. The boot is entirely on the other foot, as my sons were used to say. I am greatly indebted to you for your companionship and for bringing Arabella to visit me. It has been much too long since we have enjoyed any time together."

"Look at this drawing," Lady MacRae said again. "I own, I have not tried to sketch anything for some time, so the result is somewhat crude, but it will give you an idea of what we have been discussing."

"The dress is entirely your mother's creation," Lady Chisholm said with a chuckle. "I cannot claim to have contributed a single detail to it, and thus I can say without blushing that I think it quite beautiful."

Bab glanced perforce at the drawing her mother had made on a sheet of foolscap, and what she saw rendered her nearly speechless. Lady MacRae had enjoyed drawing before Sir Gilchrist's death, but to Bab's certain knowledge had not picked up a pen or brush since the day she had learned of that dreadful event. Still, Bab had seen many examples of her mother's talent, for the great recipe book of the

MacRaes boasted her drawings alongside recipes for puddings and liniments, as well as the housekeeping hints it contained. The book even contained amusing sketches of servants they had had over the years, and memorable events.

Now she saw a sketch of herself in a gown that would make a stunning bride gown. It took no imagination to see that it would become her well, and despite her mother's self-criticism, there was nothing in the image for which to apologize. Her ladyship's skill, if anything, had improved.

"It's beautiful," Bab said. Much as she wanted to say that she had no need of a bride dress, since she was not going to marry — now or ever — she could not say the words. If she had needed anything more to tell her how much good the notion of a wedding had done her mother, the light in her ladyship's eyes provided it. She could no more extinguish that light than she could have drowned a kitten. Clearly, she would have to find another way to stifle the notion of a wedding.

But by Sunday, she was no closer to a solution than she had been on her arrival. Chisholm had appeared only for meals, and although he greeted his guests politely, seemed content to have them as guests, and read the Sunday prayers in the castle chapel. His conversation was disinterested to the point of being terse. Even Lady MacRae's mention of wedding plans did not faze him. He said vaguely, albeit to Bab's consternation, that he was sure the ladies had everything in train.

Hoping that Lady Chisholm had simply warned him to say nothing to distress Lady MacRae, Bab wondered if she could gain any advantage by speaking to him privately. After considering the matter, she decided to hold her peace. The problem she faced in talking with Chisholm was the same as it was with his lady. She could not imagine any way of protesting to either one that she had no wish to marry their son without offending them deeply. At best, they would think her inconsiderate; at worst, unconscionably rude, so by the time Sir Alex returned late Sunday afternoon, she was fairly champing at the bit to talk with him.

Chapter 11

Sir Alex strolled into his mother's bower, having obviously taken sufficient time first to remove his travel gear and don clothing more suitable for company. The cerulean blue doublet matched his eyes exactly, and his darker blue trunk hose, slashed and puffed with pink satin, gave the outfit a particularly festive appearance.

Lady Chisholm and Lady MacRae were working at their tambour frames, and Bab, delighted to see her mother at last knotting her thread and making real progress, had been sorting threads for her on a white cloth spread across her lap.

"Allow me to assist you with that task, mistress," Sir Alex drawled amiably, drawing up a low stool beside her when he had greeted them, and sitting on it.

He seemed suddenly too near, but although his nearness created a certain tension, she did not feel that she should object to it.

Lady MacRae turned a critical eye toward him. "Some of the colors are very similar, sir. Mind that you take care, or Barbara will have to sort them over again."

He smiled at her. "I am very pleased that you have chosen to visit us, my lady. At Stirling, I scarcely had a chance to do more than welcome you before you departed for home again."

"I do not enjoy court life," she replied, returning her attention to her embroidery.

He blinked, looking from Bab to his mother but making no comment.

Lady Chisholm smiled. "I hope you found everything in order with those of our people you visited, my dear."

"More or less," he said. "I encountered tension everywhere, so I cannot say that anyone is at peace, nor do I believe that enviable state will return whilst the Dalcrosses remain in power."

"We should do something, Alex. Your father is quite right about that."

"Aye, perhaps," he said, selecting a skein of varicolored thread from those Bab had on her lap, adding as he began to unknot it, "I do not know what that 'something' might be, madam. Recall that my father also insists that any action must be lawful. Raising an army against Jamie's appointed sheriff would be little less than treason even if we could organize the few barons who have not ridden south to support him. Certainly Jamie would call it treason, and I've no wish to end on a gallows, madam, nor to see my father do so."

"No, my dear, and I suppose it would be difficult to organize the Highland gentry," Lady Chisholm said. "Many would balk if for no other reason than they believe Dalcross enjoys the support of the Pope in his determination to bring our local religious traditions in line with Rome."

Sir Alex's eyes twinkled. "I doubt that the Pope has ever heard of Dalcross. Indeed, I should doubt that he has ever heard of Inverness. I've met him, you see."

If he intended that rider to divert his audience, he succeeded.

Bab exclaimed, "Did you indeed, sir? What is he like?"

"I can scarcely answer that, mistress, for although I was honored to attend a papal audience and even kissed the papal toe, I'm afraid I found the entire experience to be something of an absurdity."

"Alexander, you should not speak such sacrilege," his mother scolded.

"Should I not? I wager you'd have been as hard pressed as I to keep from bursting into laughter had you seen that line of grown men approaching the pontiff. They do so one at a time on their knees, you see, in a sort of zigzagging lurch. At the end, one crawls on both hands and knees to the papal slipper, where some helpful soul has made a chalked cross on the exact spot one is to kiss."

"No!" Bab and Lady Chisholm exclaimed as one, both laughing. Lady MacRae continued with her neat stitches as if she had not heard him.

"I promise you, I could never have made this

up," he said. "One hesitates a moment respectfully after kissing the slipper, whilst the pontiff pontificates, and then one retreats in the same awkward, lurching manner as one has come forward, only backwards, as if from the presence of royalty."

"But why did you do it at all if you thought it so absurd?" Bab demanded when she had stopped laughing at the vision so easily imagined.

"Sakes, mistress, I wanted to see him, of course. Rather than miss that experience, I'd have kissed his —" He glanced at his mother. "I'd have kissed whatever piece of him he wanted me to kiss. One does what one must."

"I suppose you would," she murmured, returning her attention to her work.

The mood being broken, they worked in silence for several moments before Lady MacRae said abruptly, "I hope you found time to speak to your priest whilst you were out speaking to people, sir."

"About what, my lady?" Sir Alex said gently, turning his attention to her.

"Why, the wedding, of course. We must set the date, and since your mother said that you had received a letter from our Patrick, I believe you must have a good notion by now of when that should be."

With a mischievous glint in his eyes, Sir Alex looked at Bab as he said, "The only wedding Patrick mentioned in his letter was a possible one sometime in an unlikely future between your daughter and myself, but I had assumed that, as he jokes about that frequently, he was merely doing so again. Am I to understand that Mistress Barbara believes he might truly press for such a union?"

"Why, it was all arranged," Lady MacRae said matter-of-factly. "Doubtless Patrick recalled it to your attention only because he has been away this past year, but he is in Scotland again, so the time has come to get on with it. Barbara knows her duty. She will obey her father's wishes just as you will obey yours."

Bab watched Sir Alex narrowly throughout this exchange, but she could read little in his expression. He did glance at Lady Chisholm, but Bab did not think the slight shake of her ladyship's head would mean much to him.

At last, he smiled at Bab, saying, "I had not realized matters had progressed so far, mistress. You must hold me in higher esteem than I'd thought."

"You should not tease her, Sir Alex," Lady MacRae said austerely. "Why should she not hold you in high esteem?"

Uncertain whether he was baiting her or speaking sincerely, Bab held her temper and her tongue, albeit both with difficulty.

He had turned his head away again, making it difficult to read his expression, and he was pretending (she was sure) to concentrate on the separation of two red threads that were nearly but not quite identical in shade. Just then, he looked at her, and the mischief in his eyes was clear to see.

"I'd like a word with you, sir," she said. "A private word, if you please."

He leaned back in mock surprise. "Alone, mistress? Faith, do you count us as married already?"

Wishing she had a jug of water to empty over his head, Bab refused to reply in kind. Instead, carefully wrapping her threads in the white cloth on which she had been sorting them, she arose and set them on a side table. Then, she said evenly to him, "If you wish to make a game of me, sir, I cannot stop you, but it would please me if you would accord me a few moments of your time."

He, too, set aside the threads he had been sorting and stood up, but he was smiling and shaking his head in such a way that she knew he meant to continue teasing her. Before he could speak, however, his mother said gently, "Alex."

Turning to her, he smiled. "Yes, madam."

"Go with her, my dear, and see if you cannot soothe her fears. You can certainly take a turn together around the bailey without causing a scandal."

He made Bab a profound leg then and offered an arm. "There now, mistress," he murmured. "Already your wish is to be my command."

"Oh, do stop talking like a daffy," she snapped. "You make me want to shake you until your teeth fly about your head."

"Well, if you think you can . . ." he said provocatively.

Throwing up her hands, Bab turned and walked away, leaving him to follow.

As she crossed the room, she heard him murmur, "You see, madam, how she leads me a dance. I tremble to think what married life holds in store for me."

Gritting her teeth, Bab tried to ignore him. Flinging open the door and striding from the room, she caught up her skirts as she crossed the great hall dais, only to have him grab her arm as she began to step down from it to the lower hall.

"One moment, mistress," he said in his irritating drawl.

"Let go of me, sir. I do not want to have this conversation either here or in the bailey, but you will oblige me by holding your tongue. I just wish we could be private. Then, at least, if you persisted in tormenting me, I need not be answerable for my actions."

"Dear me, what a shrewish temper the lass has," he murmured. "I have no wish to stroll about the bailey in view of heaven knows how many gawkers, but we can easily stay here. I have shut the door behind us, and I trust the hall will remain empty at this hour. Therefore you may say what you will to me without delay."

She waited pointedly until he released her arm, and then she looked around and saw that gillies had already begun laying the high table for supper. Two lads came through a doorway opposite the one from the stairs just then, carrying trestles to set up the lower hall tables.

She glanced uncertainly at Sir Alex, but he had seen them.

"Leave us," he said quietly. "You may return in twenty minutes' time and still finish your tasks before supper."

"Aye, sir," one of the lads said, touching his forelock.

When they were alone, Bab faced him. "I do not know what they must think, sir. Likely, they will tell everyone that you wanted to be private with me."

"It does not matter what they think," he said. "But let us step nearer to the high table. The screens will give us more privacy, and no one will overhear what you say to me even if someone should chance to come in. You should perhaps not raise your voice, but otherwise you may shred my character as much as you like."

"I have no wish to shred your character," she said, striving to control her voice and wondering what it was about him that made her want to shriek at him like an Edinburgh fishwife one moment and apologize for her temper the next.

A stack of wooden trenchers sat at the near

corner ready to be set out, flanked by pewter mugs for ale and goblets for wine. The saltceller was in its usual place, and the claret had been decanted and left to rest in a jug near the trenchers.

"Now, mistress, what is it?"

"You must know what it is!"

"I would like you to tell me nonetheless."

"This marriage notion of my mother's is a nonsense."

"How did it come to this pass?"

She sighed. "My mother somehow got it into her head that your father and mine arranged the whole thing, but they didn't!"

"If you do not want it, you need only say so."

"Mercy, sir, do *you* want it?"

"Mistress, you must know that you put me in a most awkward position by asking such a question."

"No, I don't. You cannot want to marry me!"

"Even if that were true I could hardly say so without offering you the most egregious insult."

"I promise not to take offense. Just tell them you won't do it."

"My father would flay me alive if I said any such thing. Surely you can see that you must be the one to tell them you have no wish to marry me."

"But I cannot. My mother has scarcely spoken a sensible word to anyone since my father's death, but at the mere thought of planning my wedding, she began to emerge from her private world to inhabit the common one with the rest of us. I dare not oppose her lest she fall back into that half-world of hers again."

"Nevertheless, you need only refuse," he said. "I'll not force you into a marriage you do not want. I am well aware that you do not like me."

Annoyed though she was, Bab was nonetheless disconcerted by this blunt statement. She said hastily, "That is not true! I feel a great deal of . . . of —"

When she could not find the word she sought, he said, "Just so. You feel a great deal of loathing for me."

"Truly, sir, I do not," she said, looking away and idly fingering one of the mugs on the table. "I have long felt affection for you and for your family."

"Indeed?"

"Aye," she said, adding with a direct look and a touch more spirit, "so if it has seemed to you of late that I dislike you, mayhap you should look to your own behavior for the reason."

"*My* behavior?" He withdrew a lace-edged handkerchief from his sleeve, shook it lightly, and dabbed his lips with it.

Shaking her head at this affectation, she said, "I have scarcely recognized you since your return from the Continent, but my affection for you has not diminished. You have always been kind to me, sir, in your fashion."

"Successful marriages have been built on weaker foundations."

"The fact is that I have decided *never* to marry," Bab said. "Pray inform your parents and my mother that there is to be no wedding."

Alex dabbed the handkerchief to his nose and then to his lips again before saying apologetically, "Desolated as I am to have to disappoint you again, mistress, I repeat, I cannot do that."

The smoldering coals of her anger ignited instantly. "Why not?"

"Even if I could reconcile such a refusal with my notions of gentlemanly conduct, if you will recall, I did not arrange this marriage. I cannot call it off."

"Well, it certainly was not I who arranged it!"

"I did not say it was," he said calmly. "Nevertheless, your lady mother clearly believes that your father and mine made a contract between them, and that notion, having taken strong hold of her mind, has made her happier and more animated than anyone has seen her since Sir Gilchrist's death. I'd have to be a brute to pour disappointment on her at such a time. You will have to tell her yourself."

Since she had the same compunctions as he did, and since her guilt and frustration made her too angry to think about what she was saying, she said, "Ask your father to tell her. He must know he never made any arrangement with mine."

"But I believe they did discuss some possibilities before your father's death," he said. "Before I left to attend Jamie's proxy wedding, my father mentioned that they had discussed a union between our families, but I thought your father had suggested the union for one of my brothers and that my father had other plans. When he wrote nothing more to suggest they had spoken further about it —"

"How could he send you letters, as far away as you were?"

He chuckled, making her want to throttle him. "Surely," he drawled, "you do not think him incapable of getting messages to me. He did so easily last year, after all, when he commanded my return after Rob and Michael were killed."

She would not let him make her feel guilty about stirring that memory, not now. "Then if there had been an arrangement," she persisted, "his lordship would have sent word to you. Is that what you believe?"

"I do," he said. "Certainly he would have if I was a party to it."

"Then there was no agreement."

"But if your mother believes there was —"

"There still would be no contract, and your father could tell her so."

"He'd have to be a stronger man than he is at present to persuade her of that, as deeply as she feels about it. Moreover, she would think me a regular cheat."

"But you are no such thing!"

"I would look like one."

244

She stamped her foot. "I don't care what you look like! I won't marry you!"

"Have you even asked my father if such a discussion ever took place?"

The question brought her up short. She had not asked Chisholm anything, nor did she want to bring him into it lest he declare it a good match and suggest it to Patrick, thus taking the matter out of her hands. Thinking quickly, she said, "My mother has spoken of little else since the moment of our arrival at Dundreggan, sir, and your father has been present on more than one such occasion. Moreover, your mother knows the truth. Surely, had he wanted no part in it, he would have said so."

"Possibly he feels the same reluctance to destroy your mother's happiness that I feel."

"Or perhaps he believes he would do well to ally himself with my family now that Patrick and Kintail have become closer to the King!"

"Patrick has also managed to annoy Cardinal Beaton, I believe," Sir Alex pointed out calmly. "In these parts, thanks to the Dalcrosses, the cardinal's influence appears to be even greater than Jamie's."

Frustrated, she said, "I don't care about influence. I do not want to marry!"

"Then you need only tell your mother so and persuade her to believe it, or declare yourself unwilling when the priest arrives. That will end it, sure enough."

Feeling trapped again and infuriated by his

typically languid attitude toward so vital a subject, Bab's fingers curled into claws, but she did not realize that they had curled around the pewter mug until she had flung it at him.

Alex caught it. His eyes flashed dangerously as he stepped toward her.

Feeling a surging sense of triumph, she said, "So you do still have a temper! I thought you had left it in France, sir."

Even as she said the words, she saw that he looked mildly puzzled, the anger having vanished as if it had never been. Wondering if she could possibly have imagined the fire she had seen in his eyes, she continued to stare into his face.

He stepped nearer yet.

Too near.

She swallowed, feeling weakness in her knees that she could not remember feeling since her father's death, the same weakness, she was sure, that she had felt on those rare occasions when Sir Gilchrist had been displeased enough with her behavior to punish her. Gathering courage, she forced herself not to blink but to continue gazing steadily at him.

He was only Alex, after all.

He held her gaze for a long moment, then said quietly, "I'm not angry, lass."

"You were."

His lips twitched as if he would smile, but he did not. He said, " 'Twas only that I did not think my head or the mug would be improved by denting."

Disturbed and not a little confused, Bab said brusquely, "I should not have thrown it. Pray excuse me now, sir." And, turning on her heel, she fled.

Alex watched her go, letting the smile emerge that he had been fighting to suppress ever since he had realized he could not hide it behind a handkerchief. Still holding the mug, he hefted it, measuring its solid weight and knowing that had it made contact with his skull, it would likely have laid him out flat.

"Little termagant," he muttered. "She would probably dance a galliard round my corpse."

He had wanted to shake her, but he had not dared lay a finger on her for fear that in doing so he would reveal his increasing desire for her. He wondered if she had had any notion of how much he had wanted to take her in his arms and hold her, how much he had begun to want the marriage she was so firmly set against.

"If ye want a thing, ye must fight for it."

This time the voice in his head was so loud that he wondered for a moment if some unknown entity had taken over his private thoughts.

"Are ye willing tae fight? Ye said when ye want a thing ye must fight, and that ye'd do what ye must. D'ye no want this?"

It occurred to him that unlike the usual case with his private thoughts, the nagging voice sounded different from his.

Although he had carried on conversations

with himself in his mind for years, the accent and vocabulary of the other party in those conversations had always been the same as his own because, naturally, the thoughts were his thoughts and thus the voice his voice. He daydreamed about possibilities or thought through alternatives before making decisions just as everyone did.

The argument in his head now was different, because neither the voice nor the accent was his. He had heard the accent before though, from Scottish Borderers at court. Was his imagination playing tricks on him?

"Ye'd like tae think that, I'll wager, but ye'd do better tae think sensibly. If ye're tae gain your heart's desire, ye must leave this decision tae the lass."

It had to be his imagination. Since any other solution would require belief in things that educated men did not believe in, he dismissed the intriguing possibilities that streamed through his mind and focused on Barbara MacRae. Would she dare to confront his father and demand direct answers to her questions? His increasing knowledge of her courage led him to believe she would. Despite Chisholm's present lack of interest in most things, he was unlikely to tolerate defiance from any young woman living under his roof. The two would make formidable adversaries.

"Aye," said the voice in his head, "but the outcome o' such a battle will depend on how much yon lass wants what she asks for, dinna ye think?"

Agreeing completely but not certain that even Bab had the courage to stand against his father for long, Alex bit his tongue to keep from replying aloud and went to find his manservant.

Maggie Malloch watched Alex hurry away, wondering how much she ought to exert herself to make him heed her. He had a strong mind, to be sure, and he was the sort of educated gentleman who most strongly resisted any belief in members of the Secret Clan, but her powers were strong enough to overcome that resistance. At present, those powers told her that her son was about to join her.

"What be ye about, Mam?" Claud asked. "Ye shouldna be here."

"Pish tush," she said. "I ha' every right tae be here, because that lazy vixen Catriona ha' disappeared."

"Aye, sure, she has, for I canna find her either," he admitted.

She peered narrowly at him, but it was clear that he spoke the truth. Then, as that thought crossed her mind, she realized that he was keeping something from her.

"It isna like ye, Claud, tae be larking about without a woman, but mayhap the lack will help ye concentrate better on your duties."

As she had expected, he could not meet her stern gaze.

Her temper stirred. "Ye're in lust again, ye daftie. Who is it, and dinna lie tae me unless ye want a dose o' what your lies can bring ye."

He shuddered, as well he might, she thought.

"Who be the lass this time?" she repeated gently.

"It be Lucy Fittletrot again, Mam, but I didna ask for her help. She came tae me! She says she wants tae make up for landing me in trouble afore."

"Aye, sure she does. What did she do tae that Catriona?"

He started to shrug, but when she glared, he said hastily, "She said she put a wee spell on her, just tae make her think she'll get goat's feet like a Glaistig if she goes near tae Dundreggan, that's all."

"I see," Maggie said, her mind working swiftly to sift the ramifications of this news. "Mayhap it'll do that lass good tae learn that others can manipulate her."

"But what o' her Chisholms, Mam?"

"I'll keep me eye on 'em," Maggie said. "I must treat both sides equally though, for it looks as if the Merry Folks and the Helping Hands will make peace, but only an both sides succeed. I dinna want tae help yon Catriona, but I must if Lucy Fittletrot ha'interfered wi' her. We dinna ken who be pulling Lucy's strings though, so I'll be watching the pair o' ye, Claud, though ye needna tell her so."

He nodded obediently, but just in case,

Maggie flicked a finger. It would be just as well if he *couldn't* tell Lucy that his mother was keeping an eye on her.

Not wanting to spend a moment longer thinking about her impulsive reaction to Sir Alex's teasing, or whatever it was that had stirred her to throw the pewter mug at him, Bab went in search of Lady MacRae, determined now, whatever the consequence, to persuade her that there could be no wedding.

She found her mother in the tiny parlor that adjoined her ladyship's bedchamber, conversing animatedly with Ada MacReedy and Giorsal.

As Bab entered, Lady MacRae broke off what she was saying to exclaim, "Ada and Giorsal assure me that they can make up a new gown for you in a trice, because we have agreed that the fabric you purchased for me in Stirling, which I thought too bright a pink for me, will suit your coloring admirably. Fortunately, I brought ells of fabrics with me, though, so you may choose whatever you like."

"I shall not require a new gown, madam," Bab said gently, ignoring Giorsal's frown of disapproval.

"But of course you will," Lady MacRae said. "A bride must have a new gown for her wedding. What can you be thinking?"

"Please, madam, I —"

"If you do not like anything I've brought, I expect his lordship will be kind enough to arrange for us to visit shops in Inverness, but I cannot believe the quality of fabric there will be as nice as that lovely French silk from Stirling. Moreover, pink was your father's favorite color for you. As to fastenings, we must put our heads together with Nora, to be sure, but someone will think of something."

For a flashing moment, Bab almost yearned for a return to the days when Lady MacRae had seemed oblivious to the world around her. Horrified to think that such a thought could even formulate in her mind, she knelt swiftly beside her mother's chair and said gently, "I pray thee, madam, do not make so many plans for me. I am not worthy of such industry."

Patting her arm and smiling lovingly at her, her mother said, "My dear one, this wedding was one of your father's last wishes, and he would not want his beloved daughter to be a shabby bride. You will do him great honor."

A lump rose to Bab's throat and tears to her eyes.

Giorsal said firmly, "Mistress Bab, let me show ye the pink silk her ladyship thinks would suit ye. Ye'll likewise want to see the other drawings her ladyship ha' made today, showing how ye'll look from different angles."

Glancing at her, Bab felt a new burst of shame. Sir Alex was right. How could she even consider dousing the fires of energy and purpose that had so long lay dormant within the woman she loved most in the world? Was marrying him so great a sacrifice? Surely, a truly loving daughter would make any sacrifice to ensure her mother's happiness and mental well being.

"I am so pleased that you approve of the simplicity of this gown," Lady MacRae said, turning the new drawings toward Bab. "You have such a curvaceous figure, my love, that it would be a shame to hide it beneath too many ruffles or too wide a farthingale. The sleeker look is more elegant, don't you agree?"

"Until you showed me that first sketch, I'd forgotten how well you draw, madam," Bab said, giving her a hug. "These are wonderful, too," she added when she had looked at the others. "Any lass would be pleased to resemble these pictures on her wedding day, but —"

"You must see how well that pink silk will suit the gown, Mistress Bab," Giorsal interjected swiftly.

"Giorsal, you must not interrupt Mistress Bab when she is speaking," Lady MacRae said with a frown. "Pray, continue, dearling."

"I . . . I was just going to suggest that . . ." She glanced again at Giorsal, who had pressed her lips together but whose eyes spoke volumes. ". . . that we should show these other drawings to Lady Chisholm," she went on desperately. "She will perhaps have some suggestions to make. Her . . . her woman might have some —" She broke off, knowing that with every muttered word she sounded more as if she approved of the wedding, although she certainly had not yet come to that.

"You make an excellent suggestion," Lady MacRae said. "Let us go and seek her ladyship now. There are many other things to discuss as well, you know."

Terrified that a group appearance in Lady Chisholm's bower would only reinforce the idea that Lady MacRae's wedding plans were rapidly becoming reality in all their minds, Bab said, "Pray, madam, will you not allow me to speak privately with her ladyship first? This has all come upon me so suddenly that I scarcely know whether I am on my head or on my heels."

Lady MacRae smiled. "It would not do, I expect, for us all to descend upon her now. Before you came in, Ada was doing her best to persuade me to rest a bit before supper, and I know she is right. I have not yet regained my strength, and I do not wish to be ill on your wedding day. Do you go and discover from her ladyship if it will be convenient for us to discuss these matters after supper."

Relieved, Bab kissed her cheek and took her leave, but despite her haste, she did not miss the look Giorsal shot her. Interpreting it easily, she knew she would hear things about her character that she would not like if she upset Lady MacRae. She would not like herself much either, come to that. Still, they were planning her life. She had every right to explore any alternative she might have.

Chapter 12

When Lady Chisholm greeted Bab warmly, hope soared for a moment that her ladyship might indeed help her find a way out.

"What is it, my dear?" she said, gesturing toward the stool beside her. "I trust your mother is not ill again."

"No, madam," Bab replied, taking the indicated seat. "She is fully immersed in plans for this wedding of hers."

"Yes, so I have imagined. I must say that her energy amazes me."

"It surprises me, too," Bab said, hoping this might provide an opening. "I promise you, madam, I knew nothing about this plan until recently."

Lady Chisholm chuckled. "I do not doubt you were dismayed."

"Had *you* heard aught of such an agreement?" The thought that she might have was dizzying, and Bab had all she could do to retain her composure.

"No, my dear, not until Arabella mentioned it. Apparently, Chisholm and Sir Gilchrist did discuss some sort of a union between our families, but due to your father's sudden death, they never drew up a contract. But I must tell you, I am delighted that your mother intends to see the matter through. I cannot imagine a better wife for our dear Alex, particularly since he tells me your brother has frequently made his approval plain to him."

"I . . . I fear I am not yet ready to marry," Bab said, seeing nothing to gain by trying to persuade her ladyship that Patrick had been teasing Alex and that Alex was probably taking revenge for the pewter mug by pretending to approve now.

"Many young women marry much younger," Lady Chisholm pointed out.

"My age is not what concerns me," Bab said, striving to sound reasonable but feeling her temper stir.

"You are nervous, of course, my dear. All brides are nervous of marriage, because it is such a great step to take. It is so great, in fact, that most sensible young women leave all the arrangements to their parents."

"But surely, all brides do not leave the matter of the groom entirely to others," Bab said. "I want to have some say in that."

"I see how it is," Lady Chisholm said. "Indeed, my dear, I have a little feared that you might try to take the bit between your teeth."

Bab swallowed but managed not to look away. "If I have offended you, madam, I do sincerely apologize. That was not my intent."

Patting her hand, Lady Chisholm said reassuringly, "Don't be a goose. You have done no such thing, but I hope you will not mind if I take advantage of the closer kinship we are soon to enjoy to say that I have noted from time to time a certain independence of mind that has concerned me."

"My parents and brother have generally allowed me to think for myself."

"Yes, and *generally* that is a good thing," her ladyship replied. "However, in important matters, those in which a daughter owes both a duty and her obedience to her parents or to the head of her family, that independence of spirit may cause her heartache where none should be necessary. It becomes worse if she develops a habit of independence that may lead her to defy her husband. That will not do, my dear."

Bab remained silent, not trusting her unruly tongue to express her feelings without landing her in trouble again.

"I hope that I make my point," Lady Chisholm added gently.

"Yes, madam," Bab murmured. Inhaling deeply in another attempt to ease her frustration, she added, "My mother asked me to discover a time when you and she can discuss the matter further. She is resting, but she suggested that tonight after supper might be suitable."

"I am entirely at her disposal," Lady Chisholm said.

Taking her leave, Bab slipped her hands into the folds of her skirt to conceal the fact that they were clenched into fists. She had understood Lady Chisholm perfectly. Since Patrick would not disapprove of the marriage, if Chisholm approved, his lady would do nothing to help Bab defy her mother's wishes.

There was clearly only one course left to take, and that was to seek help from Chisholm himself. If he and Sir Gilchrist never signed a contract, surely nothing could prevent his calling the whole thing off, although she knew she would be on firmer ground if she could say she disliked Sir Alex or could accuse him of cruelty. She could do neither. She liked him, but she did not want to spend the rest of her life submitting to his wishes and putting up with his silly affectations and indolent behavior. She feared that Chisholm would be unsympathetic, though.

She was unable to speak to him until after supper, but as soon as her mother and Lady Chisholm rose to retire to the latter's bower, she asked if she might speak privately with him.

"Of course, lass. Come upstairs to my private chamber."

She saw him glance at Sir Alex, and noted a lurking twinkle in Alex's eyes that told her he had guessed the topic of their discussion.

That twinkle firmed her resolve, however, and as soon as Chisholm had shut the door of his private room, she said, "I do not want to marry Sir Alex, my lord. No one ever asked me if I did. Please, can you not help me straighten out this coil?"

"Sit down, Barbara," he said calmly.

"But —"

"Sit down, lass."

With a sigh, she obeyed, saying, "I do not mean to be uncivil, sir, but I feel as if I have been trapped into this wedding by forces wholly beyond my control."

"We will avoid the dramatics, if you please," he said, sitting opposite her. "Her ladyship has told me that she spoke with you earlier. The plain fact is that this marriage was your father's wish, and I did not oppose it. Nor do I oppose it now."

"But Sir Alex himself said there was no contract, sir. Surely he must —"

"I did not say there was," Chisholm said bluntly. "Alex had departed for the Continent when the particular possibility of his marrying you arose between your father and me. Not to put too fine a point on the matter, we had several times since your birth discussed more than one possible alliance between our families."

"But if that is the case, why did neither Sir Alex nor I hear of it?"

"Frankly, my dear, there was no reason to discuss it with you or with Alex. Our original discussions concerned a marriage to my eldest son, Robert, because he was naturally your father's first choice."

"But I was never contracted to him, was I?"

"Nay, for you were but a babe then, and Rob nearly thirteen. Moreover, I had other plans for him, grander plans."

"I see," Bab said, feeling a prick of resentment despite the fact that she would have strongly resisted a marriage to Sir Robert Chisholm. "Who was she?"

"That need not concern you, for she died when she was eleven. I was on the point of arranging another marriage for him when he was killed, but that lass ran off with a most unsuitable lover when she learned of Rob's death."

"Mercy," Bab said.

"She did not enjoy much mercy," Chisholm said with a grimace. "Her father caught up with them and sent the lover to seek his mercy before God whilst the lass — ruined, as she was — is now contemplating her sins in a nunnery."

Bab shivered.

"Gilchrist also suggested that you might marry Michael," Chisholm went on, "but Michael believed he had years ahead of him before he need choose a wife and set up a nursery, and I did not press him. Alex was my youngest, and doubtless Gilchrist therefore thought less of him than of the other two, but he believed a union would be good for both families, and so he did suggest the possibility a month or so before Kinlochewe. I said I had no objection, but I did suggest that we wait to be sure Alex returned safely from his travels before drawing up the contract."

"But matters have changed now, sir. I should think you would still prefer a much grander alliance for your heir. And since there *was* no contract . . ."

He was staring into space, but when she paused, he said, "I have learned that life is too short and real friends too few to ignore their wishes, lass."

"Then why did you not speak to Patrick at Stirling?"

"Because I could not seem to make myself care about anything," he said quietly. "Also, as you know, your father died before Alex returned, and since your brother said nothing about the matter when we did meet, I assumed that Gilchrist had not told him about our discussions. Other matters had intervened in the meantime, so until your mother broached the topic, it simply lay dormant."

Other matters, she knew, being the deaths of his two older sons. She realized then that he had lost a dear friend and two beloved sons within two years. "But surely, my lord," she said gently, "I should have some say in the matter."

He frowned. "Do you think your father would have discussed it with you? Recall that he had not discussed our other talks with you, and surely you knew that the day would come when he would arrange your marriage."

"He nearly always let me have my say in things."

"In trivial matters, perhaps. He did not hide the fact that he doted on you, lass, but he would have expected your obedience in this of all things."

She could not deny that, much as she would have liked to. As kind and loving as Sir Gilchrist MacRae had been, he did expect obedience from his children, and she knew it was a father's responsibility to provide his daughter with a good marriage. Her father would not have allowed her to make an unsuitable one.

Forcing calm, she said, "Nevertheless, sir, in Patrick's absence, I have grown accustomed to making my own decisions and looking after Ardintoul, as well."

"Then you must feel relieved that you need no longer do so," he replied. "Women are not suited by nature to attend to such matters."

"I did not mind," she said, refusing to think of all the times she had railed against her lot and wished that someone else — Patrick, by choice — would deal with the more challenging problems at home. There had been many other times, however, when resolving a particular crisis had given her great satisfaction.

"My dear," Chisholm said, clearly tiring of the discussion, "I know that in the end, as a good daughter and dutiful sister, you will obey the expressed wishes of your parents and your brother just as Alex will obey mine."

Tempted though she was to tell him that his son had promised he would not force her into a marriage she opposed, she did not. Perhaps it was his stern look or merely his confidence that she would obey, but something made it impossible to fling Sir Alex's promise in his teeth, so she said nothing.

He stood, indicating that the interview was over, and she made her curtsy. But as she turned to leave, she realized that she could not just walk away like a petulant child, so she turned back, forcing a smile.

"Thank you for taking the trouble to explain all this to me, my lord."

"Conversation with you must always be a pleasure, lass," he said, smiling. "You will see. Marrying Alex will not be such a horrible fate, but if you are still determined to refuse, you need only stand up before the priest and all the witnesses and do so. The law will support you, although your friends and kinsmen may not."

Horrified by the image his words produced, she bobbed a curtsy and fled.

Having no wish to seek out her mother, Lady Chisholm, or Sir Alex, she went to her bedchamber. When she entered to find no hot water awaiting her and realized that Giorsal must still be busy elsewhere, she used cold water from the ewer to wash her face and prepared for bed without assistance.

By the time Giorsal looked into the room, Bab was beneath the covers, and although she was not yet asleep, she did not stir.

Giorsal quietly closed the door without disturbing her, but Bab could not sleep. She could think of no way to stop the wedding other than to demand that Sir Alex keep his promise, but his casual attitude and amiable if cork-brained belief that there was no particular reason they should not marry made her fear he might fail to keep that promise. He had certainly shown no more inclination than his mother to defy Chisholm, unless of course, one counted his continual, albeit detached refusal to pit his wits against the sheriff or the sheriff's horrid son.

Bab slept restlessly and when morning came, she was bleary eyed and in no mood for Giorsal's cheerful chatter when the woman bustled in at her usual time with hot water, talking from the moment she entered the room.

"A fine morning it is," she said, "and not one for a body to be lying abed till all hours, so up ye get and wash your face whilst I fetch out your gown."

"I'll want my riding dress, Giorsal."

"Nay, for ye'll no want to ride out this morning, mistress. That devil Fox were riding again last night, because his high and mightiness Francis Dalcross ha' been making mischief again. The man's a villain and nae mistake, so I for one hope the Fox pulls his ears off and feeds them to his dogs!"

"What has Francis done now?" Bab asked, interested despite her mood. Since she was determined to avoid their ladyships and all talk of weddings, she had not known what she would do with the morning. Now she did, although Francis Dalcross's name was not the one that had piqued her interest.

Giorsal snorted in a way that she would roundly have condemned had Bab done it and said, "It seems that the grand Sheriff o' Inverness requires more funds to support enforcement o' his new laws. Therefore, he ha' taken the notion o' taking more from everyone, including the priest in Nigg, who, heaven kens, has nowt to spare. But the sheriff, or more likely that villainous son o' his, ha' decided that if the man willna share his funds, he must be punished and the funds taken."

"But surely Francis cannot do that," Bab said.

"He did do it," Giorsal insisted. "His men took by force all that the good priest had, calling everything beyond the amount required a fine for noncompliance wi' the law, if ye please. As if the Crown ever took from the Kirk!"

Well aware that for centuries there had been a running battle between governments and the holy Kirk over just such matters, and that King Henry of England had certainly taken money from the Roman Church and had for some time been encouraging his nephew to do likewise in Scotland, Bab held her tongue. She knew it would be hopeless to try to explain such matters to Giorsal when she did not understand them herself. Indeed, how Henry could think James of Scotland would ever consent to Henry's being named head of the Scottish Kirk, she could not imagine, but that was, after all, one of the primary reasons that Patrick and the others were determined to prevent an English invasion.

Instead of engaging in such a pointless conversation, she said coolly, "I do intend to ride today, Giorsal, so fetch my dark green riding dress and pray do not argue. I am in no mood for it, and I shall be quite safe, I promise you."

Giorsal opened her mouth but shut it after a swift, appraising glance, and thirty minutes later, Bab was in the stables ordering a gilly to saddle her gray.

"D'ye want me to go wi' ye, mistress?"

"Not today," she said, hoping no one had given orders to the contrary.

Apparently, no one had thought it necessary, for without further ado, the lad threw her saddle on the gray gelding and tightened its girth. Then, lifting her onto the saddle, he grinned when she thanked him and turned back to his work.

With rumors abounding that the Fox was riding, Bab did not feel certain she would succeed in leaving the castle until she was outside the gates, but no one tried to stop her. Either those with authority to stop her had not heard that the masked rider was in the area, or it had not occurred to any of them that she might dare to ride out alone. Or perhaps it was simply that the lad who saddled her horse did not know that she was to have an escort and the men at the gate likewise did not know.

She remembered only then that Chisholm

himself had warned her against riding out alone. He had not actually commanded her not to do so, however. He had said only that for a woman to ride alone was dangerous, but she knew she could not depend upon his remembering it that way. Men, in her experience, remembered such discussions the way they wanted to remember them.

But if she wanted to find the Fox, she would not do so with an armed escort, and in any event, she did not fear him, because he would not harm her. More importantly, he might help her think of a way to prevent her wedding, and in any case, she wanted to tell him about it if only to see what he would say.

Not having the slightest notion of how or where to find him but remembering that the nearest village lay near where Glen Affric met Glen Urquhart, she followed the narrow track along the fast-flowing River Affric, hoping that one or another of the villagers might have an idea where to seek him.

She soon came to a point where the river gorge narrowed considerably before plunging downhill toward Glen Urquhart. For some distance then the track led away from the rushing water and the precipitous granite walls that confined it, winding through dense woodland until it emerged on a flat, heather-clad moor.

Bab's thoughts dwelt on images of meeting the Fox and telling him of the wedding as the track sloped down through another patch of woodland. On the other side, she came upon a sight that banished all thought of the Fox from her mind.

Two horsemen had stopped a small boy with a wild thatch of red hair, and just as she spied them on the narrow track, both dismounted. One struck the child across the face and sent him sprawling to the ground.

"Stop that!" Bab shouted, giving spur to the gelding. "Leave that lad be!"

The two men turned toward her as the child sat up holding his head. She did not rein in her horse until she was nearly on top of them, making their horses shy nervously as the gelding came to a plunging halt beside them.

"How dare you brutalize that child," she cried. "You should be ashamed of yourselves, the pair of you!"

"This be nae business o' yours, mistress," the larger of the two snapped.

"It is the business of all good people to protect children. Now go on about your business and leave that child alone."

"She be a right bonnie lass," the other man murmured, putting his hands on his hips as he thrust his hips forward and leered at her.

Bab glared at him and clutched her riding whip tightly. "You keep a civil tongue in your head, sirrah," she warned him.

"And she has a fiery temper," he said, licking his lips suggestively. "Hot blood in a lass provides heat for a man, too, I'm thinking."

"Aye, sure," said the other. "Slip down off o' that horse, pretty lass, and let's ha' a closer look at ye."

"You keep your distance," Bab said. "Perhaps you do not know me, but I am Mistress Barbara MacRae of Ardintoul. My brother, Sir Patrick MacRae, is friend to King James, and I am presently under the protection of Lord Chisholm of Dundreggan. If you dare to harm me, I assure you his lordship will report you to the sheriff if he does not punish you himself."

Both men laughed, exchanging knowing looks. "Sakes, lass, we be the sheriff's own men, and if ye think he'll care if we annoy his lordship, ye dinna ken the man. Nor will his lordship interfere wi' us, for we ken well that he scarce lifts a hand to anything these days. Now, come away off that horse like I told ye."

He reached for her, but Bab struck unhesitatingly with her whip at his hand, and as he snatched it back, she screamed at the urchin to take flight. The second man leaped toward her but jumped back almost as quickly when he, too, met her slashing whip.

Seeing the child disappear into the shrubbery, she noted as well that the men's horses, startled first by the gelding and then by her screams, were loping off toward Inverness. She spurred the gelding, and it responded instantly. With whip and spurs, she urged it to a gallop back up the hill.

As she reached the crest, she was dismayed to

see that the two men below had already recaptured their horses and were about to give chase. One lifted a horn to his lips and blew two long blasts.

Hearing shouts from the far side of the heathery moor, she saw other riders, at least half a dozen, responding to the horn's signal.

Desperately seeking shelter, she rode back into the trees at the moor's edge. Then, knowing that her pursuers would expect her to ride downhill and try to slip past the two men, she firmly guided the gelding across the hillside instead, avoiding both the track and the thickest part of the woods in favor of speed. At best she was only a few moments ahead of both sets of pursuers.

Soon she saw a clearing ahead, and as she neared it, she saw in its center what appeared at first to be a dark shadow. Then she recognized the great black stallion and its rider. When he raised a hand, gesturing to her to follow, she did not hesitate, leaning low over the gelding's neck and spurring harder than ever.

Since she had been sure that riding up over the crest again was her only chance for escape, she was surprised when he followed the curve of the hillside for a short distance more before turning downhill. Surely, if the men chasing her guessed which direction she had gone, they would see both her and her rescuer as soon as they broke from the woods. Ahead, through trees beyond the dark-cloaked rider, she could already see sunlight on a grassy meadow.

The horn sounded again in the distance behind her.

"What be he a-doing now?" Lucy demanded, peering between the gray gelding's ears at the dark rider ahead. "Does he no ken that this hillside ends in a cliff above yon river. 'Tis a gey dangerous course he's taking, for the river be heavy wi' melting snow and the rains. Ye can hear the hurl-come-gush o' it from here!"

"Aye," Claud said, frowning as he clutched the gray's mane and tried to look both forward and back at once. "I dinna ken his intent, but they mustna fall victim tae the sheriff's men — no just yet, I'm thinking."

He wondered where Maggie was and hoped she was keeping watch. It did not occur to him, however, to express that hope to Lucy.

No sooner had Bab emerged from the shelter of the trees into the meadow, than she heard shouts from behind.

Looking over her shoulder toward the sound, she saw that the two groups of riders had converged and were riding toward them, spread out in a line.

"Mercy," she muttered, urging the gelding on, "they'll surround us!"

She knew she was riding at a dangerous pace, especially since she did not know the terrain. For all she knew, the way ahead led through a rabbit warren, pitted with holes to snap the leg of an unwary horse and send its rider flying. Still, she had no choice but to trust the rider ahead of her, so she rode on, trying to follow exactly where he led.

When she realized that she was catching up with him, she attributed the fact to her wild pace, but it soon became evident that he was slowing.

The hillside appeared to end abruptly just ahead.

Then she heard the roar of the water and realized that she had been hearing it for some time without troubling her brain to identify the sound. Had she thought of it, she realized, she would have expected the way to the river to be over granite, as it had been before, not ending in grass or heather. Understanding swept through her now with an icy chill of terror.

Looking back, she saw that the groups of pursuers were rapidly merging. Even if she and the Fox turned downhill, away from the water, it was too late.

As the thought crossed her mind, she saw the stallion rear and paw the air, wrenched to a halt by the strong hands of its rider. Just beyond, the hillside fell away in a sheer cliff above the raging, flood-swollen river. They were trapped.

"She kens his folly now," Claud said, "but it be too late."

"We should ha' done summat when she met them first two louts," Lucy snapped. "Whatever can we do now?"

"Nowt," he growled. "Nor could we ha' done aught afore, Lucy. We be bound by our rules, and I be in this mess in the first place through interfering wi' mortals. The only thing that might save them now would be tae make them invisible, and tae do such a thing wi' so many witnesses tae see it would mean my ruin. We'd ha' tae answer tae the Circle, ye ken, the both o' us."

"But they'll be captured, Claud. We must do summat, and quick!"

Claud frowned, thinking hard.

Bab, too, expected capture at any moment. Drawing rein beside the Fox, she looked at the tumbling river thirty feet below and gasped at the awesome sight.

"Faith, sir, what can we do?"

His gaze met hers, and she saw that his eyes were dancing. With a chuckle, he leaned toward her, and before she had any idea what he meant to do, he snatched her from her saddle and spurred the stallion forward.

Surprise left her breathless and was all that kept her from screaming as the great black horse plunged off the cliff toward the raging waters below. She clutched her arms around the Fox's neck and buried her face in his cloak, certain that she was about to die.

"I trust you can swim," he murmured, and she heard laughter in his voice.

"Not in water like that!"

She did not know if he heard her, because the freezing waters closed over them just as she finished the sentence. Her mouth full of water, choking and unable to breathe, she struggled madly, but his strong arm held her, and he did not let go. Her skirts billowed up as they submerged and then tangled around them and threatened to drag them back down again when he stroked for the surface, but she felt him kick hard, and suddenly her head was free of the water.

She came up coughing and sputtering, but he held her high enough so that she could catch her breath, and she saw with relief that they had already traveled a good distance from the cliff.

She glanced at her companion, hoping for at least a glimpse of his face, but the wet mask clung to it, revealing nothing but its shape. They were moving with the swift current, and he had evidently managed to retain his grip on the stallion's reins, because the great horse swam nearby.

"Try to catch hold of his saddle," the Fox said.

She clutched him tightly, reluctant to let go.

"Easy, lass," he said gently.

"You are mad," she retorted.

He chuckled. "In truth, I canna argue with

that. A wee voice in my head that keeps telling me daftish things said, 'Jump,' and I did. 'Twas mad indeed, but it saved us. Go on now, reach for him."

She swallowed hard, trying to breathe normally and to think clearly. The great horse, which had seemed so near only moments ago, looked miles away now, surely too far for her to catch hold of him before the current swept her away.

Calmly, as if he were finding it no trouble to swim in the turbulent water while holding her, her companion said, "If you miss or cannot hang onto him, do not try to swim to shore. Just let the current carry you until it eases enough to let you swim. Then begin angling a little at a time to your left."

"I . . . I don't know if —"

"You can. A slight bend lies ahead, and if we're lucky, we'll make landfall there. If we miss it, the river bends more sharply and widens beyond. The water is shallow there. Just worry about breathing, and let the river do the work."

"You make it sound easy," she said, cautiously reaching toward his mask.

"It *is* easy," he responded as he heaved her toward the stallion.

She went under again, but as she did, she managed to catch the girth and easily hauled herself up, although at one moment, she feared the stallion might kick her. It did not seem to notice her weight though, and it swam powerfully. She found that gripping the saddle was easier than she had expected, and she was no longer afraid. She had not really been so from the moment her head broke the surface and she could breathe again. In the Fox's company, she felt safe.

Claud clung to the gray's mane as he stared, gaping, after the crazy mortals.

"Faith, Lucy," he said, "did ye put that fool notion into the man's head? Because if ye did, I promise ye, I'll —"

"I did nae such thing," she replied, "but 'twas an excellent notion all the same, Claud. Only see how that grand leap ha' baffled their pursuers."

To be sure, the men chasing Mistress Bab had reined in hard and were now riding cautiously toward the cliff.

With the fingertips of her right hand, Lucy waved a circle above her head.

"What be ye a-doin'?" Claud demanded.

"Think, Claud. The lass willna want them louts tae ha' her pony."

He gave a gasp and stared at her as the gray plunged from the cliff with the pair of them still clinging to its mane. "Ye're mad, lass, that's what ye are!"

Lucy chuckled and blew him a kiss from the fingertips she had just waved, then flitted away, vanishing just as the gray gelding hit the turbulent water.

Chapter 13

The Fox swam alongside Bab, his head up, his powerful arms and legs moving easily. He did not even seem to exert himself.

The bend he had mentioned was swiftly approaching, and she saw that the stallion swam toward it, but she did not see how they could make landfall there. Huge boulders flanked the riverbed.

"We'll keep to the center," the deep voice beside her said, still calm.

"Aye, we will," she murmured fervently, glancing at him.

His eyes still danced, bluish-gray now, reflecting the water.

"Are you still daring to laugh at all this?" she demanded.

"Faith, lass, sometimes laughter is all we have. Look behind us."

She had looked back only the once, but now, with a touch of fear, she looked again only to stare in astonishment. "Is that my horse?"

"Aye, it must ha' missed ye, for who'd ha' thought it had such pluck?"

The laughter in his voice was unmistakable now, and the brief thrill of fear she had felt before seeing the gray swimming after them turned to delight. This was exactly the sort of event that had made *Sionnach Dubh* a legend in the Highlands.

They passed safely through the rocky bend, although Bab feared each moment that they might crash into one of the huge boulders. Had the river not been so high, she knew they could easily have been dashed to bits. Instead, the river swept them on until it broadened into a wide, shallow, much calmer pool around the bend.

She could tell when the stallion touched bottom, because it surged toward the river-bank, and somehow she managed to hold on to it until her own feet touched solid ground. The current was still strong, but her companion suddenly loomed beside her, and when he caught her arm, she knew she could safely let go of the horse. In moments, they were ashore, and she knew that no matter how swiftly the men chasing them might ride, they could not catch them now.

With a delighted chuckle, she watched the gray gelding follow them from the water and shake itself like a huge dog. She was shivering and dripping wet, but she did not care. Turning to her companion with a wide grin, she said, "That was extraordinary! I have never in my life enjoyed such an adventure. Thank you!"

To her astonishment, he caught her hard by the shoulders, and the amusement she had seen in his eyes and heard in his voice vanished.

Giving her a shake, he said roughly, "What in the name of all that is holy were you doing out alone, and what devil possessed you to draw the attention of Dalcross's men?"

She snapped, "Take care, sir, for we MacRaes have tempers, too. Two of those men were abusing a child if you must know, and so I intervened. Would you, of all people, have expected me to ride on and ignore such brutal mistreatment?"

"And just how did you intervene?" His voice was low, like the growl of a lion, and it sent chills up her spine. She had not known he could speak to her so.

"I struck them with my whip, of course, and screamed at them, whereupon their horses took fright and ran off. Unfortunately, they did not run far," she added with a grimace. "The men managed to catch them and follow me soon enough."

"What happened to the child?"

"He got away when I shouted. So, you must see that I did the right thing, but I do thank you for coming to my rescue," she added conscientiously.

"You want beating, my lass," he retorted, unknowingly echoing Kintail's words and using much the same ominous tone. "You have courage," he added, "but you lack sense. I suppose you told them exactly who you are and where you live."

"Of course, I did. I believe they will not soon

try again to harm someone under Lord Chisholm's protection."

"If that were the case, why did you have to defend yourself with your whip?"

She hesitated, but it was no use prevaricating even if prevarication had been a habit with her, so she said with a sigh, "They did not heed me. Mayhap they did not pause to consider the consequences."

"What consequences do you imagine they might fear?"

"Why, Chisholm's wrath, of course."

"You clearly do not comprehend the power Francis Dalcross and the sheriff have gathered unto themselves," he said. "Their army is greater than any other now that so many of the Highland lairds have sent their men to support Jamie. I thought that you, of all people, understood that."

Hearing the echo of her own words and the touch of sarcasm in his voice, she knew he was still angry with her.

"Most of our men are with Jamie," she said, "but no one would act against Kintail even now. No one would dare."

"Doubtless that is true," he agreed, "but the sea guards Kintail's land on the west, and the people to the north are friendly to him and they are all far enough from Inverness to ignore the Dalcrosses. Would you have the same confidence if the Macdonalds should now decide to take back the Lordship of the Isles?"

"They can scarcely do so whilst their chief entertains himself in London," she said, but she could see his point. "Has Chisholm so many enemies then?"

"No, but that is not the point. The point is the power that the sheriff wields and the use to which his son puts that power. Together they have accumulated more men-at-arms under their leadership than all of the local lairds together."

"I still do not see how anyone could object to my actions today," she said stoutly. "I was merely protecting a child from two bullies."

"You might have protected him temporarily," he said, "but you have likely angered your bullies. What do you suppose they did after they lost sight of us?"

Abandoning her defenses in a sudden rush of fear for the little boy, she exclaimed, "You believe they went after him!"

"I do," he said, "but in fairness, I doubt they will catch him today, and I can learn who he is soon enough and see that he is protected. Still, my point is good, in that your interference is more likely to cause harm than good. You don't understand the politics hereabouts well enough to take a hand in them."

"I see," she said. "I do think Sir Alex should take a hand. His lordship certainly wishes he would."

"Are you so sure of that? Not only does his lordship believe in the rule of law even when those bound to enforce it ignore it, but it is hard to imagine Alex Chisholm making much of an impression on louts like those two you met today."

The temptation to agree with him was strong, particularly since she detected amusement in his tone again and wanted to soothe his temper. And, in truth, she could not imagine Alex confronting the two bullies she had confronted. He would have protested their behavior, of course. Any gentleman would. And perhaps, had they recognized him as a member of the local gentry, they might have left her alone, but she doubted that. Still, as long as she and her mother stayed with Sir Alex's family, she would not criticize him, not even by agreeing with the Fox.

She said quietly, "You do him injustice when you speak so, sir."

"Then you will not mind telling him what you've been up to today."

"Don't be absurd. You cannot want me to tell him about this."

"He has every right to know where you've been and what has happened."

Startled, she exclaimed, "You cannot mean to tell him! Not that he would do anything horrid, but if Chisholm should hear of it, it would vex him sorely. He is not yet entirely well, you know. You could not be so unkind as to tell them."

"I won't say anything to his lordship or to Sir Alex."

"Thank heaven! I knew you could not be so unfair."

"You will tell them yourself," he said firmly. "You have your horse now, so although its saddle is likely ruined, I'll put you on its back, and you will ride straight back to Dundreggan. Once there, you will confess to Sir Alex exactly what befell you. You may have jeopardized much that I've fought for by your actions today, and I do not mean to let you do it again. Do you understand me, lass?"

It occurred to her that in his anger he spoke more like a gentleman, but she did not question the difference. The growl was in his voice again, and she did not want to linger if he was going to go on scolding her.

Grimly, he said, "I asked you a question."

"I understand what you want me to do," she said, gathering her dignity.

"Then you will obey."

"I do not know how to get to Dundreggan from here," she said, taking care not to make any promise. "I do not know this area very well yet."

"Another excellent reason not to ride alone," he said, his sternness unabated.

Bab gritted her teeth, but her silence did not disturb him. He merely caught her around the waist and lifted her to the gelding's saddle.

"Sit still," he commanded when she reached for the reins. "Leather stretches when it gets wet, and I want to tighten this girth."

"My saddle is not the only thing that got wet," she pointed out. "I'm soaked to the skin, and I must look a fright."

"Aye, lass, we're both a sorry sight, but at least we're safe for now," he said, unbuckling the belly strap, then pulling hard on it. "That will do, I think," he said as he rebuckled it. "Remember, you are to ride straight to Dundreggan, and as soon as you arrive, tell Sir Alex everything that happened. It is important, because some of Francis Dalcross's men are bound to show up at Dundreggan, demanding to know your whereabouts, and they will doubtless insist upon questioning you."

"They'll not dare to harass me at Dundreggan!"

"Aye, but they will. Recall that they saw you in my company today, and not for the first time, I'll remind you."

She had not considered that detail. Perhaps she would have to tell Alex, after all. She had not intended to do any such thing, no matter what the Fox decreed, and certainly if he did not press her further to promise him. But if the sheriff or his men came looking for her . . . Worse, if they said they wanted to question her about the Fox, she might have to tell not only Alex but also his father and mother about today.

Her companion had fallen silent, and she wished again that she could read his expressions. She hoped he was not still angry, but his eyes — stony gray again — had narrowed to slits, or else in her guilt, she imagined they had. She looked away.

"You have not given me your promise," he said.

"I agree that I must tell him before the sheriff's men arrive," she said with a sigh. Then, hoping to divert him so he would not insist on anything more exact than that, she said, "How will we go? Surely the river swept us farther away from Dundreggan, and we shall have to go back past all those horrid men."

"I know a way," he said, turning his attention to the stallion.

Bab watched him check his saddle girth as he had checked hers, then mount with the easy grace she so much admired. Without another word, he led the way along the rocky shore to the opening of a grassy glen. They were on the same side of the river as the cliff from which they had jumped, and he led her away from the water, up the glen toward the crest of the ridge.

Alone with her thoughts as she followed him, she tried to imagine her impending meeting with Alex. Reading his mind was impossible even when they were face-to-face, and trying to imagine how he might react to anything she did or said gave her a headache. She had never known anyone like him.

She tried to remember if she had ever thrown anything at Patrick and decided that she might have when she was small. But she knew exactly how he would react if she did so today, and she had definitely never thrown anything at Kintail. The very thought sent a shiver up her spine. Surely, the only reason she had dared throw the mug at Alex was that she had known he would not retaliate as most Highland men would to such an act. The thought was disturbing. Was she a coward?

They followed the ridgeline for a short time, and she thought they must be nearing the moor where they had hunted, because they were high enough now so she could see Glen Affric spread out below as she had then. When the red-and-gray towers of Dundreggan came into view, her companion drew to a halt.

"See that track," he said, pointing.

"Aye."

"Follow it back down to the river, and ye'll easily find your way. Since we're already within sight of the ramparts, ye'll be safe from our pursuers. For that matter, if they approach from that end of the glen, everyone will have warning in minutes. If ye hear the horns, increase your pace, but ride gey carefully."

"Thank you," she said, noting that his accent had returned but saying nothing about that as she extended her hand politely.

He grasped it, and she could feel the warmth of his enfolding hers even through her gloves. She had not thought about her clothing for some time, but it occurred to her now that the ride had been more comfortable than she had expected.

"You won't believe this," she said, "but my clothes are nearly dry."

"I believe it because mine are, too," he said. " 'Twas the breeze, I'll wager."

"But —"

"Dinna waste time, lass. They'll be looking for ye soon."

She nodded, not wanting to think about that.

If Sir Alex had troubled himself to miss her, he might exert himself further and send someone in search of her, but she doubted that he would feel so energetic as to seek her himself. More likely, Lady Chisholm or Lady MacRae would raise the alarm when she did not appear for the midday meal. That would not be long, though, for the sun was already high in the sky.

Clicking her tongue, she urged the gelding forward as if to follow the track but glanced back as soon as the horse moved, doing so in such a way that it would not be obvious. As she had hoped, the Fox was already turning the stallion to the west. She glanced back again a moment later, but man and horse had vanished.

Drawing rein, she listened, hearing only the wind in the trees and the distant hushing of the river below. Satisfied that she could hear no hoofbeats, and that he would not hear her either, she turned the gelding and urged it back toward the hilltop. Having noted the barest trace of a second track, one that followed the line of the wooded ridge to the west, she believed that he had followed it. Her curiosity about him greater than ever now, she decided to see where he went.

Following the barely visible track through the trees, she soon caught a glimpse of movement ahead. Relieved to know she had been right about his direction, she hoped now that she could follow him to his lair without being caught. She did not want to think about what he would do if he did catch her.

After a time, the track bent downhill, away from the river, wending its way through shadowy, silent woodland into a declivity. As the trees grew thicker, it became harder and harder to discern the track, until it was almost invisible.

No longer certain of her direction, since the thick, green canopy of branches overhead hid the sun, she followed the track as much by instinct as anything else, but she still felt safe. These were his woods, after all. If he could ride through them safely, she could, too. In any event, he would come if she screamed, and although he would be angry again, he would let no real harm befall her. In time, too, she could surely find the river again, although she had not heard it for some time.

When the sun's rays penetrated the canopy ahead, she realized she was approaching some sort of clearing. To her surprise, it proved to be a narrow side glen with a burn bubbling down through it. She saw no sign of her quarry, however, and all she could hear was gurgling water.

Her sense of direction had failed her, and the sun high overhead was no help. For no reason that she could have explained, she turned uphill along the tumbling brook, but she had not ridden far before she saw the first hoofprint in damp sand near the water. Drawing rein, she realized that if the Fox had continued to ride beside the burn, she would see him ahead of her. Since she could not, either he had taken to the woods again, or he had found a ford and crossed the burn. Boulders dotted the opposite shore, some easily large enough to conceal a horse.

She wondered if he had seen her and lay in wait. The thought gave her pause, but curiosity outweighed concern, so she rode on and soon found more hoofprints. These, as expected, turned toward the water, shallow enough at that point to ford.

Riding across, she found a discernible track and followed it, keeping watch as well as she could in that terrain for any sign of him. There were no more hoofprints. The loose scree concealed them, and because she had to concentrate to follow the track, she nearly missed the entrance to the cave.

At first, she was not sure it was a cave, for it looked like a black shadow behind one of the largest boulders. But ahead she could see that the trail ended where the narrow waterfall that fed the burn tumbled from a high rocky cliff. A nimble person in clothing other than skirts might climb it, but a horse could not. Yet neither the stallion nor its rider was anywhere to be seen.

Dismounting, she tethered the gelding to a scrubby bush. Then, drawing a few deep breaths to steady her pounding pulse, she made her way as quietly as possible across the loose stones, behind the boulder, into the opening.

The boulder had masked its size, but although she saw now that it was easily large enough for a horse to pass through, she heard no sound from within its shadowy depths. The opening penetrated a solid rock wall, and she soon discovered that the passage turned, then turned again. When she reached the second turning, the dimming light from behind had faded away. Still, she heard no sound from within.

Scarcely daring to breathe, putting one foot ahead of the other with care and concentration, she eased forward, keeping a hand on the rock wall to guide her way. Surely, she thought, a horse would make noises that would echo through a cave.

Was that a light?

Peering into the blackness, she was certain she saw a distant flame.

The way to the tiny light seemed vast. She doubted that she could go even half so far without giving away her presence by stumbling on uneven ground, kicking a loose stone, or worse, plunging into some unseen hole or crevasse. To be sure, the passageway beneath her feet seemed as flat as Dundreggan's hall floor, but she knew that the ground in a cave was unlikely to be consistently level.

Even as the thought crossed her mind, the wall she had been touching to guide her way ended so abruptly that she nearly lost her balance when her hand met empty space. Awkward moments passed before she could breathe normally again.

She took two steps forward, then stopped, realizing that to go farther without light would be so dangerous as to be sheer folly. Even that tiny, distant flame had disappeared, and might well have been only a figment of her hopeful imagination.

The place was empty, and even if it were not, only an idiot would continue without knowing what lay ahead. With a sigh, she turned to leave, only to walk bang into the solid, muscular body that barred her way.

Startled nearly out of her wits, she shrieked and nearly collapsed, but two strong hands caught her hard by the shoulders and gave her a shake.

"When you follow a dangerous animal into its lair," he growled, continuing to hold her in that iron grip, "you should be prepared to pay the consequences."

Despite the threatening words and tone, she

felt only relief. "You frightened the liver and lights out of me," she said. Her throat was dry, but her body was already recovering from the shock.

"You deserve to be frightened."

She opened her mouth to respond, but his lips claimed hers before a word left her tongue.

His mouth was hot and moist against hers but soft and sensual. She realized with shock that he was wearing neither his mask nor his cloak.

Curious to see if he would stop her, she raised a hand to touch his cheek, realizing only as she did that she still wore her riding gloves.

His tongue pressed against her lips, demanding entrance, and she submitted at once, remembering the feelings he had stirred before when he had explored it so. Her body responded to his as it always did, and if she was aware of danger, it was only the danger of her own desire. She could not doubt for a moment that whatever he demanded of her she would do, but instead of frightening her, the thought sent a new flood of yearning through her. Stretching her arms around his neck while his hands moved over her body, exploring its curves, she recklessly pulled off her gloves and dropped them to the floor, determined to do some exploring of her own.

He moaned softly, deep in his throat, and a hand moved to cup a breast, his fingers brushing its tip. The sensations he stirred made it difficult for her to think of anything else, but she wanted to touch him, too, to feel his bare skin beneath her fingertips. Accordingly, she raised a hand again to his cheek, sighing with satisfaction when she felt the prickling of a half-day's growth of beard.

His lips moved to her right cheek and then to her ear, and his tongue darted inside it, tickling. She grasped his chin and pulled it around so she could find his mouth with hers again, kissing him hungrily, pressing her body against his, knowing she was wantonly encouraging him to explore more of her.

"I rode back to Ardintoul to see you again," he murmured against her lips.

"You did?"

"Aye, but you'd already left to return to Dundreggan."

Her mouth was still against his. "Should I apologize?"

Chuckling, he said, "This rig you're wearing is a damnable thing."

"It was a very fashionable riding dress before the river soaked it."

"It's dry now," he said, "and too bad, too. I'd happily have offered to hang it to dry for you."

"What, and stand around freezing in this cave whilst we wait for it?"

He chuckled. "We'd find ways of keeping warm. Indeed, I wonder if you know your danger, lass. Your virtue is presently at great risk."

"Is it?" she asked, affecting innocence.

To her chagrin, he gripped her shoulders again. His deep voice sounded hoarse as he said, "You need a lesson, sweetheart, and you'd be well served if I taught it to you, but although I have the reputation of a villain, no one has accused me yet of raping innocent maidens, nor shall they. What I should do instead is put you across my knee and smack that pretty backside of yours till you shriek. What do you mean by following me after you promised to go straight home to Dundreggan?"

"I never promised," she said, but the words sounded hollow even to her. It was one thing to equivocate after Patrick issued an arbitrary order. She had always felt clever on occasions when she managed to avoid giving him a promise she knew she would not want to keep. But somehow, with the Fox, equivocation seemed childish. It was unworthy of her and unfair to him.

He did not reply, which made her feel worse.

She could think of nothing to say, and she wished they could just go back to kissing, but that interlude was clearly over.

"Answer my question," he prompted. His tone was stern.

"The truth is that I rode out today a-purpose to find you," she said quietly, abandoning pretense. "Giorsal, my woman, said she had heard that you were in the area. But whilst I was looking for you, I saw the sheriff's men brutalizing that poor boy, and then you rescued me, but you were so angry . . ."

She hesitated, unable to find words to describe all she had felt.

"I never took you for a coward, lass."

"I'm not!" The words stung more than she had thought words could.

"If you know of danger to someone in the glen, their need is all that should concern you. My anger should not have deterred you."

"But the need is mine," she snapped, angry herself now.

"All the greater reason," he said.

She drew a breath and let it out, hoping to soothe nerves that were suddenly raw. "I do not know how it is that you can make me so angry with so little effort," she said. "Alex can do that, too. It's the only thing you two have in common."

"Alex?"

"Don't be a daffy! Alex Chisholm, of course."

"D'ye no call him *Sir* Alex?"

She wondered if he could possibly be jealous, but she would not allow him to divert her. "Do you want to know what I came to tell you," she demanded, "or do you want to stand in the dark quibbling over stupid details?"

"I expect ye'd like me to find a light."

"I certainly would not refuse one," she said innocently. "With you standing between me and the entrance to this place, I can see absolutely nothing."

"We'll do without the light," he said. "Even if

I could trust ye no to speak if ye were to see my features, lass —"

"I would never give you away!" It occurred to her even as she exclaimed the words that his accent had grown more noticeable again.

"I believe ye wouldna betray me intentionally," he said gently. His knuckles brushed her cheek, sending enough heat through her veins to melt all her defenses.

"I'd never tell anyone." Her voice was hoarse. She cleared her throat.

"Lass, I darena trust ye. If ye can speak the truth when ye tell Francis Dalcross's men ye've never seen my face, they may believe ye. Even then, they may not, because they will want more than anything to believe that ye can lead them to me. But if Chisholm believes ye, he may be able to protect ye."

"Would he not protect me even if he did not believe me?" The thought that he might not was disconcerting. She had never considered the possibility.

His tone altered to one she could not decipher as he said, "Chisholm has nae more use than Dalcross has for the Fox. Surely, ye've learned that much by now."

She did know that. She had not thought that his lordship's opinion could affect her, but somehow, she did not feel it would improve her position to say that.

"I do know that," she admitted. "He thinks you are an outlaw."

He drew an audible breath, then said abruptly, "What was your need?"

"Need?"

"Ye said 'twas your own need moved ye to find me."

"Aye." Suddenly, she felt more vulnerable than she had when he'd had his arms around her, when she had known she could not trust her own good sense to protect her from him. She had no idea how he would react when she told him, and she had a horrid feeling that if he did not react the way she hoped —

"Well?"

Men were so impatient.

"They want me to marry him."

"Marry whom?"

"Sir Alex."

"Who wants it?"

"My mother primarily. She made her mind up to it before we left Ardintoul, when Kintail told her he was taking us to Dundreggan."

"Did you know of this the evening I visited you at Ardintoul?"

"No, not then, although I might not have told you even if I had known," she added honestly. "When my mother first said there was to be a wedding, I thought I could fix things, but it begins to look as if I cannot."

"One always has a choice, lass. Just tell them you won't do it."

"It is just like a man to say that doing such a thing must be easy."

She felt him shrug. "Scottish women have a legal right to refuse any unwanted marriage. Just tell them you won't."

"I cannot. Even you cannot believe I can simply defy Chisholm or stand up before the priest and all the guests and declare that I won't go through with it. His lordship will not support me because he wants to honor my father's wish and because it will upset my mother if the wedding does not go forward. She . . . she is different now, happier, planning it," she added with a renewed surge of guilt.

"In truth, lass, I think marriage will be good for ye."

"What?" Her guilt evaporated. "You *want* me to marry him?"

"I can think o' worse fates. Marriage to Sir Alex will keep ye safe, and it will greatly increase your status. The wife o' the heir to Dundreggan will be a person o' consequence even at Jamie's court. Such a marriage would provide well for your future and that o' your children. Surely ye must think o' that."

"I don't care about any of that! Faith, do you think money and position are so important to me?"

"I think that only a young woman o' consequence could ask that question," he retorted. "If ye had none, ye'd appreciate it more, but I ha' often heard ye say 'we MacRaes,' lass. Would ye marry a man wi' no estate? I think not."

"But I don't care about such things, truly," she insisted. "And Sir Alex Chisholm is not the man I want to marry, no matter how much money or position he might have or how safe he might be. Safe!" She snapped out the word, scorn dripping from it. "I want a man of action, sir, one who cares more about righting injustices in the world than he cares about the cut of his coat."

To her shock he laughed.

"That is not funny!"

"Aye, sure, but it is. Am I to take it that ye'd rather marry me?"

If she had thought such a thing — which, she told herself firmly, she had *not* — she would swiftly have changed her mind. "I have no interest in marrying you. Why, I don't even know who you are!"

"Aye, well, just supposing that the notion *had* crossed your mind," he went on, his knuckles stroking her cheek again, "ye must see that I canna marry anyone."

"Never?" Her voice quavered on the word.

"Just think how it would be," he said. "What would happen if some villain captured my wife or my child?"

The thought sent a frisson of fear up her spine. "That would be dreadful."

"Aye, it would. Indeed, their very existence would destroy my ability to concentrate on my work. Even now, lass, you divert me. Only see where I am at this moment and what I am doing."

His fingertips touched her lips, and she had to exert herself not to kiss them.

"You tempt me to take chances when I should be exerting every caution. That Dalcross's men have twice seen you in my company means you must guard yourself well." Touching the tip of her nose with a finger, he added, "In future, you must think what you risk for us both before you go careering over the countryside."

"That is why you were angry with me."

"Aye, that and because you risked your life. My method of evading capture might have ended badly, you know. You could have broken your pretty neck."

"You, too, but we didn't."

"No, but you must take better care of yourself, lass. I was angry this time, but I knew you had not thought about the consequences. Now that you have been warned, you would be ill-advised to ignore my counsel."

His tone had changed again, sending another shiver up her spine.

"I'll take care," she promised.

"Good," he said, kissing her lightly on the lips.

"Have you got cat's eyes that you can see so well in here?" she demanded. "You seem to know exactly where everything is."

"I know where to find any part of you, sweetheart."

His voice was low in his throat now, and she

did not ask any more questions.

"Wait here," he said. "I'll fetch Dancer and take you back to the ridge."

"Don't forget your mask and cloak," she said dryly.

He chuckled.

Half an hour later, by a roundabout way, he led her to another place on the ridge from which she could see Dundreggan and a track that led down into the glen. But this time, after he kissed her, he gave the gelding a hard smack on the rump, startling it into a trot.

She recovered quickly and looked back to see him watching her. Waving, she urged the gelding on, knowing that the man watching her would make certain she could not follow him again. She did not intend to do so, but at the first opportunity, she did mean to search for the cave again.

Chapter 14

Watching her go, he felt an odd mixture of amusement, exasperation, and admiration. She was as unlike any other young woman he knew as one woman could be, and she fascinated him, but beyond any doubt, she was riding for a fall if he could not swiftly rein her in. Francis Dalcross and his men would eat her alive.

He waited only until he was certain she would not follow him again. Then, urging the stallion to a much faster pace than he had before, and taking a route much shorter and more direct than he generally used, he returned to the cave.

She was a danger to him, he reminded himself as he dismounted. He had even forgotten his common accent with her, and although he could hope she had not noticed, he could not be sure. Yet here he was, out in broad daylight again because he had suspected she would ride out alone and had been daft enough to want to meet her if she did. Now he had to hurry lest someone seek him at home.

It would take her nearly half an hour to reach Dundreggan from where he'd left her, but that might not be enough time.

Leading the stallion into the cave, he found

Hugo awaiting him, the grim expression on the man's face making his disapproval plain.

"I know exactly what you are bursting to say," he said. "I've already heard it, and I do not want to hear it again."

"I be right, sir, and so ye ken verra well."

"Aye, doubtless you are, you rascal, but life needs spice just as good food does, and Mistress Bab provides barrels of the stuff. I am enjoying myself too, more now than I did before she came to Glen Affric."

"Aye, sure, and ye be bound for perdition, most likely."

"Perhaps, but first I have something to do and a wee task for you to perform as well. When you have finished, look after Merry Dancer." He stroked the side of the stallion's neck.

"O' course I will," Hugo grumbled. "What will ye ha' me do first, then?"

"Listen carefully," Alex said, "and I'll tell you."

Ten minutes later, Alex emerged cautiously into the chapel through a small door behind the elaborately carved-oak rood screen. Through small apertures in the carvings he saw that the chamber was empty, so he quickly made his way to the private spiral stair that led to the family apartments and thus to his bedchamber.

Finding clothing that Hugo had laid out earlier, he quickly changed, for he was looking forward to his next scene with Mistress Bab. Peering critically at himself in the glass, he saw that his excitement showed. The deception he had elected to foist onto his family and friends troubled him frequently, but it had its amusing aspects too. He fully expected the forthcoming scene to be one of them.

Picking up a scented handkerchief from his dressing table, he inhaled deeply and felt his body relax into the customary, slouching posture that his languid alter ego affected. He dared not dash about now lest someone see him, but even his most unhurried strides covered distance. When he found his father in the hall, frowning, and the noon meal still not served, he felt only relief that she had not returned yet.

"Alex, there you are," Chisholm said curtly. "Mistress Barbara seems to have ridden out alone. I thought we had explained to her that she must not do that."

Alex shrugged. "My dear sir, I fear she pays me little heed. Try as I will, I lack the knack for issuing commands with sufficient authority to impress her."

Chisholm's eyes narrowed. "You would do better to acquire that knack then, or she will lead you a dance when you marry her."

"She is spoiled, sir, that is all. She has grown accustomed to crooking a finger and seeing her slightest wish obeyed."

"Fustian. No lass reared by Gilchrist MacRae can be spoiled."

"With respect, my dear sir, did you intend to ride out to look for her?"

Recalled to his purpose, Chisholm said brusquely, "Aye, I did, and you had better come with me, I suppose."

"I am happy to oblige you," Alex said. "Indeed, you may remain here to rest if you prefer. I shall doubtless find her soon."

"Very well, but see that you do," Chisholm said. "I have told them to put dinner back an hour, so I shall expect to see you both at table by then."

"I look forward to obliging you," Alex said, turning away to hide his grin.

A short distance from the castle, Bab saw a half dozen men riding toward her with Sir Alex in the lead. She had not hurried, for the sun being directly overhead, she was sure that the household must already have sat down to the main meal of the day. When she reached the river, the temptation to ride in the opposite direction had been strong. Only the thought of the Fox's most likely reaction to defiance of his command that she go straight to Dundreggan kept her from acting on it.

Nevertheless, she was not looking forward to the inquisition she would face on her return, for someone — Chisholm, most likely, or his lady — was bound to ask where she had been. And while she could truthfully say she had ridden onto the north ridge and into the woods beyond, even that would scarcely account for the hours she had been away and would doubtless lead to exactly the sort of recriminations she particularly wanted to avoid.

She saw Sir Alex draw rein and raise a hand to halt his companions.

Bab realized that he meant to wait for her to reach him instead of exerting himself to ride even the short extra distance to greet her properly. Although his dislike of exertion was well known, his manners were generally exquisite. Had Patrick chosen to wait like that, she would have known he was exceptionally displeased with her, even punishing her, but she could never be sure what Alex was thinking. Patrick would look stern. Alex looked as he always did, precise to a pin and vaguely happy to see her.

Holding her head high, she rode toward him, although with all the men staring at her, the distance seemed longer and the time to reach them endless. Her temper stirred. How dare he make a game of her!

When she was within thirty feet of them, Sir Alex gestured toward a point behind her and said something to his men that she could not hear.

One of the men exclaimed and pointed, and she looked back to see a rearing black horse against the cloudless sky at the top of the ridge. Its black-cloaked rider raised a hand and waved.

Realizing the Fox must have watched her the

whole way, she sighed in relief that she had not let temptation sway her to defy him, but she was annoyed with him too, for not trusting her, and she struggled to control that annoyance as she turned back to face Alex.

In a doublet and hose of his favorite cerulean blue, astride his well-groomed bay, he looked very handsome and not the least bit threatening. As she drew rein before him, he said, "You lads ride on ahead of us. We'll follow at our leisure."

One of the older men said diffidently, "I warrant his lordship would want us to stay wi' ye, Master Alex, particularly if he hears that *Sionnach Dubh* be near."

"Then do not tell him," Alex said in his foppish drawl. "Go on now, all of you. I would be private with Mistress Barbara, and you are very much in the way. His lordship intends for us to wed, you know, so go."

Bab's anger increased, and she barely waited for the men to wheel their mounts and gallop toward the castle before she said tartly, "Why did you say that to them? You must know that the more you speak of a wedding, the more likely everyone is to believe it must happen. Remember, sir, you promised you would not force me into a marriage I do not want."

"I won't," he said, "and I am sorry if you do not like it that I sent the lads on ahead of us, but you were frowning so that I thought you must have something to say to me that I would liefer they not hear."

"You thought I was angry with *you?*"

"Aye, were you not? You seem always to be in a fierce temper with me."

She forced a smile. "Not always, surely."

"Always," he insisted. "What have I done to arouse your ire this time?"

She remembered then that she had been irked that he made her ride to him instead of riding to meet her. But remembering, too, that he had seen the Fox, she nibbled her lower lip, wondering if it would be best to tell him or to turn the subject to something altogether different, like the splendid weather.

"You did not seem surprised to see him," Alex said quietly.

Suddenly, it was easy. "I was surprised," she said as they turned their horses toward Dundreggan, "but not as surprised as one might expect."

"I expected you to exclaim in delight at catching sight of your legend," he said with a smile. "Instead you just glanced at him and then kept riding toward us."

"I have something to tell you," she said, "and I do think it will be better if I explain it all before we reach Dundreggan."

"Then, by all means, tell me at once."

She did so as they rode slowly along, and she found it surprisingly easy to tell him everything. He expressed no anger, only bewilderment that she would fling herself into danger by confronting the sheriff's men.

"I did not fling myself," she said. "I did not know they would behave so."

"It was kind of you, in any event, to concern yourself for the lad's sake. Not many would have done such a thing."

Even when she described the way the Fox had snatched her from her saddle and plunged the great stallion over the cliff into the roaring river, Sir Alex said only, "By my faith, you amaze me! What happened next?"

Bab hesitated.

The Fox had said to tell him everything, but he had said that while they were still on the riverbank after their wild swim. Surely, he had not intended her to admit following him to his cave. If she admitted as much, would not Alex or his father insist that she lead them to that cave? And would they believe her when she said she could not remember where it was, even though that would probably prove true?

Alex raised his eyebrows. "Well, Bab?"

"I won't lie to you," she said, "but I do not want to describe everywhere I rode afterward. You will just have to be content knowing that I returned safely."

"I can certainly *pretend* to be content if you like," he said with a slight smile, "but I warrant my father will demand to know more."

"Must we tell him?" She tried to imagine that conversation. "He won't believe we rode off the cliff like that. He may decide I've made up the whole tale."

"Perhaps, but I do not think you need fear him. He used to beat his sons soundly when they misbehaved, of course, but he is ever gentle with the fair sex."

"Even you said I wanted beating," she reminded him sourly.

His eyes widened in astonishment, and his drawl became more conspicuous than ever as he said, "My dear Bab, whatever can have put such a notion into your head? Much as one hesitates to contradict a lady, and although I do not doubt that Patrick may have said such a thing to you, that you can accuse *me* . . ."

She had already remembered that he was not the one who had said it to her, and since she would not for anything admit to him that the Fox had, she said swiftly, "I beg your pardon! You are perfectly right. Not only does Patrick say it frequently, although thankfully, he has never done it, but Kintail also expresses the same sentiments on occasion. Since I was thinking earlier about how childish I'd been to throw that mug at you, and since I know exactly how either of them would have reacted, I suppose I must have put their words into your mouth."

"I can see how you might have done that," he said, his eyes twinkling.

She grimaced. "I know you are teasing me, sir, but I do still feel guilty about flinging that mug."

"Well, I own I'd as lief you not do it again,"

he said. "As to telling my father about your adventure —"

"Must we tell any of them?"

"Would you keep it all a secret, then?"

She nodded. "*Sionnach Dubh* saved me from a frightful ordeal," she said. "I would have to be a worse villain than Francis Dalcross to repay him by giving information about him to anyone. I won't do it, not even for your father."

"Not even for me?"

She shook her head. "No."

The gates stood just ahead, so she hoped he would not press her too hard to say more. It was not his way, but she wanted him to say he would not tell Chisholm.

He did not say anything for a time, and when he did, she discerned an enigmatic note in his voice that she had not heard before.

"You were alone with him for some time."

"Aye." The word was barely audible, because her breath had stopped in her throat. She wondered how much he would demand to know, and she wondered, too, if she could manage not to tell him that the Fox had kissed her or, worse, that she had kissed him back. That thought led to the next. What if he asked if she had met the Fox more often than today and the day he rescued her from Francis Dalcross? She did not want to lie to Alex, but how much dared she tell him?

"We can talk about that later perhaps," he said.

Keeping her voice carefully calm to conceal how much the answer mattered to her, she said, "You still have not said about telling your father."

"I don't think we need to trouble him straightaway with the details of your adventure," he said. "He may, of course, hear about them from other sources."

"Who would tell him?"

He reached out then and caught her horse's bridle, bringing both horses to a standstill. "You are not employing your usual keen wit, mistress," he said, looking directly at her but still employing his normal, light drawl. "You let the Dalcrosses' men see you again in the Fox's presence. Whether they tell the sheriff or his whelp, both will certainly come to know of it, and when they do, one or the other is going to demand information from you, and they will come here to seek it."

"I won't tell them anything," she said fiercely. "I know nothing that could help them. I've never seen his face, nor has he told me anything useful."

"Faith, mistress, there is no call for such heat," he said. "We will do what we can to protect you, of course. I just want to be sure you understand that your actions today will bear unhappy consequences."

Even the mention of consequences made her glad that Patrick was miles to the south, but she realized, too, that even if Alex did not tell his

312

father that she had been with the Fox again, Chisholm would learn soon enough. Remembering that the Dalcrosses' men had seen him snatch her from her saddle and plunge off the cliff with her, she wondered how she could have thought for a moment that she could keep it quiet. That part of the story would be all over the glens before dusk.

She sighed.

"I know that you have been bored at Ardintoul and probably at Dundreggan, too," Alex said in his mild way, "but I'd like you to promise me that you will not put yourself at risk again as you did today."

"I will be careful," she said. "I did not endanger myself purposely."

"Aye, perhaps, but danger often lurks unseen, ready to pounce when one least expects it, and I do not want to have to face Patrick if aught happens to you."

"He knows me too well to blame you," Bab said.

"And I know him, mistress. He expects me to keep you safe."

She saw that the gates had opened. Several Chisholm men-at-arms gazed curiously at them, clearly wondering why they had stopped.

"We MacRaes are not cowards, sir," she said, "but I confess I do not regret missing dinner, for I am in no hurry to face your parents or my mother."

"Ah, now, as to that," he said, "my father ordered the meal set back an hour, so you have not missed it, but we will not breathe a word of your adventures to anyone until we must. We do not want to distress anyone unnecessarily."

The last bit was so completely in keeping with his usual demeanor that she smiled wryly and said, "You just want to enjoy your dinner in peace."

He chuckled. "Mistress, when they learn what happened today, all three of our parents will demand to know why I did not prevent your folly. Believe me, I will take as many meals in peace as I can get before that time arrives, because afterward I shall likely never hear the end of it."

Satisfied that he would keep the matter to himself for as long as possible, Bab made no demur when he suggested that they ride on before some of the guards came to fetch them. She felt more in charity with him at that moment than she had since she had thrown the mug at him.

Claud was thinking hard, and since he was not skilled in that particular exercise, he was making heavy labor of it. It was unfair, he told himself, that he should be saddled with the great, unpredictable wizard Jonah Bonewits as a father and the invincible, even more unpredictable Maggie Malloch as a mother and have so little power of intellect himself. At least he had only five fingers on each hand and not six like his father. Nor did his hair radiate from his head like rays of a red sun, turning yellow at the ends, as Jonah Bonewits's hair did.

That was all to the good, he decided, but he still had to make some decisions, and he did not know which course of action would best serve his Highland charge.

He was glad they had reached the castle again, because he knew Mistress Bab would be safe within its walls as long as no one came seeking her there. He wanted to talk to Maggie, but Lucy had returned as soon as he and the gray gelding had reached dry land, and was sticking to him like a cocklebur.

"She's no helping us much, that lass o' yours," Lucy said as they shook the dust of the track from themselves and hurried inside. "It be a good arrangement, this marriage ye've arranged, and she likes him. I dinna ken why she'd be against it."

Claud shrugged. "Mayhap because she doesna like others ordering the course o' her life," he said, remembering his own feelings about that sort of thing in days not long past. "But I didna arrange this marriage, Lucy. Her own mam done that, as ye heard for yourself."

"Och, aye," Lucy said with a wink. "I ken how ye do things, Claud. Ye always make it look as if the doing were summat else."

"I had nowt tae do with this," Claud said tersely. "I dinna tell lies. Nor do I plunge me

315

friends in icy water," he added, voicing his primary grievance.

"Aye, well if ye didna do it, then it were that Catriona as did," she said blithely, "and dinna think ye'll persuade me otherwise, Claud, for ye won't."

Claud did not argue. The wedding might well have been Catriona's doing, for she had said herself that she wanted them to work together, and the most likely way to arrange that was to arrange a marriage between her Chisholm and his MacRae. He thought someone else had devised the plan before Catriona was in it, however, and that was only one reason that he wanted a word with his mother.

"Dinna be wroth wi' me, Claud," Lucy said coaxingly a few moments later as she leaned close and tickled his cheek.

For once, his body failed to respond instantly to her touch, and it occurred to him briefly that he had only her word that she did not, as he had believed, share Jonah Bonewits as a father. He remembered in that same fleeting shift of gray matter that Lucy *had* lied to him before. But even as the thought popped into his mind, it faded and was no more.

Bab's satisfaction with the way things had turned out after her adventure with the Fox lasted only until ten o'clock the next morning when she went out to the stables and asked Will to saddle her favorite gelding for her.

"That gray's come up lame, mistress," the gilly said. "Sir Alex said he thought it best to let it rest its leg a day or two afore ye ride it again."

"Show me," Bab said.

When she examined the indicated leg, she could detect no swelling and found nothing lodged in the horse's shoe. She frowned, but as she did, she had a clear mental vision of the gelding struggling after her in the turbulent river.

Knowing that it might easily have injured itself in its plunge off the cliff or during its struggle to reach the shore from the swiftly moving water, she patted its nose gently, murmuring a loving apology before she turned back to Will, saying, "I don't see anything amiss, myself. Still, I agree that the leg should rest, so you may saddle another horse for me today."

The gilly shook his head. "I canna do that, mistress, for I've no other lady's horse to give ye today."

"But surely her ladyship would lend me one of hers."

"Aye, and so she would, for she be ever generous," Will agreed, "but I had me orders earlier to put her horses out to graze in the high meadow. And nae pony we ha' in the barn be accustomed to skirts, so I canna put ye on one o' them."

"I am an excellent horsewoman," Bab said firmly, beginning to understand. "I warrant I can manage any horse you have in these stables."

"I dinna doubt it, mistress, for I ha' seen ye ride, but his lordship dinna hold wi' ladies riding spirited beasts, and I ha' to answer to him, ye ken."

Knowing she could win no battle against an opponent who lacked the authority to surrender, she considered approaching Chisholm directly, but her experience with him told her that he would most likely suggest that she ask Alex to go with her. And Alex, she recalled — also from experience — had a knack for putting obstacles in her path until the only course left to her was one he had suggested.

She found him at the high table in the hall, apparently just breaking his fast, because half of a manchet loaf, a pewter mug, a basket of fruit, and a jug of ale sat before him. The rest of the hall was empty except for a pair of gillies strewing fresh rushes on the lower hall floor.

Bab strode across to the dais and stepped onto it, coming to a halt directly across the table from him. He was neatly paring an apple and looked up only when she spoke his name. He did not stand or put down his knife or the apple.

"Forgive me," he said with a smile. " 'Tis childish, I know, but I am attempting to remove this peel in a single, unbroken paring."

"I want to ride, sir," she said bluntly, "but your Will tells me your stable can provide no suitable horse for me today."

"It is going to rain," he said amiably. "I wager you'd get no more than a step outside the gates before those clouds would open and half-drown you."

"Fie, sir, it is a beautiful morning, and even should it chance to rain later, if it does more than spit a bit, I shall be astonished."

"I should think you'd want to avoid getting soaked two days in a row."

Looking quickly over her shoulder to be sure no one else was within earshot, she said, "Pray, do not speak of that here. Someone will hear you."

"What if they do? 'Twas a perfectly innocent remark."

"It did not rain yesterday," she reminded him.

He smiled. "Suffice it to say then, mistress, that because matters here require my attention, I cannot ride out with you today."

"You need not do so. I can take Will or one of the other lads if I must."

"I would prefer that you wait until I can escort you myself. As you know, my father prefers that I do."

"So it is as I suspected," she said, putting her hands on her hips. "You mean to keep me a prisoner inside these walls because of what happened yesterday."

"A prisoner?"

"You know what I mean," she said grimly.

"I know you would be wise to avoid venturing out until we know what Francis Dalcross and the sheriff mean to do," he said. "But you are not a prisoner, mistress. What devilish hosts you must think us even to imagine such a thing!"

For a brief moment, guilt stabbed her, but sharp on its heels came anger. "That is precisely how you do it," she snapped. "You *are* devilish, because you pretend to be kind and light-minded when, in fact, you manipulate others so that they must do what you want them to do. That makes you even worse than ordinary men who simply issue orders and expect them to be obeyed."

He cocked his head and said with a teasing smile, "So you think I am extraordinary, do you?"

Without thought, she snatched up the jug of ale in both hands and dashed the contents in his face, startling him so that he leaped to his feet. Knife and peel went flying in one direction, apple in the other, as he grabbed blindly for a napkin.

Still holding the jug, appalled at what she had done, Bab stared at him in horrified astonishment as he blotted the ale from his eyes and face.

When he lowered the napkin just enough to look directly at her, for an instant, the fury blazing in his eyes frightened her, but then he shut them for a long moment, and when he opened them and put the napkin down, the fury had gone.

He said, "I see that I have not lost the knack of irritating you, mistress. Pray forgive me for speaking so thoughtlessly. You have had your revenge though, because I am sure you have ruined my fine doublet."

With a sound halfway between a curse and a shriek of exasperation, she stormed from the hall.

Alex watched her go as he continued to wipe dripping ale from his face, head, and doublet. His sense of the ridiculous, while always active, extended itself only so far, and he decided that the lass should consider herself lucky on two counts. One was that the table had stood between them, and the other was that he had learned through bitter childhood experience with two teasing older brothers to control his volatile temper.

Rob and Michael had often enjoyed teasing him until he lost his temper and then dunking him in the icy river or doing some other horrid thing to teach him better manners, as they would afterward explain to him. They had toughened him with such treatment, but they had also taught him the wisdom of keeping his own counsel and playing least in sight if he wished to take revenge. In fact, he realized, his brothers had done much by their actions to make him the man he was today.

His flash of temper over, he was able to smile again. At least, Mistress Bab would not be riding into danger again before they knew exactly what Francis Dalcross had in mind for her. He would prefer simply to tell her to stay inside and explain his reasons, but her attitude toward the foppish Sir Alex was so dismissive that he doubted she would obey him and did not want to deal with the consequences if she fell into Dalcross's hands again through her own willful disobedience. That his own deceptions exacerbated the situation did not escape his notice.

As penance, he would endure Hugo's no doubt stringent comments on the spoiling of another fine doublet, and would do so without protest or rebuke.

Having managed to elude Lucy at last, Claud hurried to his mother's parlor, hoping to find her in. He did not understand the power Lucy had to winkle his thoughts away from important matters back to her twinkling self, but she certainly had that power and used it frequently. He did not usually mind, either — indeed, he had strong feelings for her that had not diminished even after learning that they shared the same father or his own dousing in the river. But he had learned, too, that things were not always as they appeared to be or as others declared they were.

The only one he trusted absolutely was Maggie Malloch.

She was not at home when he got there, but he had no sooner settled himself in his favorite chair in the parlor than she returned.

"What's amiss?" she demanded, flicking a finger to start a fire in the fireplace, and then flicking it again to light more candles in their sconces.

He watched her, biting off the urge to ask why she should assume something was amiss, because she always seemed to know what he was thinking.

She ignored his silence while she wiggled her finger again over the little white pipe she held. A thin stream of white smoke curled from it in response, and she took a deep puff before she said, "Well, lad, out wi' it now."

"I dinna ken what tae do," Claud blurted. "I thought it were a fine notion tae put Mistress Bab lass wi' the Chisholm heir. 'Twere a good match, I thought."

"Is it no a good match, then?"

He grimaced. "She doesna care for him. At least —"

"I ken your dilemma, lad," she interjected with a wave of the pipe. "She may dislike bits o' the two parts, but d'ye truly think she doesna care for the whole man?"

"She just upended a jug o' ale over the whole man! I dinna ken wha' tae do!"

"I canna help ye," she reminded him.

"Ye can if ye give equal help tae Catriona," Claud said.

"But we dinna ken where Catriona be."

"Ye still canna find her?"

"I havena looked. Since your Lucy apparently rendered Catriona helpless, I ha' given more help tae her side as I be bound, tae equal matters, but ye must still do your part alone tae succeed in fulfilling your share o' the bargain."

"But I canna decide what tae do," Claud protested. "Just when I thought I had matters in hand, the lass up and doused him wi' ale."

After taking another thoughtful puff on her pipe, Maggie said, "I dinna think I'll be breaking any rules an I tell ye a wee secret about making decisions."

"What?"

"The secret be tae think a bit and then tae make one," she said.

"But what if my thinking be wrong or I make the wrong decision?"

"If ye look tae keep the lass safe and happy, ye'll make the right ones more often than no, but 'tis better tae make a decision even an it proves wrong than tae dither and make nae decision at all. That path only opens the way for your enemies tae prevail, Claud, and that ye must never do. Now, off wi' ye, or we'll ha' half the Circle here, demanding tae ken what mischief we be brewing."

Reluctantly, he obeyed, but he could not believe her advice would aid him much, despite her vast powers and vaunted wisdom. It did occur to him, however, that keeping Mistress Bab's enemies at bay until he could decide what to do might be a good first step to take. A tiny adjustment in the weather might help with that.

Chapter 15

If Bab had not felt guilty at once, she did as she hurried up to her chamber. When Alex did not follow her, she was oddly disappointed but also relieved. What demon, she wondered, possessed her to throw things at him? In truth, he had done no more than express concern for her, and when she had railed at him for it, instead of scolding her as most men would have, he had made a joke. Why had her temper snapped as it had, and why could he stir it so easily?

To make matters worse, an hour later it began raining heavily, just as he had predicted it would. And that evening, although it stopped for a time, the skies remained ominous. For the next two days, during and between cloudbursts, the air crackled with lightning and grumbled with thunder. And when Bab found herself in a room with Alex, the air between them seemed to crackle in much the same way.

She could think of nothing to say to him that might ease the tension between them, and he did not initiate conversation other than to inquire politely how she had slept or ask if she would try some sauce or other at table. It occurred to her that she could simply apologize to him, but the thought rankled and she dismissed it.

With no sign of the sheriff or his son by Friday morning, she would have liked to ride even if it meant asking Alex to go with her. But with the weather still as heavily charged as it was, she knew that to ride for mere pleasure would be foolhardy. Her gray, like most horses, hated thunder and lightning, and it occurred to her that the intermittent thunderstorms might be why the Dalcrosses had failed so far to seek her out for questioning, if they intended to do so.

Before the skies cleared, other matters had claimed her attention.

The first occurred late that morning when, with a pause in the rain if not the thunder, and fed to the teeth with confinement, she opted to stride energetically around the bailey to enjoy the fresh air. She was not alone, of course, for besides men and lads busy with their usual chores, others engaged in swordplay, a pair wrestled near the gates, and others had set up an archery butt near the stable and were engaged in target practice.

As she rounded a corner of the keep and drew near the jutting chapel wing, a hiss startled her. Pausing, she glanced around the busy yard.

"Hsst! Here, mistress."

A two-wheeled cart containing evidence of a load of wood stood tilted in the corner where the chapel wall extended from the one by the postern door of the keep.

Movement behind the cart drew her closer until she spied a wild thatch of damp, tousled red hair and the scared face and wide blue eyes of the boy she had rescued from the sheriff's men. "You!" she exclaimed. "What are you doing here?"

"They be a-looking for me, mistress. I came here and slipped inside when they opened the gates this morning."

"Without anyone seeing you?"

"I be small, and the rain were pouring down. I slipped in beside another cart and hid till I could sneak in back here. Ye'll no tell anyone!"

"No," she said. "What is your name?"

"Gibby Cannich o' Glen Urquhart," he muttered. "What'll ye do, mistress?"

Bab thought swiftly. Dundreggan was certainly the safest place for him until the Dalcrosses' men found something else to divert their attention. But if she sought Chisholm's protection for him, would not his lordship instantly hand the lad over to them if they could claim legal grounds for detaining him?

"Dinna stare," Gibby pleaded. "They'll wonder why ye be standing here."

She had already decided what to do. "Don't move," she said, as she glanced over her shoulder to be sure no one was looking their way. Reassured, she strolled casually to the postern door and tried the latch, relieved to find that it moved easily. Opening the door, she said, "Make haste now. Slip along near my skirt and inside."

"I canna go in there! They'll hang me for a thief!"

"I won't let them. You can hide in the chapel until I find you a better place."

Claud grimaced when they went into the chapel, for he had no power in kirks or other religious places. No member of the Secret Clan did, as far as he knew, so he wished Mistress Bab would stay clear of the place. He slipped in before she shut the door, to keep watch, hoping nothing awkward would happen while he was there.

Bab quickly found a corner at the back of the chapel containing two breast-high stacks of wooden chests behind which the boy could hide. "Stay there until I return," she said. "I'll try to find somewhere better for you, but barring that, I shall at least bring you food and water."

"Aye, I'm fair gut-foundered," he said.

"And wet to the skin, I'll wager."

"Och, aye, but I'm used to that. I'll no melt."

Chuckling, Bab left him. But she soon discovered that although it was easy enough to provide a jug of water, a couple of rolls from her dinner, and a shawl of her own for warmth, finding somewhere else to hide him was not so easy, and she knew he could not stay in the chapel indefinitely. It occurred to her then to hope that he was civilized enough not to relieve himself there if his need grew strong.

Her mother and Lady Chisholm invited her to join them in the latter's bower, where she obediently took up some needlework to occupy her hands while her mind continued to busy itself with the urchin's problem. But the solution still had not presented itself when, an hour later, a maidservant entered to say that Chisholm desired a word with her.

There was nothing ominous in the words or in the maidservant's tone, but when Bab hesitated, the girl said, "His lordship did say 'straightaway,' mistress."

Glancing at Lady Chisholm and seeing her frown, Bab tried to ignore the sudden fluttering in her stomach and said, "Will you excuse me, madam?"

"Of course, my dear. I wonder what he can want with you."

Since Bab could imagine only that someone had found her uninvited guest or that Francis Dalcross or his father had arrived with a squadron of men to demand to know what she could tell them about the Fox, it was with profound relief that she entered Chisholm's private chamber to find him alone.

"You sent for me, my lord?"

"Aye, lass," he said, frowning slightly. "I've sent for Alex, too, because I want to talk to you both about this wedding of yours."

"The wedding?"

"Aye," he said. "But where the devil is the lad? I don't want to have to explain my — Oh, good, you're here," he exclaimed as the door swung open again to reveal Alex at the threshold. "Come in, come in. I was just about to tell Mistress Barbara that I think it may be wise for us to put your wedding forward."

With a gasp, Bab turned to see what Alex would say.

He stepped in and gently but firmly shut the door. Then, plucking a bit of lint from his sleeve, he murmured, "I was not aware that anyone had set a date."

"No one has as yet," Chisholm said.

"Faith, sir, and here I was, thinking that you and Lady MacRae had arranged everything for us by now," Alex said, dabbing his lips with his handkerchief.

Chisholm eyed the gesture with blatant disapproval but did not comment on it or condemn his son's flippancy. Instead, he said, "Unfortunately, I've just received word from Inverness that Sheriff Dalcross, or more likely that fiendish son of his, intends to present himself here Monday morning with a large show of arms and demand to question Mistress Barbara about the outlaw, *Sionnach Dubh*."

Alex shot a look from under his brows at Bab. Despite the gasp he had heard, she looked pale but unafraid, giving him to hope that she had herself well in hand despite her undoubted frustration at having been cooped up for days.

Returning his attention to his father, he said, "What exactly did you hear?"

"That Francis Dalcross's men reported seeing her with the Fox again. I cannot think how such rumors begin, Alex, but we can be sure that Dalcross will make the most of it, so we must do anything we can to prevent her arrest."

"Aye, Francis will arrest her if he can concoct a suitable charge."

"I don't know what has possessed the scoundrel to be spouting such nonsensical rumors," Chisholm said angrily. "That he could think our Barbara would have anything more to do with that Fox! Why, if I had my way —"

"It is true, sir," Bab said quietly.

"What?"

Alex nearly smiled. The lass never ceased to amaze him. She had courage enough for ten men, let alone for one slender lass perched on the brink of womanhood. He had admired her beauty from the moment he had become aware of it. Her quick wit and sharp tongue had long amused and entertained him, and he relished her headstrong spirit. As to her courage, he had long ago recognized it and roundly condemned it when it led her to take dangerous risks. Now, with this further proof that her integrity matched that courage, he remained silent, letting her take the lead.

Chisholm glared at her in the same forbidding way that had made a much younger Alex's knees quake with terror. Mistress Barbara, however, met his father's dour gaze without blinking.

Chisholm said, "Perhaps you would care to explain yourself, mistress."

"Frankly, sir, I'd prefer to do nothing of the sort," she said with a rueful smile. "You are going to be furious, and I cannot blame you in the least."

To Alex's surprise, his father's expression softened. "Suppose you tell me what happened, lass," Chisholm said evenly. "I shall decide whether to be angry or not after I have heard your tale."

"Faith, but I think I'd have benefited from having a sister," Alex murmured.

"Hold your impudent tongue, sir," Chisholm snapped.

"Yes, my lord," Alex said meekly.

Bab glanced at him, but when he gazed limpidly back at her, she returned her attention to Chisholm. "You were kind enough not to scold me for riding out alone the other morning or to demand to know where I went, sir," she said. "Accordingly, I failed to reveal what happened when I did."

"Happened? Faith, lass, what can you mean? Did someone harm you?"

"No, sir, because I escaped."

"Best to begin at the beginning," Alex said dulcetly.

His father looked ready to snap at him again but instead, after shooting a stern look at him from under his eyebrows, he merely gestured for Bab to continue.

She did so, telling much the same tale that Alex had heard and stopping at the same point, when she and the Fox had safely reached the riverbank.

"Bless my soul," Chisholm exclaimed, "what an extraordinary tale! If you were anyone else, lass, I must admit that I'd not believe a word of it."

"Well, if you do believe it, sir, it is more than I expected," Bab said.

"In sooth, I doubt you have experience enough to concoct such a tale."

"She does possess a remarkably vivid imagination," Alex murmured.

Bab's gaze shot daggers at him, but Chisholm said flatly, "Mistress Barbara would not lie to me."

"No, sir," Alex said.

"Thank you, my lord," Bab said. "I certainly would not."

"Aye, lass, but that puts us back where we began, for there is nothing else we can do now. I will do my possible to protect you from the Dalcrosses and their hired villains, but if you did intervene in a lawful arrest, the sheriff has the law on his side and I shall have little power against him. The only thing that might strengthen my position would be if you were indeed my daughter-in-law. Therefore —"

"But, my lord —"

"Do not interrupt," Chisholm said austerely.

Alex held his tongue, wondering how the lass would deal with this.

"I beg your pardon, sir," she said stiffly, "but I do not want to be forced into marriage merely to avoid questions into a matter that . . . that —"

"— that is no affair of the Dalcrosses," Alex interjected, hoping he would draw his father's fire to himself long enough for her to regain her wits.

"You will be silent, Alex," Chisholm said.

"Certainly, sir, but I hope you have not forgotten that I, too, figure in this wedding. I am your obedient son, as always, but I would be loath to coerce Mistress Bab into marriage or to conspire with anyone else to do so."

"You will do as I command!"

"Yes, sir, without doubt, but —"

"I will send for Parson Fraser," Chisholm said as if he had not spoken. "He can hold his kirk services here Sunday and perform the wedding at the same time."

Alex saw that Bab had turned pale.

The little voice in his head said, "It will be well, ye'll see. It be for the best, but remember, ye must hold her tae making the decision. It willna do tae take her part wi' out ye ken her true feelings, and none can ken those but herself."

For the first time, the voice had a truly feminine lilt to it, and his mind's eye presented him with a brief, hazy picture of a sturdily built little woman, holding a peculiar white implement from which a stream of smoke curled.

He blinked, rejecting interest in anything but Bab. He willed her to look at him, hoping he could somehow let her know that everything would be all right, but she stared straight ahead, her lips pressed together, her eyes flashing anger. He hoped she would have sense enough not to rip up at Chisholm. His father was much his usual self again, so no one could predict how he would react to such an eruption.

"That is all," Chisholm said, summarily dismissing them both. "You need not tell your mothers about this, either of you. I'll do that myself."

Bab had all she could do not to blurt out the angry words that leaped to the tip of her tongue, but she was not a fool, and she knew that losing her temper would only make him react the same way that any powerful man reacted to defiance.

An oblique glance at Alex's face told her he was concerned about what she might say. Well, he need not fret, for she would not say or do anything cork brained. At least she would not if she could get out of the room before anger overcame her good sense. She had stirred her father's ire and Patrick's more than once, and in her experience blatant defiance never resulted in anything good.

"Perhaps you would like to stroll along the gallery," Alex said gently.

Grateful that the tension between them seemed to have eased, she nodded, rested a hand on his arm, and let him take her from the room. They walked in silence to the far end of the gallery where it overlooked the great hall before she said, "I have not changed my mind, sir. Why do you not simply tell him that you object to being pushed into a marriage you do not want?"

"But I have no objection to marrying you," he said.

"No objection!" Somehow, those two words angered her more than anything else he had done or said. "You promised!"

"Aye, I did, and I will keep that promise. But I also said, did I not, that if you insist upon defying your mother and my father, you will have to do it on your own. I'll support your right to refuse, Bab, but I'll not start the fight with them for you."

"Are you such a coward then or just too weak to defy your father?"

"Neither, but nor do I see cause to act against my own interest when you seem to be of two minds about it yourself. You must have noticed that my father has suffered much as your mother has since Sir Gilchrist's death, and for similar reasons. First he lost his dear friend, and before he'd had time to recover, my brothers' murders left him with the last and least able of his sons to succeed him."

She barely heard anything after his suggestion that she was of two minds about their wedding. Much as she wanted to deny it, she could not form the words. As she wondered if his accusation could be true, she heard the last of what he said.

"I'm sure he does not think of you as the least of his sons."

"When I returned from the Continent," he went on quietly, "I found him as you saw him at Stirling and when you traveled here with him. Instead of the vibrant, temperamental man I had left behind, I found one who rarely cared enough to raise his voice in anger. He paid little heed to what the Dalcrosses did, other than to say he was sure they were heeding the law since it was their duty to uphold it."

"But Sheriff Dalcross does things that his lordship would never do."

"Just so, although I believe his son is the one responsible for all our ills," he said. "The sheriff is merely his cipher. Still, I trust you understand my reluctance to defy my father in this, since you feel the same reluctance to defy your mother."

"But it has been much worse with her. Your father just seems abstracted and pensive, and he sleeps more than one would expect of such a man. My mother disappears into another world and talks to beings that do not exist."

"Are you so certain that they do not?" he asked with a smile.

Bab stared at him. "Of course I am," she said. "Pray, do not mock my concern for her, sir."

"I promise you I was not doing that," he said, laying a hand on her shoulder. "It is only that I begin to wonder sometimes if we have slipped into another world."

A tremor shot through her when he touched her, and the sensation disturbed her, because it was like the feeling that swept through her body whenever the Fox touched her or stood too near. Had she turned into a woman who would react so to any man? The thought horrified her, but his hand felt warm on her shoulder, and despite her erratic thoughts, it comforted her and made it easier to think.

She looked into his eyes, finding serenity there but wondering if his concern for his father was the only reason he was willing to marry her and hoping in the same jumble of thoughts that his willingness would not prevent him from keeping his promise to her. "You will still support me whatever I do, will you not?"

"Aye, lass, I have said I will. I do not go back on my word."

"Good," she said, "because I shall depend on you to keep it."

"That lass be verra strong minded for a mortal," Lucy Fittletrot complained.

"Aye," Claud agreed. He certainly couldn't argue the point, for the harder he had tried to implant the notion of making a worthy sacrifice in Mistress Bab's mind, the more strongly did she resist it.

"At least the man seems willing enough," Lucy said.

Claud peered at her searchingly. "Look here," he said. "Ye didna put a spell on him, too, did ye?"

"Too?" She gazed innocently at him.

"Ye said ye put one on Catriona," he reminded her.

"Och, aye, I did that," she said. "And ye should be grateful, Claud. She would only ha' caused problems, as ye'd ken fine did ye but think wisely on it."

"Ye didna answer me about him, though." He was being very clever, he thought, to notice that she had not answered his question.

"I put nae spell on him," Lucy said, adding simply, "I had nae need for it."

She snuggled closer, using her fingers and lips to good purpose, and in no time he was helping her remove her gauzy lavender gown. As he moved his lips to one perfectly formed breast, she murmured, "Ha' ye decided about yon wedding then, Claud?"

"Aye," he murmured, blowing gently across the nipple and watching it pucker, enjoying her little gasp of pleasure. "Marriage will make the lass safer, and thus it be the best service we can render tae her. I ha' decided."

"And a fine decision it is," Lucy said, curling herself around him as she loosened his clothing.

Believing that her brief stroll with Alex had strengthened her resolve, Bab excused herself and returned to Lady Chisholm's bower, certain that she now had the fortitude to make her position clear even to her mother. But when she entered the room, she found the two ladies in deep conversation with Fiona Mackintosh, her erstwhile hostess at Gorthleck House, the night following her abduction.

"Mistress Mackintosh and her son Eric have been visiting cousins in the next glen," Lady Chisholm said. "The thunder having eased there, they took advantage of the lull and rode over to spend the night with us."

"I'm surprised you did not see Eric," Mistress Mackintosh said as Bab made her curtsy, "for he went in search of Sir Alex as soon as we arrived. Doubtless he found him straightaway, though, and they have been closeted together since."

Bab smiled, saying only that she had not yet had the pleasure of seeing Eric Mackintosh. Then she fell silent, striving to contain her impatience while Mistress Mackintosh chattered away, sharing all the gossip she had collected since their last meeting. Lady Chisholm's enjoyment of her guest was plain to see, and to

Bab's surprise, Lady MacRae's eyes were likewise bright with interest.

Concerned about young Gibby and what she was to do with him, Bab was about to excuse herself to look in on him when Lady Chisholm said, "Surely, Fiona, you and Eric can stay more than just one night."

"Oh, no, for we have not come so far, you know. Moreover, Mackintosh remains with my cousin's family and expects us to return there tomorrow."

"But you must stay through Sunday at least," Lady MacRae interjected. "My Barbara and Sir Alex are to be married then, and with so little time to set the news about, we will be sadly shy of guests."

Bab stared at her mother. "How did you know?" she demanded.

Mistress Mackintosh looked at her in surprise. "I should think your mother would know your wedding date before anyone else, my dear. We will certainly stay for the ceremony. Indeed, I shall send for Mackintosh to join us here."

Lady Chisholm's obvious bewilderment reinforced Bab's certainty that Chisholm had not yet had time to inform either his wife or Lady MacRae of his plan. How, then, had her mother known? Lady MacRae's belief in the date's accuracy was evident by the way she nodded and smiled.

Lady Chisholm said gently, "Are you certain that the date is set, Arabella?"

"Oh, yes," she replied. "Chisholm will tell you quite soon, I believe."

Certain that that much was true, Bab hastened to excuse herself before he could do so, wishing she could find the Fox and confer with him about what to do.

Even if he thought the match a good one, surely he would not want her to be trapped into it. Perhaps he might somehow spirit her away until she could persuade Sir Alex or her mother to call off the wedding. As that thought crossed her mind, however, the urgency she felt about it faded and her thoughts shifted again to young Gibby. Clearly, she had to find somewhere else to put him and quickly, before folks began to prepare the chapel for her wedding.

Unfortunately, the keep bustled with people, its usual inhabitants augmented by men who had escorted the Mackintoshes. It had been easy enough to spirit Gibby inside the chapel, the entrance to which lay just inside near the postern door. However, to sneak him higher into the keep would be to risk discovery at almost any turn. A peek down the stairway that led to the chapel entrance showed her that servants still bustled about on the lower level. They would continue to do so until their evening chores were done and they had sought their beds, so she would be wiser not to risk entering the chapel again until the keep had settled for the night.

At a standstill, she retired to her bedchamber

343

where she could be sure of being alone with her thoughts, but the only one of these that consoled her was the possibility that the Fox might yet take another hand in the game. Was it not his business to help people in trouble?

Having parted from Bab at the stair end of the gallery, Alex went to his bedchamber, hoping to find Hugo. The man was not there, however, so he slipped quietly down the little stairway that led directly to the chapel.

As he stepped in and turned toward the rood screen and the little door that it concealed, a scuffling sound from the rear of the chamber stopped him in his tracks.

His keen ears detected another soft sound, and he easily identified its position behind the chests of altar cloths and other furnishings at the rear. The space there, he knew, was too narrow to contain anyone very large.

The door into the chapel from the lower service area was closed, but he could hear noises indicating human industry on the other side. A shout would bring instant aid, should he require it, but he doubted that he would, and he was curious.

Moving nearer the chests, he said quietly but nonetheless authoritatively, "Come out of there at once."

Silence greeted him.

"If I must pull you out, or if you should be so unwise as to try to tip over those chests, it will be very much the worse for you," he warned. "Come out now."

"Aye, then, I'm coming. Hold your breeks on, man."

"Insolence will not avail you much, my lad," he said to the scruffy, redheaded urchin who emerged, carrying a water jug. "Who are you and what are you doing there?"

"Me name's Gibby Cannich and the lady put me here."

"The lady, eh?" Having no trouble deducing who the lady must be, Alex struggled to maintain his stern demeanor. "A gey beautiful lady with black hair?"

"Aye, she's well enough, I expect. She put me in here, though, so if ye're meaning to hand me over to the sheriff's louts, she'll be wroth wi' ye."

"I expect she will," Alex agreed, "but you cannot stay here, Gibby Cannich. I collect that you hail from Glen Urquhart, do you not?"

"Aye, then, but I'm to stay away from there till the sheriff's men forget about me," the boy said. "I didna ken where else to go, but I did learn that the lady lives here, so I came and looked for her." He hesitated, glanced at the jug, then added airily, "She gives me this jug wi' water in it, but she didna give me a slops jar, so after I drank the water, I had to piss in it. So wha' should I do wi' it now?"

Choking back laughter, Alex said, "Put it on the floor for now." When the lad had obeyed, he added, "You are an enterprising soul, but I cannot leave you here, so I think you'd better come with me. I'm going to blindfold you, though."

"Here now, ye canna do that," Gibby protested when Alex opened one of the top chests and took a purple priest's stole from the extra vestments folded therein.

"You hold your whisst," he said. "I don't want your prattling to bring anyone else in here. Now, turn around," he added as he folded the long cloth lengthwise. "I promise you'll be safe with me, for I won't hand you over to the sheriff or his men, but you must not know the route by which I take you out of here."

"Likely, ye'll murder me and fling me body in yon river," the boy muttered.

Alex chuckled but did not argue, tying the silk stole over the lad's eyes, then picking him up and walking back and forth and up the stairs and down with him until he hoped he would have no idea which way they went. Then he made for the door behind the screen, slipping through it and quietly down the dark stairway.

As he had hoped, he found Hugo in the great cavern in Dancer's chamber, brushing the splendid horse and talking quietly to it.

The man turned at the sound of his steps and stood staring at him for a long minute in disapproving silence. Then he growled, "What are ye about now, sir?"

"The lass stowed young Gibby Cannich here in the chapel to hide him from the sheriff's men," Alex said, standing the boy on his feet and stripping off the blindfold. "Gibby, this is Hugo. He is going to look after you for a time."

"I am?" Hugo frowned at the boy, who was gazing raptly at Dancer. As Gibby turned from the stallion to eye Alex more shrewdly, Hugo said, "Ye'll bring us to ruin yet, I'm thinking, wi' your impetuous starts."

"Aye perhaps, but we've time yet," Alex said, returning the lad's gaze steadily as he added, "Wee Gibby and I mean to trust each other for now. In any event, I cannot let him or the lass run tame in the chapel, and I've promised not to let him fall into the sheriff's clutches, so here's what I want you to do." He explained quickly and then, when Hugo had diverted the lad's attention by setting him to brush the stallion, Alex slipped away and returned to the chapel.

Picking up the erstwhile water jug, he carried it with him to his bedchamber where he emptied it into the close-stool pot and left the jug by the stool for Hugo to dispose of.

Young Gibby, he knew, would require watching, since it was clear that his suspicions had been aroused. But at least the lad had shown sense enough to keep them to himself and had not pelted them with questions. Hugo would watch him closely and keep him safe.

Alex found himself wondering what, if anything, he would tell Bab about the lad. She clearly cared about his fate, and he did not want her to worry or fret over what had become of him, but he could hardly explain what he had done with him.

A few moments later, a gilly rapped on the door to tell him that Eric Mackintosh had come to Dundreggan and was asking for him.

"Is he indeed," Alex drawled. "Then I must go to him straightaway."

Chapter 16

Supper was a cheerful meal, and since Bab could do nothing to address any of her concerns, she relaxed and enjoyed herself. Eric Mackintosh, a thin gentleman with pale blond hair and blue eyes, was as talkative as his mother and as charming.

When the subject of politics arose, as it often did in the glens, both Mackintoshes roundly condemned Sheriff Dalcross and his son. Therefore, the only sour note occurred when Eric expressed admiration for the Fox, and Chisholm replied curtly that the less said about that fellow, the better. Lady Chisholm deftly turned the subject, however, and the tense moment passed swiftly.

Conversation remained general and included only a brief mention of the wedding. Bab realized then that Chisholm had spoken to his lady and that everyone took it for granted that the ceremony would go forward as and when he had decreed. She hoped to find an opportunity to speak privately with her mother, but although she managed to draw her aside as they arose from the table, it availed her nothing.

"Not now," Lady MacRae said briskly. "Not when Nora needs our help to entertain Fiona

Mackintosh, who is very kind, to be sure, but she does prattle on and on, so that if one had to be alone with her, one would seek the slightest excuse to take to one's bed. Therefore, we must not abandon Nora."

It occurred to Bab that her mother was proving uncharacteristically chatty herself for once, but she said only, "Perhaps you will grant me a few private moments of your time before you retire, madam."

"Oh, not tonight, dearling, I beg you. I know exactly how it will be. When I finally reach the peaceful sanctuary of my chamber, I shall want to go straight to bed, for I am not accustomed to keeping these late hours, you know, and I want to be well rested for your wedding."

"How did you learn that it is to take place on Sunday?" Bab asked. "I did not know that myself until shortly before you spoke of it."

Lady MacRae blinked. "Chisholm must — No, it was Herself who told me."

"Herself? Pray, who is that?"

Lady MacRae looked bewildered. "Why, how strange! Her name was on the tip of my tongue, but now I cannot recall it. And so it is every time. Oh, but I do remember now that I was not to mention it to anyone. I should not have told you."

Bewildered, Bab said, "That I am to be married?"

"That the ceremony had been set for Sunday."

"Well, but that is why I wanted to talk —"

Lady MacRae hushed her with a gesture. "Not now." Her level of agitation increased noticeably as she added, "Nora is beckoning! Doubtless Fiona is talking her into a stupor, so we must not leave her any longer to bear the brunt alone."

The tone of that brittle flow of words silenced Bab. She had thought her mother had nearly recovered her normal composure, but now the mere suggestion that Bab wanted to talk about the wedding had agitated her. In the past, such agitation had signaled the onset of a period of unnatural behavior, and that was the last thing Bab wanted to induce in her now. Thus, she said no more.

She had one more day, after all. She could afford to bide her time and try to think of a gentler way to ease out of the wedding. It occurred to her then that if she could not, she would merely be making the common sort of sacrifice daughters had made for mothers or mothers for daughters since the dawn of time. And it might be much worse, for at least Alex was kind to her. Many husbands were not.

The shifting train of thought startled her, for it was as if someone else were debating the matter with her. The odd sensation dissipated, though, and after an hour of listening to the older ladies converse after Chisholm, Alex, and Eric had disappeared to other regions of the castle, she found herself idly wishing that she were male and could do likewise. Shortly afterward, Lady Chisholm yawned mightily, apologized with a laugh, and said that she for one was ready for her bed.

Bab bade the others goodnight but let them go on ahead as they left the bower and crossed the great-hall dais to the main stairway. Once she was sure they were paying her no heed, she hurried down to the chapel, hoping that anyone who saw her there would assume she merely sought a moment of solitude. She had two rolls tucked in a fold of her skirt for Gibby and hoped to find something in one of the chests that would serve as a coverlet to keep him warm through the night.

An orange glow from the flaming torches outside in the bailey lit one wall of narrow stained-glass windows and provided the only light in the chapel, but it was enough to show her the way to the stacked chests in the rear corner, and to show her that although her shawl lay on the floor behind them, the boy was not there. Nor was there any sign of him elsewhere in the chamber.

She waited a few moments, jumping at every sound, but he did not return, and she knew that she dared not wait much longer, since Giorsal would doubtless be in her chamber already and would soon begin to wonder where she was. Hoping that Gibby had hidden himself where no one else would find him, she started to place the rolls in his hiding place. But realizing that if he had slipped outside the castle wall again they would draw mice, she took them with her instead.

Giorsal was awaiting her but accepted the glib explanation that the rolls were in case Bab got hungry in the night, and quickly undressed her and tucked her into bed. Bab consoled herself again with a hope that the Fox might choose to visit her, but the night passed without incident, and she awoke Saturday morning to a day that was gray and overcast.

She found the three older ladies in the hall breaking their fast with Chisholm, who announced that he had already sent running gillies to nearby glens with orders to invite everyone to attend Sunday's morning service in the Dundreggan chapel, after which the wedding ceremony would follow.

"With trouble rife in the area, as it is, it is more convenient if Parson Fraser holds his service here than if we all venture down to the village kirk for it," he said. "I prefer to know that everyone is safe behind our walls."

Bab assumed that he hoped to keep her out of Dalcross hands in the event that the sheriff, his son, and the men were already on the way to question her.

Except for an hour during the afternoon when Lady MacRae insisted that Bab try on the wedding dress so that Giorsal and Ada could see to its final fitting, Saturday passed much the same as Friday. Bab found no sign of Gibby Cannich, and although she still was not reconciled to the notion of marrying Sir Alex, each time she hoped an opportunity might present itself to speak to her mother, something intervened to prevent private conservation with her.

When several families from Glen Affric and neighboring glens arrived before noon to take dinner with them, she learned to her shock that Chisholm had extended invitations to many of his neighbors to spend the night at Dundreggan. The visitors were merry and clearly delighted to think she would marry Alex.

At four o'clock, her kinsmen, Malcolm and Mauri MacRae from Eilean Donan, and Duncan and Florrie from Ardintoul all arrived together, announcing that Lady MacRae had sent for them days before so that they could attend Mistress Bab's wedding to Sir Alex. She did not even try to ask her mother how she had managed that. Events were moving much more swiftly than she had imagined they could, and it was becoming obvious that she might not be able to stop them.

By evening, she was as weary as if she had been traveling all day. Since she found it utterly impossible to announce to the increasing numbers of interested parties that she did not want to marry Alex, and harder by the moment even to think about declaring as much to the priest, Bab was at a loss. Knowing it would avail her nothing but argument if she informed Chisholm that she refused to marry his son, she decided at last to seek out Alex himself and ask him again to keep his promise.

Just thinking about stopping the wedding had become extraordinarily difficult, as if something were interfering with her ability to think. Whenever she tried to turn her thoughts to a way out of it, they shifted to the noble sacrifice she would be making for her mother. Nonetheless, clinging to the notion that Alex was her only hope at this point, she exerted herself to go in search of him. She was sitting with the ladies after supper, as usual, but although she had only to go from her ladyship's bower back into the hall, each step felt as if she were in the sort of dream where her feet felt too heavy to drag around with her.

Alex had lingered at the high table with Eric Mackintosh and several other men who had come with their families to spend the night at Dundreggan. When she entered, Alex raised his goblet to her but remained seated until she walked up to the table. Then, with a rueful smile he got to his feet, his movements awkward enough to make her wonder if he had already had too much to drink.

"I would speak privately with you, sir," she said.

"Mistress, I am naturally at your service," he said amiably, "but perhaps you do not realize that you are interrupting the bridegroom's ritual foot-washing."

Since their postprandial lassitude was unlike the always-boisterous foot-washings she had heard of, Bab looked pointedly at his feet, still elegantly shod.

He grinned. "We'll get to the washing eventually, but first we've a bit more claret to drink and a few more stories to tell."

"Then the others won't mind if I take you away for a few minutes."

"Nay, mistress, we'll no mind a bit," Eric Mackintosh said cheerfully. "We'll just raise a few more cups to the man whilst he's away. Where's the jug, Alex?"

"In your hand," he replied with a chuckle.

"Aye, then, so it is. Bless my soul!"

"Come, lass," Alex said. "You should not linger in such sad company as this. These lads will be ape-drunk all too soon."

He put a hand gently to the small of her back, guiding her to the stairway and on up to the gallery end where they had talked before.

"What would you discuss with me?" he asked then.

"You must know, sir."

"I have already said that I will not call it off for you, mistress."

"But I cannot do it," she protested. "So many have come, and everything has happened so fast and has built up to such a pitch that if I were to speak —"

"Bab, I know you are no coward. If you cannot bring yourself to declare an end to this wedding in the proper manner, you must not really want to stop it."

She opened her mouth and then shut it again, trying to think logically but finding it impossible. Could he be right? Her head ached with the effort to think.

Alex reached gently to cup her chin in one warm hand and tilted her face up. "Do you truly think it will be so dreadful?" he asked, looking directly into her eyes.

His lips were only inches from hers, and his touch stirred those increasingly familiar feelings in her body. For a moment, she felt dizzy and unable to reply.

His hand shifted, and his warm fingertips gently stroked her throat. "It won't be bad at all," he murmured softly. "We'll make a fine pair, I think."

She caught her lower lip between her teeth, and he moved his hand away from her throat, but she could still feel heat where his fingers had touched her.

"Look here, lass," he said in a tone firmer than that she was used to hearing from him, one that indicated he had made a decision. "I'll make you a new promise. If you still feel this strongly in the morning, you need only tell me, and even if Parson Fraser is halfway through the service, I'll find a way to stop the wedding."

"But why wait?"

"Because I must," he said. "Only consider the position you would put me in. If you do not make the declaration yourself that you want no part in this wedding, it will look as if I am the one who has cried off, which would make me a scoundrel. Some would think my father had forced me into it and I'd decided to defy him. Even if most folks accept that I'm speaking for you, some would think I'd somehow intimidated you into refusing but could not make you say the words yourself."

Feeling asleep on her feet and able only to grasp the one straw he had offered her, she said, "You will speak tomorrow, though. I need only tell you then that I am still of the same mind."

"Aye," he said. "You may depend upon me for that much, I swear. But you will still have to say the words aloud. I will not try to read your mind. Now, I warrant your lady mother expects you to rejoin her, so you had better go to her."

Bab nodded and left him. Returning to Lady Chisholm's bower, she found a cheerful group awaiting her. It was not exactly a bride party, for there were few her own age and no one to laugh with or play tricks on her, but her mother's delight in the forthcoming nuptials was evident, and she felt another stab of guilt. It was easier to move and to think now, but since her thoughts wanted to dwell solely on what an unnatural daughter she was that she could consider defying her mother even now, she excused herself as soon as she decently could and went to bed.

After Giorsal had said goodnight to her and shut the door, Bab got up again and found the silver coin the Fox had given her at Gorthleck House. Taking it back to bed with her, she lay awake, rubbing it gently between her fingers and thumb as if it were a wish token, hoping yet again that he would come to her during the night.

She savored the image for a few minutes until it occurred to her to wonder what on earth she would do if he did.

Fiddles fiddled, pipes skirled merrily, and the tempo of the music seemed fast even for one who enthusiastically danced the galliard whenever the opportunity presented itself. She was standing at the edge of the grassy ring, watching the dancers by the silvery light of a huge, round moon, and then, when she thought of the Fox again, he was standing beside her, the heat from his body stirring her blood and setting her senses atingle.

Beyond the ring and the dancers, the feasting had begun. Tables shaped like mushrooms stood laden with food and drink, and those who were not dancing helped themselves as they watched the dancers or chatted with one another. Here and there, tiny creatures riding ragwort stems, twigs, or bundles of grass swooped amongst the guests, while children darted about, trying to capture swan maidens by catching hold of their feathers.

Abruptly, the music stopped.

"It is time," he said, his voice low but carrying

easily to her ears, its sensuous timbre playing soft chords within her body and upon her soul.

She nodded and smiled, resting her hand on the arm he extended to her. Only then did she note that he was dressed all in white for the wedding. Glancing up at him, she saw that his mask was white like his clothing and covered only the upper half of his face. She could see his firm chin and his mouth, and when he smiled back at her, she saw strong, even, white teeth and longed for him to kiss her.

As if he had heard her thoughts, he said with amusement, "Soon, lass, soon." Then, gazing at her with a critical eye, he said, "I like that dress."

She had not thought about her dress, only about him, but now she looked down at herself and saw to her surprise that the dress clung enticingly to her form. It was not pink as she remembered but as silvery and glittering as the moonlight.

No one else spoke to her, but somehow she knew that the procession to the High Glen was about to begin. Feasting and dancing would continue there, and soon she would be his. Her heart was full, her body alive and aching for his. She looked up at him with a smile and saw the same hunger for her in his eyes.

The procession was solemn and slow of pace, but at last they entered the High Glen and the guests gathered around them, eager for the ceremony to begin.

The chief, a tall man, reed thin and white-

bearded, his eyes gleaming like live coals, spread his arms wide, inviting the attention of everyone there to himself and to them. He wore a long white robe and a peaked hat, and his white shoes and the hat bore multicolored tassels on their points. His voice sounded like a low rumble of thunder as he murmured, "Will the pair o' ye wed then?"

"Aye, we will," the Fox said soberly.

"And ye, lass? Will ye ha' this man?"

"Aye," Bab said without hesitation, "I will."

"Then it be done, and ye be wed. May the love ye hold in your hearts for each other now be wi' ye both for all time tae come."

As the Fox bent to kiss her, Bab saw that his eyes looked strangely pink as if they reflected the pink fabric of her gown. But then they turned pale blue, and remembering that her dress was silver, she looked down to be sure that it had remained so, and it had. Then she looked into his eyes again to see if they were still blue, and they were, but now they had turned a deeper, cerulean blue. His hand cupped her chin, holding it still, and his lips met hers, hot and demanding.

All thought of anything but his touch and his kisses vanished.

The music began again, wilder than ever, and she was dimly aware of the dancers all around them, spinning and leaping in time to it, but soon a heavy mist closed in until she was alone with him, wrapped in the music and her own heated passion for him.

His hands moved eagerly over her body, curious hands, and she felt naked beneath his fingers. The two of them seemed to be floating, both naked now, able to move together as and where they would. He kissed her lips and cheeks, and then his lips moved to the hollow of her throat and down to the one between her breasts.

His right hand slid to the curve of her hip, then to the left cheek of her bottom, pulling her closer as his lips opened around the tip of her right breast and his tongue laved its nipple, sending new, wondrous sensations through her body.

As she arched her back, gasping, and used one hand to pull him closer yet, reaching with the other to slip the mask from his face, a hoarse, elderly voice from the mist said solemnly, "Ye may place the ring on her finger now, sir."

She held tight to the edge of the mask and tried to push it up, but he kissed her again, murmuring softly against her lips, "I do have a ring for you, my love."

"Do you?" She could scarcely hear the sound of her own voice.

"Aye, sure, lass. Look here."

Reluctantly, she turned her head and saw that he held out a gold band with three beautiful rubies sparkling on it, guarded by two small diamonds.

"But I want to see your face."

"You must trust me a little longer, sweetheart," he said. "Just give me your hand now as I bid you."

Without another word, she held out her hand, and he clasped it warmly in his left one as he slipped the ring on her finger with his right. The gold felt cool at first, but he kissed her again, and the heat in her body soon warmed it.

"Ah, lassie, you are so beautiful. I want to kiss every inch of your body."

"And so you may, and whenever you wish," she said, "but first, I want to see your face." And with that, she reached again for the mask and snatched it off.

The mist thickened as she did, and as it swirled around and between them, making the world all dark and eerie, the Fox disappeared and the music stopped.

For a moment, Bab felt bereft, as if she still floated alone in an alien nether world, and then the world righted itself. Darkness changed to light, and she realized that she was kneeling before the altar in Dundreggan's chapel, facing an elderly man in priestly vestments, whom she had never seen before, as he held a cup of wine to her lips.

Heat flashed in her cheeks as she remembered believing that she was naked only moments before.

"Drink this in remembrance of me," the stranger murmured, tilting the cup.

As she raised her hand to touch the cup and perforce to drink, she felt comforted to see the ruby ring on her finger.

Then the man set down the cup, spread his arms wide, and said gravely, "Ye may rise and face your guests now, if ye will." As she obeyed, still dazed, he added in more stentorian tones, "May God bless ye both and grant ye many children. My friends, I ha' the honor to present to ye, Sir Alexander Chisholm and his lady wife!"

Lucy clapped her hands in delight. "Ye've done it, Claud!"

He shook his head, bewildered. "I did nowt," he said. "She just never said another word against the wedding. 'Twere as if a spell came over her at first light this morning and stayed upon her until yon priest pronounced them married."

" 'Twas your ain spell, ye noddy. She be your lass."

"Aye, but ye ken fine that it canna be my spell, Lucy, for we none o' us ha' power inside a kirk. Had she been under any spell o' mine afore, stepping in tae the chapel would ha' ended it."

"Oh, aye," Lucy said, looking startled. "I forgot about that."

Bab had turned with a start at the priest's announcement and was still staring wide-eyed at Alex. His doublet and hose were not white but his usual, favorite shade of blue, and he looked as he always did. But although she felt dizzy with shock at learning that she had somehow married him instead of the Fox, the feeling quickly dissipated, leaving in its wake a strong but strangely mixed sense of safety, contentment, and the sensuous, lingering memory of the Fox's kisses and caresses.

"Are we really married?" she whispered. Her tongue felt woolly and swollen, as if it were not sure that it should obey her will and speak her words.

He smiled at her as they turned toward the wedding guests. "Aye, lass," he murmured, "and I hope you will be happy as Lady Alex, for that is what everyone will call you now. I don't mind telling you, it was a profound relief to see you walking up the aisle, smiling so radiantly. I knew then that everything was all right. Until I saw you, though, I was afraid you might have taken fright and run away."

"I . . . I didn't." It was still hard to think. Surely, she had been smiling at the Fox, not at Alex, although she could hardly tell him that. What was the matter with her? How could she have married him without knowing she was doing so, and why was it that every thought and every word she spoke required such effort?

"I think they are waiting for us to lead the way upstairs," he said, cupping a hand to her elbow. "Don't forget to hold your skirt, lass. There are two steps here."

He was talking as if she were a child, but in truth, she had not noticed the steps. Silently, she caught up her skirt but then paused, staring at its pink fabric.

"What is it, Bab?"

"Nothing." She looked at his eyes, wondering if they might have changed color too, but as usual, they matched the deep, cerulean blue of his doublet. He released her elbow then and offered his arm.

She had no memory of having risen that morning and dressed, or of having walked downstairs or down the aisle of the elegant little chapel. And the ceremony there certainly had not been the ceremony she had dreamed. In her dream, she was on a greensward. There had been no rich, polished wood pilasters or wainscoting, no intricately carved rood screen, and no altar with its gold chalice and elegantly appointed tabernacle. Neither had Chisholm's banners flanked the altarpiece. Moreover, Chisholm's plump, elderly priest bore no resemblance to the tall, bearded wizard in the white robe who had so swiftly performed her dream wedding.

She wanted to pinch herself to see if she was awake, but with her skirt in one hand and the other clutching Alex's arm, and with a fascinated audience watching every move she made, she could not do it. She did feel the soft texture of his velvet sleeve, though. Did one feel texture in dreams? She could not recall at first, but then she recalled feeling naked, and heat surged into her cheeks.

Surely, though, she must still be dreaming, because if she weren't, she would react more strenuously to such a grand betrayal. For was that not what it was? Had her own mind not tricked her into believing that she was elsewhere, marrying someone else? And what had she been thinking, anyway, to marry the Fox so willingly without knowing his true identity. It occurred to her then that she might be suffering from the same odd malady as Lady MacRae. That thought did nothing to comfort her but, oddly, neither did it distress her. She seemed to have no feelings left. As that notion entered her mind, however, she realized her error.

The velvet of Alex's sleeve was soft indeed, and as she looked up at him, the sensations that his touch had stirred in her before returned stronger than ever, sending jolts of fire through her. She had married him. He was her husband and he could now do as he pleased with her. Although she had no memory of the priest's words to them, she had heard the marriage ceremony before, and she knew that she must have promised him obedience and submission. Before the night was done, he would know her physically and she would know him. That idea should have been frightening. Instead, it excited her curiosity and played tantalizingly on her nerves.

He placed his free hand atop hers where it rested on his forearm and gave hers a reassuring squeeze. Neither of them wore gloves, she realized, so they must have taken them off at some unremembered point, and his hand felt warm against hers. Meeting his gaze again, she smiled, and the intensity of his expression startled her, sending more of those beguiling sensations through her body.

As they neared the door leading to the service area and main stairway, she saw her beaming mother flanked by various other MacRaes of Kintail and Ardintoul. Bab smiled, and a feeling of peaceful warmth flowed through her as she did. Lady MacRae looked as healthy and happy as she had ever seen her.

Upstairs, the great hall was bright with spring flowers, musicians played from the gallery, and the long trestle tables groaned with huge platters of food. Tempting odors of roasted beef and lamb wafted toward them, and Bab realized that she was hungry.

She found a chance at last to pinch herself, but although she felt the pain, it did nothing to banish the sense of unreality. She could remember her dream of marrying the Fox as vividly as if it had been real, but looking at Alex, she felt more as if she were dreaming now than when she had watched pixies, elves, and gauzy green fairies swooping over the greensward on bits of ragwort and grass.

That sense of dreamlike unreality clung to her as she ate her wedding breakfast — called so despite the fact that the hour was rapidly approaching one o'clock — and continued to cling while she responded to the numerous well-wishers who had attended the festivities.

The musicians played for dancing after the meal, and she and Alex led the dancers onto the floor as soon as the trestles were dismantled and a space cleared for them. She had nearly forgotten how skilled a dancer he was, but the steps came easily to her again, and she soon found herself laughing and enjoying herself as much as any other bride.

The festivities continued through supper, and although she was finding it harder and harder to smile, the feeling was familiar and had nothing to do with fading spirits. It was simply the weariness one always felt after entertaining myriad guests for an extended period. Her face ached from smiling. Her throat was dry and sore from talking too much. Her feet hurt from dancing, and her store of pleasantries was nearly spent, but she knew her duty and made no complaint.

Putting an arm around her shoulders, Alex bent so that his lips nearly touched her ear as he murmured, "Art tired, lass? 'Tis been a long day."

"A little," she admitted, "but in truth I have enjoyed myself immensely."

Even as she wondered where the words had come from, she realized that she spoke only the truth. She had thoroughly enjoyed herself.

"We'll leave in a few moments," he said.

Suddenly her thoughts were wholly her own again, and panic surged through her. Tonight was her wedding night!

"Claud!" a familiar voice exclaimed. "At last! I thought ye'd never come."

"Catriona!" He was delighted to see her, and relieved. After Lady MacRae bade him a cheerful hello in passing, nearly startling him out of his wits, he had slipped away from the wedding festivities to try and find his mother, but Catriona intercepted him just before he reached Maggie's parlor. "Where ha' ye been, lass?" he demanded, keeping an eye out for Maggie. "I ha' searched for ye everywhere."

"Did ye? Didst miss me, Claud?" She reached to stroke his cheek.

He forgot about Maggie, as his gaze drifted downward. Catriona looked as enticing as she always did, her low-cut, gauzy green gown clinging to every delicious curve of her body. He remembered the magic in her fingers and yearned to feel them touch him everywhere.

His voice hoarse, he said, "Aye, lass, I ha' missed ye summat fierce."

"I've been busy, Claud, but I managed to slip away for a bit, 'cause I ha' missed ye, too. That gap-toothed butter whore threatened me! She said —"

"Who?"

"That viperous schemer, Lucy Fittletrot, o'

course! I'll give *her* goat's feet!"

Involuntarily, his gaze shot to Catriona's feet, concealed by her gauzy gown.

She gasped. "See there! She's even persuaded ye that I'm a Glaistig!"

"Show me your feet, lass."

"I won't! Ye should ken well that I'm no half woman, half goat."

"Mayhap ye'd like tae be, however," hissed an angry voice behind them.

Whirling, Claud beheld Lucy, her dark eyes gleaming, her golden hair practically standing on end. "Ye leave her be, Lucy," he snapped.

Turning back, determined to protect Catriona although not certain what that would entail, he saw to his consternation that she had already vanished.

"What ha' ye done wi' her, Lucy?"

"It be time tae go back tae the feast, Claud," Lucy said as she touched his shoulder. "They'll soon be bedding the bridal couple. We missed that part the last time, ye'll recall, and I want tae see what they do. Mayhap we'll learn summat."

The hiss in her voice was gone, leaving it gentle and seductive, and as she drew him toward her, her hands slid over his body before she entwined her arms around his neck and stood on tiptoe to kiss him. But for once, her touch stirred only irritation, and he drew back, his anger with her too strong to be so easily overcome.

With an angry look, she flitted away, and re-luctantly, he followed her.

Aboard the Marion Ogilvy

The winds had continued fierce and steady from the south even after they had left Spain and France behind, speeding them north toward Ireland. Kit knew they would stay to the west of it, keeping as much distance as possible between themselves and Henry's England.

The winds defied understanding, so favorable had they been. Older men who had sailed the seas from childhood said they had never seen the like.

Kit had done his work and kept to himself, speaking little to anyone other than Tam and Willie, while keeping clear of both Gibson and Sir Kenneth Lindsay. He believed strongly that the less he was seen with the ambassador's nephew the less Gibson would make him account for later. He had seen the latter eyeing him, and he knew well that there would eventually be a reckoning between them.

Long before they sighted the Irish coast, the wind eased off and shifted so that it blew from the west. It strengthened then, slowing their progress considerably.

Gibson sent him with the others into the rigging to adjust the sails, and as he scrambled to the foretop, someone above him on the main shouted, "Sails ho!"

He could see them now too, dead ahead, three huge ships of war coming straight toward them, their speed terrifying.

Gibson bellowed orders to man the gun ports, and riggers leaped to man the sheets and change the angle of the sails, turning the ship, but as quick as they were, the oncoming ships were faster, and no sooner could they make out the English flags flying from their mastheads than they heard the enemy cannons fire. Their first volley splashed short, but the *Marion Ogilvy* was broadside to them now, and the warships came on swiftly.

When the next volley exploded, he was in his usual place on the foretopmast, his view of the main clear, and he saw a ball hit the main masthead. Men screamed, wood flew in all directions, and the mast and its rigging began to crumple.

It was a solid hit. Everything above the strike point, two-thirds of the huge mainmast, began to topple toward him.

Chapter 17

Bab saw her mother and Mauri MacRae moving toward her with purposeful looks in their eyes. As they came, she saw others moving to follow them.

"What is it, madam?" she asked Lady MacRae. "Is aught amiss?"

"Nay, my dearling, 'tis but time for your bedding."

Bab's knees felt suddenly unlikely to continue supporting her, but she forced calm into her voice as she said, "What must I do?"

Beside her, Alex said with equal calm, "We will go up with them, my lady. Look to your bride laces, and keep close to me."

Remembering that the long ribbons on her sleeves were considered prizes that the men who had attended her wedding had the right to claim as she left for her bedding, Bab swallowed hard. She had heard of brides being stripped naked when they bore too few ribbons to suit the guests. She remembered something else, too.

"Will all these people attend our bedding?"

Her mother frowned, glancing around. Some of the men had been drinking freely of Chisholm's claret, ale, and an even more intoxicating drink common to the Isle of Skye called *brogac,* and they were clearly feeling sportive.

"No man in my father's house with my father at hand will step out of line," Alex said. "What ceremony there is will be simple. Your mother and the other married women will help you prepare for bed. Once you are in your bedgown and tucked in, I will enter with Eric and the other male guests. The priest will bless the bed, we'll take a cup of claret with him, and then he will shoo everyone else out of the room. It will be over before you know it, and I'll not let anyone embarrass you."

She looked at him searchingly, but he seemed sincere and the lazy drawl was absent. Still, she could not help thinking that the others were not what she worried about. She worried more about what would happen after they left.

"Hurry, Claud, I want a good place!" Lucy exclaimed, tugging his sleeve as if there had never been a moment's anger between them.

"Her ladyship will see us," Claud warned her.

"No matter if she does," Lucy retorted with a grin. "She may ha' the gift tae see us, but she has nae power tae keep us out."

"But if she chats wi' me mam, ye ken well what will happen."

"Pish tush, your mam wants ye tae keep watch over your lass, and how can ye do that an ye dinna stay wi' her?" When Claud hesitated, she said with a sigh, "Come on, Claud! If it makes ye happier, we'll just keep out o' their sight."

"D'ye think ye can keep us out o' me mam's sight?"

"Ye ken well that I can, laddie," she said with a wink. "I ha' done it afore."

He had suspected as much at least once, and he wondered again what magic Lucy had that seemed to protect her against Maggie's vast powers.

As she turned to follow the bridal couple and he moved to follow her, one of the guests who had enjoyed his *brogac* a trifle more freely than the others chose that moment to cast the remaining contents of his mug carelessly over his shoulder as he shouted for claret to toast the bride. Lucy was just passing by, and the potent brew nearly caught her in its path. With a deft move, she managed to avoid it but turned with an angry shriek and raised her hands menacingly.

"Lucy!" Claud bellowed. "No!"

She turned to him, her fury swiftly turning to impishness. "I were just going tae let him enjoy the rest o' the night as a wee frog," she said demurely.

"Ye ken fine that we canna do such things," Claud scolded. "If ye turn him into a frog, others will see him vanish. Moreover, I'll ha' tae take the blame for it, and I'm meant tae settle this affair without doing aught tae make known our presence here. I dinna want tae face the Circle again, lass, until I succeed."

"Aye, well, I dinna like getting wet, and that villain well nigh drowned me."

"I thought ye were in a hurry tae see the bedding," Claud reminded her.

"I am," she said, disappearing up the stairs and leaving him again to follow.

This time it was with a sigh of profound relief that he did.

Aboard the Marion Ogilvy

He had thought he was about to die, for the mast appeared to be toppling straight toward him and he had nowhere to go, but as he gritted his teeth and clung tightly to the foretopmast, he felt and heard the sounds of a great wind blowing up. It had shifted direction again and now filled every sail, so that suddenly they were running with the wind to the northeast, and it blew so powerfully that it seemed even to right the falling mast. Or perhaps he had only imagined the mast was falling toward him. Confused, his mind sought reasonable answers for what he had seen.

Perhaps the wind had picked up moments before and so quickly that the entire ship had tilted with increasing wave action, and all before he had noticed.

In any event, he was not going to question it.

He could tell by the reactions of other riggers that many had seen what he had seen and feared what he had feared. Nonetheless, they hastened now to check the mainmast shrouds, those heavy, paired ropes, chained and dead-eyed to the rigging rail that held the mast in place.

They were off course and heading into the Irish Sea, between Ireland and England, but they were easily outrunning the English ships. With luck, oncoming darkness would keep them safe and allow them to reach the North Channel between Scotland and Ireland before dawn. And then, thanks to the shorter distance to Dumbarton, they would get there faster than anyone had anticipated.

He looked skyward and sent up a silent prayer of thanksgiving to the ancient gods who watched over sailors on the high seas. The ones responsible for the *Marion Ogilvy* had apparently forgotten her for a while, but someone had remembered them in time, and he was grateful.

The women hustled Bab upstairs to Sir Alex's bedchamber ahead of him, with the other gentlemen following. It had been easy for them to separate her from Alex. They had merely urged her onto the spiral stairway ahead of him and then eased in between, so she now had a solid wall of wide skirts protecting her as she hurried up the stairs, following Lady

MacRae with Mauri right behind her.

The procession was merry, accompanied by much boisterous laughter and a few ribald remarks, but the latter were few and generally tame, owing to Chisholm and his lady trailing behind the rest of the merrymakers.

When they reached the landing near Alex's bedchamber, Mauri bustled ahead, clearly having acquainted herself earlier with the room's location. She pushed open the door, looked inside, and gestured for Bab to precede her.

While Mauri paused at the door to see that only the ladies entered, Bab stared around the room with interest.

Alex's bedchamber was not what she had expected. His deep interest in his attire, and in fabrics and colors, had led her to expect a far more elaborately decorated chamber. By comparison with what she had imagined, the room was nearly Spartan. The dark blue-velvet bed hangings and window curtains, corded back with ordinary twisted and tasseled white cotton rope, were simple and plain, lacking even modest embroidery. The room was nonetheless comfortable, for a cheerful fire crackled on the hearth, and myriad candles and oil-burning cressets on the walls provided a rich golden light throughout.

Bab's bedgown and wrapper lay ready on the high bed, which stood against the wall opposite the fireplace and was both wider and longer

379

than the one she had been sleeping in. Giorsal and Ada MacReedy stood waiting by it to assist her.

The clamor outside the door grew louder and then was muted when Mauri firmly shut it, leaving the gentlemen outside.

The room was spacious, but teeming with chattering women as it was now, it seemed to be far too small for the purpose at hand. Lady Chisholm's voice quelled the clamor as she said in a quiet but nonetheless carrying tone, "Hush now, ladies, lest we deafen poor Bab."

Someone suggested that it would be a pity for her not to hear Sir Alex's words of love when the time came, but Bab had no need to comment, for Giorsal was guiding her to the washstand, where a towel and warm water awaited her, along with other amenities that were supposed to render her pleasing to her husband.

It seemed almost natural then to let herself be divested of her wedding dress and prepared for bed. Her face and hands were soon washed, her teeth cleaned, and while her assistants dabbed fresh perfume behind her ears, on her wrists, between her breasts, and in other places where she had never thought to put perfume, she chewed a bit of mint to freshen her breath. Then they helped her into the soft lawn bedgown and the voluminous red velvet wrapper that had been wedding gifts from her mother. Somehow, in the crush of completing her pink gown, Giorsal and Ada had found time to make them, too.

Someone had removed her bridal headdress and someone else had loosened her hair from its plaits. Now Giorsal brushed it out quickly, knowing that the men outside the door would be growing impatient.

Fiona Mackintosh folded down the coverlet and quilt and stood aside.

"Climb you in, my dearling," Lady MacRae said quietly at Bab's side. "I trust you know what will happen tonight."

Bab stared, wondering why her mother would have such trust. "In truth, madam," she murmured with fire in her cheeks, "I have but the vaguest notion."

"Why, you simply do your duty and submit to your husband's will." With a smile, Lady MacRae kissed her cheek and stepped back, adding, "You may let the gentlemen in as soon as her ladyship has climbed into the bed, Mauri."

Automatically, Bab glanced at Lady Chisholm before she realized the title was her own. Then, obediently, she used the bed steps to climb into the high bed and scooted to the inside where pillows had been piled for her to rest against, so that she could sit up comfortably for the forthcoming proceedings.

The women arranged the quilt over her, drawing it to her waist, and as Mauri MacRae admitted Sir Alex and the other men, the women stood aside to give Alex an unimpeded view of his bride.

To Bab's surprise, he had already changed his clothing, or his friends had changed it for him. In place of the elegant doublet and hose he had worn for their wedding, he wore a dressing gown of blue brocade with gold cording and tassels.

Glowering at the rowdy men who had followed Alex, the priest stepped up beside him. Alex smiled at Bab, and she felt her tension ease, for whatever else anyone might say about him, he was kind and gentle, and he would not harm her.

When at last the priest could make himself heard, he said formally, "We must bless this bed before Sir Alex can be permitted to join his bride and consummate this marriage." Then, in a harsher tone, he added, "Ye'll be quiet, the lot o' ye men, or I'll put a curse on ye that'll make your eyes rot in your heads!"

Exchanging muttered comments and grins, the men in the company nonetheless grew quiet enough to allow him to continue with the blessing. As soon as he finished, Eric Mackintosh, who had served as Alex's best man, produced a jug of claret and four goblets, which he proceeded at once to fill.

Passing one to the priest, two to Alex for Bab and himself, and keeping one, Eric raised his and said with a grin, "I offer a toast to the beautiful young Lady Chisholm and to her ugly husband.

It is our fond hope that they may be happy together for the rest of their days, although how she can be with such a pawky dunderclunk for a husband is more than I can say."

Laughter broke out again, and everyone cheered.

Alex raised his goblet to the company, grinned, and took a sip. "You must drink the toast, lass," he said.

"But they are toasting us," she protested. "I did not think one —"

Interrupted by loud cries to "Drink!" she took a tiny sip.

Alex offered a toast to the crowd and another to Parson Fraser, but after the latter, the priest said brusquely, "That will do, that will do. Out now, the lot o' ye!"

Moments later, with the clamor on the other side of the closed door and fading in the distance, they were alone.

"Now they'll be getting on wi' it," Lucy said with satisfaction as she settled comfortably against Claud to watch. "Ha' ye seen this sort o' thing afore, Claud?"

"Aye," he said, remembering when he and Catriona had been party to such a scene. "Lucy, what did ye do wi' Catriona this time?"

"I told ye," she said without taking her eyes from the other couple. "The wench be afraid o' me, so she fled. Now hush. I want to hear what he says tae her."

"He'll no say anything yet," Claud said, looking at the two in the bed. "He'll urge her tae drink her wine. It'll relax her if she be afraid."

"I dinna think she is afraid," Lucy said wisely.

"Lucy, how did ye make her ha' that dream?"

"I think ye must ha' done it yourself. Mayhap, even in the chapel —"

"Ye ken fine I didna do it. Why d'ye no answer, Lucy? Art lying tae me?"

"Lucy Fittletrot does not lie," she said. "She had nowt tae do wi' the dream that eased that marriage ye wanted so greatly."

"I did want it," Claud admitted.

"Dinna fret," Lucy advised. "Nae one but your lass kens aught about that dream, so ye broke nae rules wi' the doing."

"But I —"

"Hush now, he's going tae say summat tae her."

Alex shifted a little to give himself the pleasure of gazing at Bab, astonished as always at her beauty. The golden glow of the candles and firelight only enhanced it and made her dark blue eyes look huge and dark.

She gazed at him, her eyes wide now and wondering, and he marveled that she was not afraid of him. He doubted that she knew much about coupling, but he was surprised by her courage. She had shown it often, and she had discretion, too.

How much danger had he put her in? For, whatever happened next, it would be his fault for succumbing to his yearning for her. And sooner or later they would have a reckoning between them. If she declared his deceptions unforgivable, what would he do then?

He remembered the first time he had seen her, at Ardintoul, when his family had traveled there to visit hers. She had done something to annoy Patrick, who was nearly ten years older, and three years older than Alex. She had faced her brother, a wee termagant of four, hands on her hips, eyes flashing, daring him to punish her.

At the thought, he smiled, and she smiled tentatively back at him.

"Do you know what I was thinking?" he asked her.

"No," she said. "How could I?"

"Sometimes I feel as if you see right into my head and read my thoughts."

"Do you? I feel the same about you when I want to do something you do not approve and you put obstacles in my path without ever saying a word to me."

"Art still annoyed with me for keeping you within the walls this week, lass?"

"I do not like being confined," she said.

Something inside him winced at those words though he could not have said what caused it. "I'm sorry," he said, "but you were safe here, and I could not know what you might face outside the walls. Have you finished your wine?"

Color leaped to her cheeks, and he no longer believed she was calm. Gently he took the goblet from her and placed it with his own on the bed-step table. Then, slipping his arm around her shoulders, he drew her close, pleased when she did not resist. "I'm glad you decided to marry me after all," he said.

"I did not decide," she murmured. "I'm still not sure how it happened."

"Tell me," he said.

"It was exactly like a dream," she said, watching him as if she would gauge his belief or disbelief of what she said. "I dreamed I was in a fairy glen, and the chief of the fairies was performing a wedding." She paused, and her gaze slid away from his as she added, "I was there one moment, and the next I was facing Parson Fraser and he was telling me to drink the wine in the chalice."

She was blushing now, and he nearly asked whom she had married in this dream, but he believed he knew, and if he was wrong, he did not want to hear about it. So instead, he said, "I hope you are not sorry it was real, Bab. I am not."

"No?"

"I have been more than willing to marry you ever since the subject arose," he said, meaning every word. "I truly believed you had changed your mind. Women do that frequently, I think."

"Men like to think that," she said, nodding.

"What I'd like is to kiss my wife."

Her lips parted, and her eyes widened even more. The moment was irresistible. He bent toward her and captured her mouth.

"Ah," Lucy said. "That's better. Wi' luck they'll nae talk so much now."

"Whisst, will ye whisst?" Claud felt a prickling sensation and recognized it as a warning that his mother was nearby. "If ye can make us invisible tae me mam, lass, ye'd best do it straightaway."

Lucy vanished without saying a word, evidently having forgotten to take him along, because he was suddenly facing his mother.

"What be ye a-doing here?" Maggie demanded, hands on her hips.

"Ye said I should watch over the lass!"

"Aye, well, but ye're fortunate that her ladyship didna see ye here."

"Lucy hid us so she couldna see us." As the admission slipped off his tongue, he wished fervently that he could snatch it back.

Maggie's face reddened. She leaned forward, putting her face right in front of his. "Lucy is it? D'ye mean that spawn o' Satan, Lucy Fittletrot?"

"She said she isna Jonah Bonewits's daughter, so she's no my sister neither."

"What does that matter?" Maggie demanded. "She ha' been under his wicked spells afore, so he could bind her more easily now. I'll wager she's responsible for yon wedding that married your lass wi' Alex Chisholm."

"Ye ken there were a spell?"

"Aye, o' course, I do. I might ha' stopped it afore she stepped into that chapel, but by then she seemed to have accepted it, and it set well wi' me that she should marry him. She loves him, ye ken. She just doesna understand it yet."

"Oh, aye, that be plain as day," Claud said glibly, hoping it was true.

"They'll do well on their own for now," Maggie said. "Your presence becomes an unnecessary intrusion."

And with a snap of her fingers, Claud found himself sitting in his favorite chair in her parlor, alone, staring at the flickering fire. With a sigh, he decided that his love life was rapidly turning to ashes.

Responding with eager curiosity to Alex's kisses and caresses, Bab wondered what sort of woman she was that she could respond to two men as she did. Perhaps, she thought, all kisses were the same and were meant to stimulate a person to couple, because her body was certainly responding. But she dismissed that thought when a memory presented itself of Francis Dalcross kissing her. That had not stimulated anything but fury, so plainly, all kisses were not the same.

Nonetheless, Alex's touch was as stirring as the Fox's, and her body ached for him to continue caressing her. When he reached for the ribbons of her wrapper and loosened them, she raised a hand to help and then wondered at her boldness.

While his fingers were busy with the ribbons, he continued to kiss her, so she scarcely noticed when he pushed the wrapper from her shoulders and reached for the ribbons of her bedgown. But when his hand moved to her bare skin, the sensations were nothing like her dream. She did not feel at all as if she were floating. Indeed, the sensations were stronger, more blood stirring, and when Alex's hand cupped one bare breast and his thumb stroked its nipple, she gasped again, and his tongue took that opportunity to slip into her mouth.

A moment later, her bedgown was off, and Alex's hands began to explore her body. "You may touch me, too, you know," he murmured against her cheek.

She did not know what to do. "Must I?"

His hands became still. "I collect that you know little of coupling," he said. "Did your mother not tell you what to expect?"

"She said I should do my duty and submit to my husband," Bab said.

He chuckled. "I wish I may see that."

She was silent for a long while, trying to sort her thoughts, expecting him to say more. When he did not, she wondered if he had fallen asleep.

"Sir?"

"You may call me Alex, madam."

"Madam." She listened to the echo of the

word in her mind. "Are you vexed with me?" She had been calling him Alex in her thoughts for weeks, but she could not quite bring herself to say it aloud yet. One was trained from birth to call men sir, and she had always done so even with Patrick.

He had not answered her. "Are you vexed?" she asked again.

"I am trying to imagine why you think I should be."

"Should brides not be eager to explore all the secrets of the marriage bed?"

"I don't know," he said. "I have never been a bride, but I think they are what they are, and after all, you did not come to this bed altogether willingly."

It was her turn to be silent, but her silence was brief. She said, "It seems silly, does it not? A girl is supposed to marry, and few of us are given much choice in a husband. Moreover, I like you very well, sir. I cannot think of another gentleman I would prefer to have married." That was true enough, for despite his occasional attempts to sound like one, the Fox was hardly a real gentleman, and despite her feelings for him and the delicious dream that had led to her marrying Alex, she knew she could never have married the Fox.

"Dear me," he said in the drawl she disliked so much, "do you throw mugs and cast jugs full of ale over other gentlemen? Because if you do," he added before she could reply, "I must tell you that as your husband I shall take a dim view of such conduct."

"It is when you speak like that that I most want to douse you with ale," she said tartly. Then, with a sigh, she went on, "In truth, sir, I do not know myself. I was reeling with confusion one moment and then dancing and chatting happily the next. Then all manner of qualms set in when the ladies hurried me up here and began to undress me, and now the confusion has returned, but despite that, I am content to be lying here beside you, talking with you like this."

"I feel that, too," he said. "And do not think that I cannot understand your alarm about today, for I'm a little overwhelmed by it myself. Everything happened so quickly, and there is still much to be resolved. If you are not quite ready to consummate this marriage, I'll be disappointed, but I will understand. We can wait a night or two until you become more accustomed to being my wife."

His words were reasonable, and his tone was friendly, so why, Bab wondered, did she feel such a surge of disappointment?

"I will do as you think best, of course," she said.

"Ah, Bab," he said with laughter in his voice. "I think we should wait until your thoughts are your own again. I do not know this submissive woman."

"You *are* vexed."

"Nay, lass. I admit that I would like nothing better than to make you mine at once, but I want you to enter into the spirit of things with me. I do not want to push you where you are loath to go." He threw back the covers.

"Are you leaving?"

"I am just going to snuff the lights and put another log on the fire."

A moment later, the room was darker, and when he climbed back into bed, she realized that he had taken off his dressing gown and wore nothing beneath it.

"I want to hold you, lass," he said, suiting action to words.

She could almost hear her own heart beating, but she let him hold her close to him, and the feeling of his body against hers was pleasant. His caresses were gentle at first, soothing, as if he were stroking a cat, and she felt herself relaxing, savoring the sensations his touch aroused in her. His hand moved lower, to the juncture of her legs, to the place that no one touched save herself.

"Relax now," he said. "I won't hurt you."

"I know you won't, but my body wants to jump," she said.

He chuckled again, and knowing that she had intended him to, she smiled and then gasped when his fingers touched a remarkably sensitive part of her. His hand moved away and back, touching her breasts again. Then he kissed them, and his mouth teased one nipple while his hand became busy where it had been before.

Her body began arching, begging him to continue until sudden waves of pleasure captured her, rendering all thought impossible. She could only react, and the sensations lasted for several moments. When they eased, she lay beside him, deeply relaxed, with her head on his shoulder.

"What happened?" she murmured.

"Nature happened," he said.

"Did we consummate our union then? I thought —" She stopped, not sure she ought to put that thought into words.

"We did not," he said. "We've only just begun, lass. I wanted you to know the pleasure of coupling, although that was but a token."

"Goodness," she said, wondering how it could have been more powerful.

He kissed her. "Sleep now, and sleep well. We'll talk more tomorrow."

She did not argue, but neither did she sleep, not for a long while.

She had always known her own mind, and she had always spoken her mind even when the speaking got her into trouble. So why, now, was it so difficult to understand her feelings? She was no longer suffering from the sluggishness she had felt before. Her thoughts were clear and crisp. They just made no sense.

Beside her, Alex lay suffering, telling himself that he ought to feel noble if only because he had not taken further advantage of her. But he knew things were only going to become more difficult. It was one thing to play hero when he had no one to account to or for but himself. It was another to have brought Bab into it.

If he did not set matters right before Patrick learned of it, he did not want to think what the consequences would be. For that matter, he did not want to think about what Bab would say. She was no meek nun's hen, nor would he have her so.

He had other problems, too, including young Gibby, who had certainly recognized Dancer.

"Art asleep yet, lass?"

"No."

"I found something of yours in the chapel last night."

"You did?" He felt her stiffen, and despite his guilty conscience, he smiled.

"Aye, and I should tell you that your Gibby Cannich is quite safe. My man Hugo is looking after him and will keep him out of the sheriff's clutches."

She relaxed again. "Thank you, sir. I was worried about him. I shall sleep more comfortably, knowing he's safe."

He said no more, hoping that sleep would come soon but certain that it would be a long time before he was truly comfortable again.

Bab slept at last and well enough, but she awoke with the first light of dawn, uncertain how she was to go about dressing, since her clothing was in her own bedchamber. But less than a half-hour later, the door opened, and a man entered silently. He looked taken aback to see the bed curtains open and Bab watching him, but he was carrying her clothes, so she smiled.

Bowing, he left as silently as he had come in.

A moment later, Giorsal entered, and just as Bab realized that she could not get out of bed without disturbing Alex, he opened an eye and looked at her.

Then he opened the other and muttered, "Is it morning already?"

"Aye, sir, and Giorsal is here. Pray recall that we are to break our fast with Eric Mackintosh and your cousin Eileen. We must not tarry."

"I remember."

It was tradition that on the first morning of their new life together a bride and groom took breakfast with their best man and best maid, and young Eileen had served Bab in the latter capacity because she lived near and there had been no time to make other arrangements. Still, it would not do to disappoint her, for unmarried as she was, she had not been permitted to attend the bedding.

Bab arose at once to let Giorsal help her dress, and when she was decently clad, Hugo returned to help Alex. Soon both were ready to go down to the hall.

Eric and pale, blond Eileen were already

there, the high table already set, the privacy screens in place. But no sooner had Alex and Bab taken their places than an eruption of noise at the entrance heralded visitors, and someone shouted, "Sheriff Substitute Francis Dalcross demands entrance, master."

Bab glanced at Alex who grimaced but did not respond.

"I do demand it," Francis snapped, striding across the hall with two of his minions. He stepped past the privacy screen onto the dais without awaiting permission. "I would have speech with Mistress Barbara MacRae."

"Faith, Dalcross, have you no manners?" Alex drawled. "You interrupt us before we have even broken our fast. One trusts that you have good reason."

"Good enough. That damnable Black Fox murdered the sheriff on Friday."

Exclamations from three of the four at the table greeted his news, but Alex said only, "May the devil fly away with him then. Are you certain it was the Fox?"

"Aye, for the villain left one of his damned silver coins by my father's body for all to see. I have come to discover all the lass can tell us about him."

"I am sorry to learn of your loss," Alex said, adding with a distinct edge to his voice, "but the *lass* is now my wife, Dalcross, so take care how you speak of her, and have the goodness to show proper respect."

Dalcross allowed himself a cursory bob in Bab's direction saying, "So that is how it is, is it? Well, it makes no difference what games you play here at Dundreggan. I've come to take Mistress . . . that is, to take your lady wife back with me to Inverness so I may question her properly."

"That will not be necessary," Alex said evenly. "You may ask her any questions you like right here."

"Very well," Dalcross agreed.

Bab's relief at that decision was short lived, however, for he added, "You should know that I am now the acting sheriff, and shall remain so until the King appoints a new man, if he does. So you may believe me when I tell you that if she refuses to answer me, I shall arrest her as an accomplice to the murder."

Chapter 18

A chill swept over Bab at hearing Francis Dalcross's threat. That they had found one of the Fox's signature coins stunned her, but she refused to believe he could be a murderer.

Beside her, Alex remained silent.

She heard a muffled whimper of alarm from his cousin Eileen, but no one heeded her discomfort. Beside her, Eric watched Alex steadily and said nothing.

Bab said, "You cannot think that I had aught to do with your father's tragic death, Francis Dalcross."

"I do not know for a fact that you did not," he said, returning look for look.

Alex's left arm touched her right one, so she felt him stiffen, but when he spoke, it was in his habitual light drawl. "But you amuse me, Dalcross," he said. "You are a bigger fool than even I have suspected if you seek a woman for this crime. Or was your father poisoned at table? Poison might indeed indicate a feminine hand at work, but I should be looking for his present leman and not someone so patently innocent as my lady wife."

"I do not say that she is the killer," Dalcross said. "Rather, let us say more accurately that I have no reason to believe she killed him with her own hands but every reason to believe she knows much about the man who did."

"What fustian is this you spout, Dalcross?" Lord Chisholm snapped as he stepped onto the dais from the lower hall, having clearly over-heard the previous exchange. He glowered at the unwanted intruder, awaiting his reply.

"My father is dead, my lord, murdered."

"If you expect sympathy from me, you'll not get it," Chisholm retorted. "You and he have set clan against clan and everyone in the glens against you this past year, so you have no one to thank for this outcome but yourselves. Now, what is this I hear about your wanting to question my daughter-in-law?"

"As you heard me say, sir, I have reason to believe she knows much about *Sionnach Dubh*. I warrant you would not want her protecting that outlaw."

"No, indeed, if she is guilty, but if she is doing any such thing, I am at a loss to know how. She lives here, sir, as does her mother. Do you think she keeps him hidden in her bed-chamber?"

"I would not reject an offer to search this castle," Dalcross said slyly.

"Do not try my patience, sir. You'll get no such permission, and well do you know it. If you have questions to ask her, ask them and get out."

"I want to take her back with me to Inverness."

"I warrant you do, but I shall not allow that unless you can show me that she has broken the law. Put your questions to her now, or take your men and leave."

"I would prefer somewhere less public then," Dalcross said, his manner curt and no less confident than when he had entered the hall.

"I'll clear my lads out of here if yours go with them," Chisholm said.

Dalcross nodded but said, "I want at least one to remain so that I am not the sole Crown witness to what she tells me."

"That is reasonable," Chisholm said. He gestured to Eileen to leave, but Eric remained at Alex's side and Dalcross made no further objection.

Bab looked from one gentleman to another until her questioning gaze met Alex's steady one. Her hands were clasped together beneath the table in her lap, and as she gazed at him, he put one large, warm hand atop hers and let it rest there.

Drawing a deep breath and releasing it, forcing herself to relax, she turned to Francis Dalcross. "What would you ask me, sir?"

"Who is the Fox? What is his true name?"

"Godamercy," she said, widening her eyes. "I do not know that."

"I warrant you do, madam. You have been seen twice in his company, and I have no reason to think you were with him either time because he'd abducted you."

400

Bab stared at him, astonished by his audacity, but she managed to keep her voice calm as she said, "Only one man has ever been villain enough to abduct me, sir, and that villain is you."

"Oh, well said, lass, well said," Alex drawled. "Now, take care, Dalcross, lest you undo yourself."

"Hold your tongue," Dalcross said crossly. "You accomplish no good by baiting me. As for you, mistress, if you cannot tell me his true name, you can at least tell me what he looks like and where he led you."

"I cannot describe him, nor will I tell you anything else about him," Bab said firmly, making her decision. "I do not believe the Fox had anything to do with your father's unfortunate death."

"Now, that won't do, lass," Chisholm said sternly. "Dalcross is the acting sheriff, so he has every right to ask his questions. You must answer him truthfully."

"With respect, my lord, and truthfully, I know naught that can help, for I've never seen his face, and I will not speculate. Nor will I speak of discussions we had, for indeed, I have greater cause to be grateful to the Fox than to Francis Dalcross."

"A point to the lady, I believe," Alex said dulcetly.

Dalcross shot him a look of pure hatred. "She may win a point or two, but I hold the winning hand, I believe." Turning to address Chisholm, he said, "The law supports me, my lord. As you know. *Sionnach Dubh* was declared outlaw years ago, and witnesses have seen her in his company. I saw her with him myself."

"I am astonished that you dare to admit that," Bab said. "When you speak of lawbreakers, sir, I say you should name yourself amongst them!"

"Therefore," he went on, ignoring her and speaking directly to Chisholm, "since she plainly knows more about him than anyone else does, she is in clear violation of the law if she refuses to answer all questions put to her. I can and I will charge her with being an accomplice to murder, and she will share his fate."

"I believe that to make such a charge, you must first prove that he committed the crime and that she knows facts material to your case," Alex said.

Chisholm nodded. "That is true."

"It is also true," Dalcross snapped, "that I can arrest her if she refuses to speak, and take her to Inverness for questioning. Is that not so, my lord?"

"Aye, it is," Chisholm agreed reluctantly.

"Then, my lady, you have a choice. You can answer my questions now without equivocation, or I will take you to Inverness. Which shall it be?"

Bab was silent.

Chisholm said earnestly, "You must answer

him, lass. I cannot prevent his arresting you if you do not." When she hesitated, he added roughly, "By our lady, Alex, command her to answer the man!"

Alex looked at Bab. "You should, you know. It is only sensible."

"I have nothing useful to tell him and no wish to aid him," she repeated.

"Faith, Alex, do you call that a command?" his father demanded.

With a little smile, Alex said, "If you recall, sir, you have already noted that my lady wife is not a properly biddable female. If I must be honest, and in this case I sincerely believe I must, it is a lack that I particularly admire in her."

"Not always," Bab muttered.

"No, not always," he agreed, his smile widening. "Are you quite sure that you cannot bring yourself to answer his impertinent questions?"

"I am sure," she said.

Alex turned back to Dalcross and shrugged. "There you have it, I believe."

"Then I am placing you under arrest, my lady. Please stand up."

"She has still not broken her fast," Alex reminded him.

"That is not my fault," Dalcross snapped. "I warrant you'd as lief I convey her safely to Inverness before nightfall."

"Aye, that is a point to you. You will not

take her alone, however."

"I cannot stop you if you choose to follow us," Dalcross said, "but you may not accompany us, nor will I grant you access to her when we arrive."

"Here," Chisholm protested, "you'll not keep a gently raised female in the Inverness Tolbooth! 'Tis unheard of!"

"She will stay at Sheriff's House," Dalcross said. "As you know, it possesses several quite adequate cells that have held quality visitors before."

"You do not possess any female staff at present, however," Alex said.

"That is not so," Dalcross said. "My father employed a respectable housekeeper, and I mean to keep her on there."

"My lady wife, if she is indeed to accompany you, will quite naturally take her own waiting woman with her, however," Alex said blandly.

Dalcross nodded and then said to Bab, "I would like to leave at once, my lady. I will accept your word of honor if you give it that you will accompany me without the necessity of manacles or other indignity. You may also take a few moments to apprise your maidservant that she is to accompany you, and you may break your fast if you can do both with some dispatch."

"I will give you my word, sir, if you will give me yours before these men that I will be safe in your company. I have reason, as you know, to doubt that."

He grimaced. "I owe you my profoundest apologies for what occurred between us, madam. I misunderstood our relationship, I fear. Now, pray do not tarry, lest nightfall find us still on the road."

Bab heard a sound from Alex that sounded suspiciously like a growl, but when she glanced at him, he met her look as mildly as if Dalcross's intrusion in their day were but a ripple in the sands of time. He did not offer to accompany her upstairs, but that did not surprise her. With enemies in the castle, although he disliked confrontation, he would not turn his back.

After Bab had departed for Inverness with Dalcross and his men, Alex listened to his father read him a dismal description of his character, the better part of which he agreed with completely. Then he excused himself, saying he could not see what he might gain by hurrying after her as Chisholm recommended, when he could do nothing for her in Inverness. With his father's reproaches still ringing in his ears, he left the hall and hurried to his bedchamber, hoping to find Hugo there.

Although his lordship, clearly disgusted with his son's lack of enterprise, had promptly ordered a number of his own men to follow Dalcross's party and ensure that Bab arrived safely at the Sheriff's House in Inverness, he had not spared her character either. Alex agreed with much of what he said on that head, too, not least of which was a flat declaration that someone ought to have taught the wench obedience to authority long before her eighteenth birthday.

On the other hand, he decided, no one could fault her for a lack of discretion.

Entering his bedchamber, he found it empty, and nearly certain that Hugo must have returned to the cave, he flung open one of his wardrobe chests and began searching through it for clothing that would be more practical for the hours ahead.

"I dinna approve o' deceiving the lass. Were ye a son o' mine I'd see ye well skelped for such duplicity."

Grimacing, Alex told himself that his guilty conscience was getting sadly out of hand. It had begun to sound increasingly like an indignant female, and how his own thoughts could sound so passed his understanding.

"Ye'd understand well enough did ye ever open your eyes, me fine lad."

"Me eyes *are* open," he protested, speaking aloud this time.

"Nay, then, for were they open, ye'd see me. I be right here in front o' ye."

An oblique sense of movement drew his eye toward the bed, but no one was there. Then, through a smokelike mist, he saw a plump little woman perched near the foot of the bed, leaning against the bedpost.

The smoke cleared as it gathered into a single stream issuing from an odd-looking white implement that she held in one hand. She eyed him with disapproval.

He stared, for where she might have come from, he could not imagine. "I would have sworn that no one else was in here," he said.

"Then ye'd ha' been wrong," she said.

"Who are you?"

"Me name's Maggie Malloch, but we've nae time now tae go into me antecedents. What d'ye mean tae do about your lass?"

"I'm going to do what I do best," he said.

"Aye, that's good, but take the lad wi' ye."

He did not have to ask which lad. "I'll have to take him, because I'll need Hugo, and I dare not leave young Gibby to his own devices whilst I'm gone."

"Aye, ye're a canny one and nae mistake, but ye'll ha' tae tell her the truth gey soon now, ye ken."

"I am not looking forward to that," he admitted. "Even now, I am not persuaded that it is the best plan, because her safety may yet depend upon being able to say with all sincerity that she knows nothing."

"Aye, 'tis true, that, but ye've deceived her!"

"If you are saying that I'm a scoundrel for doing such a thing, I agree w—"

"Nay, nay, I'm no saying any such thing. All men deceive women. It be their nature, and women's nature tae deceive men. I'm just saying that there be consequences ye may no wish tae face."

"What business is this of yours?" he asked.

"I'm tae watch, is all."

"Watching does not require speech or the purposeful interference with the very thoughts in my head," he pointed out. "You will note that I have not demanded more details of your identity. I'm nearly afraid to ask *what* you are, but I do recall Lady MacRae once mentioning a woman no one else seemed to see, who rode pillion with Lady Kintail on her journey here. Was that you?"

"Aye, for she could see me until I took steps tae prevent it," Maggie said. "Kintail can see me, too, but I took steps straightaway wi' him, so he never did."

He nodded but resisted asking more questions about that. Instead, he said, "Why are you watching me?"

"Not only ye, but others, too. There be mischief afoot," she said. "I aim tae see fair play, and tae that end, I'll see that your sword protects ye as it should."

"With respect, may I point out that it rarely fails me?"

She puffed on one end of the white implement and exhaled smoke before she said, "Ye dinna ken what lies ahead or who may try tae cast a spell on ye or your personal effects, but I can protect yon sword and yourself against evil spells."

"Can you not simply see that it does not fall into the wrong hands?"

"I canna interfere so obviously wi' other mortals, but sithee, others o' my world be watching, too — me son, Claud, for one. Unfortunately, he be beset as usual by females, poor lad, and whenever he falls in lust, he makes mistakes."

The door opened before Alex could reply, and Hugo entered. When Alex looked back at the bed, the little woman was gone.

"Claud," Lucy said urgently, shaking his shoulder. "Wake up, Claud!"

Starting, Claud rubbed his eyes and saw green. The canopy of leafy branches overhead and the damp, earthen smell of the woods made him think at first that he had somehow been wafted to Catriona's bower, but a second thought and the lack of the burn's gentle babbling suggested otherwise.

"Where am I?" he asked, blinking his eyes as if he might find himself safely back in his mother's parlor by doing so.

"Ye be here wi' me, ye great daffy," Lucy told him.

"But how did I get here?"

"D'ye no ken this place?" Lucy countered.

He shook his head. "I thought it was Catriona's glade, but a wee burn runs through that place, and there be a mirror pool, too."

"I told ye, I dinna like water," Lucy said with a grimace.

"Good lack, ha' ye dried them up, then?"

"I like the place better this way. Dinna ye like it, Claud?"

"Nay, I do not!"

"Well, nae matter. I woke ye 'cause they're taking your lass tae Inverness, and if she doesna tell them what they want tae ken, they'll put her on trial for her life and hang her. We must stop them, Claud, or ye'll fail in your task, and the Circle will give ye over tae the wicked Host."

Claud shuddered. "But what can we do?"

"I think we should winkle her away from them and hide her."

"We canna do that," Claud said. " 'Twould be tae show our power where mortals would see it. Breaking that rule all by itself would mean failure, lass."

"Nay, Claud," she said, moving seductively against him. "I'll show ye a way we can do it without harm tae our —"

She disappeared without finishing, and Claud instantly became aware of the prickling sensation that of late had heralded his mother's arrival.

Maggie stood in front of him before he could brace himself. Her face was close to his. "D'ye never learn?" she snapped. "What were ye doing here wi' that wicked baggage?"

"I dinna ken," he admitted. "I were sleeping

410

in yon parlor, then I were here."

"There be mischief afoot, lad," Maggie said with unwonted gentleness. "Go wi' your lass and seek help from nae one ye dinna trust absolutely. And, Claud, dinna forget that if ye meet wi' evil, ye must call it by its name tae defeat it."

"Aye, Mam, I'll remember."

With that, she dismissed him and he hurried to find Mistress Bab.

Bab's journey to Inverness was accomplished without incident, because once they were out of Glen Affric, the tracks from Strathglass through Glen Urquhart and north along Loch Ness to Inverness were more heavily traveled. Although she had lost all respect for Francis Dalcross on the day he abducted her, she had little fear that he would molest her on the way, particularly with Giorsal riding at her side.

She could even sympathize with his bereavement, certain that he must feel it sorely. Even so, she could not bring herself to believe that the Fox had had anything to do with Sheriff Dalcross's death.

She had learned more along the way, because the men in his tail talked among themselves about it. Apparently, the sheriff had been riding from Sheriff's House to Bothyn Castle, the Dalcross family seat near the village of Beauly on the Beauly Firth, when he was attacked and stabbed to death.

What caused discussion, aside from the discovery near the body of that telltale silver coin, was that the sheriff had apparently been alone, his customary tail of six men-at-arms having been diverted at the critical time to give chase to a man on a large black horse. The men escorting Bab assumed the rider to have been a decoy, allowing the true Fox to lie in wait and murder the sheriff.

To Bab, on the other hand, that decoy was proof that the Fox had had nothing to do with the murder. If he were going to kill someone, she was sure he would face his opponent man-to-man and doubtless with a grim smile on his face beneath his mask. But she listened to all that they said and said nothing herself.

As dusk fell, they crossed the wooden bridge over the River Ness to enter Inverness, and shortly afterward they reached the gates of Sheriff's House in the High Street. Although Bab looked about her with interest and even admired the great stone castle on Castle Hill to the south, she sighed with disappointment that she had seen no sign of the Fox along the way.

Giorsal said, "I warrant his lordship will ha' ye out o' this place in a trice."

Bab nodded silently, not having the heart to tell her that his lordship believed in the rule of law and had already admitted that in this case the law was on Francis Dalcross's side. Her strongest hope had lain with the Fox.

When they drew rein and Dalcross dismounted, he made no attempt to approach her, signing to two of his men to assist both women in dismounting and then commanding those same men to take them to the cells. These proved to be small, dank chambers below the house, where there was little light by which to see.

"There be a pail in yon corner, my lady," one of the men said as the other used a tinderbox to light a cresset on the wall. "Sheriff Dalcross ordered the bench and bed removed, but I warrant someone will be bringing ye food afore long."

She had not thought about food, but she did now, for she had had little but a crust of bread and some water since leaving Dundreggan, and she was hungry.

The men left, and Giorsal said, "This be a dreadful place, Mistress Bab."

"Aye, and I'll not be surprised if it grows more dreadful before dawn."

"D'ye no think they'll feed us, then?"

Bab did not know, but they were soon to find out, for not ten minutes had passed since the two men had left them to themselves, when a key sounded in the lock and Francis himself thrust the door open, filling the doorway.

"Welcome to Sheriff's House, my lady."

"It will avail you little to have me here," Bab said. "I know nothing that will aid you in your search, and even if I did I would not tell you."

"We'll see soon enough what you know, my

sweet, because before this time tomorrow, I promise you, you will be begging me to let you speak."

"Do you mean to torture me then? Even that cannot aid you, since I cannot tell you what I do not know."

"Just think of the possibilities, though," he said, smiling in a way that made her wish she could smack him. "I am a creative man, and I will bend my abilities to the task of making you tell me everything you know. If necessary, pressure can be brought to bear on your woman here whilst you watch to see how she enjoys it."

A chill shot up Bab's spine at the thought that they might hurt Giorsal, but she forced herself to remain silent. Common sense told her she might well be begging him before long, but she would not begin now.

His smile widened. "I suppose you expect the Fox to rescue you," he said. "He won't succeed, of course, but I certainly hope he tries. Sheriff's House is closely guarded in ways he would never suspect. However, if he does come to me, at least you will be spared the ordeal of my questioning."

"You will not catch him," she said. "Better men than you have tried."

He chuckled. "I will leave you to contemplate the future, lass. It would be a shame to spoil your beauty, but one way or another, I will soon know all you can tell me about the man who murdered my father. That cresset on the wall

414

contains enough fat for another hour or so. You'll not get more. Nor will you have food, although I may, out of mercy, allow you water tomorrow before we begin." With that, he stepped back and shut the door, and again they heard the key in the lock.

Bab turned to find Giorsal regarding her grimly, and said, "I'll not let them hurt you, Giorsal. Francis and his men will do as they like with me, but if they threaten you, be sure that I'll tell them what little I know."

"I thank ye for that, Mistress Bab, though I doubt it will avail us much. That villain doesna look as if he'd believe ye'd told him all ye ken even when ye had."

That was not Bab's fear. Hers was that he would continue to threaten Giorsal until she told him she had visited the Fox's cave and promised to do all she could to lead him there. Surely, though, if he took her out to hunt for the cave, the Fox would rescue her then. She decided that she should give that matter more thought.

" 'Tis a pity Sir Alex is no the avenging sort," Giorsal said with another sigh. "He and his lordship, between them, should be able to gather men to storm this place and set us free."

"His lordship would not allow that," Bab said. "He believes in the law, Giorsal, and if this comes to a trial, he believes the law will set me free." She had a nagging suspicion that Alex was not so sanguine as his father. Amiable

415

though he was, she did not think he would be content to leave her in Francis Dalcross's clutches But what he could do to alter the situation, she could not imagine.

"Ye'd think a gentleman would provide a seat for a lady in a place like this," Giorsal said. "Yon Dalcross does pretend to be a gentleman, does he not?"

"We'll just have to sit on the floor, Giorsal," Bab said. "At least, the weather has warmed, so we can use your cloak to put under us and mine to put over us, and perhaps we'll be able to get some sleep. At least, if means to let me ponder his methods of torture until morning, it is unlikely that he will disturb us tonight."

"Aye, if we can trust his word," Giorsal said darkly. But she took off her cloak and folded it so they could sit upon it now and lean against the wall.

They talked for a time, and when the cresset sputtered and died, and the chamber grew colder, they spread the cloak on the hard stone floor and wrapped Bab's heavy crimson one around them as well as they could. The floor was cold.

Bab was sleeping fitfully when the rattle of a key in the lock awoke her. Sitting up, she shook Giorsal, whispering her name. "Someone's coming!"

"It'll be that villain," Giorsal said. "I wish we had a good, stout club."

Bab wished it, too, for the thought of what

Francis might do terrified her. The chamber was pitch dark now, but she could not stand the thought of him finding her on the floor, so she stood up and clutched her cloak around her. Giorsal stood beside her, gripping her arm.

Bab sensed rather than saw the door swing open. Whoever stood there had no light, but even so, she felt herself relax.

"We're here," she said softly.

"Aye, well, ye're quiet as mice in a mill, so I did wonder," he said in his deep, authoritative voice. "Would ye no like to leave now?"

"We would," Bab said, smiling for the first time since she had left Dundreggan.

"But who is that, my lady?" Giorsal muttered. "Likely, he'll be one o' that Dalcross's men, trying to trick us."

"It is no trick, Giorsal, for I recognize his voice. 'Tis *Sionnach Dubh,* and he will not harm us. He aids people in trouble, and we certainly need his help."

"The Fox!"

"We've nae time for chatter," he said. "Come now at once. Take my hand, lass, and ye, Mistress Giorsal, take her ladyship's hand. I canna show a light down here, for they'd see it sure, through those wee windows near the ceiling."

They stepped out of the chamber and waited while he relocked the door.

"However did you come by that key?" Bab asked.

He chuckled. "I thought ye knew by now

417

that I ha' my ways, lass."

His commoner's accent seemed thicker tonight, and she wondered if he was affecting it for Giorsal's sake. At first, she had believed he aped her own manner of speech, but she had come to wonder if he might not be of gentler birth, aping common folk as a way to disguise himself.

When he tugged her hand, she moved to follow but remembered what Francis had said. "He's set guards to watch for you. He hoped you would come!"

"Dinna fret, lass. I ken well how the man thinks. He'll no catch me tonight."

Reassured, she followed where he led, holding tightly to his hand and to Giorsal's. She could see only shadows and denser shadows. There were no windows in the corridor outside the chambers, only a small one high in the wall at the end of it. What light strayed through that one came from the stars, for she saw no sign of a moon. At all events, they were moving from dimmest light into blackness.

He paused, released her hand, and without the sound of another door opening, she felt a sense of space where there had been none before. He continued to move forward a few steps with confidence, but a moment later, he paused again and urged her and Giorsal to pass him.

"I'll just shut it again," he murmured.

They were in a passageway now that smelled of earth, and when Bab reached out she touched a rough-hewn post. Feeling around it, she found a dirt wall. "We're in a tunnel," she whispered.

"Aye," he said. " 'Tis gey convenient, that, I say."

"But how did you —"

His finger touched her lips, silencing her. "Nae questions. We still ha' to get shut o' this place."

His finger stayed right where it was, so she muttered against it, "How do you always know exactly where my —"

Chuckling this time, he slid the finger down to tilt her chin up as he said, "D'ye never obey, lass? Hush now, and follow me."

He clasped her hand in his, and she followed with Giorsal trailing silently behind her, clinging to her skirt. The tunnel was long, but at last, Bab smelled fresh air ahead, and soon after that, the dense darkness lightened, and then they were outside, breathing cold night air, tangy with salt from the Moray Firth.

The Fox paused, and Bab knew he listened as intently as she did. She had no exact idea where they were, but from their relationship to Castle Hill and the sound of the River Ness nearby, they were at the perimeter of the town somewhere near the bridge. Windows still showed lights, and torchlight from the Hill revealed the shapes of houses in the town, but there was rustling shrubbery nearby as well.

"Here, master."

The words came from their right, and the Fox quickly led them toward the speaker. Bab could not see the man's features or judge his shape, for he wore a long cloak like his master's, but she heard whuffling sounds and pawing of impatient horses. A moment later, she saw them, five of them.

Realizing that he must have at least two companions, she looked for the second one and discerned a much smaller figure close to the horses. Even as she saw him, however, the Fox caught her around the waist and swung her onto one of the horses. A moment later, Giorsal too was mounted.

"Let's go, lads," he muttered. "Not a sound now until we're well away."

He waited until they had crossed the bridge before he said in a normal tone, "Ye lads ride on ahead wi' Mistress Giorsal. I want a private word wi' her ladyship."

Without comment, they obeyed.

"Thank you," she said. "I feared you would not come. I'm glad you did."

"Ye do recall that I warned ye this would happen," he said.

"Aye, but I could not stop it. Francis Dalcross —"

"Ye need not explain Francis Dalcross to me," he said.

"You do not ask me if I told him anything."

"I know ye did not."

A warm feeling spread through her at hearing

that he had trusted her so. Nonetheless, she said frankly, "It was as you said though, for he promised to do whatever he had to, to make me talk. He . . . he threatened to hurt Giorsal."

"I hope you would have had the good sense to tell him anything you knew long before it came to that point," he said roughly.

"I am afraid I would have," she admitted.

"There is no shame in that, lass."

They were silent for some moments, and then he said more calmly, "I warned ye, too, that any sort of relationship with me might be hazardous, but the situation is a wee bit different now, is it not?"

"How so?" she asked.

"Ye be a married lady."

"Aye, and you said you approved of the marriage, if you will recall."

"I did, and I do. Things can be gey different now, lass. Ye love adventure, and I — if I may say so — represent adventure as nae one else could. Moreover, I think I ha' fallen in love wi' ye, and I think perhaps ye love me a wee bit, too."

He paused, but when she could not bring herself to say the words he so clearly hoped she would say, he went on. "Although ye could scarcely marry *Sionnach Dubh* or live safely wi' him, now that ye have a gey safe husband in Sir Alex Chisholm, we can certainly see more o' each other and perhaps become even more intimately acquainted."

Chapter 19

Bab did not speak. Delighted as she was to hear the Fox admit that he loved her, she was disappointed that he would make such a proposition.

At last, quietly, she said, "I take my marriage vows seriously, sir. I took them before God and before a priest of the Scottish Kirk. I could never betray my husband in the manner you suggest, not even for you."

"No one need know," he said.

"I would know. Indeed, your suggesting this makes me wonder if you encouraged me to marry Sir Alex in the hope that I would then become your mistress. If you did, I can only say that you were mistaken in me. The sort of clandestine relationship you propose is not an adventure but a mortal sin, and so you should know." As she said the words, the memory of her wedding dream stirred, but it quickly faded and she felt no guilt. It had been only a dream.

"I ha' disappointed ye," he said. "I hope ye can forgive me."

Something in his voice sounded out of place under the circumstances, but she could not put her finger on what it was. Then she realized that although he had expressed concern, he did not sound upset. In fact, he sounded almost cheerful.

Nonetheless, the proposition shadowed her opinion of him a little more. Each time he had criticized Alex or condemned his lack of action, she had felt obliged to defend him. At first, she had thought it was merely what one did when a friend was criticized, but each time it happened she had disliked it more.

At the same time, she was as sensually aware of the Fox's nearness as she ever had been, and she was grateful that they were on horseback. Had they been standing face-to-face, had he put his arms around her or kissed her, she was not certain she would have had the strength to deny him.

They were such different men, the two of them. Alex was wealthy, well traveled, and accustomed to having whatever he wanted without having to exert himself much to get it. The Fox apparently did as he pleased and took what he wanted, but he did not seem to mind exertion in the least. He was quick to fight, had all the qualities of a born rebel, and believed in both violence and humiliation as means by which to punish his enemies. She would never forget his punishment of Francis Dalcross, when he had sent the man scurrying naked into the shrubbery.

Just the thought of that scene made her glance at him. Clearly aware of her attention, he turned toward her, but he did not speak. He had been silent since her rejection of his proposition. Remembering now what he had done to Francis made her glad she had refused to answer Francis's questions about him. If Francis ever got his hands on the Fox, he would hang him for that incident if for nothing else.

She thought of Alex, charming and kind. He wore beautiful clothes and was an excellent dancer. She could not imagine the Fox gracing the King's court, let alone dancing a galliard. And although Alex had been known to travel in his silly chair borne by servants, and was more apt to react to outrage with a limp "dear me" than to strap on his sword and seek vengeance, he forgave her faults easily and casually, and had not lost his temper even when she had flung things at him. His eyes had flashed briefly on occasion, to be sure, and she had feared for a moment that he might retaliate. That he had not had proven a bit of a disappointment at the time, but at least Alex had never threatened to beat her, as the Fox had.

He wondered what she was thinking. Doubtless, she was condemning his stupid proposition almost as severely as he was himself. Although he had been silently berating himself since making it, he knew that what had impelled him to test her in such a fashion was the same imp in him that had stirred him to attempt his imposture in the first place, and that was his own self-doubt. But he had not expected to feel such overwhelming guilt at the result.

Bab was true. She was discreet, courageous, and wholly trustworthy. She was a pearl among women, and he was a swine not to be truthful with her. But he had already put her in danger and he would put her in much more if he revealed the truth about the man she had married. Regardless of what that odd little woman, Maggie Malloch, had advised, that danger was real now, and it would remain real for as long as Francis Dalcross lived and the Fox remained active. He heard no voice arguing with him in his head now about that.

Nonetheless, deceit was and had always been contrary to his nature. For months, it had seemed necessary, but with Bab in his life, it seemed only dishonest. He had long believed that he was protecting himself and his family the best way he knew, but he was rapidly coming to realize that, instead, he had merely been testing himself, his father, and now, most recently, testing the woman he had come to love.

Bab wished he would say something. Was he angry with her? It did not feel as if he were. Perhaps if she spoke first, the tension between them would ease. She wondered how he had known about the tunnel at Sheriff's House, but he had made it clear that she should not ask him questions about things like that.

"I should not have said that."

His voice after such a long silence startled her, but she did not have to ask him what he meant. "No," she said, "you should not."

"Art vexed wi' me, lass?"

"Not now, but pray stop using that silly commoner's accent. I know you can speak as properly as I do, for you have done so any number of times. I will not ask who, in truth, you are, but 'tis plain to me that you were gently bred and educated."

"You are too wise for your own good," he said. "How long have you known that, and what else have you deduced, I wonder."

"You need not sound as if you would like to throttle me," she said. "I know you would not, for I am quite sure that you did not murder Sheriff Dalcross. Indeed, I doubt that you have ever murdered anyone."

"So you do not subscribe to the popular belief that if Chisholm's cousin did not murder his two sons, I must have done so."

"No, and that must certainly be nonsense, for no one has even suggested you had a motive. One might as well accuse Sir Alex of murdering his own brothers!"

"One might indeed."

"You need not say it in that tone of voice, as if it were possible," she said. "Recall that he was in France at the time."

"Italy."

"Well, on the Continent, at all events."

"So you believe Christopher Chisholm murdered his cousins, then."

"I do not know him, but men say he did, so I suppose he must have."

"I do know him. He did not."

"Then where is he? Why did he not come forward?"

"That I do not know, but I would wager that our recently deceased sheriff and his son know more about that whole business than they have ever admitted."

"I thought Dalcross did not become sheriff until after the event."

"He did not, but the event propelled him into the office. Someone suggested to Jamie that since Chisholm could not keep his own sons from being murdered, he was unfit to continue as Sheriff of Inverness. The result is as you have seen.

"Dalcross and his son turned the office into a lucrative business, much to the detriment of the people it is supposed to serve. Politics entered into it, of course, and Chisholm himself was in no shape after his sons' deaths to contest the Dalcross appointment, certainly not with your precious Alex as his sole remaining heir."

"I wish you would not continually belittle Sir Alex," Bab said testily. "Pray, recall that he is my husband."

"I never forget it, lass, but you are right. I should not speak so dismissively of him in your company. Forgive me?"

427

"Aye, for that and for many things," she said. "Will we reach Dundreggan before morning?"

"Aye, we've time to spare if you can stay in that saddle, for it cannot be much after ten yet."

"Mercy, I thought it must be much later. Were you not afraid you might encounter Francis Dalcross, entering Sheriff's House so early?"

"Nay, for my lads were watching him. He took himself off to his favorite alehouse not half an hour after he deposited you in your cell at Sheriff's House. I was only waiting for full darkness to fetch you."

"You were following us, then? How did you learn he had arrested me?"

"I told you, I have my ways."

"I expect someone along the way told you. We saw any number of people."

"The moon will be up in a bit," he said. "We'll travel faster then."

Aboard the Marion Ogilvy

Riding the tail of the incoming tide, they docked at Couroch soon after midnight. Located near the upper end of the Firth of Clyde, Couroch was the nearest seaport to Dumbarton and thus to Stirling and Cambuskenneth Abbey, where Sir Kenneth Lindsay would deliver his messages to Cardinal Beaton.

The winds had remained favorable all the way, and despite sailing perilously near England's coast at times, they had seen no further sign of enemy ships and had easily made the North Channel by dawn that morning. Now, working by lantern light, the men quickly furled the sails and lashed them to the yards.

As soon as the moorings were fast, Sir Kenneth took his leave, and as he walked down the gangplank to the torchlit dock, Gibson turned and looked at Kit, who had been keeping an eye on him.

Many of the regular crewmembers were preparing to go ashore, because the ship would stay at Dumbarton for a sennight to take on supplies. Kit, Willie, and Tam would remain aboard, as usual, and Kit believed Gibson would take the first opportunity to finish the flogging Sir Kenneth's orders had postponed.

Resigned to the inevitable, he headed below to get supper and to sleep if he could. As he passed under the afterdeck gun port, he saw Tam coming toward him.

"Come quickly, lad," the older man said, gesturing urgently. "Willie's dropped a line off one o' the main shrouds from the chain wale."

"How did he get out there?" Kit demanded, because the chain wale was a heavy plank bolted edgewise to the outside of the ship to increase the spread of its shrouds. The usual access to it was by sliding down a pair of the shrouds from the afterdeck. It was unlikely, even at midnight and with much of the ship's crew hastening to go ashore, that Willie could have done such a thing without being seen.

"The men pulled one o' them cannon back tae poke about in its innards after it misfired at them pesky English yesterday, and they havena shoved it back yet," Tam said. "Willie climbed through the port, and he says there be room for us tae squeeze through, too, do we want tae go wi' him. I'm for doing it. Will ye come?"

Glancing back to where he had last seen Gibson, Kit saw that he was watching them. There was no time to ponder the wisdom of Willie's plan. They would not be near Scottish soil again for months, and they were unlikely ever to get another chance like this one.

"I'll do it," Kit said.

Tam turned on his heel and led the way into the shadows beneath the afterdeck. A lone lantern burned midway, casting enough light for men to see where they were going but not enough to encourage lingering along the way.

They went toward the stern gun port on the side opposite the dock. From even a short distance, the gun there was not obviously out of position, but when they reached it, Kit saw that it sat more than a foot from the porthole, which was easily large enough for wiry Willie Armstrong to slip through. Whether stocky Tam or the much larger Kit would be able to do so was another question.

"I'll fit if I ha' tae shed my clothes," Tam

said, eying the porthole grimly.

"Go on, then. We won't have much time before someone sees us."

Outside, Willie also encouraged Tam to make haste, so he put his head and shoulders through the hole, and with Willie tugging and Kit pushing, managed to squeeze the rest of himself through.

"It'll be easier for ye, 'cause ye're slimmer in the middle," he told Kit. "If ye can get them shoulders o' yours through, the rest will come easy as winking."

The deed proved easier than Kit had expected, and once on the wide plank, the rest was just as Willie had promised. His line was stout, well tied, and reached to the waterline. It would be merely a matter of shinning down it and swimming across the River Clyde to its opposite bank.

Commanding the other two to go first, Kit waited until Willie was in the water with Tam close behind him on the line. He was about to swing onto it himself when a strong hand reached through the porthole and grabbed his arm.

"Tell your friends tae swim back here right now," Gibson growled, "or I'll blow your fool head off first and then send me lads in tae fetch 'em both back here, so's I can hang each one from his own yardarm."

Without a thought, Kit yanked his arm free and dove. Although he heard a gun discharge, he hit the water unscathed. When he came up for air, he saw Tam and Willie splashing wildly for the opposite bank. Above them, Gibson had climbed out onto the plank and was taking careful aim at him.

As he drew breath to dive again, the man above suddenly lurched as if he had tripped, and plunged toward the water with a terrified scream.

Hitting hard and shoulder first, Gibson came up once, splashing wildly, and shrieked, "I canna swim!" Then he submerged again.

Wanting nothing more than to let the bastard drown, Kit nonetheless swam powerfully toward the place where he had seen him disappear. The water was calm, and the night around him was oddly silent. Neither Willie nor Tam dared shout to him, lest they draw unwanted attention, but he was astonished that no one above seemed to have heard either the gunshot or Gibson's terrified scream.

He dove several times, swimming underwater with sweeping strokes, feeling his way in the dark water for any part of Gibson, but to no avail. The first officer did not surface again or disturb the water with his struggles. He had vanished.

With no sign yet that anyone above had missed Gibson or the three of them, Kit swam to join Tam and Willie.

If Bab had hoped that when the moon arose and they rejoined the others, she would catch a

432

glimpse of at least two of her rescuers' faces, she was disappointed, for they, too, wore concealing cloaks and hoods. All she could discern was that one was much smaller than the other. Neither said a word.

The Fox waited until the moon rose to increase the pace, so when they joined the others, Giorsal exclaimed with relief, "Faith, Mistress Bab, I feared he ha' made off wi' ye, after all, and these men wouldna say a word tae me."

"I'm sorry you worried, but I told you we could trust him," Bab said.

Conversation after that was limited, for both women were tired and focused their energy on staying in the saddle and making as much speed as they safely could. The result was that they reached Dundreggan nearly two hours before dawn. The Fox and his henchmen parted from them a short distance from the gates.

"You'll be safe from here, lass," he said. "Just shout when you come within earshot, and they'll let you in. We'll watch, just to be sure."

"Thank you again, sir," she said. "It has occurred to me, though, that Francis Dalcross will come after me, will he not?"

"If he does, you must tell that husband of yours to spirit you away. I doubt he will be such a fool as to let you fall into Dalcross's clutches again, though. If he does, he will answer to me, as will you if you do anything so foolish as to put yourself in that villain's path or in any other sort of jeopardy."

His grim tone sent a little shiver up her spine, and she resolved to be particularly cautious, for a time at least.

Claud was pleased that Mistress Bab was safely back at Dundreggan. Obedient to his mother's wishes, he had kept close watch over the lass while she remained locked in the Sheriff's House cell. She was safe enough there, but he had wondered what he would do if Francis Dalcross had begun to torture her. The rules of the Clan were strict about interfering between mortals, and he had already tested those rules beyond what members of the Circle would accept, so he was relieved that he had not had to make any such a decision. As it was, he had done little other than help her sleep a bit and feed her needed energy for the long ride home.

He wondered where Lucy was. He had not seen her since Maggie's arrival had frightened her away. Nor had he seen Catriona, but he knew he would not see her as long as he had had to stay at Dundreggan. She would not risk growing goat's feet, so he would have to search elsewhere for her. He wondered if the little burn was bubbling again in her glade, or if Lucy's rearrangements would be permanent.

Bab had no trouble gaining entrance to Dundreggan. The men on the wall were delighted to open the gate for her, and the captain of the guard escorted her into the keep and protested when she refused to allow him to wake the household.

"Morning is quite soon enough to let them all know I am safe," she said. "I pray you, captain, do not disturb his lordship or anyone else."

"I doubt his lordship will be sleeping well under the circumstances, my lady. I'll just tell his man though, if ye dinna want me to wake him."

"Do as you think best, but I am going to bed."

Giorsal said sternly. "You should go to Sir Alex, mistress."

"I'll see him in the morning, too," Bab said.

"But he is your husband, and he must be anxious about you!"

"I want to think, Giorsal, and if you would assist me, you will not argue or scold. You may say all you like to me in the morning. For now, I prefer peace."

"Yes, my lady."

Bab knew from that formal response that she had offended her, but they were both worn out, and all she wanted to do was to sleep.

They went immediately to her bedchamber, where she performed cursory ablutions and climbed into bed in her shift. Despite her comment about wanting to think, however, she was asleep before Giorsal shut the door.

So exhausted was she that she barely stirred when an hour later, Alex climbed naked into the bed beside her and drew her into his arms. Sighing comfortably, she settled against him and slept until sunlight from the window wakened her and she found herself snuggled close with her back to him. Surprised, she turned to face him and found him smiling sleepily at her.

"How did you — ? That is, when did you — ?"

"You must learn to complete your sentences, sweetheart. How did I, or when did I what?"

"You know perfectly well what I meant. This happens to be my bed, sir."

"And I am your husband, madam. I have every right to be in your bed."

"You do not even ask how *I* come to be in it," she said. "Do I collect that the captain of the guard wakened you even after I asked him not to disturb you?"

"He did not waken me," Alex said. "I was already awake."

"My point, sir —"

"I know what your point is, lass. I also know how you returned home."

"Oh."

"I doubt there is anyone at Dundreggan who does not know by now. There is really no other way you could have returned here at four in the morning without a proper escort other than for *Sionnach Dubh* to have brought you."

"I suppose not," she said.

"So he is once again your rescuer."

She heard a note in his voice that made her look at him narrowly, but as usual there was nothing to read in his expression. Softly, she said, "He rescued us, yes, and I should think you'd be grateful to him, sir. He said you should take care that I do not fall into Dalcross hands again."

"Never fear, lass. I won't let that happen again," he said. "I know you must think little of me for letting it happen even once."

"You could not stop it," she said, "but if you think he has become a great hero to me, Alex, it is no such thing. I am grateful to him, but he has many faults. Nonetheless, and despite that coin Francis Dalcross said they found, I am sure the Fox did not murder the sheriff."

"He has killed before, lass. Men have seen him do so."

"But not in cold blood, sir. The one who dies always dies with a sword in his hand, and rather than kill his opponents, the Fox is more likely to humiliate them as he did the first time he rescued me when he stripped Francis of his clothing. I have heard all the tales, and no one has ever called him murderer or coward except for Francis Dalcross. Moreover, whatever the Fox may be, Alex, you are my husband."

"Am I, lass? Not quite yet, I think."

She leaned close and kissed him on the lips. "Marriage is forever, so I can think of no good reason to delay any longer. We should consummate our marriage before aught else interferes. And if such thinking is wanton of me, then so be it."

"It is not wanton, sweetheart, but there are certain things we must discuss."

"Faith, sir, do you not *want* to consummate our marriage?"

He groaned. "Oh, Bab, what a thing to ask me! Of course, I do."

"Then tell me what to do."

"Very well, but we must have a serious talk before this morning is over."

She snuggled against him again. "I'll do exactly as you say, sir, now and afterward. At least, I'll try. Now, explain this consummation business to me."

She was so soft and pliant, pressing her body eagerly against his, and the lawn shift she wore was so thin that she might as well have worn nothing at all. Alex decided that it would take a stronger man that he would ever be to resist her in this mood, although he did not doubt that he would pay a price for putting off his confession, just as he would pay for the outrageous proposition he had made to her on the way home from Inverness.

In the end it had been the proposition that decided the matter, for he realized that as long as he continued to deceive her, he would find it far too tempting to test her, and although that was not fair, it would be irresistible. She continued to surprise him and to soothe the place in him that still struggled to compete with his brothers. Since he would never best either of

438

them now, they would forever remain in his memory the superior beings they had been in his youth. But neither Rob nor Michael could ever have Bab, and that put their deaths in a certain new perspective for him. He had mourned their loss from the day he had learned of it, but he had mourned something else as well. Whatever that was had vanished the first time he had taken her in his arms.

As he slipped her shift off over her head now and began to caress her, beginning with her silky shoulders and breasts, he realized that she had never professed to love him — not as himself or as the Fox. But neither had he confessed to her that he had fallen in love with her, although as the Fox he had admitted that he thought he was. That scarcely counted, though, considering the circumstances.

He had feared to admit his growing love for her, knowing that she saw only the man he pretended to be since his return from the Continent and fearing that she could never truly love such a man. He had not thought himself a coward before, but even more than he feared that she did not love him now did he fear that his deceit might render him ineligible to claim her love for all time to come.

When the chance to marry her had arisen, he had leaped like a salmon at spawn to snatch at it. She was his now, or she would be when they consummated the union, no matter what happened in the future. And that she was his must always be accounted as an asset. But much as confession would relieve his soul, just the thought of it loomed as a monstrous obstacle between them. How would she react?

Ruthlessly suppressing these thoughts, he bent to kiss her breasts, taking one erect nipple into his mouth to suckle it, savoring her soft mews of pleasure. He would not play the fool tonight. He would give of himself, the real Alex, with all his passion and his love. And if, as a result, she recognized him for who and what he really was, they would deal with that then. But although he could not bring himself simply to blurt out the truth to her now and hope for the best, he would not deceive her in any other way, not any longer.

She clutched his hair now in one fist, her breath coming in little gasps as he moved a hand down her belly to the juncture of her legs and stroked the soft curls there. The nerves in his fingertips seemed supersensitive, as if he could feel her throbbing pulse beneath every inch of skin he touched.

His own body was ready, eager to claim her, but he wanted her ready first.

His fingers probed the opening between her legs and found that her body's natural defenses had already responded. She was ready for him. Still, he stroked her more, stimulating her and increasing her passions so that he would not hurt her any more than necessary when he took his first possession of her.

Each time he touched her, his own desire swelled more within him until he felt he would explode if he did not satisfy it soon.

Bab eagerly accepted his attentions, delighting in each new sensation and discovery. She had never suspected that her body hid such secrets, so many sensitive places. It amazed her that all Alex had to do was touch her, and her body would leap in response. One moment she felt as if she were melting into the feather mattress, and the next as if she were in a world where all was heady passion.

Her mouth felt hot and hungry, and she wanted to kiss him everywhere. Her hands moved over him, seeking to learn more about him and to excite him as he excited her. When his hand moved between her legs, she nearly cried out, but curiosity held her silent. As he caressed her and his fingers gently penetrated her, her tension increased until her body hummed from her breasts to her toes, and when he moved at last to claim her, she welcomed him. She was conscious of a brief dull ache and then he was inside her, hot and pulsing.

Alex was still for a moment, as if he were judging her reaction, and when she kissed his cheek and sought his lips, he began to move, gently at first and then more urgently for a time, until with a gasping moan he collapsed atop her.

Bab could scarcely breathe. It was not his

weight that stifled her but the increasingly aching desire in her body that had not yet been quenched. She wanted to urge him to continue, but she feared that, Alex being Alex, he had already exerted himself beyond all reason.

Hearing him draw a long breath heightened her concern, but then he shifted his weight to one side and began to caress her lightly, first with just his fingertips, drawing them downward from the side of her neck over her breasts to her waist and lower belly. Then he used the palm of his hand, stroking her, pausing at one breast to cup it gently, teasing her nipple with his thumb. Then his palm moved lower, stopping when it reached the curls at the juncture of her thighs and resting there.

When she opened her mouth to tell him to keep going he kissed her, thrusting his tongue inside, and at the same time fingering her soft nether lips, making her tense involuntarily. His palm moved to her thighs, stroking them until they relaxed, whereupon his fingers invaded her again, stroking and teasing until she moaned for release. Then he caught her hand and moved it so that it touched him, clasped him, and began to stroke and squeeze his stiffening flesh.

Fascinated by the way he moved within her grasp, Bab continued to caress him, and when he raised himself over her so that his hips were between her thighs again, she helped him insert himself. He began to move inside her then with tantalizing slowness, and she resisted the urge to beg him to move faster, savoring each new sensation, even the slight, continuing ache that accompanied all of them.

His kisses became more probing, and her tongue responded to his. Her hands clutched him, pulling him closer until her body leaped to meet his. Where first it had ached, now it had caught fire, but she felt no pain, only urgency. They found a natural rhythm together, climbing higher and higher until she thought she could bear no more. And then, all of a sudden, warm waves of pleasure flooded through her, great pulsing, muscle-contracting waves such as she had never known before.

When the sensations eased, she sighed and smiled at Alex. "What an amazing thing! Can we do it again?"

He chuckled deep in his throat and kissed her ear, his warm breath tickling it as he murmured. "Soon, sweetheart, but not instantly."

She snuggled against him, relaxing deeply with her head in the soft hollow of his shoulder. As they lay together, sated with pleasure, holding each other, and delighting in their new-found intimacy, someone rapped on the door.

Chapter 20

Pulling the quilt up so that it covered Bab to her chin, Alex said, "Enter."

Hugo put his head in, said apologetically, "Begging your pardon, Master Alex, but his lordship requests your presence below in the great hall."

"The devil fly away with his lordship," Alex said heartily. "Go and tell him that if he will contain his soul in patience, I shall be with him in half an hour. You may tell him that I am with my lady wife and have no wish to leave her any sooner. Couch that in whatever diplomatic phrases you like, Hugo, but tell him."

To Bab's surprise, Hugo remained stolidly where he was. "Wi' respect, sir, his lordship said ye was to come at once."

"A pox on his lordship, then," Alex said, but this time with less heat in the words, and Bab looked narrowly at him.

He smiled at her, and she noted that something in his manner was different. She considered it in the few seconds before he swung his legs out of the bed and gestured for Hugo to bring him his dressing gown. Then the answer came to her. He had set aside his affectations.

The drawl was gone, as was the sleepy look in

his eyes. It was as if their coupling had stripped away his outer shell and left the inner man. She liked the result. What she did not like was the way he exchanged looks with Hugo, as if they were communicating silently, keeping secrets from her.

"What is it?" she demanded. "What is going on, sir?"

Alex smiled again. "Naught to worry yourself about, sweetheart. I promised, remember? I won't let him take you back to Inverness."

His voice was different without the drawl, deeper and pleasant to her ear, but she felt her temper stir. "It is Francis then. Take care, sir. I won't be coddled."

"I'll have Hugo send Giorsal in so you can dress," he said as he left.

She carefully cleaned away the evidence of her coupling with a cloth and cold water from the ewer on the washstand, splashed more water on her face, and scrambled into her shift, petticoat, and bodice, leaving the lacings loose. Then she flung clothes from her chests until she found a skirt she could wear. By the time Giorsal arrived, there was little left to do but to tighten and tie Bab's laces.

Handing her mistress a silver-linked belt, Giorsal watched her fasten it, adjusted her skirt to her own satisfaction, and then stepped back to view the result.

"That will do, I expect," she said. "I'll just brush your hair now, mistress."

"Never mind my hair," Bab said. "Hand me that cap."

Knowing better than to argue with that tone, Giorsal did as she was bid.

Hastily, Bab slipped her feet into a pair of embroidered slippers, wrapped her tousled plaits into a knot atop her head, and crammed the lacy cap on over the whole. Then with a glance at Giorsal to assure herself that she had left no unseemly bare parts showing, she hurried down to the hall.

Having dressed so quickly and being certain that Alex would take his usual time, she fully expected to find his lordship pacing the floor, commanding all and sundry to tell him what the devil was keeping his son, but to her surprise Alex caught her on the stairway just before she reached the great-hall entrance.

"You are not to go in there, lass," he said, his tone uncompromising.

She met his gaze steadily. "I want to know what is happening."

"I do not know that myself yet," he admitted, "but Francis Dalcross is here, and Hugo said this time he has brought a whole troop of his men with him."

" 'Tis as I thought then and he's come to take me back." The thought made her shudder, but Alex had said he would not let Francis take her away again, and she did not think he would have said it had he not believed he could stop him.

He said now, "If be that is why he has come, I do not want him to see you. That was our error last time, but no one will have told him you are here unless my father did, and I am not sure he even knows."

"He does," Bab said. "The captain of the guard told me last night that he would wake his manservant and tell him I was safe."

"All the more reason to keep out of sight then," he said. "Don't defy me in this, Bab. I want your word that you will not show yourself until I give you leave."

"Very well," she said, glad that he had not ordered her back to her room. She was not certain she would have obeyed such an order, for much as she disliked defying him, she intended to see what happened.

She noted as Alex entered the hall that he walked in the languid, mincing manner she disliked so much, but that did not matter now. Hurrying back upstairs to the gallery, she went directly to the laird's peek, determined to see and hear for herself exactly what Francis wanted and what he meant to do.

As she reached the peek, she heard his voice easily. "So there you are at last, Sir Alex," he said. "Where is your lovely wife?"

"Faith, Dalcross, you amaze me," Alex drawled. "Have you misplaced the lass already?"

"I have not. I know exactly where she is, as do you."

447

Chisholm said sternly, "Speak your piece, man. You said you had a message for my son, and I have produced him for you. If you have misplaced her ladyship, you cannot expect us to help you find her again."

"Oh, I have not misplaced her, my lord. She has served the exact purpose I meant her to serve, for she has led me to *Sionnach Dubh,* just as I intended. Sir Alexander Chisholm, in the name of his grace, the King, I place you under arrest and charge you with the murder of my father. You will answer to that charge and to all the others laid over the years against your alter ego, *Sionnach Dubh.*"

Bab gasped and clapped a hand over her mouth so she would not cry out.

"Have you lost your senses, sir?" Chisholm snapped. "My son is hardly the man you seek. Do you not recall that your outlaw Fox is an expert with sword and pistol? To accuse Alex would be absurd were it not such an insult."

"I do you the courtesy to believe that he has deceived you just as he has deceived everyone else," Dalcross said. "But only a man who had himself lived at Sheriff's House would know its deepest secrets, unless you yourself revealed to the Fox the location of its hidden tunnel — a secret, I might add, that you did not see fit to impart to my late, esteemed parent or to myself."

"I have told no one," Chisholm snapped. "But clearly you know of it."

"I discovered it only tonight, however. My people were watching the bridge, knowing he would most likely cross the river there since it is still in spate and difficult to cross elsewhere. It was by sheer accident that we then found the tunnel. Someone had carelessly left the entry ajar, and one of my men felt the draft."

Bab frowned at hearing this. She was certain the Fox had fastened the door.

Claud, watching from his perch on the dais in one of the privacy-screen carvings, also frowned. Recalling his mother's warning about mischief afoot, he had watched Mistress Bab's escape with particular concern, relaxing his vigil only after the riders had crossed the bridge. Despite the darkness, he had seen her rescuer shut the hidden door carefully. He had, moreover, bolted it on the tunnel side.

Setting himself furiously to think, Claud hoped that for once he would find his mental faculties adequate to the task.

Francis said bluntly, "That the Fox was able to enter and leave with her ladyship in the dead of night without so much as showing a light speaks for itself and is clearly sufficient cause for his arrest."

Peeping around the archway into the hall, Bab saw him sign to two of his men to shackle Alex. She nearly demanded from the gallery that they unhand him, but remembering his command, she decided that she would do better to bide in peace until she had thought everything through more carefully.

Alex laughed in Dalcross's face as his captors clapped manacles on his wrists. "No one will believe this," he said. "Faith, Dalcross, but mayhap I should thank you. Such an accusation is bound to enhance my reputation to a vast degree."

Francis ignored him, gesturing for his men to take him away.

As they did, Alex said over his shoulder to his father, "Doubtless this matter will be resolved quickly, sir, but I'd be grateful if you would tell my lady wife that I love and adore her. I left her a token by which to remember me in the wee carved box that resides in the compartment in my bed-steps. Hugo knows the place."

"By heaven's might, I'll not stomach this," Chisholm said. "I will *not* lose another son to the whims of fate."

" 'Tis no whim, my lord," Dalcross said as he took his leave. "You will lose him by virtue of his own acts to the King's justice and the Inverness gallows."

Determined to avoid Chisholm lest he impose restrictions on her that she could not obey, Bab hurried upstairs without revealing to him that she had witnessed the entire scene. Going straight to Alex's chamber, she thrust the door open, catching the two people inside by surprise.

"Gibby," she exclaimed, "how relieved I am to see you! You cannot know what a fright you gave me by disappearing as you did."

"I didna disappear," the lad protested.

"We never meant to frighten ye, my lady," Hugo said. "Master Alex found him in the chapel and gave him to me to look after."

"Yes, he told me he had done that. Thank you for keeping him safe."

"I didna mind," Hugo said, favoring her with a searching look.

Thinking she knew the reason for it, she said soberly, "They have arrested Sir Alex. That idiotish Francis Dalcross believes him to be the Fox, which I know cannot be true, because I was with Sir Alex myself one day when we saw the Fox on the ridge above us."

Gibby and Hugo, their expressions wooden, said nothing.

"That reminds me, Hugo," she went on. "As Sir Alex was leaving, he said you would know of a certain compartment in his bed-step table where I might find a small carved box. He said it contains a gift for me."

"A gift, my lady?"

"Aye, a token by which to remember his love," she said softly.

"I ken the place," Hugo admitted. "I'll show ye."

Bab followed him to the head of the bed, where he squatted by the bed-step table and turned a small knob that formed part of the decorative carving. When an opening appeared, Bab reached in and slid out a wooden box.

Lifting its lid, she gasped, for the box was two-thirds full of silver coins. Some revealed the side with the fox's mask, others that with the sprig of heather.

She stared at them for a long moment without speaking as shock warred with fury in her unspoken thoughts, and then she looked at Hugo and said, "There can be but one meaning to these being here."

"Aye, mistress," he replied, watching her warily.

"Your master is very lucky that he is not standing here right now, but oh, how I wish he were, for I should like to teach him what I think of his deceits."

Wisely, this time Hugo remained silent.

She was amazed at the calm that seemed to have banked her fury but was certain that it must be false. Much as she wanted to rail at Alex, she could not do so until he was free again, and since Francis was determined to hang him . . . Suppressing that unwelcome thought, she said, "You knew the truth, of course."

"Aye, mistress. 'Twas m'self ye saw riding Dancer on the ridge that day."

She glanced at the boy and back, asking her next question silently.

"Aye, he kens the truth. But only since master found him in the chapel," Hugo added hastily. "The lad saw Dancer in the cave, ye see, and that horse be as well known as the Fox. He's true though, Wee Gibby is. He were with us last night and he'll no break faith wi' the master."

Bab gazed down at the coins in the box, saying with a sigh, "They found one of these on Friday beside the sheriff's body, Hugo."

"Aye."

"He could not have left it there on Friday, because he was here."

"Nay, my lady, he did not."

"Most people he has given them to tend to keep them, do they not?"

"Aye, they do and all."

Bab nodded. "I know of at least one man who possesses one of these coins who also had easy access to the sheriff's body after they discovered it."

"Aye, my lady, only he has more than one o' them coins, and 'tis me own belief that he put one where they found it to make it look as if the Fox had committed the murder. But there be no way to prove aught o' Francis Dalcross and much danger in trying, both to ourselves and to Master Alex."

"We must get help then," Bab said. "I know that many of the gentry hereabouts who would be willing to support any Chisholm against Francis Dalcross and his men, have gone south with their armies. But there must be some left who would help us, Hugo. Even if powerful men are few, there must be any number of others who would fight to protect the Fox from harm."

"Aye, sure," Hugo agreed.

"But my lady," Gibby said, "we canna tell them they'd be aiding the Fox. 'Tis a great secret, that."

"You are quite right, Gibby," Bab said, recognizing at once the error in her thinking. "Dear me, but this is a coil."

" 'Tis no matter," Hugo said. "Without a proper leader, nae one will dare stir a foot against Dalcross anyway. Dinna forget, mistress, that his men be better armed than most hereabouts."

"Nevertheless, we must do all we can. We'll simply tell them Chisholm's son has been accused and has not the least chance of getting a fair trial, because the jury will be men handpicked by Francis Dalcross."

"Aye, that'll anger them, right enough, and it be gey true, too," Hugo said.

"Do you still think they'll refuse to take up arms against Francis?"

"We'll ha' to see," Hugo said, but his tone made his skepticism clear.

"Gibby can help, too," Bab said.

Hugo nodded but said, "I answer only to Sir Alex and thus to ye, mistress, but we canna send others out without we first gain permission from his lordship."

"Could you put the matter to him, do you think?"

"It would come better did ye ask him, my lady."

Bab hesitated but quickly made her decision. "I think he would listen to you as easily as to me, Hugo, perhaps more easily. You traveled on the Continent with Sir Alex, after all, and I am only a woman. Moreover, if I go to him, he almost certainly will order me to stay here, and I cannot do that because I believe I can be of more use persuading folks to help. It will be harder for them to deny me, I think."

"But ye shouldna leave Dundreggan, my lady. Sir Alex wouldna like it."

"I know he would not," she said with a rueful smile. "He warned me to do nothing foolish or dangerous, and I am certain he would count this as both, but I'd rather see him angry and threatening all manner of punishment than see him hang. And if we cannot prevent it, Hugo, I am sure that Francis Dalcross will hang him. I'd never forgive myself if I sat obediently with our mothers and let that happen."

"And if aught should happen to ye whilst ye was trying to help him, d'ye think he'd be glad that ye helped?"

"He can say what he likes about that if we can just get him free again," Bab said. "He should recall before he rebukes me, however, that I have some few things to say to him as well, for deceiving me as he did."

"Aye, he did that, but 'tis sure he's trusting ye now," Hugo said.

She looked down at the coins. "He is, is he not? Then he should trust me to do as I think best, and so must you, Hugo."

"Aye, perhaps, but I think I'll show ye how to shoot Master Alex's pistol and ask a few o' the lads I trust to look after ye, rather than let ye ride out alone," Hugo said. "Getting ye outside the wall will be easy enough. I'll just tell the captain o' the guard that Master Alex said ye could go wi' me and a few others wha' be armed, or we can get out through the caverns, o' course, but that'll make for trouble should anyone seek ye whilst we're away."

"Then we'll follow your first plan," Bab said. "And, Gibby, I want you to see if you can persuade your people in Glen Urquhart to help Sir Alex."

"Aye, I'll try an ye want me to, but me dad did say I wasna to go back there whilst the Dalcrosses be looking for me," the boy reminded her.

"The only Dalcross left will not concern himself with you whilst he has Sir Alex to keep him busy," Bab said. "How long do you think we have, Hugo?"

"Not long, mistress. Francis Dalcross will want to have the whole business over and done in a twinkling, but he'll want folks to see what he'll call a fair trial, too, so he'll give his lordship time to travel to Inverness, and he'll want word to reach all the neighboring glens that he's caught the Fox and be trying him. I'm thinking we ha' four, maybe five days, but I'd not want to count on longer."

She nodded, feeling chilled at the thought that in less than a sennight Alex could be dead. The possibility had been lurking in her subconscious ever since she had heard Francis declare him under arrest, but now it threatened to overwhelm her, for she realized that the last thing she wanted was to lose Alex just as she had come to know him. She had much more yet to learn about the man she had married. She could not let Francis Dalcross deprive her of that fascinating, endearing prospect.

Loch Tarbert, the Kintyre Peninsula

By noon, Kit and his companions were helping a score of other men drag a west Highland galley across the quarter-mile strip of land between the Firth of Clyde and Loch Tarbert — a track much used over centuries for that purpose and worn smooth by the many hundreds of boats dragged across it. Its use eliminated the need to sail around the entire southern half of the Kintyre Peninsula and thus shortened the journey from Dumbarton to the Great Glen by nearly eighty miles.

Having easily decided that the quickest way from the north bank of the Clyde to the Highlands was by water, it had taken Kit only until shortly after first light to find a suitable galley

and persuade its captain to take on three unknown oarsmen. His good fortune continued,
however, for if anyone had been searching for
three escaped prisoners from the *Marion
Ogilvy*, he saw no sign of it.

He had expected to have to change boats
more than once in order to reach his destina-
tion. However, to his great satisfaction, their
congenial captain announced that he was
making first for the village of Oban on the east
shore of Loch Linnhe and thence for the even
smaller hamlet of Gordonsburgh at the head of
the loch, where the River Ness emptied into it.
That route according exactly with Kit's own
plan, he and his two companions had agreed to
row for their passage.

The galley's crew of thirty-two, like that of
many such boats, was primarily comprised of
landless adventurers and broken men, the latter
cast out of their clans for misbehavior, but no
one complained at the addition of three men
who could easily pull their weight, and no one
questioned their antecedents.

Kit had expected Willie and Tam to head for
the Scottish Borders as soon as they touched
home soil, but both men informed him that
they had agreed to cast their fortune with his.

"But I'm for the Highlands, lads," he said.

"Aye, and that'd be a fine thing," Tam said.
"I ha' never seen 'em afore."

"Me neither," William said, and so it was decided.

All three adapted quickly to their duties on the galley. Quick, light, and easy to beach, galleys were general-purpose boats which could carry troops or goods as occasion demanded, and were particularly suitable for West Highland travel. The combination of sails and oars made them extremely versatile. Sails added to their speed and allowed the oarsmen to rest, while the oars gave them often-needed independence from wind and tides. They could even row against contrary winds for short distances, such as when it became necessary to round a headland or sail into a bay against the tide.

The boat which Kit, Tam, and Willie presently found themselves helping to haul across the strip of land between the firth and Loch Tarbert carried little cargo but it would carry Highland hides, wood, and fish on its return trip to Dumbarton.

By that time, Kit expected to be well on his way to Glen Affric.

Maggie was pleased with the way things were going. The Merry Folk and the Helping Hands were peacefully waiting to see if their representatives would succeed or fail in providing acceptable service to their respective mortals. Claud, at least, seemed to be doing well enough with Mistress Bab, and since her arrest, he had watched her carefully, all the while managing to avoid undue interference.

The one niggling worry Maggie had was over

Claud's womenfolk, Catriona and Lucy Fittletrot. Both seemed for the present to have disappeared, which Maggie would not normally have considered a loss, but she wanted to know what mischief each was up to. Retiring to her parlor to give the matter some thought, she was just realizing who might have sufficient power to keep her from finding either one, when the curl of smoke from her pipe began to take a substantive form.

First, it curled to the floor, assuming the shape of a man, and then the white took on color. His hair appeared, dark at the roots, reddish as it grew out, and fair at the tips. Radiating from his head like rays of the sun, it stuck straight out, framing his long, narrow face and glittering with tiny jewels. The face was not remarkable, unless one counted the thin yellow, green, red, and blue streaks on each cheek, but his dark eyes gleamed and his smile was mischievous.

"You!" Maggie exclaimed. "What brings ye here, Jonah Bonewits?"

All of him was visible now, his body swathed in flowing, pale-blue fabric bedecked with twinkling ornaments. When he fluttered a hand in Maggie's direction, he revealed that it had six fingers, each bearing a colorful ring.

"As I warned ye, Mag, I take a powerful interest in everything ye do," he said, his voice deep and spellbinding. "I havena abandoned ye or my amiable son."

"They banished ye," Maggie reminded him.

"Aye, but only from the Circle, lass, as ye ken verra well, and I'll soon be back. Sure and d'ye no recall that I said I'd be taking a hand in this business."

"But why should it interest ye?" she asked, knowing the answer but wanting to see if he would admit it.

He did, saying dulcetly, " 'Cause ye ha' vexed me, Mag, and sorely. I'll no forget it till ye ha' paid the price for all your meddling."

"What d'ye want?"

"Why, 'tis simple, Mag. I want ye tae fail, and what I want I will have." With that, having said what he had come to say, he vanished.

With Hugo's help, Bab was able to set her plan into action, but she did not think she accomplished much good. Although the men with whom she spoke personally on Tuesday and Wednesday seemed outraged that Francis Dalcross had arrested Alex, and promised to do what they could do to help, she could not persuade herself that anyone truly meant to set himself in opposition to Francis.

That the commoners were frightened of the power the late sheriff's son wielded was clear. No one else in the glens had so much manpower; and those who did wield considerable authority, such as Chisholm and the Mackintoshes, lacked both the manpower and the will to act against Dalcross when it meant going against the King's law as well.

She soon discovered, however, that Chisholm had not remained idle. In the face of his son's arrest, his lordship put aside his melancholy and threw himself into action, but his efforts bore no more tangible fruit than Bab's. To be sure, everyone to whom he sent word promised to attend Alex's trial, so perhaps they could hope that the number of watchers would encourage Francis to act fairly. But Chisholm admitted to Bab that the acting sheriff would just pick a tame jury and magistrate to assure that Alex's case would be lost before it could be won.

They had less time than she had hoped to drum up support, because word came Thursday morning that his trial would begin Friday at one. Chisholm made only a token objection to her declaration and his wife's similar assertion that they would accompany him, but both women insisted, and they barely had time to pack for the journey before he was ready to depart. Lady MacRae evinced no interest in riding to Inverness, and no one tried to persuade her to change her mind.

So lively had her ladyship become that Bab had feared she would insist upon going with them, but when the subject arose, Lady MacRae said simply that she did not wish to see her new son-in-law in chains.

When Bab bade her goodbye and assured her that she would obey Chisholm and do nothing foolhardy, Lady MacRae patted her cheek and said, "You have made me very proud, my dearling, and you would have made your father proud, too. Sir Alex will make you an excellent husband, as you will see once this little matter is properly resolved."

With tears welling into her eyes, Bab quickly made her adieux and hurried to join the others. Neither Hugo nor Gibby had been at Dundreggan when the word came and neither had returned before Bab and the others left, so she gave hasty but nonetheless strict instructions to the captain of the guard to inform Hugo of the turn of events as soon as he returned. After that, she kept her mind firmly on her horse and the track ahead or chatted determinedly with Lady Chisholm, not wanting to spend a minute more than necessary pondering Alex's likely fate.

Certain that Mistress Bab would be safe while she was traveling with Lord Chisholm and his men-at-arms, Claud seized the opportunity to search again for Catriona. Returning to her glade, he found it as he had left it and thought at first that no one was there.

He heard only the birds twittering to each other and the wind whispering in the leaves of the trees overhead. The merry burn in the center was still dry and silent. As he sighed his vexation, he heard feminine humming.

"Lucy, where are ye and what are ye up tae now?" He knew he sounded angry, but perhaps it would give the mischievous lass pause to know that he *was* angry. This was Catriona's private bower, as personal and sacred to her as Maggie's parlor was to Maggie and to him. Lucy had trespassed, and worse, she had defiled the lovely glade by killing Catriona's merry, tumbling burn and the little pool.

The humming sounded again, and before he could determine its direction, he heard the unmistakable gurgle of water. A scant moment later, he saw it. First it trickled slowly into the dry, rocky bed, washing dust from the stones and eddying around their bases. Then it inched higher and moved faster until the gurgle became a chuckle, and Catriona's merry burn tumbled through the glade again.

"Good lass," Claud said. "Now come out here. I would speak wi' ye."

He saw movement in the shrubbery near the place where the burn normally bubbled forth from the ground, but he saw no flash of lavender from Lucy's gown, only green, as Catriona stepped into view.

They stared at each other for a long moment before she said, "So ye had naught to do wi' this prank, eh?"

"I did not," he said, moving toward her. "I wouldna spoil this place, Catriona, not for anything. I ha' too many fond memories tae do that."

She moved to meet him, looking as fresh and delicious as she always did in her flowing, gauzy green gown. "Do ye, Claud? Then what o' yon Lucy Fittletrot? Ye'll no tell me she had naught to do wi' this."

"Never mind Lucy now," he said, reaching for her. When she stiffened, he hesitated, realizing that she wanted to hear the truth. "Sakes, Catriona, I dinna ken what tae say about her. The minute ye think ye ken someone well, ye're bound tae find out that ye dinna ken them at all. I liked her. I canna say I did not. But there be summat about her since this business began, even more since yon wedding, and when I saw what she did here . . . How did ye start the water again?"

"Lucy only stopped up the source," Catriona said. "The water was already trickling through again but running away from the glade. It was easy to fix that."

He nodded, reaching for her again, and this time she walked into his arms. "Ah, lassie," he murmured, pulling her close and hugging her tight, "I'm just sorry she interfered and caused ye tae fail in your task. I'll tell them o' the Circle what happened, though. They canna blame ye when it were Lucy's doing."

To his surprise, Catriona chuckled. "I willna fail, Claud. I ha' done what they asked o' me, and barring any more wickedness, all will be well in the end."

"But how?"

When she told him, he laughed aloud and whirled her around the glade in a dance that would have astonished Lucy of the twinkling toes.

Chapter 21

Having experienced the grandeur of Stirling Castle and seen the Stirling Tolbooth on Castle Hill in that royal burgh, Bab had expected Alex's trial to take place in some official-looking chamber in Sheriff's House or in a public building in central Inverness. It was something of a shock therefore to discover that the jury would determine his fate in a common alehouse.

She had never been inside an alehouse before, and thus her curiosity was high as she followed Chisholm and his lady into the low-ceilinged taproom, but it seemed a horrid place in which to decide if a man would live or die.

Most of the spectators were men, so she understood why his lordship had tried to persuade her — and his lady, too — to remain at Dundreggan. As it was, she was glad Lady MacRae had decided to stay behind.

The room was not only crowded but it fairly vibrated with the din of mostly masculine conversation, and it stank of stale ale and sweating bodies.

Rows of rough-hewn benches faced the fireplace, at one side of which sat a plain table and chair. On the opposite side, a second chair faced the audience, and between the benches and the rear door, five or six tables stood side-by-side with men perched on them as if they were higher benches. In the front corner nearest the magistrate's table, two benches extended at right angles to the audience, and on these sat ten men who chatted and laughed amongst themselves as boisterously as anyone else in the room.

At first, Bab feared that she and her companions would have to stand to see anything of the trial, but she soon saw that Eric Mackintosh had saved places for them on the front bench. She was by no means certain this was an advantage though, since everyone in the room stared as they edged their way to the front.

The din had increased and was overwhelming, for everyone seemed to have an opinion to express. That his neighbor spoke at the same time deterred no one.

Bab would have liked to cover her ears as she made her way to the seat Eric had reserved for her, but she did not, choosing to retain her dignity instead. Despite the number of spectators, she could not see that her efforts had produced many supporters for Alex. Aside from Chisholm's own people, she recognized no one to whom she had spoken in the past two days, and she knew that many in the room must be Francis Dalcross's men.

One of his men-at-arms strode into the tap-room through a doorway behind the single chair near the hearth, and before the door shut behind him, she caught a glimpse of a tidy sitting room, allowing her to deduce that the alemaster and his family, if he had one, lived on the premises. The man-at-arms carried a long-handled pike and banged the handle end on the floor to demand order.

With much shuffling of feet, coughing, sneezing, and fading chatter, the people in the room eventually took heed of him, and if they did not become silent, at least he could make himself heard when he shouted, "All stand for his worship, Sir Archibald Daviot, the King's magistrate!"

As the onlookers noisily got to their feet, a sinewy man of middle age with wire-rimmed spectacles entered through the same door and went without ceremony to stand beside the table and its chair.

"Sit, sit, sit," he commanded in a voice that sounded too big for him.

With much shuffling and comment, everyone obeyed.

"You there, Robert Fraser, shut your maw so a body can think!" he said testily, adding to his baillie, "Bring in the prisoner now and sit him in yonder chair. Watch him closely, mind. We'll ha' nae escapes from this court today."

Sir Alex entered next. His father having provided him with a clean blue-velvet doublet and fresh hose, he entered with much of his usual aplomb despite the shackles on his wrists and ankles. When his gaze met Bab's, his eyes narrowed, making her swallow hard to think he might be angry with her for coming, but then he smiled ruefully and shook his head at her as if he knew it would have been useless for his father to insist that she not do so.

She hoped he was not displeased, but it made no difference, for she could not have stayed away. She had done all she could to help him, and apparently her efforts had come to naught, so if anyone should be rueful, it was she. Hugo and Gibby were doubtless still trying to rouse supporters, but she doubted that they would succeed. Folks were too frightened of the Dalcross power to confront it.

"Faith, but ye must set another chair for our witnesses," Sir Archibald said to his baillie. "Did ye think we'd make them stand to give their testimony?"

The man hurried to set a second chair beside the magistrate's table, whereupon Sir Archibald snapped, "Call the case!"

"Aye, your worship." Turning to the audience and squaring his shoulders, the baillie proclaimed in stentorian tones, "A bill being proffered to attaint Sir Alex Chisholm o' Dundreggan Castle and Glen Affric, here present, for murder and other nefarious crimes, this properly-constituted jury o' his peers will now proceed to determine his guilt or his innocence."

Sir Archibald glanced at Alex. "How do you plead, sir?"

"Not guilty, your worship," Alex said quietly.

"Swear the jury!"

The baillie gestured to the ten men sitting on the two benches in the corner, and all ten stood again, looking properly solemn as he recited the oath and they echoed it. When they had resumed their seats, the baillie declared without further ado, "Sheriff Substitute Francis Dalcross will speak now for the Crown and for his sovereign grace, James, fifth o' that name to reign as High King o' the Scots!"

Bab watched Francis cross the room to stand by the magistrate's table, walking as haughtily as if he instead of James were King. He glanced at her, smiling faintly, and she knew he savored his victory. Doubtless, he believed he had already proven to her how wrong she had been to marry Alex instead of submitting to his own advances. She returned the look steadily, wishing she possessed magical powers and could make him vanish before he could present his case to the jury.

She could do nothing to stop him, however, and the room fell silent at last.

With a dramatic sigh, his gaze sweeping the audience before resting on the jury, Francis said, "Mine own father fell to this villain's murderous hand. Sir Alex Chisholm, also known as *Sionnach Dubh*, the Highland Black Fox, besides robbery, interference with his grace's lawfully appointed authorities, and other crimes, has egregiously broken the King's peace by ending a life more honorable than his own. This man walked amongst us, pretending to be our friend, and then committed a heinous murder. God on High may forgive him for it. I shall not."

Muttering filled the courtroom as Francis called his first witness, but Bab could not tell if the muttering was aimed at Alex or at Francis. It quickly became apparent, however, what Francis's strategy would be.

One after another, he called his own men-at-arms, the first of whom swore that he had seen the Fox lurking near Sheriff's House on the night of the murder. Two others swore they had seen him follow Sheriff Dalcross as he rode toward Bothyn Castle but had paid little heed, since the sheriff's own men rode with him as usual. A member of that escort next testified that the sheriff's men had given chase to a masked man on a black horse, thus leaving the sheriff alone at the pertinent time. And a fifth one of Dalcross's men swore that the Fox had several nights later most daringly helped a prisoner escape from Sheriff's House. That witness insisted that no man but Alex Chisholm, who had lived there off and on since childhood, knew Sheriff's House well enough to have effected that escape.

At one point, hearing Lady Chisholm gasp, and turning to put a comforting hand on hers, Bab feared briefly that her ladyship might believe the worst of the wicked testimony. But her fear proved needless.

"Such villains to speak so," Lady Chisholm murmured, glowering at the witness. "God should strike him down for uttering such horrid lies."

As lies piled upon half-truths and the magistrate apparently accepted every word as evidence, Bab wilted with despair. Francis's tame jury would hardly find Alex innocent in the face of such testimony, and his advocate, although clearly a respectable and learned gentleman, seemed unable to shake a single one of Francis's witnesses from their carefully crafted tale.

Every man supported the one before him, and no one stepped forward to speak for Alex except members of his clan and friends such as Eric Mackintosh, none of whom could provide an alibi for him on the night in question other than to swear he was at Dundreggan, an alibi at which Francis and his jury openly scoffed.

When the last witness had spoken, Francis stood to sum up his case, saying with authority, "The Crown has proven beyond any doubt that Sir Alexander Chisholm, in the guise of *Sionnach Dubh,* killed my father and is thus guilty of many more crimes as well. I know you jurors will see your duty plain and will declare him guilty so that he may be taken from this room and hanged forthwith. Then we shall be done with the Fox and his dastardly acts forever."

"I fear 'twill take more than hanging Alexander Chisholm to be done wi' all that," a deep voice declared from the back of the room. "That ye choose to dislike him, Francis Dalcross, doesna make him the murderer o' your father, nor will it, for he didna kill the sheriff, as I'll wager ye ken better than most."

The audience, turning as one, gasped in astonishment. So firmly had Francis Dalcross's attention been fixed on the jury and everyone else's fixed on Francis, that no one had noticed the door at the rear of the taproom slowly opening, or seen the entrance of the black-cloaked, black-masked figure who stood there now.

Bab glanced at Alex to be sure he still sat in his chair, and then looked again at the newcomer, wondering at the familiar sound of his deep voice.

Could she have been wrong? Might there be some other explanation for the silver coins in the box in Alex's bedchamber? But no, Hugo had admitted the truth.

The room being dimly lit and the corner near the door dark and shadowy, she could just make out the familiar, cloaked figure, like another dark shadow against the wall. His mask concealing all but his eyes, he stood still for a moment before, with a swirl of his cloak, he revealed the sleek-looking sword in his right hand.

Dalcross, clearly stunned, quickly recovered his wits. "That man must be an impostor," he cried. "The Fox sits before us, proven guilty as charged!"

"Ye lie, Francis Dalcross," snapped the newcomer. "The only villain in this room be yourself, and if murder ha' been done, 'tis no Sir Alex who ha' done it."

"We have witnesses," Dalcross retorted.

"Aye, but your witnesses claimed 'twas the Fox, did they no? I ha' two more witnesses outside who agreed after a wee bit o' persuasion to swear ye killed your own father for the purpose o' inheriting his wealth and taking his place as Sheriff o' Inverness-shire. Moreover, they say, 'tis no the first time ye had done murder!"

Gasps and cries of shock and consternation from the gallery greeted this statement, but Dalcross remained undaunted. "You can have no such witnesses!"

"Aye, but I do. I'll grant ye, this honest jury o' yours might wonder if my witnesses be as tainted as your own, but I'll give ye a personal trial m'self, fair and square, if ye still want this case to stand on the testimony ye've contrived for it."

Dalcross sneered. "Dare we guess how you propose to effect such a trial?"

"Why by the sword man, by the sword! If ye're telling the truth, which me very presence here declares a lie, surely God willna let me defeat ye. Sakes, if ye be telling the truth, I'm an impostor and lack the skill to defeat ye, for ye ha' been telling everyone ye be the finest swordsman in the glens. What say ye to that?"

"I have no need to fight you," Dalcross said. "This jury of sensible men will certainly find Sir Alex guilty of the murder, because he is guilty, and you — whoever you are — can have no affect on that outcome." Turning to the jury, he said belligerently, "I trust that you *have* reached a verdict, have you not, lads?"

The jurors looked at one another, but before their spokesman could respond, the masked man at the rear of the room said quietly, "Afore ye declare your verdict, the lot o' ye, I'd ha' ye ken that there be a mob o' folks outside who support Sir Alex. They be armed and ready to take matters into their own hands, knowing that any jury beholden to Francis Dalcross be most likely to produce whatever verdict he demands. They'll no allow ye to proceed to a hanging on that verdict unless . . ."

When he paused dramatically, so quiet did it become in that room that one might have heard a mouse sneeze.

Belligerently, Dalcross snapped, "Unless what?"

"I'm offering ye a chance to make your case before the folks outside," the masked man said. "This lot can join them there, and my lads will see fair play whilst ye and I let our swords speak for us. If ye win, I'll let stand whatever verdict your jurors declare. If ye fail to win, Sir Alex goes free."

Dalcross looked at the jury, the members of

which were eyeing each other, showing no resolution one way or another.

"Aye then, I'll fight you," he declared angrily. "Fetch my sword, someone."

"Nay," Lucy cried, appearing suddenly in front of Claud and Catriona, who were observing the interesting activities in the courtroom from the lintel over the door into the little sitting room. "Where did *he* come from?"

Catriona smirked. "Ye think ye're so smart, ye idle weed. I warrant ye want poor Alex Chisholm tae hang, thinking that if he does, I'll ha' failed."

"Ye *have* failed, ye fliperous puffkin. Ye're no fit tae be wi' Claud, but the Host will look after ye well enough."

"Is that why ye did this, Lucy?" Claud demanded. "Sakes, but ye must be the one that opened the door tae the tunnel so yon Dalcross would suspect Sir Alex!"

"Aye, I did that and more, and why not? If Sir Alex hangs, then she'll ha' failed even an she doesna see it yet, and if both men hang . . ."

"Then I'll ha' failed as well," Maggie Malloch said, taking form beside Claud. "Is that what be at the root o' this mischief, Lucy Fittletrot?"

Lucy did not speak but flitted away into the crowd of mortals.

As Francis gave the order to fetch his sword, Bab noted an odd, calculating look in his eyes, and as everyone else in the room turned excitedly to a neighbor to comment on the newest turn of events, she saw him stoop and reach into his boot. In a flash, he drew his dirk and leaped toward the still-shackled Alex.

Recognizing his intent, Bab threw herself forward, shrieking like a banshee as she thrust herself between them.

Francis's dirk plunged toward her.

Staring into his eyes, terrified but determined, she believed for that single instant that Francis, rather than Alex, would be the last thing she saw in this life.

Dalcross's furious gaze collided with hers, and in mid-arc, with a groan of frustration, he cast the dagger aside. Many hands grabbed him, pulling him away. Although his gaze remained riveted on her, she turned her back to make sure that Alex was unharmed.

He was gazing at her in stark horror.

"Seize him," Dalcross bellowed, and Bab turned sharply to see him rip himself free of those who had grabbed him and point at the masked figure still standing patiently at the back of the room. "Seize the impostor!"

"So ye're nobbut a timorsome hen-heart after all, a gutless, cringing feardie," the latter said, his voice carrying, as he had before, despite the increased noise in the crowded room. "Dinna forget ye've an armed mob outside, hungering to riot."

"I warrant that my men outnumber them,"

Dalcross snapped, his cheeks reddening nearly to purple. "Still, I'll meet you if only to unmask you and prove that you are not who you pretend to be. Then we'll hang you alongside the Fox."

"I want to see this," Alex muttered.

Realizing that she was the only one who had heard him, because everyone else was crowding toward the exit, determined to witness whatever scene took place outside, Bab gestured to a nearby man-at-arms. Summoning her sternest tone of command, she said, "Escort Sir Alex outside at once. Indeed, if you have a key to those horrid fetters and manacles . . ."

He hesitated, looking around for the magistrate's baillie, who was in the crowd pressing close behind Dalcross. Respectfully, the man-at-arms said, "I ha' nae such key, my lady, even did I dare to unlock him."

His willingness to help gave her hope that the tide of opinion had turned in Alex's favor. But all depended on the man in the cloak, and since she had no notion who he could be, her hope was small.

As she turned to ask Alex if he knew the man, Chisholm and his lady joined them, and his lordship moved quickly to help the man-at-arms aid Alex. Between them, he was able to hobble to the doorway, but no one paid heed to Bab's question. Following them, Bab felt a tug on her sleeve and turned back to find the magistrate holding out a key.

"You may unshackle his feet, my lady. I doubt that he will try to escape, and no one has a better right to witness the outcome of this little play."

Snatching the key, Bab called to the others to stop and quickly bent to unlock the fetters. When she stood to undo the manacles, the magistrate said, "Nay, my lady, we'll await the outcome afore taking that step, if you please."

Grimacing, she met Alex's gaze and then relaxed when she saw the twinkle in his eyes. They hurried out to the cobblestoned yard together, and to her surprise — for she had thought the impostor must have lied about the armed mob — she saw men with whom she had spoken over the past days, men who had insisted they dared interfere with nothing in which Francis Dalcross took a hand.

Two of them were standing together, sharing a dipper of water from the alehouse well, chatting as if they attended a fair. There were many others, too, nearly all of them armed, their weapons varying from pitchforks to swords, pikes, and axes. Many, however, still looked a bit fearful.

Bab could not blame them for their fear, because she had her own. Everyone knew that Francis Dalcross was the best swordsman in the Highlands save one, and she believed that one exception stood silently beside her. The impostor would soon be unmasked, and whoever he was, if he failed, she knew that Francis would make sure he paid the same high price that Alex would pay.

"Do you know who he is?" she murmured to Alex.

He shrugged, his gaze fixed straight ahead where the crowd was forming a ring around Francis and the masked man. Spectators parted to make a path for him and for Bab, his parents, and the magistrate. When they reached the front, the swordsmen were facing each other.

Two of Dalcross's men stepped forward threateningly, but the masked man held up his free hand, and they hesitated.

"We'll have a fair fight, lads," the masked man said gently.

They glanced as one at their master, who jerked a nod without taking his narrow-eyed gaze from his opponent.

Claud stood atop the well housing with Catriona, trying to watch every direction for Lucy, certain that she would attempt more mischief.

"I'll not let her harm my lad, Claud," Catriona said.

The men by the well had joined the crowd, and from her perch, Claud could see the two swordsmen eyeing each other.

There was no sign of Lucy Fittletrot.

As his searching gaze moved around the alehouse yard again, he noted in passing that the dipper rested in the bucket on the rim of the well and that the bucket was more than half full of water.

The two swordsmen circled warily, each measuring the other to judge his expertise. Their movements were graceful, but Bab saw that the masked man's long cloak eddied around his legs as he moved. By contrast, Francis had removed the short black cloak he had worn while presenting his case and wore only his shirt, doublet, hose, and boots. Surely, the less restricted man would enjoy the advantage.

As the thought crossed her mind, the masked man shrugged his cloak back from his shoulders and said tauntingly, "Come at me then, Dalcross, if your coward's feet will carry ye."

Francis seemed to have lost his voice and his bluster, but at this taunt, he recovered swiftly and lunged.

His opponent, clearly anticipating the move, deftly parried it, and the fight was on. Both men moved lightly and with grace, and each seemed well taught.

For a time, Bab worried that Francis seemed much the better swordsman, and at one point, when he lunged and his sword slid between the masked man's left arm and side, she heard Alex catch his breath beside her. She was sure then that Francis would win and she would lose the man she had come to love. Tears sprang to her eyes at the thought, but she could imagine no way to alter the outcome. Without thinking, she reached for Alex's hand and met the cold iron of a manacle instead.

She glanced up at his face, but his gaze was still fixed on the swordsmen. She could tell by the muscle twitching high in his cheek that his jaws were clenched and that he fervently wished he rather than the impostor faced Dalcross. As she turned back to watch them, their swords clanged together, but this time it was the masked man who leaped forward, putting Francis on the defensive at last.

So swiftly did the man move, and so hard did he press Francis, that the ensuing flurry of swordplay forced the crowd to part and let them through. The cobblestones made their footing difficult, a point that Bab realized only when Francis stumbled. Instead of pressing the advantage, however, the masked man held back, allowing him to regain his balance before continuing the attack.

Claud saw Lucy at last, swooping toward the swordsmen, her hands outstretched, her lips moving.

"Lucy, no!" he shrieked, summoning the water pail into his hands and flinging it. It sailed high overhead, so that as Lucy turned toward the sound of his voice, the water was already spilling out of the pail.

She had no warning before it cascaded over her.

With an eldritch shriek, Lucy Fittletrot disappeared and a terrifying new shape took her place. The sight was all Claud needed to confirm his suspicions.

In that same moment, Maggie appeared with her hand outstretched. Pail and water vanished before either could hit anyone in the crowd below.

The monstrous shape turned toward her, looming close, threatening her.

At the top of his lungs, terrified, Claud shouted, "Jonah Bonewits, show yourself, ye loathsome coward!"

The shape twisted and thinned, taking the form of a man, and the next thing Claud knew his father was standing before him, enraged. Although most folks had hidden depths, evil did not, Claud decided. When one recognized it and called it by name, evil had to reveal itself in its natural form.

As the thought crossed his mind, he saw Jonah Bonewits point toward him, heard Catriona shriek, and saw the flames blazing toward them. He flung himself in front of her and, in that instant, felt a sharp, burning sensation and then nothing.

If Francis felt any gratitude for the respite, he did not show it. Indeed, he looked angrier, Bab thought, as if he resented his opponent's sense of fair play. His strokes became wilder, more daring, but his opponent seemed to be toying with him now, and when the masked man's sword lightly touched Francis's chest only to disengage at once, Bab became certain of it. Shouts and cheers greeted the move, but more than one man bellowed, "Put an end to the dastard!"

"Skewer him!"

"Spit him!"

Suggestion followed grisly suggestion, and no one could doubt now which man the audience supported. Francis's men shouted, too, but in the general din, Bab could not tell if they all supported their master or if some supported his opponent.

A stroke of the latter's sword sliced near Francis's throat, and she could attribute only the masked man's skill for the fact that it did not decapitate him. Even Francis realized as much, for he raised his free hand to his neck tentatively, as if he were checking to be sure he had not been cut.

"Sakes, man, finish this before it becomes a mockery," Alex muttered just loud enough for Bab to hear.

But the masked man clearly had another goal in mind. As Francis began to look desperate, as even his staunchest supporters saw that he could not win, the masked man continued to toy with him, as if to emphasize his own superior skill.

At last, as the crowd grew quiet, knowing how it would end and waiting with surprising patience, the masked man said, "Art enjoying yourself now, lad?"

"End it, damn you," Francis croaked.

"Nay, not yet a while, for I'm thinking that first ye should tell all gathered here who the filthy murderer be that killed your father."

"Be damned to you then, for I won't!"

"Aye, but I wager ye will, given time, and I've time and all to spare." The man did not even seem tired, Bab thought. His voice was as steady as if he were enjoying normal conversation, at leisure. His stamina was astonishing, and the sword looked light in his hand, whereas Francis's weapon looked heavy and moved sluggishly. They had been fighting now for nearly ten minutes, a long time for a swordfight, as she knew from watching her brother practice.

She noted that Alex had relaxed upon hearing the masked man's words. A slight, understanding smile tugged at his lips now as he critically watched the two.

Francis remained stubborn for only a few moments more before gasping, "All right then, it was I, just as you said. I hated the man! Now, make an end!"

"Nay, for I'll warrant ye've more to tell us. There ha' been other murders hereabouts, and other innocent men accused o' committing them."

"What murders? When?" Staggering, wheezing openly now, Francis seemed barely able to get the words out.

"Over a year ago," the masked man said. "Two brothers died, as I recall."

Bab glanced at Alex, but he continued to watch the swordsmen.

Lord Chisholm, beside him, frowned heavily but did not comment.

Francis shook his head, resisting for only a moment before he gasped, "Aye then, I did it, but my father ordered it done and I was but —"

As he said the words, he suddenly thrust himself forward, his sword jabbing swiftly, dexterously, to engage his opponent's. Then, with a deft flick of his wrist, he sent the masked man's sword flying into the air toward Bab and lunged, his own sword aimed right at the masked man's heart.

As the sword flew through the air toward Bab, Alex automatically thrust a hand up to keep it from striking her. To his astonishment, the irons fell from his wrists, leaving them free in the split second before his right hand grasped the familiar shape of the sword's hilt.

"Dalcross!" he bellowed.

In the instant that Dalcross hesitated, the masked man grabbed a handful of his cloak and whirled it forward, catching the point of the blade that sliced toward his heart and deflecting it.

Francis snatched the sword back, glanced at Alex, then back at his opponent.

"I am the one you want," Alex said quietly. "You are tired and would be wise to put down that fine new Italian sword of yours and yield to justice. But even if you cannot bring yourself to do the wise thing, would you murder an innocent man before all these witnesses? The masked man is unarmed now."

In answer, Francis leaped toward him. "This is all your fault," he snarled as he thrust wildly at Alex. "You and the people of these glens stirred us to act as we did when you refused to yield to our authority as sheriff."

Alex did not answer, lightly parrying the attack. He knew the expression on his face was probably grim, for he felt grim as he maneuvered Dalcross back to the center of the ring before his wild swordplay could injure any innocent bystander.

As he moved, he saw the masked man ease his way into the crowd as if to watch with the others. One moment the man was there. The next he was gone.

Although Alex did not think anyone else had noted his disappearance, he kept Dalcross occupied in order to give his champion a few more minutes to escape, hoping that Dalcross would employ the time by coming to his senses.

At last, though, he stepped back and raised his sword point, dodging another wild thrust as he did and saying, "Have done, Dalcross! You cannot win this."

"I'll not grant you the satisfaction of seeing

me yield!" Dalcross growled.

With a sigh, Alex steadied his blade again and, with a single gesture, easily disarmed the other man. When Dalcross's sword struck the ground, Alex stuck the point of his own through a curl of the hilt to prevent the weapon's being picked up again. As he did, several men hurried forward from the crowd and pinioned Dalcross's arms to his sides, rendering him helpless.

Beside Bab, the magistrate, regarding Alex's manacles in his hand as if he had no idea how he came to be holding them, turned to Chisholm and said quietly, "My lord, I hope you will agree to take up the duties of sheriff again until his grace the King troubles himself to appoint a new man. I can assure you that all of us in Inverness-shire would be most grateful if you would."

"I will, and gladly," Chisholm said, but he was staring at his son as if he had never seen him before. Visibly giving himself a shake, he said to the men holding Dalcross, "Place that man under arrest, you lads, and lock him in the Tolbooth."

Alex turned away, looking for Bab and finding her exactly where he had left her. When she smiled, he forgot everyone else.

Bab flew to meet him, running into his open arms and hugging him tight, relieved beyond measure that he was free and safe at last. When his arms closed around her, she sighed with contentment, but the moment was brief.

"Faith, Alex Chisholm, where did ye learn to wield a sword like that? The last time I saw ye wi' one in hand, ye near cut off your left foot!"

Turning to greet the speaker and others who made similar teasing comments, Alex shrugged, saying lightly, "I took some lessons whilst I was in France, but the Fox had worn the poor man out. I hope you'll excuse me now," he added. "I've spent the past three days locked up in a heathenish cell, and I want to spend a few hours alone with my wife, if you will permit me that pleasure."

Laughing, they agreed to it, but his mother said that if his father meant to take over the duties of sheriff, they, all of them, should repair at once to Sheriff's House to order supper and see what had to be done to set the place to rights so they could sleep there that night.

"I pray you will forgive me, madam," Alex said quietly, "but I'd as lief not spend another night in that place — not for some time, at least. I'd prefer to take my wife home. You are welcome to come with us if you like, and I'll wager that my father would grant his permission, for he'll likely be busy here for days."

"Nay, my dear," she replied. "I'll not abandon him at such a time as this. His health is vastly improved, to be sure, but he will not look after himself properly if I am not at hand. By all means, though, take your beautiful bride home with you."

Looking down at Bab, Alex said with a smile, "I will, unless she objects."

"She does not," Bab said firmly. She had no wish to remain in Inverness, where the sole entertainment for the next several days would likely be the trial and hanging of Francis Dalcross and his henchmen. Shooting him a direct look, she added, "She would rather be at home with her husband, sir, for they have certain matters to discuss, and well do you know it."

"Then let us not waste another moment, my sweet," he said. "We have only to find horses, and we can be off."

Chapter 22

"What happened to Claud?" Catriona wailed.

Maggie felt like wailing herself, but she could not. First, she owed Catriona an apology, and then she would let her fury reign free.

"And where did that horrid man go?"

Struggling to maintain an even tone, Maggie said, "Jonah Bonewits vanished whilst we gaped at the air where Claud had been standing only a moment before. As tae Claud himself, I canna tell ye, but I dinna feel his presence here, and I can always feel him when he's about."

"He's dead," Catriona said tearfully. "He stepped in front of me, or I'd have been the one to go up in flames."

"Aye, that be true enough," Maggie said. "I'd no wish that on ye, Catriona."

"Ye dinna like me," Catriona reminded her, sniffling.

"Still, I misjudged ye, and I must apologize for it," Maggie said. "I thought I knew ye, but ye ha' shown me another side. When I said ye should look after the Chisholms, I expected ye'd look tae Sir Alex, and when ye didna do that, I believed ye'd let that Lucy Fittletrot scare ye away and were doing nowt, but I were wrong."

"*Was* she Lucy Fittletrot?" Catriona asked. "Was she *ever?*"

"Aye, I believe she was until the wedding," Maggie said. "But I should ha' realized that only Jonah Bonewits has power enough tae ha' put Mistress Bab under a spell in the wee kirk. I warrant Lucy were under one even before he shifted into her shape. Sithee, Claud figured out about the water, so mayhap she helped reveal its power over Jonah. If we find them, we'll ask. But in the meantime, ye ha' kept your word, Catriona, and so has Claud. At the next meeting o' the Circle —"

"I don't care about the Circle. I want Claud!"

Maggie pressed her lips together, fighting a sudden onslaught of fury as tears welled in her eyes. Ruthlessly, she pulled herself together, saying gruffly, "Control yourself, Catriona. Our work isna done yet."

Fresh horses were easily come by, thanks to Eric Mackintosh, who had already foreseen the need, so dismissing all offers of company or men-at-arms, Alex and Bab bade everyone farewell and were on their way.

To Bab's surprise, the trial and its aftermath had consumed less than two hours, so they crossed the bridge over the River Ness shortly after three.

"It will likely be late before we get home, sweetheart," Alex said. "I warrant you must be tired since you only arrived in Inverness last night."

She hesitated, wondering how much to reveal about her efforts to gain support for him, and decided that if she did not want to be scolded all the way home, or worse, she should say as little as possible now. "I am not tired," she said.

"I was thinking that perhaps we ought to find a place to spend the night and ride the rest of the way tomorrow," he said with a meekness in which she no longer believed. "You cannot have had much sleep this past sennight, for you journeyed to Inverness twice and did not sleep much the night before my arrest. And you must have worried so. I, on the other hand, am well rested, having had little else to do."

" 'Tis most odd," she said, reflecting, "but I truly am not tired. I should be, certainly, for it is just as you say, but I feel as if I've had all the sleep I require. Doubtless, I feel so only because you are safe now," she added with a smile.

"Did that matter so much to you, sweetheart?" He spoke more like he spoke as the Fox, but she was rapidly growing accustomed to the notion of being married to two men in one.

Quietly, she said, "You know it mattered."

"Can you forgive me for deceiving you?"

"Will you promise never to do so again?"

"With all my heart," he said. "You have become precious to me, Bab. Although I have enjoyed much about playing the Fox, I did not enjoy deceiving you or my parents. But I believed it was safer for all of you not to know the truth."

"Your parents still do not know the truth, although I'll wager they suspect it," she said. "Who else does know, besides Hugo and Gibby?"

"I'd have said no one before an hour ago."

"Well, that was not Hugo pretending to be the Fox, sir, as it was on the hillside that day. That man is taller than you are, and he is broader across the shoulders, too. Nevertheless, he rode away from the alehouse on Dancer."

"So you saw him leave, did you?"

She nodded.

"Aye, well, if he's the man I believe he is, he's always been a great bear of a fellow, albeit light on his feet. With my brothers dead and Fin and Patrick in the Borders, I know of only one other whose skill with a sword might match my own and who might feel he had a stake in all this. Also, he would be in a position to acquire my horse, cloak, mask, and sword."

"To learn about the secret cavern, in fact."

"Aye, my wise one, even that."

"And Dancer would accept him?"

"The man has an uncanny knack with horses."

"But you are the true Fox, are you not?"

His grin was boyish, even mischievous, as he reached across the gap between their horses to put an arm around her and hug her. "I thought you were convinced of that, my love. Ha' ye doubts the noo?" he added, slipping easily into the common accent his alter ego had affected.

"How did this other man learn the Fox's true identity?" she countered.

"I do not know that yet," he admitted, "but although his knowing proves that one should never grow complacent, we cannot complain about the outcome."

They made good time after that, for the horses seemed no more tired than Bab felt. Eric had wisely packed a supper for them to eat as they rode, and since they had much to talk about, the hours flew by.

Bab carefully kept the conversation on Alex's activities and well away from her own. He explained that when Chisholm had sent word to him of his brothers' murders and ordered him home, the tone of the letter made it clear that he expected little of his third-born son other than that he return. Upon discovering the extent to which the Dalcrosses and their men had assumed authority over the glens, Alex had decided to take certain matters into his own hands.

"I knew no one would suspect me," he said. "I had learned long since that my brothers would not tease me if I did not try to compete with them but attended to my studies. So I simply exaggerated my earlier behavior by imitating fashionably foppish men I'd met in

France and Italy and neglecting to mention to anyone that I had become adept with a blade whilst studying in those countries."

"What made you work so hard to improve your swordsmanship?" Bab asked.

The boyish grin contained a rueful quality this time. "I wanted to show them up," he said. "My brothers always enjoyed lording it over me, and from childhood, I'd hoped one day to best them. I thought just this once I'd surprise them." He grimaced. "Instead, mine became a sword of vengeance."

They continued talking, and their pace continued brisk even after dusk fell, for the moon soon rose and the way remained clear before them.

Bab enjoyed talking with him. It was as if Alex and the Fox had each been but half a man before, and now the man beside her was whole. If Alex had faults, and she knew he did, his own gentle virtues and the Fox's determination and strength of purpose made them seem as nothing to her. She wondered if she had known in some hidden, unreachable place in her mind, that the two men were one. She had certainly felt the same stirring of the senses for each one.

When the gates of Dundreggan loomed ahead of them, it was barely nine o'clock, and she might have been sorry their ride was at an end, were it not for the one matter still unresolved.

Alex's thoughts clearly matched hers, for as they entered the hall, he said, "Now, sweetheart, let us see if we can unmask him."

"You think he is here?"

"I do. Come with me unless you are too tired."

"I would not miss this, but should we not tell my mother we are back?"

"She will have retired after her supper," he said. "Now, come."

"But where are we going?" she asked at the main stairway when, instead of going upstairs, he went down.

"To the chapel. It contains a secret passage."

"The chapel? Then that is how you found Gibby!"

"Aye," he said. "I could not leave him there after he'd seen me, so I took him with me to the cave, to hand him over to Hugo, but he no sooner clapped eyes on Dancer than I'm sure the lad guessed all my secrets."

"I think you can trust him, though," she said.

"I agree, because whatever he may think of me, he's mad about the horse."

She chuckled. "But do you just go into the chapel whenever you mean to visit the cavern? Don't folks wonder at how pious you must appear to be?"

"There is another stairway from the family chambers that ends behind what looks like a carved panel near the rood screen," he explained. "One of my ancestors liked secrets, so he constructed it."

"His love of secrets seems not to have died

with him," she observed.

"We'll keep silent now," he said. "This business is still not for all to know."

In the chapel, he showed her the hidden stairway. Then, leading the way behind the rood screen, he drew her into the alcove behind it. To Bab's astonishment, what looked like an ordinary painting of St. Andrew pulled away from the wall to reveal a hidden doorway.

"Come," Alex said, holding out his hand.

Taking it, she followed him down more dusky stairs, lit somehow by faint yellowish light from above. Counting the flights, she knew they had descended some distance below the level of the great hall when at last they came to the bottom of the stairway, having to feel their way down the last few steps.

"Wait," he murmured. She feared for a moment that he meant to leave her, but she heard a scraping sound as of metal on rock, then another sound that she easily identified as flint against a tinderbox. Sparks danced, then smoldering tinder, and a moment later, he lit a taper for her and another for himself from the first, and she was able to see the niche in the rock wall where the items had been stored. Other candles lay there and another tinderbox, as well.

"Now, mind your step," he said quietly. "This passage floor is remarkably even, but there are places where an unwary person might stumble, and it is not wide enough for us to walk side-by-side."

"Even if this tunnel leads outside the wall, won't we need horses?"

"The tunnel leads directly to the cavern," he said.

"But that cavern is miles from here!"

"The outer entrance is just over the hill behind Dundreggan," he said. "You came upon it by a roundabout way that day, so it seemed farther away than it is."

"Especially since you led me back to the ridge by just such another roundabout way."

"I did," he admitted. "I did not want you meddling by returning to the cavern too easily. Now, hush, lass, for we do not want to advertise our arrival, although I warrant he'll be expecting at least one of us."

"Won't you tell me who he is?"

"I want to be certain. If I am wrong, Hugo has much to answer for."

They did not speak again for some time, and it seemed to Bab that they had walked for miles, but she still had unusual energy, and she knew that the spooky passageway made the journey seem longer than it was. Her candle was less than half burned when Alex suddenly snuffed his. His body blocked her view, so she could not tell if he saw something ahead of them or was merely taking precautions.

He turned, smiling, and just as she opened her mouth to ask what amused him, he pinched the flame from her candle, making her gasp at the sudden darkness.

"Your eyes will adjust if you close them for a moment," he whispered. "But do not speak."

She still seemed to see the flame when she closed her eyes, but the image soon faded, and when she opened them, she saw a faint golden glow beyond Alex's shadowy bulk.

He stood sideways to her and the glow outlined his hand as he raised it and lightly pressed a finger to her lips.

Without thinking, she kissed his finger.

His arms came around her then, and he pulled her close, hugging her and kissing her ear, her neck, her cheek, and then her lips, thoroughly. She arched her body against his and wrapped her arms tightly around him.

Although she would have liked to enjoy more of his caresses, when he pressed his tongue against her lips, she pushed him away, urging him to continue along the passageway. As he obeyed, she heard his deep chuckle.

He moved so quietly that she could not hear his footsteps. Her slippers were quiet, too. The glow brightened ahead, and she could discern details of the arched opening beyond them. Her heart pounded, and it occurred to her that the person — if there was indeed someone awaiting them — might not be a friend.

Alex wore his sword, but as certain as she was that he was the Fox, and despite having seen him wield the weapon with great dexterity, she still could not quite imagine him whipping it out in Foxlike fashion and vanquishing an enemy. Try as she might to reconcile all her notions of Sir Alex Chisholm with her notions of the Fox, and although it had become easier, she could not always do it. Here in the darkness of the passageway, it was easier to think of him as the Fox.

No sound came from the chamber ahead, but the golden glow flickered, telling her that it came from flames of one sort or another, most likely candles. She doubted that the light came from a fireplace, because surely she would smell smoke if it did. In any event, the cavern would not boast a chimney. Imagining the most likely reaction of anyone coming upon a hole in the ground from which smoke billowed forth made her smile. Upon just such events were legends built.

Alex paused at the opening. He did not speak, but someone else did.

"Damnation, man, you still move as silently as a shadow! Had I not been on the watch, I'd never have noted your presence."

The voice, deeper than the Fox's, was nonetheless similar enough so that Bab was not surprised that earlier she had found it familiar.

"I remember you used to creep up on your brothers when we were small," the speaker added. "Did you hope I'd have a seizure so you'd inherit my holdings?"

"Since we are only second cousins, you have many heirs before me," Alex said, "but apparently you do know that your father died whilst you were gone."

501

Silence greeted this observation before the other man said, "No, I did not know that. Had I known, I would not have let Francis Dalcross live long enough to hang for his sins."

"I'm sorry to have broken the news so abruptly then, but how are you, Kit? Did it not occur to you your family might have liked to know you were in the area before you acted your little play today?"

"Faith, I only arrived in Glen Affric yesterday, and since your Hugo was the first man I met, it did not seem sensible after that to announce my presence. My original intent was to persuade you and your father of my innocence and then to confront the damnable Dalcrosses to clear my name, but I began hearing rumors of your arrest from the time I reached the head of Loch Linnhe. At first, it was only that the Black Fox had been captured. Imagine my astonishment when I began hearing about the trial of Sir Alex Chisholm!"

"I warrant you suffered severe palpitations," Alex drawled.

"Faith, is that how you talk to folks now, like an idle poop-noddy? No wonder folks seemed so shocked at your unmasking. But who is that winsome lass hiding behind you?" he asked as Bab peeped out to get a better look at him.

"This is Barbara, my wife," Alex said, drawing her forward. "This is my cousin, Christopher Chisholm, Bab, now Laird of Ashkirk and Torness, which makes him only half a Highlander, so you need not be too polite to him."

Still gazing curiously at the large man, she said, "I am pleased to meet you, sir. You saved his life, and I warrant he is more grateful to you than he pretends to be. It is his habit to make light of things, as you must know."

"Aye, your ladyship, none better. Our family is close, although we own land in five counties and half of us live in the Borders. When I passed my place, Alex, I found it teeming with men-at-arms, and since I recognized none of them and know naught of what transpired in my absence, I came on to Glen Affric. Are those men at Torness yours, Dalcross's, or has my uncle sent his own men up here?"

"They are ours," Alex said. "When I returned to Scotland from the Continent and learned of my brothers' deaths, the first thing I wondered was who could benefit from the situation. I was certain that you had not killed them, and my father was skeptical, so although he could not imagine who else might have done it, he made no objection when I saw to it that your land was guarded."

"I thank you."

"Where the devil have you been hiding yourself all year, ye great stump?"

"Hiding myself! That's a good one. The villainous Dalcrosses captured me and handed me over to Cardinal Beaton's men, claiming I'd be an obstacle to their attempts to reform the

Highland Kirk. They taunted me, insisting that were they to turn me loose, they'd be signing my death warrant, because I'd then be tried for your brothers' murders. I have been all the way to Rome and Venice, my lad, and to a few other places I'd as lief never see again."

"But why did they not simply put you on trial or make an end to you?"

"Recall that your father was still Sheriff of Inverness," the other said. "In any event, they preferred the mystery to the trial, or they feared folks on an Inverness jury might believe my word over theirs. I'm not a stranger here, after all, and the Dalcross methods were known even then. As to murdering me, I think from things I overheard that they feared some of their own men might speak up if they did that."

"But once Dalcross became sheriff . . . He had his tame jury, after all."

"Aye, but I was aboard the *Marion Ogilvy* by then, I think, and had I not been, even with such a jury, had Chisholm himself spoken for me —"

"Do you think he would have?"

"I do not know, but he is an honorable man, and he holds his family dear. My father was his closest cousin. Had Francis Dalcross arrested me properly and charged me with your brothers' murders, I warrant your father would have made it his business to speak to me before they tried me and certainly before they hanged me. Do you think I could not have persuaded him that I spoke the truth?"

Bab heard a touch of laughter in Alex's voice as he said, "Faith, you were always able to persuade him of your innocence, even when you were as guilty as Satan. I suffered more than once from the effects of your glib tongue."

"You got your own back often enough."

"But what drove Francis Dalcross to murder my brothers?"

"I have thought about that for a year," Kit said. "Both Dalcross and his son were power mad and jealous of the power of families like the Chisholms, Frasers, and Mackintoshes. Francis had inched close enough to Beaton to know he was seeking support throughout Scotland, and particularly in the Highlands, to keep the Scottish Kirk under Rome's influence. Francis wanted not only to oust Chisholm but to render him harmless, and he believed . . ."

"What?" Alex demanded when his cousin paused and looked rueful.

"Forget it, Alex; it isn't important."

"It is to me," Alex said grimly.

"As he handed me over to his minions to deliver to the *Marion Ogilvy*, Francis said nothing would hurt your father more than losing his two stalwart sons and being left with . . . with only you to inherit his titles and estate." Kit grimaced. "The man was a murderer and a fool, Alex, and he'll soon hang. Whatever he thought, he was wrong, as any of us could have told him."

Bab saw that Alex had pressed his lips together, and a muscle twitched high in his cheek. She put a hand on his arm and felt the muscles tense beneath his sleeve. "He is right, my love," she said gently.

He glanced at her, and she saw surprise in his gaze. Then his expression softened, and he put an arm around her, drawing her close. Nonetheless, his tone was sad when he said, "Had I not been childishly jealous, had I worked harder to be like them when I was young —"

"You, too, would be dead, my lad, and that is the plain and the short of it," Kit Chisholm said sternly. "Use those sharp wits of yours, Alex! Had the Dalcrosses believed for a moment that you were cut from the same bolt as your brothers, they would have deprived your father of all three of his sons. The reason the scoundrels spared your life when you returned to Scotland was only because they erroneously believed Chisholm was ashamed of you."

"What makes you think he was not?" Alex demanded. "You cannot have spoken to him since your return."

"Nay, but I did before it all happened. Did you never know why he chose you instead of Rob or Michael to represent him at the King's proxy wedding?"

Alex shrugged. "I assumed he thought Jamie's second wedding was a matter of lesser importance. Why else would he send his third and youngest son?"

"Because he feared his eldest son might take

offense at something and start a fight or his second son would play pranks on someone with the same result. You, he said, could be depended upon to do the thing properly and without shaming him."

Alex was silent for a long moment. "I wish he had told me," he said.

"That is not his nature," Kit said. "He admires your intelligence."

"I infuriate him more often than not."

"Aye, sure, you infuriated all of us more often than not." The big man grinned as he held out his hand, adding, "I'm glad to see you safe, Alex. I trust the Fox will retire now until such time in the distant future as he may be needed again."

"He will, indeed," Alex promised.

Bab said, " 'Tis a pity your parents are still in Inverness, sir. They would be glad to see your cousin and to know he is responsible for saving you."

"Not alone," Alex said, giving her shoulders another squeeze. "I know who my friends are, sweetheart, even those who are so foolhardy as to fling themselves between me and a would-be murderer. She did that, Kit, little fool that she is."

There was an edge to his voice that she did not quite like, so she was glad when Kit said, "She sounds very brave to me. I don't think it wise for anyone else to see me just yet," he added abruptly. "It can do us no good for folks

507

to begin wondering at my appearance just when we have proved that you are innocent of playing the Fox. Francis Dalcross would certainly leap to all the right conclusions if he were to learn of it, and he could still do you some damage."

"Aye, that's true," Alex agreed. "But if you must play least in sight until tales of the Fox's exploits grow rarer, where will you go?"

"Well, I cannot stay in this cave," Kit said. "I've two lads with me who chose to throw their lots in with mine, but I did not think it wise to bring them in here. Hugo and the youngster with him are keeping them safe and Hugo brought us supplies as well as a horse I've left yonder with your Dancer. Since the men at Torness are yours, I think I'll head there and take my two men with me. I'll have to head south soon, in any event, to sort out my father's affairs and my own."

"Aye, you were promised to some lass as I recall."

"I was," Kit agreed. "If they haven't rearranged matters, I still am." He held out his hand and as Alex shook it, he added, "I'll be on my way then. Since you've been locked up these past few days, I wager you'll want to reacquaint yourself with your bonny wife."

"I do, indeed," Alex said, casting a look at Bab that stirred tremors through her body. Whether they were tremors in anticipation of passion or punishment, however, she could not be sure. "Tell Hugo I want to see him," Alex added. "I expect I shall have to forgive him for giving away my secret."

"Aye, I'll tell him," his cousin promised. Smiling at Bab, he bowed and said, "It is a pleasure to meet you, my lady. Alex has done very well for himself."

She thanked him, and when he headed in the opposite direction from the way they had come, she said to Alex, "Just how many chambers are there, sir?"

"Six," he said promptly. "You saw only the outermost one before, but another one serves as Dancer's stable, and there are others, too."

She was silent then, wondering what to say next, but he took the lead by saying, "You must go to bed, lass. I'm amazed that you're not asleep on your feet."

"Really, sir, I —"

"I do not think you should debate the matter with me right now," he said. "I'll take you back to the chapel and you can go up and get ready for bed while I wait to talk with Hugo. I'll come to you afterward, and if you're still awake, we'll decide what we want to talk about then."

That edge being in his voice again, Bab thought it wiser not to argue.

The green glade was as it had always been, peaceful and welcoming. The happy burn gurgled over its stones, and the mirror pool lay in its usual place, gleaming where a stray, mote-laden sunbeam danced on it.

Catriona drew a long breath, basking in the familiar atmosphere, waiting for the peace she always felt upon entering her bower to wrap its arms around her. But the feeling did not come. A piece of her had been torn away, and she had not known how much she would miss it until it was gone forever.

Sensing another presence, she whirled hopefully and then sighed when she saw Maggie Malloch.

"I'd hoped . . ."

"I ken fine what ye'd hoped, lass," Maggie said, albeit without her usual energy. "It speaks well o' ye, Catriona, but I ha' nae news about Claud. I do bring ye word from the High Circle though, lass, and ye willna like it."

"But I did my part," Catriona said. "Ye said I did!"

"Aye, and I thought it were true, but there be them in the Circle what live tae be obstreperous, your own Red Annis and Grogan Capelthwaite tae name but two."

"They must ken that I nearly failed Christopher Chisholm then."

"Ye did?"

"Aye, twice, when I left him to seek out Claud. The first time a ship's mast nearly fell on him, and the second time, the English navy nearly captured his ship."

"Well, they ken nowt about such things," Maggie assured her, "for they said only that since ye chose tae aid Christopher when they'd expected ye tae aid Sir Alex, your task canna be finished until Christopher Chisholm be settled happily back in his ain life, and ye'll ha' tae admit he's by nae means settled there yet."

"Aye, that be true," Catriona said. "But what difference can it make with Claud gone? There canna be peace betwixt the tribes, and even Red Annis and Grogan Capelthwaite must see that that be the fault o' Jonah Bonewits."

"They be little more than henchmen o' his, and nae friends o' ours," Maggie said. "And they do be still trying tae reclaim his place in the Circle for him."

"Even after all he has done?"

"Aye," Maggie said grimly. "There be nae accounting for politics in the High Circle or anywhere else. As for Jonah himself, nae one kens where he might be."

Catriona sighed unhappily and said, "Can no one match the power that dreadful wizard wields?"

"Aye," Maggie said. "I can, and 'tis the one thing that makes me hope we might find our Claud again."

For the first time since seeing the flames shooting toward her, Catriona felt a twinge of hope. "Then ye dinna think Jonah gave him tae the Host?"

"Nay, nay, because Claud be Jonah's son as well as mine," Maggie said. " 'Twas ye he wanted tae stop, thinking ye were trying tae aid

Sir Alex, and that your failure would mean mine. He be powerful enough tae ha' protected Claud even at the last minute though, and if he did, there be only one place he might ha' sent him where I'd no feel his presence."

"Where?"

"Into the mortal world," Maggie said. " 'Tis said that when we o' the Secret Clan pass on, 'tis sometimes into their world."

"We'll never see him again, then."

"Och, we may though. Jonah Bonewits kens that soon or late I'll winkle out the truth, and he must be hopeful that it will be soon, for he's sought a reckoning between us for ages past. If Claud be in the mortal world, he'll be where I can find him."

"Then why d'ye no confront Jonah now?"

Maggie stiffened. "Ha' ye any notion o' what could happen did the two o' us be so lost tae all else as tae pit our strength against each other until one o' the other o' us is nae more?"

Catriona shook her head.

"I dinna ken either, but we'll likely find out soon enough, the both o' us."

Chapter 23

Giorsal was waiting for Bab in her bedchamber. "Good evening, my lady," she said. "You must be relieved that you and Sir Alex are safely home again."

"Indeed, yes," Bab said, but she said little more, deflecting Giorsal's eager questions simply by saying firmly that they could talk about it all tomorrow.

Many of her own questions had been answered, but she still did not know if her husband would react to her recent activities as Alex or as the Fox. As Alex, he was casual and forgiving, apparently caring little about what she did. As the Fox, he was temperamental and far more unpredictable. Recalling at least two instances in which her actions had stirred his fury, however briefly, she rather feared that she had married the Fox's temper.

Automatically, she went through her usual bedtime ritual, but her mind was back in the cavern, wondering if he was coming to her yet. She was not a coward, but neither was she a fool. If Alex had been playing a role to fool the Dalcrosses and people of the glens, then most likely the Fox's personality was the true one, and the Fox had promised to put her across his knee if she put herself in jeopardy again.

"Surely, he knows that I only did what I had to do," she murmured.

"What's that, my lady?" Giorsal asked. "I didna hear ye."

" 'Tis nothing. I fear I was talking to myself," Bab said. "Mayhap I am growing to be like my mother."

Giorsal laughed. "I warrant ye'll no talk to the wee folk like she does."

"No," Bab agreed, letting the woman slip her nightdress over her head. "You may brush my hair now, and then I'll go to bed."

"Be Sir Alex no taking ye to his bed, then?"

"He'll be along shortly, I expect," Bab said, sitting on the stool in front of the cheerful little fireplace and holding her hands out to the warmth.

Giorsal picked up the hairbrush and began to brush Bab's long hair. Soon its tresses hung in a thick, shining tumble of curls to her waist.

"Let me finish that, Giorsal."

Bab started at hearing his voice. She had not heard the door open and wondered how long he had been watching them.

Alex smiled when she turned toward him, his expression warm, the look in his eyes sensual. He stepped forward and took the brush from Giorsal's hand. "You may go now," he said to her. "I'll look after your mistress."

"Aye, sir. Good night, then." A moment later, the door shut behind her.

After a momentary silence, he said, "I've had rather a long chat with Hugo."

"Have you?" Apprehension stirred icy prickles along her spine.

"Aye." He smacked the business end of the hairbrush against his palm.

"Alex, I —" She started to stand, but his hand on her shoulder stopped her. His grip was hard, insistent. She swallowed, trying to think how best to explain.

"Don't get up, sweetheart. I want to brush your hair." His voice was gentle, but it lacked the Alex-like note of languid indifference that she had hoped to hear.

His brush strokes were firm, and the rhythm was soothing, but the silence hung heavy between them. She wished he would say something.

The fire crackled, and a shower of sparks leaped high as a log broke apart and the two atop it shifted.

"Alex, we . . ."

At the same time, he said, "Sweetheart, we . . ."

Bab turned to look at him, and as she did, he set the brush on the table against the wall and reached for her, pulling her to her feet.

For a moment, they looked at each other, and then he pulled her close, holding her tightly against him.

She sighed. "I was afraid you were really angry."

"Nay, lass, how could I be angry with you

after deceiving you as I did?"

She chuckled, her face pressed against his soft doublet. "Easily. I've seen how easily. It must have been difficult for you to pretend indifference to my taunts."

"Indifference?" He held her a little away so that he could look into her eyes. "Never indifference, my love. If I chose to play the fool . . ."

"Oh, never the fool," she said. "To be sure, I thought so at first, but you were always so kind to me! I would have had to be the hardest-hearted woman alive to ignore that, and I could not. Why, every time you apologized, I felt guilty, for I knew I had been rude. I warrant Patrick would have slapped me for many of the things I said to you if I'd ever said them to him."

"He'd best not try slapping you whilst I'm about," he said evenly.

She chuckled. "In truth, he has done so only once or twice in my life, and I'd venture to guess I deserved it when he did. He and my father both were more likely to send me to my bedchamber than to smack me for my misdeeds."

"Much more sensible," Alex murmured, kissing her ear. "Although I would take you to my bedchamber, rather than send you to yours."

"There is something I want to tell you," Bab said.

"More confessions, lass? You should know

that I've about reached my limit of forgiveness. I do understand that instinct that led you to fling yourself between Dalcross's knife and me and even the need to go riding all over the glens in search of support for me, but —"

"I had an armed escort and your pistol, Alex. This is about a dream I had, the one about my wedding in the fairy glen. I still do not understand how I could have stayed asleep and dreaming at such a time, but it must have been some sort of brainstorm, because I was marrying you in the dream, too, only you were the Fox."

"I suspect I may know how that happened," he said. "I'll explain it another time, though, and tell you something of my own strange experience. Presently though, I think you should sleep."

"No, my love, I want to show you what else happened in that dream, but first you have to take off your clothes and come to bed."

Interest leaped into his eyes. "Faith," he said in his Alex drawl, "this begins to intrigue me."

"I thought it might," she said demurely.

"I warrant you had no clothes on in that dream either," he murmured, grinning as he pulled her bedgown off over her head and stood gazing raptly at her.

In minutes, his own clothing was off, and he carried her to the bed, where before they slept she showed him all she had learned in her wedding dream.

Dear Reader,

I hope you enjoyed *The Secret Clan: Highland Bride*. If you recognized bits of the Black Fox, it is because I used elements of legendary heroes such as the Scarlet Pimpernel, Zorro, and others in creating him, but I hope you will agree that he managed to develop an identity all his own.

As always, I know that there are those of you out there who would make fine editors because you question every detail. In an attempt to answer some of the questions most likely to pop into your heads, let me just say first that Kit's journey from Rome to Dumbarton, although aided by Catriona nearly all the way, nonetheless took place in a plausible amount of time for the period.

According to Denis Rixon (*The West Highland Galley*, Edinburgh 1998), a medieval ship traveled at approximately two miles per hour in a light breeze, four to five miles per hour in a fresh breeze, and seven miles per hour in a strong breeze. The journey from Rome to Dumbarton is approximately 2500 miles. A Highland galley's speed was generally at the top end of this and was even greater for short distances, so the journey from Dumbarton to the Highlands is also plausible.

As for the Fox's sword and swordplay, by 1530 gentlemen commonly wore swords as part of their everyday dress, and many carried a dirk as well. Most swords were still of the thrusting variety, with slender long blades and an elaborate cage of slender bars or a cup to protect the swordsman's hand (the basket hilt).

The art of fencing was still new in 1541, but for gentlemen, rapiers had become more fashionable than broadswords, and Italian fencing masters had begun setting up shop in major cities throughout Europe. For more information on the history and various manners of swordplay, I highly recommend *Arms in Action: Vol. 3, The Sword* (VHS Documentary, Cat. No. AAE-40463, ©1998 A&E Television Networks: The History Channel). The superiority of French swordplay over Italian no longer stirs controversy, but it certainly did in the sixteenth century.

Once again, I want to express my heartfelt thanks to Pam Hessey and also to Charlie Kaiser, both of the California Hawking Club, for taking me hunting with the ever spectacular Cowboy, Mojo, and Modoc, so that I could see for myself how hawks hunt in the field. It was a grand day and one I'll long remember. Any errors or omissions in the hawking scenes are all my own, as usual.

Many thanks also to my agent, Aaron Priest, and to his wonderful assistant Lucy Childs, and to my editors, Beth de Guzman and Karen Kosztolnyik. Your efforts and support are always greatly appreciated.

As for Kit Chisholm and Maggie Malloch,

you will meet both again when Kit returns to his father's home after his year-long absence to find that everyone believes he must be dead and the lass to whom he was engaged is about to marry someone else. Moreover, that someone is the uncle who believes he has inherited Kit's fortune and estates, and he intends to keep them and the girl if he can. Look for *The Secret Clan: The Reiver's Bride* at your favorite bookstore in September 2003. In the meantime, *slàinte mhath!*

Sincerely,

Amanda Scott

website: http://home.att.net/~amandascott

About the Author

Amanda Scott, best-selling author and winner of the Romance Writers of America's RITA/ Golden Medallion and the *Romantic Times'* awards for Best Regency Author and Best Sensual Regency, began writing on a dare from her husband. She has sold every manuscript she has written. She sold her first novel, **The Fugitive Heiress** — written on a battered Smith-Corona — in 1980. Since then, she has sold many more, but since the second one, she has used a word processor. More than twenty-five of her books are set in the English Regency period (1810–20), others are set in fifteenth-century England and sixteenth- and eighteenth-century Scotland. Three are contemporary romances.

Amanda is a fourth-generation Californian who was born and raised in Salinas and graduated with a bachelor's degree in history from Mills College in Oakland. She did graduate work at the University of North Carolina at Chapel Hill, specializing in British history, before obtaining her master's in history from California State University at San Jose. After graduate school, she taught for the Salinas City School District for three years before marrying her husband, who was then a captain in the Air

Force. They lived in Honolulu for a year, then in Nebraska for seven years, where their son was born. Amanda now lives with her husband in northern California.